Elizabeth Lowell

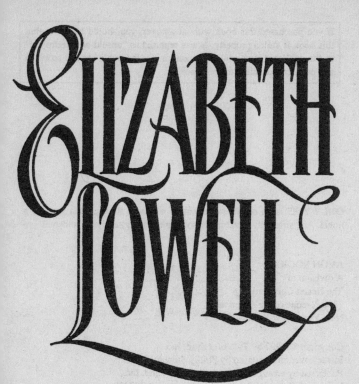

ELIZABETH LOWELL

Only You

AVON BOOKS ◆ NEW YORK

ONLY YOU is an original publication of Avon Books. This work is a novel. Any similarity to actual persons or events is purely coincidental.

AVON BOOKS
A division of
The Hearst Corporation
1350 Avenue of the Americas
New York, New York 10019

Copyright © 1992 by Two of a Kind, Inc.
Inside cover author photo by Phillip Stewart Charis
Published by arrangement with Two of a Kind, Inc.
Library of Congress Catalog Card Number: 91-92439
ISBN: 0-380-76340-0

First Avon Books Printing: July 1992

AVON TRADEMARK REG. U.S. PAT. OFF. AND IN OTHER COUNTRIES. MARCA REGISTRADA. HECHO EN U.S.A.

Printed in the U.S.A.

RA 10 9

THE "ONLY" FAMILY

Sarah and Edward Moran

Caleb Black m. Willow
ONLY HIS

Matt (Reno) m. Evelyn Starr
ONLY YOU

Rafe (Whip) m. Shannon Conner Smith
ONLY LOVE

Lord Robert Stewart----Shy Wolf
(Cheyenne)

Wolfe Lonetree m. Jessica Charteris
ONLY MINE

1

Canyon City, Colorado
Late summer 1867

Out of money, out of luck, alone, and frightened, the girl known as Evening Star did the only thing she could think of to stay at the saloon's poker table.

She bet herself.

But first Eve shuffled the deck with dazzling speed, subtly arranging the cards as she had been taught to do by Donna Lyon. While she worked, she tried not to look at the dark-haired stranger who had sat down at her table without warning. The man's hard good looks were unsettling.

Outlaws like Raleigh King and Jericho Slater were enough for any girl to deal with. She didn't need a handsome stranger to make her sore hands shake.

Eve took a secret, steadying breath and said, "Five-card draw. Table stakes. Ante up."

"Just a minute, little lady," Raleigh King objected. "You're busted. Where's your ante?"

"Sitting right here."

"Huh?"

"I'm the ante, Mr. King."

"You're betting yourself?" Raleigh asked in disbelief.

Reno Moran didn't have to ask. He had read the determination in the girl's posture when he sat down and took cards. It had been her combination of steady eyes and slightly trembling lips that had lured him across the room.

Whatever happened, he knew she meant every word.

"Yes, I'm betting myself."

Eve glanced at the jewelry and coins stacked around the table in front of each man.

"I'm worth as much as anything any one of you has now," she added.

Then she smiled a brilliant, empty smile and continued shuffling.

Silence spread out from the poker table, followed by a rush of whispering as the other men in the room asked one another if they had heard correctly.

The whispers told Reno that a lot of men had wanted the girl, but none had gotten her. A cynical smile shifted the line of Reno's black mustache. There was nothing new in that particular game. Girls had been teasing and promising and then withholding their bodies for a long time.

Reno glanced from the deck of cards in the girl's hands to the girl herself. In the saloon's dim interior her eyes were a clear, uncanny gold that matched the lantern light rippling through her tawny hair. The cut of her dress was demure enough, but it was made of a crimson silk that set a man to thinking about what it would be like to unfasten all the gleaming jet buttons and touch the luminous skin beneath the fabric.

The direction of Reno's thoughts irritated him. He was old enough to know better. He had been taught and teased by the most expert female since Adam's wife fed him the forbidden fruit.

Looking at Reno, Slater stirred the pearls and gold coins he had just won from Eve.

"I figure this should match the ring you won off of Raleigh," he said to Reno, "and be worth a damn sight more than that journal you've got left," he added to Raleigh.

"The hell you say," Raleigh retorted. "I have it on good authority that this here old journal contains a gen-u-ine Spanish treasure map worth more than all the pearls in the Orient."

Slater looked coldly at the book but didn't object to Raleigh's statement.

Reno picked up the elegant, ancient ring he had won earlier from Raleigh. Emeralds flashed subtly, surrounded by gold so pure it took the imprint of his fingernail.

The stones were pretty enough, but it was the gold that held Reno's interest. To him the feel and weight of gold was like nothing else. Women's flesh was sweet and soft, but women were as fickle as a spring wind. Gold never changed, never corrupted, never turned out to be less than it seemed.

Silently Reno measured the ring against the girl whose name was as improbable as the innocence in her golden eyes.

It was Raleigh who expressed Reno's doubts aloud.

"Huh," Raleigh said to Eve. "So you figure you're worth as much as the ring, the pearls, or the treasure map? You must know some pretty fancy tricks."

The smile he gave Eve was frankly insulting.

"Give the little lady what she wants," Slater said coldly. "One way or another, she'll pay up. At Denver prices, a month of her time should cover it."

Eve barely managed not to shudder at the thought of being at the mercy of a man like Jericho Slater for a single night, much less for a month.

Silently she told herself she didn't have to worry. She wouldn't have to pay off the bet, because she had no intention of losing.

For once the idea of cheating at cards didn't make Eve squirm with unhappiness. If anything, there was a certain rough justice in cheating Slater and his gang. Everything of value on the table had been stolen a few days ago by Raleigh King. If she had to cheat to get everything back, she would.

Her only regret was that she could do no worse than that to the man who had murdered Don and Donna Lyon.

With outward casualness, Eve continued shuffling while she waited for the third player to agree to the unexpected bet. When no agreement came, she glanced cautiously at the man from beneath her thick eyelashes.

The green-eyed stranger had taken a seat at the table an hour ago, just before Eve had begun to deal the first hand. A single look at the stranger had told her two things: She had never seen a man who appealed more to her; and she had never seen a man more dangerous.

She suspected that the stranger's Virginia drawl was as misleading as the seeming indolence of his movements. There was no laziness in his green eyes. Wariness was as much a part of him as his black hair and powerful body.

Yet Eve's instincts kept whispering that this man was somehow different from men like Slater and Raleigh, cruel men who cared nothing about hurting or destroying those who were weaker than themselves.

"Just one thing," Slater added coldly. "Make damned sure all the cards you deal yourself come from the top of the deck."

Eve forced herself to smile despite the ice condensing in her stomach. She had no doubt that Slater would kill a woman he caught cheating just as quickly as he would kill a man.

"Are you accusing me of cheating?" Eve asked.

"You've been warned" was all Slater said.

Reno shifted slightly. The motion brought the butt of his six-gun closer to his left hand. Silently he measured the catlike elegance of the girl with the determined eyes and the soft mouth.

"You sure you want to bet yourself, Miss . . . what was the name again?" Reno asked, though he knew very well.

"Star," she said softly. "My name is Evening Star."

Eve's voice was much calmer than she felt. She had lied about her name so often, she no longer hesitated over it. In any case, the lie was meaningless; no one alive remembered her as Evelyn Starr Johnson.

"All right, Miss Star," Reno drawled. "Are you sure you know what you're doing?"

"What do you care?" Raleigh demanded. "She's old enough to have everything a man needs, and pretty enough to make taking it a pleasure."

"Miss?" Reno repeated, ignoring the other man.

"I'm sure."

Reno shrugged, outwardly indifferent. Beneath the table his left hand settled on his six-gun.

The saloon's hush changed into a humming of male voices as people left their drinks at the bar and focused on the poker table where the potential stakes now consisted of a rope of pearls, an ancient emerald ring, a Spanish treasure map . . .

And a girl called Evening Star.

Reno was certain the ring was real, had his doubts about the treasure map and pearls, and wondered how the girl with trembling lips and steady gold eyes had ended up as table stakes in Canyon City's most infamous saloon.

"Five-card draw," Eve said quietly. "My deal. Agreed?"

"We already agreed," Raleigh said impatiently. "Deal."

"You're really sweating to lose the rest of your money, aren't you?" Reno asked carelessly.

"Listen you son—"

"Shut up, Raleigh," Slater interrupted coldly. "You can get killed on your own time. I came here to play cards."

"The only one doing any dying will be this here rebel turncoat," retorted Raleigh.

"I don't see any rebel turncoats," Reno said, smiling lazily. "Do you?"

The wolfish quality of Reno's smile, plus Slater's blunt warning about getting killed, told Raleigh he had made a mistake by dismissing the lazy-looking stranger as no threat.

"No offense meant," Raleigh muttered.

"None taken," Reno said easily.

Both men were lying.

Eve's heart threatened to choke her as the moment approached when she would have to stop shuffling and deal. Given a choice, she would have gotten up and walked away from the grimy saloon and the three dangerous men. But there was no real choice.

She had nowhere to go, no money to pay her way, her stomach was growling from hunger; and most of all, a desire for vengeance burned in her blood like acid. Raleigh King had killed the only two friends Eve had.

And she had just thought of a way to return the favor.

Praying that the green-eyed stranger was as deadly as she suspected he was, Eve took a deep, invisible breath and began dealing cards with great care and dazzling speed. The cards made a crisp sound as she placed them facedown, one at a time, in front of the three men and herself.

Slater and the stranger watched Eve's hands. Raleigh watched the place where red silk swelled outward over her breasts. Though the neckline of the dress was modest, the fit left no doubt there was a female beneath.

While Eve dealt, she avoided looking at Jericho Slater, for she knew his cold blue eyes would be telling her that she wasn't going to get away with bottom-dealing good hands to herself any longer. With her fingers still sore and blistered from burying Don and Donna Lyon, she simply wasn't fast enough to hold her own for long against a gambler of Slater's skill.

Nor was the derringer concealed within the pocket of her red silk dress going to be much help against the heavier handguns worn by both Slater and Raleigh.

It has to work, Eve thought desperately. *Just once, the weak have to win out over the cruel and the strong.*

Eve didn't look at the green-eyed stranger again. A man that handsome would have been unsettling under any circumstances, much less when a girl's life depended on her concentration.

Five cards now lay facedown in front of each player. Eve set aside the deck and picked up her own cards, wondering what she had dealt to herself. From the corner of her eye she watched the stranger. If the possibilities of the hand he had been dealt excited him, it didn't show on his face or in the light green crystal of his eyes.

Eve wasn't surprised when Slater opened the betting, for she had dealt him two pairs. Nor was she surprised when Raleigh jumped in with a raise, for she had dealt him a straight. The stranger simply called for that round, as did Eve.

Without a word she dealt each man the one or two cards he requested and swept the discards to the bottom of the deck. She permitted herself a brief glance at each man's face as he looked at his hand.

The stranger was good. Not a flicker of emotion showed on his face as he picked up his single new card.

Nothing showed on Eve's face, either.

The cards she had were uninspiring. A jack, a nine, a six, a three, and a two. The suits were a complete mismatch. About all the cards were good for was to conceal the fine trembling of her fingers as she waited for the shooting to begin.

Dear God, let the stranger be as quick as he is handsome. I don't want his death on my conscience.

Raleigh's death, however, was another matter. Eve had no scruples about that. Anyone who could torture an old man to death while his dying wife looked on helplessly deserved a much more painful death than he was likely to get from the stranger's six-gun.

Slater began the betting by throwing two twenty-dollar gold pieces into the pot. Raleigh called and then raised. So did the stranger.

Eve threw in her cards and waited for the shooting to begin.

On the final round of betting, Slater pushed the pearls into the center of the table. Raleigh followed with the journal. Reno tossed the ring into the pot.

"Call," Reno said coolly.

Slater fanned his cards face-up at the table. "Full house. Kings and aces."

Slater's blue eyes began appraising Eve the way a man appraised a strange mare he planned to ride.

Raleigh crowed and turned over his cards.

"Four nines and a queen," he said triumphantly. "Looks like the little lady is mine."

"What about you?" Eve asked quickly, turning to the stranger.

Reno gave her an odd look. Slowly he began turning over his cards one at a time with his right hand. Beneath the table, his left hand lay relaxed and close to his gun.

"Ten of hearts," Reno said. "Jack. King. Ace."

As he turned over the last card, he watched Slater's hands. The royal flush gleamed like blood on the table.

"Queen of hearts."

For an instant there was only silence. Then Raleigh and Slater went for their guns. Slater was much faster than Raleigh, but it didn't matter.

Reno moved with stunning speed. Before Slater could draw his gun, Reno upended the card table and slammed it into the other men with his right hand. With his left he reached for his own gun.

Eve scooped up the ring, the pearls, the journal, and the coins before any of it hit the floor. Instantly she sprinted for the back door of the saloon, racing past men who were too surprised to stop her. Just before she reached the door, she risked a fast glance over her shoulder, wondering why no one was shooting.

Slater had known immediately that he was no match for the stranger. Hands held away from his sides, he watched Reno with reptilian intensity.

Raleigh was neither as bright nor as fast as his friend. He believed he could draw and shoot quicker than Reno could. Raleigh died before he understood his mistake.

As the abrupt thunder of gunshots exploded in the room, a man called Steamer stepped partway between Eve and Reno. She watched, horrified, as Steamer drew his gun to shoot Reno in the back.

There was no time for Eve to pull her derringer free of its hidden pocket. She jammed her hand in the skirt pocket, grabbed the small pistol, and pulled the trigger. The layers of red silk didn't slow the bullet one bit, but the hasty shot almost missed.

The bullet burned across Steamer's thigh. He gave a startled cry, his arm jerked, and the shot he triggered went into the ceiling.

Before Steamer's finger could squeeze the trigger again, Reno turned and shot him in a single fluid motion. As Steamer fell dead to the floor, Reno spun back around to face Slater.

Shocked by the stranger's lethal speed, Eve stood and stared for a moment before common sense took over. She bolted for the nearby stable.

Eve had prepared well for this moment. She had traded the battered Gypsy wagon that belonged to the Lyons for an equally battered saddle and saddlebags. She had been surprised to discover that, once free of the traces, the gentle old gelding called Whitefoot was both fast and eager for the trail.

Whitefoot was saddled, bridled, and ready to go. All of Eve's possessions were in the saddlebags and bedroll tied behind the saddle. Later she would take time to change into trail clothes. For now, speed was more important than modesty. She jammed the ring on her right hand, pulled the rope of pearls over her head, and stuffed the journal and gold coins into a saddlebag.

In a wild swirling of crimson silk, Eve threw herself into the saddle, spun Whitefoot on his hocks, and headed out of town at a dead run. By the time Whitefoot passed the saloon, the scarlet skirt had climbed to Eve's thighs.

From the corner of his eye Reno glimpsed a flurry of crimson and a breathtaking length of leg clad in cotton pantalets so sheer, they were little better than going naked. The drumroll of horse's hooves filled the ringing silence that had followed the crash of gunfire.

Slater smiled grimly at the man who was watching him over the barrel of a six-gun.

"Looks like she suckered both of us," Slater said calmly.

"Looks that way," Reno agreed.

"Friend of yours?"

"No."

Slater grunted. "Just as well. Man would have to be crazy to turn his back on that bit of scarlet."

Reno said nothing.

Slater fell silent. It was dealer's choice, and the man with the six-gun was the dealer.

Without looking away from Slater, Reno assessed the men remaining in the saloon. Raleigh and Steamer were dead.

"Friends of yours?" Reno asked.

"Not particularly. I don't cotton to stupid men."

"But you ride with them."

"No," Slater corrected. "They ride with *me*."

Reno's smile was sardonic.

"Well, you'll be riding a little light," he said, "but not for long. God must have loved fools and horseflies. Sure to hell he made a lot of them."

Reno's ice green eyes counted the men remaining in the saloon. Three of them were drifters. The rest were part of Slater's gang. All of them were being careful not to give Reno a reason to shoot.

"Might your name be Reno?" Slater asked.

"Some folks call me that."

A sound went through the men in the saloon. As one, they eased backward, giving Reno all the room he might want and then a bit more just to be safe.

The only move Slater made was to nod as though a private guess had just been confirmed.

"Thought so," he said. "Only a few men can move like that."

Slater paused, then asked with real interest, "Is the Man from Yuma still hunting you?"

"No."

"Too bad. Hear he's fast. Really fast."

Reno smiled. "You heard right."

"Did you kill him?" Slater asked. "Is that why he isn't hunting you anymore?"

"I had no reason to kill him."

"I do."

"So I hear. Pity you weren't with your twin brother, Jed, when he died. Then Wolfe could have made it a clean sweep."

Slater became very still. "You were the third one there that day. The one with a six-gun."

Though it wasn't a question, Reno nodded.

"I was there. Best piece of work I've done. Whole lot of folks are sleeping more easy now that Jed and his boys are pushing up daisies."

Slater's face went still and hard.

"Lie facedown on the floor, boys," Reno said calmly. "I'm feeling a mite nervous right now, so don't do anything to startle me while I take your guns."

There was a muted surge of motion as the men in the saloon went facedown on the floor. Reno moved among them quickly, gathering guns. As he worked, he kept an eye on Slater, whose right hand was inching toward his belt.

"After I gather up all the loose iron," Reno said casually, "I'm going to wait outside the door for a while before I ride on. Whenever you feel lucky, you just lift your head and see if I'm still around."

None of the men seemed in a hurry to take Reno's offer.

"Slater, I hear you keep a little hideout gun behind your buckle," Reno continued. "Maybe you do, maybe you don't. Now, I'd hate to kill an unarmed man, but not as bad as I'd hate to be shot in the back by a coyote who beats women and cheats at cards enough to put Satan to shame."

Slater's hand stopped moving.

Reno went through the room, drawing guns and shucking bullets onto the saloon floor. His passage was marked by the sound of the bullets falling and bouncing across the uneven wooden boards.

When several minutes had passed without the noise of more ammunition falling, one of the men eased his face off the floor and looked around.

"He done left," said the man.

"Check the street," said Slater.

"Check it yourself."

By the time one of Slater's men got up the nerve to check the street, Reno was four miles away, riding at a dead run as he followed the trail of the girl called Evening Star.

2

AFTER the first two miles of hard running, Eve pulled Whitefoot back to a slower pace and began looking for the landmark Donna Lyon had described with her dying words.

All Eve saw to the west was the steeply rising Front Range of the Rocky Mountains. No ravine or shadowed crease in the land looked more inviting or more passable than any other. In fact, had she not already known that there was a pass through the looming peaks, she would have thought none existed. The rugged stone summits thrust straight into the blue afternoon sky, with little more than a notch here or there to hint at possible ways through the ramparts.

Nobody rode nearby. There were no houses, no farms, no settlements. All Eve could hear above the sound of Whitefoot's deep breathing was the long sigh of the wind from the granite peaks. Pearly clouds wreathed some mountaintops, hinting at the afternoon and evening storms that flashed through the Rockies in summertime.

Eve had hoped for a good hard rain to hide her tracks, but she wasn't going to be that lucky. The clouds weren't nearly thick enough to help her out.

"Sorry, Whitefoot. We'll have to keep running," she said aloud, stroking the horse's hot brown shoulder.

Her eyes searched the landscape once more, hoping to see El Oso, the bear-shaped mound of boulders described by Donna and the old journal.

No such pile of stones lay within view. There was nothing to suggest which way Eve should go to find the entrance to the ravine that would ultimately lead to a pass through the massed peaks.

Anxiously she turned and looked over her back trail. Behind her the rumpled land fell away in shades of green until the horizon came down on the plains, blurring everything into a gauzy, glittering blue.

Abruptly Eve stiffened and shaded her eyes, peering over her back trail.

"Perdition," she muttered. "I can't tell whether that's men or deer or wild horses or something else entirely."

What Eve's eyes couldn't make out, her instincts did. With her heart wedging in her throat, she kicked Whitefoot into a canter. She wanted to go at a fast gallop, but the land was too steep. If she ran Whitefoot any harder, she would find herself afoot before sunset.

Earth spurted and rocks rolled as Whitefoot cantered along the vague trail that ran parallel to the Front Range. In some places the trail was wide enough for a wagon. In others it unraveled into footpaths leading to sheltered places where people could camp out of the endless wind.

Each time Whitefoot crested a rise, Eve looked

back. Each time the men following her were closer. If she didn't do something, they would catch her before dark. The thought was enough to chill her more deeply than the wind blowing down from icy peaks.

Finally Whitefoot came to a ravine that held an odd pile of boulders and a brawling little stream in its bottom. The boulders didn't particularly look like a bear to Eve, but Donna had warned her that the Spaniards who drew the map had been alone in the wilderness so long that they saw fanciful things.

Eve urged Whitefoot around the mound that might or might not be El Oso. Once past the rocks, she turned her horse in to the stream and kept him in the water until the going got too rough. Only then did she allow the gelding to splash out across a swath of stony ground. Whitefoot's hooves left small marks and scrapes across pebbles to mark his passage, but it was better than the clear trail he had left in softer ground.

Zigzagging, guiding the horse alongside or actually in the stream, heading ever deeper into the wild mountains, Eve rode into the thick gold light of afternoon. Her legs were chapped from the rubbing of the old saddle and cold from exposure to the wind, but she didn't dare stop long enough to change into Don Lyon's old clothes.

As soon as the way became less steep, Eve reined Whitefoot back into the stream. This time she kept him wading for more than a mile before she found stony ground that wouldn't take hoofprints.

She checked the journal and looked around unhappily. She was at the limit of the countryside covered by the journal. Soon she must turn and take a long, winding valley westward, following the grass like a river to its source high in the peaks, a divide marking one side of the range from the other.

But before she crossed that divide, she had to lose the men who were following her.

SLATER stood in his stirrups and looked down his own back trail. Nothing moved but the wind. Even so, he couldn't shake the feeling that he was being followed. Slater was a man accustomed to listening to his instincts, but he was getting tired of having his spine itch when there was nothing more to show for it than an empty back trail stretching all the way to Canyon City.

"Well?" he asked impatiently as his best Comanchero scout rode up.

Crooked Bear held his cupped right hand to his mouth and then brought his hand across to his right shoulder in the sign for river.

"Again?" Slater asked in disgust. "Her damned horse must be part fish."

Crooked Bear shrugged, made a sign for wolf, and then for small.

Slater grunted. He had already had a sample of the girl's cleverness at the card table. He didn't need any further proof that she was as fast and wary as a coyote.

"Did you see that red dress of hers?" Slater asked.

Crooked Bear signed an emphatic *no*.

Slater looked at the clouds. "Rain?"

The Comanchero gave a Frenchman's shrug.

"Crooked Bear," muttered Slater, "someday you're going to piss me off. Go over the ground again. Find her. You hear me?"

The half-breed smiled, showing two gold teeth, two gaps, and a broken tooth that hadn't hurt enough to be pulled.

SHIVERING with a combination of cold and fear, Eve watched the Comanchero quarter the stream banks one last time, looking for her tracks. When he dismounted, she held her breath and looked away, not wanting to somehow call attention to herself by staring at him.

After a few minutes, the temptation to look was too great. Eve peered carefully through the greenery and rocks that studded the long slope between her and the stream. The low cry of the wind and the mutter of thunder from a distant peak shut out any sounds the men below her made.

Slater, Crooked Bear, and five other men were quartering the stream bank. Eve smiled slightly, knowing she had won. If Crooked Bear couldn't find her tracks, no one could. The Comanchero was almost as famous throughout the territory for his tracking abilities as he was for his savage reputation with a knife.

It was an hour before Slater and his men gave up. By then it was almost dark, a light rain was falling, and they had thoroughly trampled whatever signs Whitefoot might have left coming out of the river.

Breath held until it ached, Eve watched Slater's gang mount and ride out of sight up the stream. Then she scrambled back off the slope and went to Whitefoot, who was waiting patiently, head down, more asleep than awake.

"Poor boy," she whispered. "I know your feet are sore after all those stones, but if you had been wearing shoes, Crooked Bear would have found us for sure."

Despite the urgency driving Eve to get over the Great Divide, through the San Juan Mountains and down into the stone maze described by the Spaniards, she knew she had to make camp within a few miles. Whitefoot had to have rest, or he wouldn't be able to take her over the Great Divide.

Once the divide was behind her, somewhere between the summit and the stone canyons the journal described, she had to find a way to get Whitefoot shod, buy a packhorse, and gather the supplies she would need for the trek.

But what Eve really needed to buy was a man she could trust, someone who would guard her back while she hunted for the lost mine of Cristóbal Leon, ancestor of Don Lyon, descendant of Spanish royalty and holder of royal permission to seek gold in the New World holdings of the Spanish Crown.

I might as well wish for a fairy godmother as for a strong man I can trust with gold. Weak men cherish and strong men destroy.

Makes a woman wonder what God was thinking of when He created man.

As soon as Slater rode off, Reno collapsed the spyglass, wriggled down off the rocky rise, and went back to where his horse and the three pack animals loaded with winter supplies waited. His mare's black nostrils flared at his scent. She snorted softly and extended her muzzle to him for a bit of rubbing.

"Hello, Darlin'. You get lonely while I was gone?"

Soft lips whuffled over his fingers, leaving a feeling of tickling warmth behind.

"Well, you won't be lonely much longer. Crooked Bear finally got fed up with the game. If we hurry, we'll be able to pick up her trail before sunset."

Reno climbed into the saddle, stroked the mare's

neck with a strong, leather-clad hand, and reined
the blue roan toward a steep slope. Working
quickly, the horse zigzagged down into a ravine
that ran roughly parallel to the place where
Crooked Bear had lost the trail. The packhorses
followed without being led.

"If we're really lucky," Reno said, "before breakfast we'll see if that girl knows any more tricks than
cold-decking, bottom-dealing, and setting men up
to be killed."

FROWNING, edgy despite the
empty back trail, Eve held Whitefoot still and listened. She heard nothing but the hushed rustling
of raindrops sliding over leaves.

Finally she turned and led Whitefoot toward the
vague notch where the journal assured her there
was a place to camp at the base of a cliff. There
was shelter from the rain, a small spring set amid
moss and ferns, and a view of the surrounding
countryside. All she would need was someone to
stand guard while she slept.

It was full dark before Eve and the footsore gelding reached the campsite. The flat white disc of the
rising moon had just cleared the peaks.

Talking softly to Whitefoot, feeling more alone
than she had since Don and Donna Lyon died, Eve
tended to her horse, ate a cold supper, and fell into
the meager bedroll she had scrounged from the
contents of the Gypsy wagon. She was asleep immediately, too exhausted by the sorrow and danger
of the past week to keep her eyes open.

When she woke up at dawn, the stranger with
the light green eyes and fast gun was calmly going
through her saddlebags.

Eve's first thought was that she was still dream-
ing, for the man's accusing eyes had haunted her

sleep, making her twist and turn restlessly. In her dreams she had been trying to get closer to the handsome stranger by dealing perfect hands to him, but each time he had seen the heart flush, he had thrown in his cards and walked away from the poker table, leaving her alone.

Now that Eve was awake, getting closer to the dangerous man who was going through her saddlebags was the last thing on her mind. Beneath the blankets, her hand began easing very slowly toward the shotgun that had been Donna Lyon's preferred weapon. Following Donna's example, Eve had slept with the shotgun alongside her bed since Donna's hands had become too crippled to hold the weapon.

Through barely opened eyes, Eve assessed the intruder. Her breathing didn't change. Nor did she shift her position in any noticeable way. She didn't want the gunfighter who was so coolly rummaging through her possessions to know she was awake. She remembered all too well how fast he could draw and shoot.

There was a faint whisper of sound as the man pulled his hand out of the saddlebag. Pearls gleamed like moon-drops in the pale early morning light.

The sight of the jewelry draped across his lean, long-fingered hand intrigued Eve. The contrast between smooth and pale, tanned and powerful, sent an odd cascade of sensation from her breastbone to her belly. When he let the sleek, cool strands slide between his fingers as though savoring the pearls' curves and texture, another sensation rippled through her.

Gusts of wind sighed through the hidden camp, setting the pines to swaying and murmuring among themselves. Beneath the moving boughs,

sunlight retreated and returned, concealing and revealing the stranger's features.

Eve tried not to stare, but found it impossible.
She reminded herself that she had seen more at-
tractive men, men with more perfect features, men
with gentle eyes and mouths eager to smile. There
was no reason for this hard stranger to appeal so
deeply to her senses. There certainly was no reason
for him to have haunted her dreams.

Yet he had. Without the dangerous card game
to distract Eve, she was even more curious about
him than she had been when he first sat down and
took cards in the poker game.

Reno ran the pearls through his fingers one more
time before he slipped them into a fawnskin bag
and put them in his jacket pocket.

The next thing his fingers encountered in the
saddlebag was a length of soft leather wrapped
around something and tied with a worn leather
thong. Curious, Reno pulled out the bundle and
unwrapped it. Two long, slender metal rods with
a notch in the blunt tips fell into his palm with a
faintly musical sound.

Be damned, Reno thought. *Spanish dowsing needles.
Wonder if she's skilled enough to use them.*

Thoughtfully Reno wrapped up the large, blunt
"needles" and put them back in the saddlebag.

The next thing his fingers encountered was the
worn, dry leather of the Spanish journal. He
opened it, flipped through it quickly to make certain it was the right one, and transferred it to his
own saddlebags.

The rest of the contents of the girl's saddlebag
made Reno feel frankly uneasy about reclaiming
his winnings from the pretty little cheat. All she
had in her kit was a boy's jacket, the scarlet dress,
another dress made of flour sacks, and a boy's ruf-

fled white shirt and black pants. The gold ring was nowhere in sight. Nor was the handful of coins she had scooped up with the ring.

It was obvious she was way down on her luck. On the other hand . . .

"You keep moving your fingers toward that shotgun," Reno said without looking up, "and I'm going to drag you out of that bedroll and teach you some manners."

Eve froze, stunned. Until that instant she would have sworn the man hadn't even known she was awake.

"Who are you?" she asked.

"Matt Moran." As he spoke, he stuffed clothes back into the saddlebag. "But most folks call me Reno."

Eve's eyes widened to startled pools of gold. She had heard about the man called Reno. He was a gunfighter, but he never looked for battles. Nor did he hire out his lethal skills. He simply went his own way through the wild country, looking for placer gold during the high-mountain summers and for Spanish gold in the red hush of desert winter.

For a few crazy moments, Eve thought of bolting into the underbrush and hiding until Reno gave up and rode away. Almost as soon as the idea came, she abandoned it.

Reno's aura of lazy grace no longer fooled her. She had seen him move in the saloon, his hands so fast they blurred. The Lyons had often praised Eve's quick fingers, but she had no doubt that the man called Reno was faster than she was. She wouldn't get three steps from her bedroll before he caught her.

"Don't suppose you'd want to tell me where my ring is?" Reno asked after a moment.

"*Your* ring?" Eve asked indignantly. "It belonged to Don and Donna Lyon!"

"Until you stole it and lost it to Raleigh King, and I won it from him," Reno said, shooting her a glance out of eyes like green ice. "Then it became my ring."

"I didn't steal it!"

Reno laughed.

It wasn't a warm sound.

"Sure, *gata*," he said sardonically, "you didn't steal the ring. You just won it in a card game, right? Was it your deal by any chance?"

Anger rippled through Eve, driving out the odd sensations that had bothered her since she had seen the delicate pearls held so gently in Reno's hand. With the surge of anger came a diminishing of her caution. Once more her hand eased toward the shotgun that lay just beyond her blankets.

"Actually," Eve said in a clipped voice, "the ring was taken at gunpoint from a dying man."

Reno gave her a disgusted look and went back to rummaging in the saddlebag.

"If you don't believe me—" she began.

"Oh, I believe you, all right," he interrupted. "I just didn't think you'd be so proud of outright robbery."

"I wasn't the one holding the gun!"

"Had a partner, did you?"

"Damn you, why won't you listen to me?" Eve demanded, furious that Reno thought her a thief.

"I'm listening. I'm just not hearing anything worth believing."

"Try shutting up. You might be amazed at the things you learn with your mouth closed."

The corner of Reno's mouth lifted slightly, but it was the only sign he gave that he had heard Eve. Almost absently he groped in the saddlebag, searching for the ring. The cool, unmistakable feel of a gold coin brought his full attention back to his search.

"Didn't think you had time to spend anything," Reno said with satisfaction. "Old Jericho didn't let any grass grow under his feet before he—"

The words ended abruptly as Reno tossed aside the saddlebag and uncoiled in a swift lunge that ended with the shotgun being yanked from Eve's fingers.

The next thing Eve knew, she had been jerked from beneath the covers and was dangling from Reno's powerful hands like a sack of flour. Fear shot through her. Without thinking, she brought her knee up fast and hard between Reno's legs as Donna had taught her to do.

Reno blocked the blow before it could do any damage. When Eve went for his eyes, he buried his face against her throat and took her down to the ground.

Before Eve knew what had happened, she was stretched out flat on her back, unable to fight, unable to defend herself, unable to move at all except to take tiny, shallow breaths. Reno's big body covered every bit of hers, driving the air from her lungs and the fight from her body. The bedroll's thickness did little to cushion her from the hard ground beneath her.

"Let me go," she gasped.

"Do I look like a fool?" he asked dryly. "God only knows what other nasty little tricks your mama taught you."

"My mama died before I ever knew her face."

"Uh-huh," Reno said, obviously unmoved. "I suppose you're a poor little orphan child with no one to look after you."

Eve gritted her teeth and tried to get a grip on

her temper. "As a matter of fact, I am."

"Poor little *gata*," Reno said coolly. "Stop telling me sad stories or I'll cloud up and cry all over you."

"I'd settle for you getting off of me."

"Why?"

"You're crushing me. I can't even breathe."

"Really?"

Reno looked at the flushed, beautiful, furious face that was only inches from his own.

"Odd," he said deeply, "you're not having a bit of trouble talking at thirty to the dozen."

"Listen, you overgrown, overbearing gun-fighter," Eve said icily. Then she corrected herself. "No, you're not a gunfighter. You're a thief who makes his living robbing people who are too weak to—mmph!"

Eve's words had been effectively cut off by Reno's mouth closing over hers.

For an instant she was too shocked to do any-thing but lie rigid beneath his warm, overwhelming weight. Then she felt the sure thrust of his tongue between her teeth and panicked. Twisting, kicking, trying to throw him off, she fought with every bit of strength in her body.

Reno laughed without releasing Eve's mouth and deliberately let himself sink down over her, pinning her to the ground with his much greater weight, absorbing her struggles without in the least stopping the sensual probing of his tongue within her mouth.

Eve's wild, futile fighting did nothing but wear her out and make her desperate for air. Yet when she tried to breathe, she couldn't, for Reno's weight was too great to shift from her chest even the bare inch she needed.

The world began to go gray, then black, receding from her in a rush, spinning away.

The small, frightened sound Eve made as she felt herself fainting did what none of her struggles had accomplished. Reno lifted his head and body just enough to allow her to breathe.

"That's your second lesson," Reno said calmly when Eve's dazed gold eyes focused on him once more.

"What—what do—you mean?" she gasped.

"I'm faster than you are. That was your first lesson. I'm stronger than you are. That was your second lesson. And the third lesson . . ."

"W-What?"

Reno smiled oddly, looked at Eve's trembling lips, and said huskily, "The third lesson was mine to learn."

He saw her wide, confused eyes and smiled again.

This time Eve understood why the smile seemed odd to her. It was much too gentle to belong to a man like Reno Moran.

"I learned that you taste hotter than whiskey and sweeter than wine," he said simply.

Before Eve could say anything, Reno lowered his head once more.

"This time give it back to me, *gata*. I like it hot and deep."

"What?" Eve asked, wondering if she had lost her mind.

"Your tongue," he said against her open mouth. "Take that quick little tongue and rub it over mine."

For an instant Eve thought she had heard wrong.

Reno took her sudden stillness for agreement. He lowered his head and made a husky sound of pleasure as he tasted her once more.

The sound Eve made was pure surprise at the gliding caress. For the space of a heartbeat she felt like a pearl being delicately held by a powerful hand. Then she remembered where she was and who Reno was and all the warnings Donna had given her about the nature of men and what they wanted from women.

Eve jerked her head aside, but not before she had felt the hot, textured surface of his tongue rubbing over her own.

"No," Eve said urgently, frightened again.

But this time it was herself she feared, for a curious weakness had shot through her at the caressing touch of Reno's tongue.

Donna Lyon had warned her bond servant about what men wanted from women, but she had never warned Eve that women might want the same thing from men.

"Why not?" Reno asked calmly. "You liked kissing me."

"No."

"Like hell, *gata*. I could feel it."

"You're—you're a gunfighter and a thief."

"You're half-right. I've fought with my gun. But as for being a thief, I'm only taking what is rightfully mine—the pearls, the ring, the journal, and the girl with the golden eyes."

"It wasn't a fair poker game," Eve said desperately as Reno bent down to her once more.

"Not my fault. I wasn't the one dealing."

Reno brushed his mouth lazily over Eve's and listened to the surprised rush of air between her lips.

"But—" she began.

"Hush," Reno said, cutting off Eve's protest by biting her lower lip gently. "I won you and I'm going to have you."

"No. Please, don't."

"Don't worry." Slowly Reno released Eve's lip.

"You'll like it. I'll see to it."

"Let me go," Eve said urgently.

"Not a chance. You're mine until I say otherwise."

He smiled and kissed the frantic pulse in her throat.

"If you're real nice," he said in a low voice, "I'll let you go after a few nights."

"Mr. Moran, please, I didn't mean to lose the bet. It's just that Mr. Slater was watching too closely."

"So was I."

Reno lifted his head and looked down at Eve curiously.

"You dealt every card of mine off the bottom of the deck," he said. "Why?"

Eve spoke quickly, trying to keep Reno's attention on anything but the sultry, sexual heat that made his eyes burn like gems.

"I knew Raleigh King and Jericho Slater," she said. "I didn't know you."

"So you set me up to be killed while you ran off with the pot."

Eve couldn't help the guilty flush that crept up her cheeks.

"I didn't mean it to turn out that way," she said.

"But it almost did, and you didn't do a damn thing to stop it."

"I shot at Steamboat when he was drawing down on you!"

"With what?" Reno scoffed. "Did you throw a gold coin at him?"

"My derringer. I keep it in my skirt pocket."

"Handy. Do you have to shoot your way out of many card games?" Reno asked.

"No."

"Pretty good cheater, huh?"

"I don't cheat! Not usually, anyway. I just . . ." Her voice died.

Amused and skeptical at Eve's difficulty in finding the right words to explain how she was innocent when both of them knew she wasn't, Reno lifted one black eyebrow and waited for her to continue.

"I didn't know until too late that Slater knew I was cheating," Eve admitted unhappily. "I knew he was cheating, but I couldn't catch him at it. So I lost to you when I should have stayed in and called Slater."

"The emerald ring," Reno said, nodding. "With the cards you threw in, you should have hung around for at least one draw. But you didn't. So I won that hand, because Slater hadn't had time to deal himself the rest of his full house."

Eve blinked, surprised by Reno's quickness. "Are you a gambler?"

He shook his head.

"Then how did you know what Slater was doing?" she persisted.

"Simple. When he dealt, he won. Then you started dropping out too soon, and I started winning hands I shouldn't have."

"Your mama didn't raise any stupid children, did she?" muttered Eve.

"Oh, I'm one of the slow ones," Reno said in a lazy drawl. "You should see my older brothers, especially Rafe."

Eve blinked as she tried to imagine anyone faster than Reno. She couldn't.

"All through explaining?" Reno asked politely.

"What?"

"This."

Reno bent just enough to cover Eve's mouth with his own. When he felt her tighten beneath him as though to fight again, he settled more heavily on her, reminding her of the lesson she had already learned: When it came to a contest of strength, she didn't have a chance against Reno Moran.

Tentatively Eve relaxed, wondering if Reno would release her if she didn't fight him.

Immediately the overwhelming pressure of his body lifted until it was little more than a warm, disturbingly sensual contact from her shoulders to her feet.

"Now kiss me back," Reno whispered.

"Then you'll let me go?"

"Then we'll negotiate some more."

"And if I don't kiss you?"

"Then I'll take what is already mine, and to hell with what you want."

"You wouldn't," she whispered weakly.

"Care to bet?"

Eve looked into the cool green eyes so close to her own and realized that she never should have allowed Reno Moran to sit down at her poker table.

She was very good at reading most people, but not this man. Right now she couldn't tell if he was bluffing or telling her the simple truth.

Don Lyon's sage advice rang in Eve's mind: *When you can't tell if a man is running a bluff, and you can't afford the ante if you lose, then fold your cards and wait for a better deal.*

3

WITH trembling lips, Eve lifted her head to give Reno the kiss he had demanded. After a quick pressure of her mouth against his, she retreated, her heart beating wildly.

"You call that a kiss?" Reno asked.

She nodded, because she was too nervous to speak.

"I should have guessed you'd cheat with your body the same way you cheat with cards," he said, disgusted.

"I kissed you!"

"The way a frightened virgin kisses her first boy. Well, you're no virgin, and I'm no wide-eyed country boy."

"But I—I am," she stammered.

Reno said something beneath his breath, then added in a cutting voice, "Save the wide-eyed act for a pup that's still wet behind the ears. Men my age know everything worth knowing about wom-

33

en's tricks, and everything we know, we learned the hard way."

"Then you didn't learn enough. I'm not what you think I am."

"Neither am I," he retorted dryly. "I haven't been taken in by that look of wide-eyed innocence since I was innocent myself. That was a long time ago."

Eve opened her mouth to further argue her innocence, but a single look at Reno's face convinced her that he had already made up his mind on the subject. There was nothing of comfort in his ice green eyes or in the flat line of his mouth beneath his mustache. He believed she was a saloon girl and a cheat, pure and simple.

Even worse, she couldn't wholly blame him. She *had* cheated him. Although she hadn't started out to use Reno in her deadly game with Slater and Raleigh, in the end she had risked Reno's life without so much as warning him of what was at stake.

To add insult to injury, she had run off with the very pot she had cheated to give to Reno. The fact that he had survived at all was due to his own unusual skill with a gun. She hadn't even known who he was, so she could hardly say that she was certain he would be able to fight free of the trap he had walked into.

A kiss seemed a simple enough apology to a man whose death she had nearly caused.

Lifting up again, Eve put her lips over Reno's. This time she didn't retreat instantly. Instead, she increased the pressure of the kiss gradually, learning the smooth resilience of his lips in a silence that was bounded by the frantic beating of her heart.

When Reno made no move to deepen or to end the kiss, Eve hesitated, wondering what she should do next. Though Reno didn't believe it, she had told the truth about her innocence. The few times she hadn't been fast enough to dodge a kiss from a cowboy, there had been nothing gentle or pleasant about the embrace. They had grabbed, she had fought free, and that had been the end of it. If there had been any sensual enjoyment in the experience, it hadn't been hers.

But Reno wasn't grabbing, and Eve had agreed to this kiss. She just didn't know how to go about it. The realization perplexed her almost as much as the discovery that kissing Reno affected her in an entirely unexpected way.

She liked it.

"Reno?"

"Keep going. I'll get an honest kiss out of you yet."

Tentatively Eve's hands crept around Reno's neck, for she was becoming tired of holding herself in a half-upright position. At first she was reluctant to trust her weight to his strength, but the temptation was too great to resist for long. Gradually the pressure of her arms around his neck increased as she allowed him to support more and more of her weight.

"Better," Reno said in a deep voice.

His lips were very close to Eve's. The warmth of his breath sent a glittering wash of sensation over her. For an instant her own breath hesitated, then came back quickened. She arched her body to close the remaining distance between her mouth and Reno's.

The first touch of his lips was already familiar, as was the frisson of pleasure that went over Eve when their mouths met. The silken brush of his mustache over the edge of her upper lip was also a pleasure she had known before. Yet each time she felt it, the intensity of the sensation grew greater, shortening her breath even more.

"I wouldn't have guessed," Eve whispered.

She was so close that each word was a separate brush over Reno's mouth. It was the same when he spoke to her, each word a caress.

"What wouldn't you have guessed?" he asked.

"That your mustache would feel like a silk brush."

Eve wondered at the ripple that went through Reno, but had no time to think about it, for his arms were sliding around her. She stiffened, expecting to be grabbed and held down once more.

But Reno made no further move to force her. He simply held her so that she didn't have to make any effort at all to stay close to him. Slowly she relaxed, letting his arms support her.

"I'm still waiting for my kiss," Reno said.

"I think I've kissed you more than once."

"And I think you haven't kissed me at all."

"What was I just doing?"

"Teasing," he said bluntly. "Nice enough, but not what I had in mind, and you know it as well as I do."

"No, I don't. I'm not a mind reader," she retorted, irritated that he hadn't been half so unsettled by the slow, gliding kiss as she had.

"I know what you are. You're a saloon girl with fast hands who promised me the one thing she can't deliver—an honest kiss."

Eve opened her mouth to ask Reno what he thought an honest kiss should be. Then she remembered what he had said about kissing.

I like it hot and deep. Take that quick little tongue and rub it over mine.

Before Eve could lose her nerve, she brought her lips against Reno's open mouth and touched his tongue with her own. The nubby, velvety texture

she felt intrigued her. Tentatively she ran the tip
of her own tongue over him once more, tracing the
shape of his mouth. In the course of her explorations she discovered how smooth and silky the
underside of his tongue was.

She didn't notice the gradual tightening of Ren-
o's arms or the quickening of his breathing. She
didn't notice that she was being lured more deeply
into the kiss with every speeding heartbeat. All she
knew was that Reno's taste and warmth were more
intoxicating than the French brandy Don and
Donna had so loved.

Eve didn't question the growing urgency that
claimed her. She simply tightened her arms around
Reno's neck, trying to get even closer to him, seeking a more complete merging of their mouths.

Suddenly the ground pressed up hard beneath
Eve's body. She was on her back once more, and
Reno was covering her like a warm, heavy blanket.

This time Eve didn't protest, for the position allowed her to get even closer to Reno. Her fingers
searched through his hair, knocking aside his dark
hat. Restlessly she combed her fingers through his
hair, enjoying the thickness and texture and
warmth of it.

Reno shifted and arched against her like a great
cat, silently telling her that he liked the feel of her
nails against his scalp, his neck, the bunched muscles of his back. He liked the taste of her too, sweet-
ness and a heat that grew greater the more he
tested it.

Reno's tongue probed deeply into Eve's mouth
as his weight settled between her thighs, separat-
ing them until he could press the ache of his arousal
into the soft nest that was made to receive him.
He felt the sensual ripple that went through her
body at the contact and wanted to groan at the

savage thrust of his response.

He hadn't meant to get this aroused. He certainly hadn't meant to show her just how badly he wanted her.

But it was too late now. She would know exactly what that hard ridge of flesh pressing against her meant, and she would know exactly how to use it against him to get what she wanted. All that remained of the game was to see how far she would let him go before she tried to stop him.

And what she would offer to make him stop.

Reno's hips moved again, pressing more intimately against Eve's yielding body. A sweet fire blossomed in the pit of her stomach, making her moan. Instinctively her arms tightened around him, seeking to keep him close. She was rewarded by a sinuous movement of his hips, his body retreating and returning to hers in the same primitive rhythms of his tongue moving within her mouth.

Long fingers slid from Eve's shoulders to the lacy camisole and pantalets that were all she had worn to sleep in. He stroked from her ribs to her hip and then up again, not stopping until one breast was filling his hand. His thumb moved, discovered the velvet hardness of her nipple, and tested it with a sensuous, twisting pressure.

Pleasure speared through Eve, taking her completely by surprise. Instinctively she arched, increasing the sweet pressure of his hand, twisting against him like a cat.

With a husky sound of triumph, Reno increased the caress, capturing Eve's nipple and rolling it between his fingers, drinking the whimpering cries that rippled from her mouth. When he could resist the temptation no longer, he tore his lips from hers and dragged a path of fire down her neck and breast, seeking the berry that had ripened to fullness at his caress.

The liquid heat of Reno's mouth sinking through the thin camisole to the naked flesh beneath shocked Eve back to her senses. Dazed, uncertain about what had happened, she fought for breath, only to have it taken from her once more when his mouth tugged on her nipple and fire whipped through her body.

His hand moved and laces came undone, threatening to bare her in an intimacy she had never known before with any man.

"No!" Eve gasped.

Before she could say another word, Reno's mouth was over hers and his tongue was thrusting deeply into her mouth, making it impossible for her to speak. The hungry rubbing of his tongue against hers sent the world spinning away from Eve once more, leaving only Reno's heat and strength as an anchor.

Before he lifted his head again, she was clinging to him, her instinctive protest drowned beneath the heady pleasure he was giving her.

Reno stripped Eve's camisole away with a smooth movement of his arm, revealing the creamy curves and tight coral tips of her breasts. His breath came out with a low sound of need. She glistened with the heat of his mouth, and each rapid breath she took made her breasts shiver invitingly. She had looked so slender, so like a young girl, that he hadn't expected her to be so much a woman.

Without really intending to, Reno bent down to Eve once more.

"Reno, don't, I—"

Eve made a broken sound that was part fear, part fire, as he ignored her small struggles. Slowly his hands slid beneath her back. Then his arms tightened and she was arched like a bow in the instant before he opened his lips and began to suckle and tease the nipples he had aroused.

A low moan was torn from Eve. She shivered as lightning arched her body even more deeply into Reno's hungry mouth.

"What are you doing to me?" she asked brokenly.

His only answer was to turn his head and pull her other nipple into the sultry, unexpected paradise of his mouth.

The sensation of pleasure was even more violent this time. It dragged another cry from Eve as her body arched to meet the demands of the man who held her with such fierce care.

Then Eve felt Reno's hand between her legs.

Fear burst, driving out pleasure, quenching her passionate fire with the icy certainty that Reno wasn't going to stop short of taking her.

"No more!" she said desperately, trying to twist away. "No! Stop! You said a kiss, and I kissed you just the way you said you liked it, didn't I? I've kept my part of the bargain. Please, stop. Reno, *please.*"

Slowly, very reluctantly, Reno lifted his head. The lingering, sensual release of Eve's nipple from his mouth sent a helpless wave of response through her.

He closed his eyes and clenched his teeth against an involuntary groan. The hand he had pressed between her legs was surrounded with the kind of fire he had never drawn so quickly from any woman.

He flexed his fingers, savoring Eve's passionate heat, drawing a cry that wasn't wholly fear from her flushed lips.

"Why should I stop, *gata*?" Reno asked huskily,

watching her. "You want it damn near as much as I do."

His hand moved again, and again she cried out, for her pantalets had no center seam. There was not even the frail barrier of cotton to dull the sensation of his hand curved possessively around her.

Eve grabbed Reno's wrist, trying to drag it from between her legs. She couldn't. He was much stronger than she was.

"You said you would stop if I gave you an honest kiss," Eve said, raggedly. "Wasn't that an honest kiss? Wasn't it?"

The desperation in Eve's voice was unmistakable, as was the sudden stiffness of her body and the hard arcs of her nails digging into his wrist.

Yet at the same time she was a fire surrounding Reno, luring and burning him with each caressing instant.

"If that kiss had been 'honest,' I'd be hilt deep in you right now and you'd be using those sharp little claws on me in a different way, and we'd both be loving every last bit of it," Reno said flatly.

"Is that the only honesty you know?" Eve demanded. "A girl giving herself to every man who wants her?"

"*You* wanted *me*."

"And now I don't! Are you going back on your word, gunfighter?"

Reno took a deep breath and called himself twenty kinds of fool for wanting the expert little cheat from the Gold Dust Saloon. He thought he had been teased by the world expert, one Savannah Marie Carrington. She had tied him in sexual knots and then dragged promises from him before she would let him so much as kiss her hand again.

But each time the promise she really wanted—a settled life in West Virginia—wasn't forthcoming, she had buttoned her bodice with calm fingers and left him. It hadn't been that easy for Reno to turn passion on and off. Not at first. But he had learned. Savannah Marie was a good teacher.

"I didn't promise to stop," Reno said coolly. "I just said we'd negotiate after one kiss. Offer me something, *gata*. Offer me something as interesting as this."

Reno's hand moved once more, pressing against Eve, caressing her. Again she tried to push him away.

"The mine," Eve said. "The Lyons' gold mine."

"Spanish treasure?"

"Yes!"

Reno shrugged and bent toward Eve again.

"I already won that, remember?" he asked.

"Just the journal. It's no good to you without the symbols," she said quickly.

He paused, watching her through narrowed eyes. She might have been eager for his kisses earlier, but now she was eager only to be free of his touch.

Abruptly Reno removed his hand from Eve. He was damned if he would allow himself to be teased into wanting a girl more than she wanted him. That was the kind of mistake a smart man never made more than once.

"What symbols?" he asked skeptically.

"The ones Don Lyon's ancestor carved along the trail to mark dead ends and dangers and gold and everything else that would help."

Slowly Reno moved back, giving Eve more room. But he was careful not to get beyond arm's reach of her. He had seen Eve move. She had an unsettling speed, every bit as fast as a cat.

"All right, *gata*, talk to me about Spanish gold."

"My name is Eve, not cat," she said.

She grabbed the camisole that Reno had tossed aside and yanked it on.

"Eve, huh? Somehow I'm not surprised. Well, my name isn't Adam, so don't try feeding me any apples."

"Your loss, not mine," she muttered. "I'm told my apple pie is the best to be found west of the Mississippi and north of the Mason-Dixon line, and maybe south of it as well."

Hurriedly Eve fastened the camisole with fingers that were unusually clumsy. She knew she had just had a narrow escape.

And she was grateful that gunfighters kept their word.

"I'm more interested in gold than I am in apple pie," Reno retorted. "Remember?"

He stroked Eve's thigh. The action was both a caress and a threat.

"Don Lyon was the descendant of Spanish gentry," Eve said quickly.

Then she looked from Reno's hand to his eyes, plainly reminding him of their bargain. Slowly he lifted his hand.

"One of his forebears had a license from the king to explore for metals in New Mexico," Eve said. "Another ancestor was an officer assigned to guard a gold mine run by a Jesuit priest."

"Jesuit, not Franciscan?"

"No. It was before the Spanish king threw the Jesuits out of the New World."

"That was a long time ago."

"The journal's first entry is dated in the fifteen-fifties or eighties," Eve said. "It's hard to tell. The ink is faded and the page is torn."

When Eve didn't say anything else immediately, Reno's hand went to her belly. He spread his fingers wide, almost spanning her hipbones.

Her breath came in with a rushing sound. It was as though he were measuring the space for a baby to grow.

"Go on," Reno said.

He knew his voice was too deep, too husky, but there was nothing he could do about it, any more than he could control the heavy running of his desire, no matter how foolish he knew it was to want the calculating little saloon girl.

The heat from her body was like a drug seeping through his skin and being absorbed into his blood, making it harder with each heartbeat to remember that she was just one more girl out to get whatever she could by using her body as a lure.

Then Reno realized that Eve had said nothing more. He looked up and saw her watching him with yellow cat's eyes.

"Going back on your word so quickly?" Eve asked.

Angrily Reno lifted his hand.

"I think it must be 1580," Eve said.

"More like 1867," Reno retorted.

"What?"

Without answering, Reno looked at the frail cotton of the camisole, which served only to heighten rather than to conceal the allure of Eve's breasts.

"Reno?"

When he looked up, Eve was afraid she had lost the dangerous game she was playing. Reno's eyes were a pale green, and they burned.

"It's 1867," he said, "summer, we're on the eastern edge of the Rocky Mountains, and I'm trying to decide if I want to hear any more fairy tales about Spanish gold before I take what I won in a card game."

"It's not a fairy tale! It's all in the journal. There was a Captain Leon and someone called Sosa."

"Sosa?"

"Yes," Eve said quickly. "Gaspar de Sosa. And a Jesuit Priest. And a handful of soldiers."

Through a screen of thick brown eyelashes, she watched Reno warily, praying that he believed her.

"I'm listening," he said. "Not real patiently, mind you, but I'm listening."

What Reno didn't say was that he was listening very carefully. He had tried to retrace the trail of the Espejo and Sosa expeditions more than once. Both expeditions had found gold and silver mines that had yielded vast wealth.

And all of their mines had been "lost" before their riches ran out.

"Sosa and Leon were given license to find and develop mines for the king," Eve said, frowning as she tried to remember all that she had learned from the Lyons and the old journal. "The expedition went north all the way to the land of the Yutahs."

"Today we call them Utes," Reno said.

"Sosa followed Espejo, who was the one who gave the land the name of New Mexico," she said hurriedly. "And he was the one who called the routes leading out of all the mines and back to Mexico the Old Spanish Trail."

"Nice of them to write in English so you could figure all this out," Reno said sardonically.

"What do you mean?" Eve asked, giving him a quick glance. "They wrote in Spanish. Funny Spanish. It's the very devil to puzzle out."

Reno's head lifted sharply. Eve's words, rather than her body, finally had his full attention.

"You can read the old Spanish writings?" he asked.

"Don taught me how before his eyes got too bad to make out the words. I would read them to him, and he would try to remember what his father had said about those passages, and his grandfather, too."

"Family tales. Fairy tales. Same difference."

Eve ignored the interruption. "Then I'd write down what Don remembered in the journal's margins."

"Couldn't he write?"

"Not for the past few years. His hands were too knotted up."

Unconsciously Eve laced her own slender fingers together, remembering the pain the old couple suffered in cold weather. Donna's hands had been little better than her husband's.

"I guess they spent too many winters in gold camps where there was more whiskey than firewood," she said huskily.

"All right, Eve Lyon. Keep talking."

"My name isn't Lyon. They were my employers, not my blood relatives."

Reno had caught the change in Eve's voice and the subtle tension in her body. He wondered if she was lying.

"Employers?" he asked.

"They . . ." Eve looked away.

Reno waited.

"They bought me off an orphan train in Denver five years ago," she said in a low voice.

Even as Reno opened his mouth to make a sarcastic remark about the futility of tugging on his heartstrings with sad stories, he realized that Eve could easily be telling the truth. The Lyons could indeed have bought her from an orphan train as though she were a side of bacon.

It wouldn't have been the first time such a thing had happened. Reno had heard many other such stories. Some of the orphans found good homes.

Most didn't. They were worked, and worked hard, by homesteaders or townspeople who had no cash to hire help, but had enough food to spare for another mouth.

Slowly Reno nodded. "Makes sense. Bet their hands had started to go bad."

"They could barely shuffle, much less deal cards. Especially Don."

"Were they cardsharps?"

Eve closed her eyes for an instant, remembering her shame and fear the first time she had been caught cheating. She had been fourteen and so nervous, the cards had scattered all over when she shuffled. In picking the cards up, one of the men noticed the slight roughness that marked aces, kings, and queens.

"They were gamblers," Eve said tonelessly.

"Cheats."

Her eyelids flinched. "Sometimes."

"When they thought they could get away with it," Reno said, not bothering to hide his contempt.

"No," Eve said in a soft voice. "Only when they had to. Most of the time the other players were too drunk to notice what cards they were holding, much less what they were dealt."

"So the nice old couple taught you how to cold-deck and bottom-deal," Reno said.

"They also taught me how to speak and read Spanish, how to ride any horse I could get my hands on, how to cook and sew and—"

"Cheat at cards," he finished. "I'll bet they taught you a lot of other things, too. How much did they charge for a few hours with you?"

Nothing in Reno's voice or expression revealed the anger that churned in his gut at the thought of Eve's beautiful body being bought by any drifter

with a handful of change and a hard need filling
his jeans.

"What?" Eve asked.

"How much did your *employers* charge a man to
get under your skirt?"

For an instant Eve was too shocked to speak.
Her hand flashed out so quickly that only a few
men would have been able to counter the blow.

Reno was one of them, but it was a near thing.
Just before her palm would have connected with
his cheek, he caught her wrist and flattened her
out on the bedroll beneath him in the same violent
motion.

"Don't try that again," he said harshly. "I know
all about wide-eyed little hussies who slap a man
when he suggests they're anything less than a lady.
The next time you lift a hand to me, I won't be a
gentleman about it."

Eve made a sound that could have been a laugh
or a sob. "Gentleman? You? No gentleman would
force himself on a lady!"

"But then, you're not a lady," Reno said. "You're
something that was bought off an orphan train and
sold whenever a man was interested enough to
hand over a dollar."

"No man, *ever*, paid for anything from me."

"You just gave your, uh, favors away?" Reno
suggested ironically. "And the men were so grateful, they left a little present on the bedside table,
is that it?"

"No man ever got under my skirt, with or without paying," Eve said icily.

Reno rolled aside, freeing Eve. Before she could
move away, his hand settled at the apex of her
thighs, where a bronze thicket guarded her sultry
core.

"Not true, *gata*. I've been under your skirt, and I'm a man."

"Go to hell, gunfighter," Eve said through clenched teeth, her voice steady despite the tears of shame and rage in her eyes.

Reno saw only the rage. It occurred to him that he would be wise not to turn his back on his little saloon girl until she cooled off. Eve was quick, very quick, and at the moment she looked fully capable of picking up the shotgun and emptying both barrels into him.

"Mad enough to kill, aren't you?" he asked sardonically. "Well, don't worry. Nobody ever died of it. Now, talk."

Eve watched Reno through glittering golden slits. He lifted one black eyebrow.

"If you don't feel like talking," he said, "I can find something else for that quick little tongue of yours to do."

4

"**S**OSA found gold," Eve said, her voice vibrating with anger. "He paid the King's Quinto and bribed the other officials and kept the truth about the mines to himself."

Reno looked away from Eve's flushed cheeks and pale lips, feeling something close to shame for pushing her so hard. Then he cursed himself for feeling anything at all for the saloon girl who had done her best to get him killed while she stole everything in sight and ran to safety.

"What was the truth about the mines?" Reno asked roughly.

"All of them weren't listed for the tax collectors. The silver mines, yes, and the turquoise mine and even two of the gold mines. But not the third one. That one he kept to himself."

"Go on."

Though Reno wasn't looking at Eve any longer, she thought he sounded truly interested for the first time. She drew a discreet, relieved breath and kept talking.

"Only Leon's eldest son knew about the secret gold mine, and then that son's eldest son, and so on until the journal came into Don Lyon's hands at the turn of the century," Eve said. "By then, Spain was long gone from the West, the Leon name had become Lyon, and they spoke English rather than Spanish."

Reno turned back to look at Eve, drawn by the shifting emotions in her voice.

"If there's a gold mine in the family," he asked, "why was Don Lyon making his living cheating at cards?"

"About a hundred years ago, they lost the mines," Eve said simply.

"A hundred years. Was that when the Jesuits were thrown out?"

Eve nodded.

"The family was closely tied to the Jesuits," she continued. "They had enough advance warning to bury the gold that had been smelted but not shipped. They covered over all signs of the mine and fled east across the mountains. They didn't stop running until they came to the English colonies."

"Didn't any Leon ever try to find the gold they had left behind?" Reno asked.

"Don's great-grandfather did, and his grandfather, and then his father. They never came back." Eve shrugged. "Don always wanted the gold mine, but he didn't want to die for it."

"Smart man."

She smiled sadly. "In some ways. He was far too gentle for this world, though."

"A gentle cheater?" Reno asked ironically.

"Why do you think he cheated? It was the only way he had any chance at all against men like you."

"A gambler who's that bad at cards should find another profession."

"That's not what I meant," Eve retorted. "Don was a small man. He didn't have the strength to fight with his fists, the speed to fight with a gun, or the greed to be a good cardsharp. He was a kind man rather than a strong one.

"But he was good to Donna and to me, even through we were weaker than he was. That's more than I can say of the big men I've met!"

One of Reno's black eyebrows rose. "I suppose if you had been cheating *for* rather than against me, I might feel more kindly toward you myself."

Eve's smile was as small and cold as the spring hidden against the cliff.

"You don't understand, gunfighter."

"Don't bet on it, saloon girl."

She tossed her head, sending her deep gold hair cascading over her shoulders.

"I thought you were different from Raleigh King, but you're not," she said. "You haven't the least idea what it's like to make your way in a world that is stronger, harder, and more cruel than you could ever be."

"You won't get into my good graces by comparing me to the likes of Raleigh King."

"I'm not trying to get into your good graces."

"You'd better start."

Eve took one look at Reno and bit back the angry words that were crowding her tongue.

There was no gentleness now in Reno's eyes or in the line of his mouth. He was dead angry. When he spoke again, his voice was as cold and remote as his ice green eyes.

"Be grateful Raleigh needed killing," Reno said flatly. "If you had set me up to kill a country boy, I'd have let Slater have you. You wouldn't have liked that. Slater isn't one of those kind men you so favor."

"He can't be any worse than Raleigh King," Eve said bleakly, remembering the night she had come back late from one of Canyon City's saloons and discovered what Raleigh had done to the Lyons. "No one could be worse than him."

"Slater has a reputation with women that's too sordid to repeat—even to a saloon girl who cheats at cards."

"Did Slater ever torture an old man who had tried to sell a gold ring to pay for medicine for his dying wife?" Eve asked tightly. "Did Slater ever pull the truth from an old man one fingernail at a time while his wife watched helplessly? And after the man was dead, did Slater ever take his knife to an old, dying woman and . . ."

Eve's voice crumbled into silence. She clenched her fists and fought for self-control.

"What are you saying?" Reno asked in a low voice.

"Raleigh King tortured Don Lyon to death while he dragged out the truth about where the emerald ring was hidden, and the journal with the treasure map. Donna tried to stop Raleigh, but the wasting disease had left her too weak even to lift her derringer."

Reno's eyes narrowed. "So that's how Raleigh knew about the map."

Eve nodded tightly. "When Raleigh was finished with Don, he turned on Donna."

"Why? Didn't Raleigh believe her husband had told the truth?"

"Raleigh didn't care," Eve said bitterly. "He just wanted . . ."

Her voice dried up into a painful silence. No matter how many times she swallowed, she couldn't force out words to describe what Raleigh had done to Donna Lyon.

"Don't," Reno said.

He put his palm gently over Eve's lips, sealing in the bitter words she was trying to speak.

"I guess he and Slater were well matched after all," Reno said softly.

Eve grabbed Reno's hand, but not to push him away.

"Tell me," she said urgently. "You killed Raleigh King, didn't you?"

Reno nodded.

She let out a long breath and whispered, "Thank you. I didn't know how I was going to be able to do it."

All gentleness vanished from Reno's expression.

"Is that why you set me up?" he demanded.

"I didn't set you up. Not in the cold way you mean."

"But you saw the chance and you took it."

Eve's mouth tightened. "Yes."

"And then you grabbed the pot and ran."

"Yes."

"Leaving me to die."

"No!"

Reno made a sound that was too hard to be a laugh.

"We came closer that time, *gata*. We almost had it."

"What?"

"The truth."

"The truth is, I saved your life," Eve retorted.

"Saved it?" Reno demanded. "Girl, you did your best to get me killed!"

"When I didn't hear any shooting—" she began.

"Disappointed?" he interrupted.

"I turned back to see what had happened," she said, ignoring his interruption. "Then Raleigh drew and you shot him, and a man called Steamer pulled his gun to shoot you in the back. I shot him first."

Unexpectedly, Reno laughed.

"You're good, *gata*. Really good. The wide eyes and the earnest, trembling mouth are first-class."

"But—"

"Save those lips for something better than lying," Reno said, bending over Eve once more.

"I shot Steamer!" she protested.

"Uh-huh. But you were aiming for me. That's why you turned back. You wanted to be dead sure I wouldn't follow you to collect my winnings."

"No. That's not the way it was. I—"

"Give up the game," Reno said curtly. "You're trying my patience."

"Why won't you believe me?"

"Because a man who believes a liar, a cheat, and a saloon girl is more of a fool than Reno Moran is."

His fingers closed around Eve's thigh once more. And once more she wasn't able to break away from his touch.

"I'm not a liar," she said hotly, "and I hate being so weak that I have to cheat, and I was a bond servant with no choice about what kind of work I did or where I did it or what I wore while I did it!"

Eve's voice shook with anger as she continued, not letting Reno interrupt.

"But you believe only the worst about me," she said, "so you should have no trouble believing this—my biggest regret about yesterday is not letting Steamer shoot you in the back!"

Surprise loosened Reno's grip for an instant. It was all Eve needed. She jerked from beneath his hand with a speed that startled him.

She stood, taking a blanket with her. With hands that showed a fine trembling, she wrapped the blanket around herself, concealing everything of her body but the hot flags of anger and humiliation burning on her cheeks.

Reno considered taking the blanket away from Eve. He had liked looking at the satin curves and velvet shadows beneath the old, thin cotton fabric of her underwear. Her anger both surprised and intrigued him. Women who were caught in lies usually became all soft and wary and eager to make amends.

But not the girl called Evening Star. Her eyes were measuring him for a shroud.

Wryly Reno admitted to himself that whatever else he could say about Eve—and none of it good— she had grit. He admired that in men, women, and horses.

"Don't be so quick off the mark," Reno drawled. "I might just get up and ride out of here, leaving you for Slater."

Eve hid the shaft of fear that went through her at the thought of Jericho Slater.

"Pity you didn't shoot him, too," she said beneath her breath.

Reno heard. His ears were as acute as his hands were quick.

"I'm not a hired killer."

Her eyes narrowed warily at the flatness of Reno's voice. "I know."

His cold green glance searched her face for a long moment before he nodded.

"See that you remember it," he said curtly. "Don't ever set me up as an executioner again."

She nodded.

Reno came to his feet in an unhurried, graceful movement that reminded Eve of the cat he accused her of being.

"Get dressed," he said. "We can talk about the Lyons' mine while you cook breakfast."

Reno paused. "You do know how to cook, don't you?"

"Of course. Every girl can."

He smiled, remembering a certain redheaded British aristocrat who hadn't been able to boil water when she married Wolfe Lonetree.

"Not every girl," Reno said.

The gentle amusement in his smile fascinated Eve. It was as unexpected as a hot day in winter.

"Who was she?" Eve asked before she could think better of it.

"Who?"

"The girl who couldn't cook."

"A British lady. Prettiest thing a man ever did see. Hair like fire and eyes like aquamarines."

Eve told herself that the feeling snaking through her couldn't be jealousy.

"What happened?" she asked offhandedly.

"What do you mean?"

"If she was that fetching, why didn't you marry her?"

Reno stretched and looked down at Eve from his much greater height.

She didn't back up an inch. She simply stood and waited for the answer to her question as though there were no difference in size or strength between herself and the man who could have broken her like a dry twig.

In that, Eve reminded Reno of Jessica and Willow. The realization made him frown. Neither Jessica nor Willow was the kind of girl to cheat, steal, or work in a saloon.

"Wouldn't the pretty aristocrat have a gunman like you?" Eve persisted.

"I'm not a gunman. I'm a prospector. But that's not why Jessi wouldn't have me."

"She liked gentlemen?" Eve guessed.

To conceal his irritation, Reno grabbed his hat and pulled it down over his unruly black hair.

"I *am* a gentleman."

Eve looked from the crown of Reno's black hat to the worn fleece-lined leather jacket that came to his hips. His pants were dark and had seen hard use. His boots were the same. He wore blunted brass cavalry spurs. Their metal had been so long without polish that they no longer were the least bit shiny.

Nothing about Reno gleamed or flashed, and that included the butt of the six-gun he wore. The holster was the same; it had been oiled for use rather than for looks. The bullets, however, were quite clean.

In all, Reno didn't appear to be a gentleman. He looked every bit the dangerous gunfighter Eve knew him to be, a man drawn in shades of darkness rather than light.

Except for his eyes. They were the vivid green of early spring leaves, as clear and perfect as cut crystal against the sun-darkened skin of his face.

But a person had to be close to Reno to discover the light in his eyes. She doubted that many people got that close.

Or wanted to.

"Jessi is married to one of my best friends," Reno said flatly. "Otherwise, I'd have been happy to try my hand at courting."

" 'Courting.' "

Eve looked at the tangled bedroll where she had known her first taste of passion.

"Is that what you call it?" she asked dryly.

"Courting is for a woman you want to make your wife. That—" Reno jerked his thumb at the bedroll "—was a little rolling around before breakfast with a saloon girl."

The blood left Eve's face. She couldn't think of anything to say except the kind of words that would give Reno a lower opinion of her than he already had. Silently she turned to her saddlebags, grabbed a shirt and a pair of jeans, and started walking away.

Reno's hand shot out with startling speed, grabbing her arm.

"Going somewhere?" he asked.

"Even saloon girls need privacy."

"Tough. I don't trust you out of my sight."

"Then I'll just have to pee in your boots, won't I?" she asked sweetly.

For an instant Reno looked shocked. Then he threw back his head and laughed.

Eve jerked free of his fingers and stalked off into the nearby forest as Reno's words followed her.

"Don't be long, *gata*, or I'll come hunting you— barefoot."

WHEN Reno came back from the forest with more dry wood, he looked approvingly at the small, hot, nearly invisible fire Eve had made. Woodsmoke from the hat-sized fire drifted no more than a few feet into the air before it dissipated.

He dumped the fuel near the fire and sat on his heels by the small, cheerful flames.

"Who taught you to make that kind of fire?" he asked.

Eve looked up from the frying pan where bacon sizzled and pan biscuits turned crisp brown in the fat. Since she had returned from the forest dressed in men's clothing, she hadn't spoken to Reno unless asked a direct question. She had simply gone about preparing breakfast under his watchful eyes.

"What kind of fire?" Eve asked, looking away from him.

"The kind that won't attract every Indian and outlaw for fifty miles around," Reno said dryly.

"One of the few times Donna Lyon took a cane to me was when I put wet wood on the fire. I never did it again."

Eve didn't look up as she spoke.

Irritation prodded Reno. He was tired of being made to feel as though he had offended the tender sensibilities of some shy little flower. She was a cardsharp, a cheat, and a hussy, not some cosseted child of strict parents.

"Did the Lyons have a price on their heads?" Reno asked bluntly.

"No. If they had, they wouldn't have worried about attracting outlaws and gunmen and thieves to their fire, would they?"

Reno made a noncommittal sound.

"They just would have shot a buck and roasted it whole," Eve continued acidly, "and then robbed everyone who followed the smell of cooking meat back to their camp."

"Too bad Donna didn't tell you about the difference between honey and vinegar when it comes to attracting flies."

"She did. I've been using vinegar ever since. What sane girl would want to draw flies?"

A smiled flashed beneath Reno's dark mustache.

For an instant he thought how much Willow and Jessica would have enjoyed Eve's tart, quick tongue—right up until the time she cheated or lied or stole something from them. Then he would have to explain to them, and to their irate husbands, why he had brought a saloon girl in red silk to their home.

Eve pulled a piece of bacon from the pan and put it on her battered tin plate.

Silently Reno admitted to himself that Eve didn't look like a slut at the moment. She looked more like some waif blown in by the wind, worn and sad and frayed around the edges. Her clothes had once belonged to a boy, from the look of them— too narrow in the chest and hips, and too loose everywhere else.

"Whose clothesline did you steal that outfit from?" Reno asked idly.

"They belonged to Don Lyon."

"Lord, he was a small man."

"Yes."

Reno stopped, struck by a thought.

"I didn't see any new graves when I passed by Canyon City's graveyard on the way in, but you said the Lyons were killed by Raleigh King."

Eve said nothing in response to the implied question.

"You know, *gata*, sooner or later I'm going to break you of lying."

"I'm not a liar," she said tightly. "I buried the Lyons at our campsite."

"When?"

"Last week."

"How?"

"With a shovel."

With a speed that startled Eve, Reno straightened and grabbed one of her hands. After a single look at her palm, he released her.

"If you handled cards that deftly with a mess of broken blisters," Reno said, "I'd hate to take cards in a game with you when your hands heal."

Saying nothing, Eve went back to tending breakfast.

"You should wash them with soap and hot water," Reno added.

Startled, Eve looked up. "The biscuits?"

He smiled unwillingly.

"Your hands. Jessi says washing wounds prevents infections."

"I washed before I went to bed last night," Eve said. "I hate being dirty."

"You used lilac soap."

"How did you know? Oh, you found it when you searched my saddlebag."

"No. Your breasts smelled like spring."

A wash of pink went up Eve's cheeks. Her heart turned over as she remembered the feel of Reno's mouth on her breasts. The fork she had been using on the bacon jerked, and hot grease spattered on the back of her hand.

Before the pain of it registered on Eve, Reno was there, looking to see how badly she had burned herself.

"You're all right," he said after a moment. "It will smart for a bit, that's all."

Numbly she nodded.

He turned her hand palm up and looked at the abraded skin once more. Silently he took her other hand and glanced at the palm. There was no doubt that her hands had been hard used, and recently.

"You must have worked a long time to chew up your hands like that," Reno said.

The unexpected gentleness in his voice made

Eve's eyes burn worse than the skin that had been scored by hot grease. A wave of memories swept over her, making her tremble. Preparing the Lyons for burial and then digging their grave was something she would not soon forget.

"I couldn't leave them like that," she whispered. "Especially after what Raleigh did . . . I buried them together. Do you think they minded not having separate graves?"

Reno's hands tightened over Eve's as he looked at her bent head. The acute sympathy he felt for her was as unexpected as it was unwelcome. No matter how often he reminded himself that she was a saloon girl, she kept sliding beneath his guard as easily as the fragrance of her lilac soap was absorbed into his body with every breath he took.

He took a deep breath, trying to control his physical reaction to Eve. The breath didn't help. Her soft, golden hair smelled of the same lilac soap that her breasts did. He had never been especially fond of scent—any scent—but he suspected that lilac would haunt him almost as much as the memory of her nipples rising eagerly to his mouth.

Reno wanted Eve more than he had any woman in a long, long time. But if she discovered his weakness, she would make his life a living hell.

Reno dropped Eve's hands and turned away to the fire.

"Tell me more about my mine," he said curtly.

Eve took a deep breath and banished the Lyons from her mind as Donna had taught her to banish all things she couldn't control.

"Your *half* of the mine," Eve said, and waited for the explosion.

It wasn't long in coming.

"What?" Reno asked, spinning around to face her.

"Without me deciphering the symbols along the trail, you won't be able to find the mine."

"Don't bet on it."

"I have no choice but to bet on my skill," she said. "And neither do you. Without me, you'll never find the mine. You can have all of nothing or half of the gold mine that rightfully belongs to me."

There was the kind of silence that precedes thunder after the arc of lightning from sky to ground. Then Reno smiled, but there was no humor in the thin curve of his mouth.

"All right," he said. "Half of the mine."

She let out a soft rush of air in relief.

"And all of the girl," Reno added flatly.

Relief congealed into a lump in Eve's throat.

"What?" she asked.

"You heard me. Until we find the mine, you'll be my woman whenever I want you, however I want you."

"But I thought if I told you about the mine, you would—"

"No buts," Reno said coldly. "I'm getting damned tired of bargaining for what is already mine. Besides, you need me as much as I need you. You wouldn't last two days out in that desert alone. You need me to—"

"But I'm not what you think I am, I'm—"

"Sure you are," he interrupted. "Right now you're wriggling like a worm on a hook, trying to find a way out of keeping your word. Only a cheat would do that."

Eve closed her eyes.

It was a mistake. The tears she had been trying to hide slid from beneath her lashes.

Reno watched, savagely shoving down all feeling of sympathy, telling himself her tears were just one more in the arsenal of female weapons. Yet it was nearly impossible for him not to soften. The longer he was with Eve, the more difficult he found it to remember what a conniving little tart she really was.

For the first time in his life, Reno was grateful for the past's cruel lessons in the ways a woman managed a man. There had been a time in his life when he would have believed Eve's silver tears and pale, trembling lips.

"Well?" he said roughly. "Is it a deal?"

Eve looked at the dark, oversize gunfighter who was watching her with eyes as hard as jade.

"I—" Her voice cracked.

Reno waited, watching her.

"I was wrong about you," Eve said after a moment. "I'm not strong enough to fight you and win, so you'll take what you want from me, just like Slater or Raleigh."

"I've never taken a woman by force in my life," Reno said flatly. "I never will."

Eve let out a long breath. "Truly?"

Despite himself, Reno felt a wave of compassion for Eve. Cheat or not, saloon girl or not, no girl deserved the kind of rough usage she got from men like Slater and Raleigh King.

"You have my word on it."

Reno saw the relief in Eve's golden eyes and smiled thinly.

"That doesn't mean I won't touch you," he continued. "It just means that when I take you—and I will—you'll be screaming with pleasure, not pain."

A tide of crimson replaced the pallor of Eve's face.

"Do we have a deal?" Reno asked.

"You won't touch me unless I—"

"I won't *take* you," he corrected instantly. "There's a difference, saloon girl. If you don't like that bargain, we can go back to the first one—I get all of the mine and all of the girl. Take your pick."

"You're too kind," Eve said through her teeth.

"Doubtless. But I'm a reasonable man. I won't keep you forever. Just for as long as it takes to find the mine. Deal?"

Eve looked at Reno for a long moment. She reminded herself that he had no reason to trust her, many reasons *not* to respect her, was quite capable of taking what he wanted and to hell with her protests; yet he was willing to treat her better than any inhabitant of the Gold Dust Saloon would have, given the same opportunity.

"Deal," she said.

When Eve turned away to tend breakfast, Reno moved with his customary speed. She froze as his hand closed over her wrists.

"One more thing," he said.

"What?" Eve whispered.

"This."

She closed her eyes, expecting to feel the heat of his mouth over hers.

Instead, she felt Don Lyon's ring sliding from her fingers.

"I'll keep the ring and the pearls until I find a woman who loves me as much as she loves her own comfort," Reno said.

Then he added sardonically, "And while I'm at it, I'll find a ship made of stone, a dry rain, and a light that casts no shadow."

Reno pocketed the ring and turned away. "Get

saddled up. It's a long way over the Great Divide to Cal's ranch."

"Why are we going there?"

"Cal is counting on the winter supplies I'm bringing. And unlike some people I've met, when I say I'll do something, I do it."

5

BEYOND the Great Divide, the massive wall of mountains slowly changed, breaking into chains and clusters of ragged peaks rising in stone waves against the endless blue sky.

Even in late August, the peaks were streaked with glittering snowfields. Creeks rushed down steep folds in the sides of the mountains, combined forces on the flats, then wound down long valleys and through basins like ropes of liquid diamonds beneath the sun. The vivid green of aspens and the darker greens of fir, spruce, and pine made a velvet robe across the mountain flanks. In the clearings, grasses and shrubs added their own bright shades of green to the land.

Once Reno and Eve had ridden through the first pass beyond Canyon City, there were few signs of men traveling over the land, and even fewer marks of permanent residence. Wild animals abounded. Mustangs fled like multicolored clouds before a storm wind when Reno and Eve rode into lonely valleys. Elk and deer glided out from cover to browse along the margins of the clearings.

Though wary of man, the deer weren't as quick to flee as the wild horses. The pure, keening cries of eagles floating on the wind were woven like bright threads through the day.

Reno was more wary than any of the animals. He rode every moment as though expecting attack. He never cut across a clearing unless it would take them miles off their course to circle along the margin where forest and grass met. He never crested a rise without pausing just below the rim to see what was on the other side. Only when he was satisfied that there were no Indians or outlaws nearby did he reveal himself against the skyline.

He never rode into a narrow canyon if he could avoid it. If avoidance was impossible, he slipped the thong on his six-shooter and rode with his repeating rifle across the saddle. Often during the day he would retrace part of their back trail, find a vantage point, and simply watch the land for any signs that they were being followed.

Unlike most men, Reno rode with the reins in his right hand, leaving his left hand free for the six-gun that was never beyond his reach, even when he slept. Every night he checked his weapons for trail dust or moisture from the afternoon storms that swirled through the peaks.

Reno didn't make a fuss about his precautions. He didn't really even notice them anymore. He had lived alone in a wild land for so long that he was no more aware of his skill at it than he was of his skill in riding the tough blue roan he called Darlin'.

Eve didn't think the mare was anyone's Darlin'. She was a hardy mustang with the temperament of a wolverine and the wariness of a wolf. Should anyone but Reno approach the mare, she flattened her ears to her skull and looked for a place to sink her big white teeth into flesh. With Reno, however, the mare was all nickers and soft whuffles of greeting.

Darlin' was constantly testing the breeze for the scent of danger. At the moment her head was up, her ears were pricked, and her nostrils were flared as she drank the wind.

Out in the sunlit meadow a bird called sharply and cut aside to fly into the forest. The silence that followed the bird's retreat was total.

Eve didn't wait for Reno's signal to go into hiding. As soon as the bird veered aside, she reined Whitefoot deeper into the cover of the forest and waited. Breath held, motionless, she watched the meadow through the screen of aspens and evergreens.

A solitary mustang stallion walked warily into the clearing. The half-healed wounds of a recent fight were clear on the horse's body. He lowered his muzzle into the creek and drank, stopping every few moments to raise his head and sniff the breeze. Despite his wounds, the stallion was fit and powerful, just coming into his full maturity.

Compelled by the young horse's muscular beauty, Eve leaned forward in the saddle. The faint creaking of leather carried no farther than Whitefoot's ears, yet the stallion seemed to sense her presence.

Finally the wild horse drank again, looked up, and walked slowly away from the stream. Soon he began cropping grass. His vigilance didn't end while he ate. Rarely did a minute go by that the stallion didn't pause, lift his head, and test the breeze for enemies. In a herd his constant checking wouldn't have been necessary, for there would have been other ears, other eyes, other wary horses to scent the breeze. But the stallion was alone.

It occurred to Eve that Reno was like the mustang stallion—ready for battle, wary, trusting nothing and no one, completely alone.

Eve sensed movement behind her. When she turned in the saddle, she saw the catfooted blue roan coming through the forest toward her.

A breeze wound through the evergreens, drawing a sigh from their slender green needles. Whitefoot stirred, made uneasy by the scent of the stallion on the wind. Silently Eve stroked the gelding's neck to reassure him.

"Where are the packhorses?" Eve asked in a low voice as Reno rode alongside.

"I left them tied up the trail a piece. They'll raise a fuss if anything tries to creep up on us from that direction."

Reno stood in the stirrups and looked across the meadow. After a moment he settled back into the saddle.

"No mares," Reno said quietly. Beneath his mustache, his lips shaped a thin smile. "From the looks of his hide, that young stud just learned the first lesson of dealing with women."

Eve looked questioningly at Reno.

"Given a choice between an old stud that knows where to find food and a young stud so crazy for a woman that he doesn't know which end is up," Reno drawled, "a female will take the old stud and comfort every damned time."

"A female that trusted the promises of every young stud with rutting on his mind wouldn't last through the winter."

"Spoken like a true woman."

"Imagine that," Eve shot back.

Unwillingly, Reno smiled. "You have a point."

Eve looked at the stallion and then back at Reno,

remembering what he had said as he pocketed the emerald and gold ring he had taken from her finger.

"Who was she?" Eve asked.

One of Reno's black eyebrow's lifted in silent query.

"The woman who chose her own comfort over your love," Eve said simply.

The line of Reno's jaw tightened beneath the stubble that had grown over the days on the trail.

"What makes you think there was only one?" he asked coolly.

"You don't strike me as the kind of man who has to learn something twice."

The corner of Reno's mouth kicked up. "You're right about that."

Eve waited, saying nothing, but her intent golden eyes asked a hundred questions.

"Savannah Marie Carrington," Reno drawled finally.

The change in his voice was almost tangible. There was neither hate nor love in the tone, simply a contempt that was chilling.

"What did she do to you?" Eve asked.

He shrugged. "The same thing most women do to men."

"What's that?"

"You should know, *gata*."

"Because I'm a woman?"

"Because you're damned good at the kind of teasing females use to get men so hot and bothered they'll say or do almost anything to get what they want."

Reno's eyes narrowed as he added, "Almost anything, but not quite."

"What wouldn't you do? Love her?"

He laughed humorlessly. "Hell, that was the one thing I did do."

"You still love her," Eve said.

The words were an accusation.

"Don't bet on it," Reno said, giving her a side-long glance.

"Why?"

"Are you always this nosy?"

"Curious," Eve corrected instantly. "I'm a cat, remember?"

"That you are."

Again Reno stood in the stirrups to check the surrounding land. The stallion grazed on hungrily, undisturbed by anything he could scent or sense. Birds called across the grassy clearing and flew from tree to tree in normal patterns. Nothing moved along the vague trail the horses had left at the margin of the meadow.

Reno reined Darlin' around, ready to resume the ride to Caleb and Willow's home in the San Juan Mountains.

"Reno? What did she want you to do? Kill someone?"

He smiled tightly. "You could say that."

"Who?"

"Me."

"What?" Eve asked. "That doesn't make any sense."

He said something profane beneath his breath and looked over his shoulder at the girl whose golden eyes, soft breasts, and lilac scent haunted his dreams.

"Savannah Marie wanted to live in West Virginia, where our families had farms before the war," Reno said, clipping each word. "But I had seen the true West. I had seen places no man ever touched, drunk from streams as pure as God's smile, ridden over passes that had no names . . . and I had held the solid gold tears of the sun in my hands."

Motionless, Eve watched Reno as he spoke, wondering at the emotion that made his voice both resonant and husky when he talked about the land.

"The first time I left Savannah Marie," Reno said, "I missed her so much I damn near killed two horses riding back to her."

He said no more.

"But she hadn't waited for you?" Eve guessed.

"Oh, she'd waited," he drawled, but there was no warmth in his voice. "At the time, I was still best catch for a hundred miles around. She came running up to me with her blue eyes all sparkling with tears of happiness."

"What happened?"

He shrugged. "The usual. Her family threw a party, we went for a walk in the garden, and she gave me just enough to make me wild for her."

Eve's hands tightened on the reins. The contempt in Reno's voice was like a whip.

"Then she asked if I was ready to make a home and raise horses on the acreage her daddy had set aside along Stone Creek. I pleaded with her to marry me and head West, to a land bigger and brighter than anything along Stone Creek."

"And she refused," Eve whispered.

"Oh, not right away," Reno drawled. "First she whispered about the fun we'd have if I'd just agree to live along Stone Creek. All I had to do was say 'yes' and she'd do anything I wanted. Hell, she'd do everything, and be grateful for the chance."

Reno shook his head. "God, there ought to be a law against boys falling in love. But no matter how much she teased me," he continued, "I was smart enough not to make promises it would kill me to keep. I'd go yondering and I'd come back hoping, and each time I was gone longer, and each time Savannah Marie would be waiting for me. . . ."

Reno took off his hat, raked long fingers through his hair, and resettled his hat with a swift tug.

"Until I came back and found her three months married and four months pregnant by a man twice her age."

At Eve's shocked sound, Reno turned and gave her an odd smile.

"Shocked me, too," he drawled. "I was plumb flummoxed. I couldn't figure out how old man Murphy had gotten under Savannah's skirts in a matter of months when I had been courting her for years. So I asked her."

"What did she say?"

"That a woman wants comfort and security from a man, and a man wants sex and children from a woman," Reno said succinctly. "Old man Murphy was well fixed. When she got him hot enough to take her maidenhead, he agreed to marry her, because a decent man marries the girl he ruins."

"Sounds like she had all the passion of a merchant's scales."

"That about covers it," Reno said dryly. "But it's a good thing for a man to learn."

"All women aren't like that."

"I've known only one girl in my whole life who gave herself for love rather than a wedding ring," Reno said flatly.

"Jessi of the fiery hair and gemstone eyes?" Eve guessed.

He shook his head. "Jessi trapped Wolfe into marriage rather than be forced into a marriage with some drunken English lord."

"Perdition," Eve muttered.

"Wolfe felt the same way at first," Reno said, smiling. "He came around."

"But you forgave Jessi for caring more for her own comfort than for Wolfe's," Eve pointed out.

"Wasn't my place to forgive or not. Wolfe did. That's all that matters."

"But you like Jessi."

Anger swept through Reno at Eve's persistence. He didn't like thinking about Jessi and Wolfe, Willow and Caleb. Their happiness kept making Reno wonder if he wasn't missing something, if he shouldn't find a woman and take a chance on getting burned twice by the same fire.

Once burned, twice shy, he told himself.

And forever cold.

Abruptly Reno reined his mare around so that Darlin' stood head to tail with Eve's horse. The horses were so close together that his leg brushed against Eve's. Before she could move away, his hand shot out, pushing her hat aside until it hung down her back, suspended by the leather chin thong. His gloved hand slid between her bright braids and wrapped around her nape.

"I understand that women have to make up in cunning what they lack in strength," Reno said angrily. "But understanding isn't the same as liking."

His glance went from Eve's unusual eyes to her full lower lip.

"On the other hand," he said deeply, "there are some really fine uses for women. Especially a girl with golden eyes and a mouth that trembles with fear or passion, inviting a man to protect and ravish her."

"I'm not," she said quickly.

"I tasted you. You were sweet and hot. And you tasted me."

Eve's breath stopped at the look in Reno's eyes.

He smiled, reading her response in the rapid beating of the pulse in her neck.

"Think about it, *gata*. I sure as hell have."

Reno released Eve and nudged the blue roan with his heels.

"Shake a leg, Darlin'. We've got a lot of ground to cover before we get to Cal's ranch."

THOUGH small, the campfire's gently dancing flames fascinated Eve. Like her thoughts, the flames were both intangible and very real.

She hadn't meant to take Reno's advice and think about her unexpected sensuality. But she had thought about it, and about him. That could be dangerous.

An owl called from the dark wall of fir trees that rose beyond the campfire.

Eve started.

"Just an owl," Reno said from behind her.

Eve jumped again and whirled around.

"Would you mind not sneaking up on me?" she snapped.

"Anyone who sits and stares at fire the way you do has to expect to be taken by surprise from time to time."

"I was thinking," she said stiffly.

Reno bent over the campfire, picked up the small, battered coffeepot, and poured a bit more in the mug he was holding. When he finished, he sat on his heels beside Eve, sipped the coffee appreciatively, and watched firelight draw burning patterns of gold through her hair.

"Penny for your thoughts," Reno said.

Heat climbed up Eve's cheeks, for she had been thinking of the time when Reno had kissed her lips, her neck, her breasts . . . She was too honest to deny that she was attracted to him; if she weren't, she would never have made the unholy bargain for half of the mine.

But that meant she was in the uncomfortable position of not quite trusting her own reactions. It left her feeling edgy and adrift, for all her life she had trusted her instincts when it came to dealing with other people. The Lyons had come to trust her instincts, too; they had often praised her ability to see beyond the surface of other card players to the emotions beneath.

At the same time, Donna Lyon had warned Eve more than once about the nature of man and woman.

Only one thing a man wants from a woman, make no mistake about it. Once you give him that, you better be married, or he'll go off down the trail and find another foolish girl to spread her legs in the name of love.

"Two pennies," Reno said dryly.

The sudden flush on Eve's cheeks made Reno wonder if she had been thinking about the one time he had let his own desire overcome his common sense and tried to seduce her.

God knew that time had been on his mind. When he wasn't looking over his shoulder for shadows on the back trail, he was thinking about the moment when he had first breathed in the scent of lilacs and tasted the velvet hardness of her nipples.

But thinking and remembering was all that he had done, despite the temptation of their evening campsites, where firelight beckoned and stars glittered against a black sky. He hadn't been able to shake the feeling that he was being followed. Rolling around on the ground with a saloon girl was the kind of distraction that could be fatal—especially if Slater was the man dogging Reno's trail.

If that wasn't enough to cool Reno off, there was the fact that they would reach the ranch tomorrow. His conscience was giving him a bad enough time as it was about bringing a saloon girl to his sister's home.

And yet . . .

Reno turned and looked at the silent girl who was watching him with eyes the color of gold.

"Three pennies?" he offered.

"Er, I was thinking about Donna Lyon," Eve said, the only half of the truth she was willing to talk about. "And being partners."

Reno's mouth thinned. A flick of his wrist sent the last drops of coffee in his cup arcing into the darkness beyond the fire.

"Gold, huh?" he said sarcastically. "I should have guessed. Money is all girls ever think about. Well, we're a long way from finding any gold."

"And we'll stay that way unless you let me look at Cristóbal Leon's journal," Eve retorted.

Reno rubbed the stubble on his chin and said nothing.

"Surely you can't be afraid I'm going to cut and run with the journal," she said. "Even if poor Whitefoot were shod, he wouldn't be any match for your mustang."

Reno looked at Eve. In the firelight his eyes were as clear as spring water. Without a word he came to his feet and walked away from her. He came back a moment later, carrying the journal in his hands. Still saying nothing, he sat cross-legged by the fire and opened the journal.

When Eve didn't move, he glanced aside at her. "You wanted the journal. Here it is."

"Thank you," Eve said, holding out her hand.

Slowly Reno shook his head.

"Come and get it," he said.

The look in Reno's eyes warned Eve. Warily she scooted sideways until she was sitting next to him. By bending over his arm and craning her neck, she was able to see the journal's faded, spidery script.

A dia vente-uno del ano de 15 . . .

The opening words were so familiar she could read them effortlessly.

"In the day of—"

"You're cutting off my light," Reno interrupted.

"Oh. Sorry."

Eve straightened, peered again, and made a frustrated sound.

"Now I can't see."

"Here." Reno handed her the journal.

"Thank you."

"You're welcome," he said, smiling in anticipation.

Before Eve's fingers had done more than close around the soft leather, Reno picked her up and settled her in his lap with her back to his chest. When she tried to move off his lap, he held her in place.

"Going somewhere?" Reno asked.

"I can't see this way," Eve said.

"Try opening the journal."

"What?"

"The journal," he said dryly. "It's hard to read through the cover."

When Eve started to move off his lap, Reno held her in place with offhanded ease.

"I said I wouldn't force you," he reminded her in a calm voice. "And I said I wasn't going to keep my hands off you. I'm a man of my word. What about you? Do you keep your word like a woman or a saloon girl?"

"I keep my word, period," Eve said through her teeth.

"Prove it. Start reading. The light's good enough now, isn't it?"

She muttered agreement, took a secret breath, and opened the journal to the first page. The words wouldn't come into focus. All she could think of was the feel of Reno's body against her back, her hips, her thighs.

Long arms reached around Eve as Reno took the journal from her hands and opened it.

"Read aloud," he said.

His voice was as casual as though he spent every night with a girl in his lap reading books.

Maybe he does, Eve thought.

"I should point out," Reno drawled, "that if what I hear doesn't interest me, I can always find something else to do that does interest me."

The sensual threat in his voice was unmistakable.

"'In the twenty-first day of the year fifteen...'" Eve said quickly, hoping Reno didn't hear the unevenness of her voice. "It's blotched there. I can't tell if the year is... is..."

Her voice fragmented as she felt the collar of her jacket tugged down in back. The warmth of Reno's breath on her neck made her shiver.

"What are you doing?" she asked.

"Keep reading."

"It just says who authorized..."

The brush of his mustache against Eve's nape took her breath away.

"Read."

"I can't. You're distracting me."

"You'll get used to it. Read."

"...who authorized the expedition, and how

many men and what arms and . . ."

Eve's words stopped as Reno's teeth tested the softness of her skin with ravishing delicacy.

"Go on," he whispered.

". . . and what the purpose was."

The tip of his tongue circled her nape. He felt the tremor that went through her and wondered whether it was fear or anticipation.

"What was the purpose?" he asked.

Eve reminded herself that a bargain was a bargain. She had agreed to let Reno try seducing her.

She hadn't agreed to his success.

"Gold, of course," she said curtly. "Isn't that what the Spanish always wanted?"

"I don't know. You've got the journal. Read to me."

"That wasn't part of our bargain."

The heat of Reno's mouth on Eve's nape made her heart turn over. The hot suction and fine edges of his teeth sent wildfire through her nerves.

Reno felt the shudder that went through Eve, and wondered once more whether fear or sensuality moved her, for he had seen both in her topaz eyes as she watched him through the long days on the trail.

There was no doubt whether fear or sensuality ruled Reno. The taste of Eve's naked skin and the feel of her hips snug between his thighs was a pleasure hot enough to burn. He shifted slightly, increasing the sweet pressure against his rapidly hardening flesh.

"They—the Spanish were supposed to baptize Indians, too," Eve said hurriedly.

She tried squirming off Reno's lap. Each movement she made only served to increase the intimate contact.

She became very still.

"Were they?" he asked in a lazy voice.

"Yes. It says so right here."

"Show me."

Eve tried to find the page, but her fingers were clumsy, and Reno was holding the journal in such a way that she couldn't turn more than one or two pages.

"Your thumb is in the way," she said.

Reno made a throaty, questioning sound that ruffled her nerves almost as much as a physical touch.

"I can't turn the pages," she explained.

The rest of Eve's words were lost in a stifled gasp as Reno's mustache moved like a silk brush along her hairline. Goose bumps coursed up and down her arms.

"Then you hold the journal," he said in a deep voice. "But if you try climbing off my lap again, I'll lay you out on the ground, instead."

Eve took the journal from Reno's hands and began turning pages as though her life depended on finding out what the rest of the royal instructions to the Cristóbal Leon expedition had been.

Reno's long, deft fingers began unbuttoning her jacket.

"Saving souls," she said quickly. "They were trying to save souls."

"I believe you mentioned that already."

The jacket began to open, allowing the cool night air to wash Eve's throat. She closed her eyes and tried to breathe past her heart, which was lodged halfway up her throat.

"Somewhere he . . . he writes about seeking an overland route to the Spanish missions in California," she said.

"Exploration," Reno said deeply. "Man after my own heart. Go on, *gata*, read to me about undiscovered territory and treasures hidden within darkness."

"They started up from New Spain and . . ."

Eve gasped softly as the last button on her jacket gave way beneath Reno's gentle urging. The worn white gambler's shirt that had once been Don Lyon's glowed in the firelight as though made of satin.

"Don't panic," Reno said. "I'm not doing anything that we didn't do before."

"That's supposed to make me feel better?"

"The Spanish started from New Spain," was all Reno said. "And then what?"

"Then they came at the Rockies from the east . . ."

Her breath rushed out when long fingers stroked her throat lightly, caressing the frantic race of her pulse.

". . . or maybe the west. I don't know. I can't . . ."

Reno released the first button of her shirt.

". . . can't remember which direction they . . . they . . ."

Another button gave way. Then another.

"What did they find?" Reno asked softly as he pulled her blouse apart. "Gold?"

Eve dropped the book and grabbed the edges of her blouse. It was too late. Reno's hands were already stroking bare skin, luring her body with promises of pleasure.

"Not right away. They found . . . they found . . ."

Eve's voice frayed into a soft, ragged cry as her breasts changed in a rush, answering the caress of Reno's hands.

"Stop," Eve said.

But even she couldn't have said if she meant the word for Reno or for herself. The sensual pressure of her hardened nipples was nudging against his palms.

"Pleasure, not fear," he breathed against her neck. "We'll burn down the mountains, *gata*. And then we'll burn down the night."

Eve twisted aside, all but falling to the ground as she pulled free of Reno's knowing hands.

"No!"

For a few tense moments, Eve thought Reno was going to pull her right back onto his lap. Then he let out an explosive breath that was also a curse.

"It's just as well, *gata*. If I keep touching you, I'll have you." He shrugged. "I don't want to take my fancy lady into my sister's home."

Eve drew her jacket together with fingers that shook, but it was anger, not passion.

"That won't be a problem, now or later," Eve said.

"What?"

"My being your fancy lady."

Reno's eyelids flinched at the bitterness in her voice, but all he said was, "Going back on your word so soon?"

Eve's head came up and her eyes burned as hotly as the fire.

"I agreed that you could *try* to seduce me," she said tightly. "I didn't guarantee your success."

"Oh, I'll succeed," he drawled. "And you'll be helping me every inch of the way. It will be the most fun you ever had paying off a debt."

The white flash of Reno's smile infuriated Eve.

"Don't count on it, gunman. No girl wants a man who makes her feel like a slut."

6

THE change that came over Reno when he rode into the wide valley where Caleb and Willow made their home astonished Eve. The narrowed eyes and predatory alertness dropped away from him, revealing a man who was relaxed and quick to smile. She had thought Reno to be over thirty; now she decided he was years younger and worlds less hard.

Reno's transformation alone was enough to make the valley appeal to Eve, but there was more. The setting itself was exceptionally beautiful, for the valley was open rather than crowded between towering mountain flanks. A silver-blue river glittered between banks graced by cottonwood trees. On the far side of the wide, lush valley, a cluster of mountain peaks rose in stark grandeur against a sapphire sky.

The snake-back rail fences that divided part of the valley into pastures looked as though they were only a season or two old. Fat cattle grazed calmly as Eve and Reno rode by, followed by the three packhorses. From a nearby pasture, a muscular red stallion trumpeted a call and galloped over to the visitors with his tail raised like a banner.

As the stallion approached, Whitefoot flicked his ears uneasily and stepped up his pace to hurry past. Reno's mare wasn't the least bit worried. She lifted her head to whinny an enthusiastic greeting to the red horse.

"Not this year, Darlin'," Reno said, smiling as he reined in the dancing mare. "You're the best dry-country horse I've ever had. Time enough for you to have Ishmael's colts after I've found Spanish gold."

Darlin' chewed the bit resentfully, snorted, and made a halfhearted attempt to unload her rider.

Laughing, Reno rode out the mare's displeasure with the same deceptively lazy ease he did so many things. Then he spurred Darlin' lightly, sending her galloping up to the big log house where a woman wearing a white blouse and a full green skirt was just running out into the yard.

"Matt?" she called out to the rapidly approaching rider. "Is that you?"

"It's me, Willy," Reno said.

He reined the mare to a dancing stop and added dryly, "If it weren't, Cal would have emptied Darlin's saddle while we were admiring your Arabian stallion."

"That's a fact," Caleb said, stepping out from the house.

"Still being bothered by Comancheros?" Reno asked, noting the rifle in the other man's hands.

Caleb shrugged. "Drifters, Comancheros, gold hunters. Even had a pack of lords and ladies through while you were gone. Country's getting too damn crowded in the summertime."

"Lords and ladies, huh? Bet Wolfe didn't think much of that."

"Wolfe and Jessi weren't here," Willow said. "They're still out seeing the sights."

Reno smiled. If he had been Wolfe, he would have done the same thing—taken his beautiful young bride off in the wilderness and spent a lot of time alone.

"We heard they were over to the west," Willow continued, "somewhere down in that maze of stone canyons. Jessi swore the honeymoon wouldn't end until she had seen all of Wolfe's favorite hideaways."

"Maybe I'll run into them in the red rock desert," Reno said. "What about Rafe? Is he back yet?"

Willow shook her head, making her blond hair gleam in the high-country sunlight.

"He's still off yondering, looking for a way through the canyon Wolfe told him about, the one so wide and so deep only the sun can cross it," Willow said.

"How old is that news?"

"Just last week," Willow said. "A drifter who had met him on the Rio Verde stopped by here yesterday."

"He was after some of Willow's biscuits," Caleb added wryly. "Said he'd been told they were worth riding a hundred miles out of his way to get."

"Damn," Reno muttered. "I was hoping to sign Rafe on for a little gold hunting."

Willow looked from her brother to the pack-horses and the slender rider who were just now coming into the yard.

"Did you hire a boy to help you?" she asked.

The change in Reno's expression was noted instantly by Caleb.

"Not quite," Reno said. "That's my, uh, partner."

Eve was close enough to hear Reno's words. She reined her tired horse next to his and took over the introductions that he was plainly reluctant to make.

"My name is Eve Starr," she said quietly. "You must be Reno's sister."

Willow's cheeks pinked and she laughed. "Oh, my. I'm sorry, Miss Starr. Yes, I'm Willow Black, and I should know better than to assume everything in pants is a male. Jessi and I both wear pants when we ride."

Caleb looked at the worn, ruffled gambler's blouse and faded black twill pants on Eve, and knew that he would never have mistaken her for a man. There was something too essentially feminine about the shape beneath the loose clothes for any man to mistake it.

"I'm Caleb Black," he said to Eve. "Get down and come inside. The trail over the Great Divide is long and hard on a woman."

"Yes, do get down," Willow said quickly. "It's been months since I had a woman to talk to."

Willow's generous, welcoming smile was like a balm on Eve's pride. Her answering smile included Caleb, who was as big as Reno but seemed a good deal more gentle, especially when he was smiling as he was now.

"Thank you," Eve said. "It was a long ride."

"Don't get too comfortable," Reno said curtly as she dismounted. "We're only staying long enough for you to switch horses."

Caleb's eyes narrowed as he sensed the tension just beneath the other man's calm voice, but he said nothing.

As always, Willow said what was on her mind. "Matthew Moran, where are your manners? Not to mention your common sense!"

"Someone might be following us," Reno said. "I don't want to bring him down on you."

"Jericho Slater?" Caleb guessed.

Reno looked surprised.

"Men don't have much to talk about out here except other men," Caleb said dryly. "One of my riders has a Comanchero, er, friend. Her brother is Slater's tracker."

"Not much gets by you, does it?" Reno muttered. "Yes, it's probably Slater on my trail."

The feral smile that came over Caleb's face made Eve swiftly revise her idea of his gentle nature.

"And here I thought you'd forgotten my birthday," Caleb said. "It's really fine of you to bring a Slater to share around. Damn few of those boys left."

Laughing softly, Reno shook his head and accepted the inevitable.

"All right, Cal. We'll stay to supper."

"You'll do more than that," Willow said quickly.

"Sorry, Willy," Reno said. "We've got too much ground to cover."

"What's the rush?" Caleb asked. "Is Slater that hard on your trail?"

"No."

Caleb's dark eyebrows rose at the curt answer.

Reno shifted in the saddle and thought of what he could say that wouldn't be a lie and wouldn't be the truth: he was damned uncomfortable bringing a saloon girl into his sister's home.

"It's late in the season to be taking on the high country," Reno said, "and we've got a lot of rock desert to cross before we even get to the Abajos."

"Abajos, huh? That's a mighty lonesome group of mountains you've picked out to explore."

"Not me. The Jesuits. At least, I assume that's

where we're headed," he added, looking sideways at Eve.

"You assume?" Willow asked, confused. "Don't you know?"

"I'm not real good at making out the old-style Spanish, and I'm plumb useless when it comes to the Lyons' private family code. That's where my, uh, partner comes in."

"Oh." Willow still looked confused.

Reno looked like a man who was through making explanations.

Caleb shaded his eyes and stared across the meadow to the closest peak. High on its rugged side, a handful of aspens burned with the yellow torch of fall.

"You've got some time yet before the high country closes," Caleb said easily. "Only a few of the aspens on the north-facing slopes have turned."

Reno shrugged. "I'm not betting against an early snow."

The set of Reno's mouth said more than his words. He wasn't going to stay at the ranch one moment longer than he had to.

"Gold fever, huh?" Caleb said without rancor. "Been expecting it."

Reno nodded curtly.

"Well," Caleb said, "you might think about your partner. She looks a little frazzled to be galloping off after fool's gold. Maybe you should leave her here to rest up while you reconnoiter."

Though nothing in Caleb's voice or expression suggested he thought there was something unusual about a girl riding alone through the wilderness with a man who wasn't her husband, fiancé, or blood relation, Eve's face colored.

"It's my map," she said.

"Not quite," Reno retorted.

Caleb's dark eyebrows lifted.

"It's a long story," Reno muttered.

"Best kind," Caleb said, his voice bland.

"Then it will take a long time to tell, won't it?" Willow demanded.

"Willy—" Reno began.

"Don't you 'Willy' me, Matthew Moran," she interrupted, putting her hands on her hips and planting herself in front of her brother.

"Now, just a min—" Reno began.

It was no use.

"Even if you swapped saddles like a Pony Express rider and galloped until sunset," Willow said, talking over her brother, "you wouldn't get more than a few miles down the road. You're staying for a time, and that's that. It's been too long since I've had a woman to talk to."

"Honey, it's—" began Caleb.

"You stay out of this," Willow said. "Matt's been living on his own too long. He's got no more manners than a wolf."

Eve watched Willow with a combination of fascination and horror as she faced down the two large men. If Willow realized that her husband and brother were a foot taller and far stronger than she was, it didn't slow down her tongue one bit.

Yet neither man struck Eve as the kind to step back for anyone, much less for someone who was half their weight and a third their strength.

Caleb and Reno looked sideways at each other while Willow took a breath. Caleb smiled, then began laughing softly. It took Reno longer, but in the end he gave in to his little sister.

"All right, Willy. But only one night. We're pulling out at dawn."

She started to object, looked at Reno's eyes, and knew more arguing would be pointless.

"And only if you make biscuits," Reno added, smiling as he dismounted.

Willow laughed and hugged her brother.

"Welcome home, Matt."

Reno hugged her in return, but his eyes were shadowed as he looked beyond Willow's blond head to the house and the meadow where livestock grazed. He was welcome, but it wasn't his home. He had no home.

For the first time in his life, the thought bothered him.

THE kitchen smelled of Willow's biscuits, beef stew, and the dried apple pie that Eve had insisted on making for dinner. Willow hadn't put up much of a fight, readily accepting that Eve preferred to be treated as a neighbor or a friend rather than as a guest.

Reno hadn't been pleased to find Eve in the kitchen when he came in from choosing horses and readying the pack saddles for an early start tomorrow, but it was too late to object. Eve and Willow were sharing the kitchen and talking together like old friends.

Eve had bathed and changed into the old dress Reno had found in her saddlebag while searching for much more valuable things. The dress was wrinkled, all but worn-out, painfully clean, and obviously had been made from flour bags. The cloth had been washed in harsh soap and dried in the sun so many times that the makers' names had faded to an illegible wash of pink and pale blue. Either the material had shrunk over time, or the dress was a hand-me-down, for it fit too snugly across Eve's breasts and hinted too much at the flare of her hips.

It made a man want to measure the slender waist

with his hands, and then peel off the coarse cloth
to get at the silky woman beneath.

But it was better than the crimson silk saloon
dress Reno had first seen on Eve. He had been
afraid she would wear it in Willow's house as a
way of getting back at him for saying he wouldn't
take a fancy lady into his sister's house.

He hadn't meant the remark as a insult; it was
simply a fact. He had too much respect and love
for his sister to parade fallen women through her
home.

"Oh, blast," Willow said. "I forgot Ethan's dia-
per."

"I'll get it," Eve said.

"Thanks. It's in the bedroom next to yours."

Eve turned and saw Reno's disapproving eyes.
She straightened her shoulders, lifted her chin, and
walked past him without a word.

His cold glance followed the unconscious swaying of her hips until he could see them no longer.
Only then did he turn back to his sister and his
nephew, who was at present being bathed near the
warmth of the kitchen stove.

The baby's whiskey-colored eyes were an exact
match for Caleb's. Though not yet six months old,
Ethan Black was already bigger than most children
at ten months. He made an armful for his mother
as he splashed and paddled enthusiastically in a
basin of warm water.

"Here," Reno said. "Let me take care of him.
You make biscuits."

"I've already made a triple batch," Willow said.
"The last of them are baking right now."

"Those are for tonight. I was talking about biscuits for the trail tomorrow."

Laughing, Willow stepped aside.

Reno picked up the soft washrag, rubbed soap

into it, and began washing his nephew. The baby made a happy sound and reached for Reno's mustache with chubby little fingers. Reno drew back, but not quite enough. Ethan grabbed hair and pulled.

Wincing, Reno moved to disentangle the small fingers. Despite the baby's happy yanking, Reno was careful not to truly discourage his nephew. He eased the fingers from his mustache, gave them a smacking, tickling kiss, and laughed when Ethan's eyes widened with surprise and delight.

The baby crowed and made another grab for Reno's mustache. This time Reno had the baby's range and ducked successfully.

"If you don't beat all," Reno said as he washed his squirming, energetic nephew. "I'm gone less than a month, and your arms grow half an inch."

Ethan's arms windmilled, sending water everywhere. Willow looked up from the flour she was sifting, saw her child's delight, and shook her head.

"You spoil him," she said, but there was no censure in her voice.

"One of the pleasures of my life," Reno agreed. "That, and your biscuits."

With a glad shriek, Ethan launched himself at Reno's chest.

"Easy there, little man."

Gently he restrained the baby so that Willow's kitchen wouldn't end up as wet and slippery as a bathhouse floor.

Ethan tried to wriggle free, but couldn't. Just when he was clouding up for a good cry, Reno distracted him by picking up one of his little hands, pressing his mouth against the palm, and blowing hard. The fruity noises that followed delighted the baby.

No one noticed Eve standing in the doorway to the kitchen, watching Reno with both disbelief and yearning in her eyes. She had never imagined that much gentleness lay beneath Reno's hard body and lethal speed with a six-gun. Seeing him bathe his nephew made her feel as though she had stepped from one world into another one, a world where anything was possible. . . .

Even tenderness and strength combined in the same man.

"Damn, you're as slippery as an eel," Reno said.

"Try rinsing him off," Willow said without looking up.

"With what? Most of the water is on me."

Willow laughed. "Hang on. There's warm water on the stove. I'll get it as soon as I finish sifting this batch of flour."

"I'll get it," Eve said as she stepped into the kitchen.

A subtle change came over Reno at the sound of Eve's voice behind him, a tightness that wasn't there before.

Willow saw it, noted it, and wondered why Reno was so ill at ease with the girl who was his partner. There was none of the relaxation between the two of them that Willow would have expected of a couple involved in a courtship or a liaison of a more physical sort.

Nor was there any flirtation. Reno treated Eve as though she were a virtual stranger—and a male stranger, at that.

That surprised Willow, for Reno was normally both gallant and appreciative of women. Especially women with wide golden eyes, a generous smile, and a feline grace of movement that was frankly, if unintentionally, sensual.

"Thank you, Eve," Willow said. "Ethan's towel

is warming on that peg just beyond the stove."

From the corner of his eye, Reno watched as Eve retrieved both towel and warm rinse water for the baby. When she bent over, the worn fabric of her dress cupped her breasts with breathtaking closeness, revealing every curve.

The fierce shaft of desire that went through Reno angered him. His sexual appetite hadn't ever been this unruly. Deliberately he looked away from Eve to the strapping, healthy baby wriggling between his hands.

"He may have Caleb's eyes," Reno said, studying Ethan, "but they're set like yours. Same catlike tilt."

"I could say the same about your eyes," Willow said. "Lord, but the girls used to fall at your feet like overripe peaches."

"That's Rafe you're thinking of."

Willow snorted. "It's both of you. Savannah Marie was like a donkey between two carrots."

Silently Eve began pouring a trickle of water over the slippery baby Reno was holding.

"It wasn't our looks," Reno said. "It was our farm bordering her father's that she liked."

The steel edge buried in Reno's voice made Willow look up from her biscuits.

"Do you think so?" she asked.

"I know so. All Savannah Marie was interested in was her own comfort. That's all most women are interested in."

Willow made a protesting sound.

"Except you," Reno added. "You never were like other girls. You had a heart as big as a barn—and no more sense than a hayloft."

Willow laughed.

When Eve looked up, she was caught by Reno's pale green eyes. He didn't have to say a word; she knew he included her in the category of women out for their own comfort and to hell with what anyone else needed.

"Honestly, Matt," Willow said. "You shouldn't say such things. Someone who doesn't know you might believe you meant it."

The look Reno gave Eve said she had better believe him.

"Tilt Ethan's head back," Eve said in a low voice.

Reno shifted his nephew until Eve could rinse his silky, dark hair without getting soap in his eyes.

When Ethan began to protest, Eve bent down and spoke to him in a soothing voice as she rinsed his hair. Her deft, skillful hands soon had his head as clean of soap as the rest of him.

"There, there, little sugar man. Don't fuss. I'll have you warm and dry before you know it. See? All finished."

Eve took the towel from her shoulder, wrapped it around Ethan's sturdy body, and lifted him from the shallow bath basin. She set him on the counter and went about drying him with an easy skill that told its own story. As she worked, she tugged gently on his toes and recited snippets of old rhymes she hadn't thought of in years.

". . . and *this* little piggy had none . . ."

Ethan gurgled with delight. The piggy game was one of his favorites, second only to peekaboo.

". . . and *this* little piggy went whee! whee! whee! all the way home."

Ethan laughed, and so did Eve. She wrapped the towel around him and lifted him into her arms for a hug and a kiss.

Eyes closed, lost in memories and dreams, Eve swayed from side to side with Ethan wrapped in her arms, rocking him and remembering a time years ago when she had hungered for her own home, her own family, her own child.

After a few moments Eve realized the kitchen was very quiet. She opened her eyes to find Willow smiling gently at her. Reno was watching her as though he had never seen a woman handle a baby.

"You do that very well," Willow said.

Eve set Ethan back on the counter and began diapering him with matter-of-fact skill.

"There were always babies at the orphanage," Eve said. "I used to pretend they were mine . . . a family."

Willow made a low sound of sympathy.

Reno's eyes narrowed. If he could have thought of a way to prevent Eve from telling her heart-tugging lies, he would have. But it was too late. She was talking again, and Willow was listening with wide hazel eyes.

"But there were too many older children in the orphanage. Each time the orphan train left, the oldest were shipped off to the West. Finally it was my turn."

"I'm sorry," Willow said softly. "I didn't mean to bring up unhappy memories."

Eve smiled quickly at the other woman. "That's all right. The people who bought me were kinder than most."

"Bought . . . ?"

Willow's voice faded into an appalled silence.

"Isn't it time to put Ethan to bed?" Reno asked curtly.

Willow accepted the change of subject with relief.

"Yes," she said. "He fretted all through his nap today."

"May I put him to bed?" Eve asked.

"Of course."

Reno's eyes followed Eve every step of the way out of the kitchen, promising retribution for wringing his sister's soft heart.

7

Ethan's cry came clearly into the kitchen, where Eve and Willow were just finishing the evening dishes.

"I'll take care of it," Reno said from the other room. "Unless he's hungry. Then he's all yours, Willy."

Willow laughed as she wrung out the dishrag. "You're safe. When I finished nursing him an hour ago, he was as full as a tick."

Caleb's voice came from the long table just off the kitchen where he and Reno had been working over the Leon journal and that of Caleb's father, who had been a surveyor for the army in the 1850s.

"Eve," Caleb called, "aren't you finished polishing plates yet? Reno and I are having a devil of a time with your Spanish journal."

"I'm on my way," Eve said.

A moment later she walked up to the table. Caleb stood and pulled out the chair next to his own.

"Thank you," Eve said, smiling up at him.

Caleb's answering smile changed his face from austere to handsome.

"My pleasure," he said.

Reno scowled at them from the bedroom door, but neither one noticed. Their heads were already bent over the two journals.

Reluctantly Reno went on into the room where Ethan howled over the injustice of being put to bed while the rest of the family was up and about.

"Can you make out this?" Caleb asked Eve, pointing to a tattered page.

She pulled the lantern a bit closer, angled the journal, and frowned at the elaborate, faded script.

"Don thought that abbreviation meant the saddleback peak to the northwest," Eve said slowly.

Caleb heard the hesitation in her voice.

"What do you think?" he asked.

"I think it referred back to this."

Eve turned back two pages and pointed with her finger to the odd symbols marching down the margin.

One of the symbols was indeed labeled with an abbreviation that could have been the same as the one on the other page. The letters were so faded it was hard to tell.

"If that's so," Caleb said, "Reno is right. It could be referring to the Abajos rather than the Platas."

Caleb opened his father's journal and turned pages quickly.

"Here," he pointed. "Coming up from this direction, the terrain reminded Dad of a Spanish saddle, but . . ."

"But?"

Caleb flipped pages until he came to the map he had made combining his father's explorations with his own.

"These are the mountains the Spanish called Las Platas," he said.

"The Silver Mountains," Eve translated.

"Yes. And where there's silver, there's usually gold."

The excitement stealing through Eve showed in her smile.

"If you come in this way," Caleb continued, "at a distance these peaks look a bit like a Spanish saddle, too. But you could say that about a lot of peaks."

"Did they actually find silver in the Platas?"

Caleb shrugged. "They found silver somewhere on this side of the Great Divide."

"Nearby?"

"No one knows for sure."

Caleb pointed to scattered clusters of mountain peaks on the map. Some rose like islands from the red rock desert to the west. Others were part of the Rocky Mountains. At the base of one cluster, Caleb's ranch was marked in.

Nothing showed at the base of the other mountains but question marks where old Spanish *vistas* may have been located centuries before. Yet the land wasn't quite naked of man's presence. Drawn in with dashed lines, like the tributaries to an invisible river, rumored Spanish trails led down out of the mountain groups, came together in the canyon country, and headed south to the land that had once been called New Spain.

"But here," Caleb said, pointing to the heart of the canyon country, "a week's hard ride to the west, pack trains loaded with silver wore trails in stone that you can still see today."

"Where?"

"Down on the Rio Colorado," Reno said from

behind them. "Only, the Spanish called it the Tizón in those days."

Startled, Eve looked up so quickly her head nearly knocked against Caleb's.

Reno stared at her, his green eyes shimmering with an anger that had grown every time he glanced out of the bedroom and saw the dark gold of Eve's hair brushing against the thick black of Caleb's hair as they pored over the journals.

Reno's anger came as no surprise to Eve. He had been furious with her ever since Willow had insisted that they stay for supper and the night.

What did surprise Eve was the baby gurgling happily in Reno's muscular arms. It occurred to her that she had rarely seen Reno without his nephew in the hours since they had arrived.

In a man as gentle and giving as her father had been, such pleasure in a baby wouldn't have surprised Eve. In a man like Reno, it was a revelation that astonished Eve every time it occurred. Nothing in her past had prepared her for it. The hard men she had known were just that—hard. They used their strength for their own ends, and the devil take the hindmost.

Unfortunately, Reno reserved the gentle side of his nature for his family, period. Eve had no illusions that a saloon girl would get the benefit of his relaxed teasing and flashing, beguiling smiles. Nor would she get the benefit of the protective love that he extended to his sister.

Reno was obviously furious with Eve for insinuating herself into Willow's house and Caleb's courtesy. Eve knew it each time she looked up and saw Reno watching her with fierce green eyes.

At least he was careful not to let Willow or Caleb see his anger. Not that Eve thought Reno's restraint was for her benefit. He just wanted to avoid raising any questions he didn't want to answer about saloon girls and his sister's home.

"Is that where we're headed?" Eve asked Reno. "The Colorado River?"

"I hope not," Reno said curtly. "I've heard the Spanish knew a shortcut between here and the Abajos. If they did—and we find it—we'll cut several weeks off our travel time."

Caleb muttered something under his breath about fools, lost mines, and a maze of canyons that had no name.

Oblivious to all, Ethan leaned forward and made a swipe at the bright scarf that was holding Eve's loose chignon in place. When he missed, he protested. Loudly.

"Bedtime," called Willow from the kitchen.

Eve slid the scarf from her hair. Immediately her chignon came undone, sending a cascade of dark golden hair down her back. She caught up her hair and bound it in a loose knot. Then she deftly reshaped the scarf into a doll with a knot for a head, other knots for arms, and a flaring skirt below.

"Here you are, sugar man," she whispered to Ethan. "I know how lonely those nights can be."

The baby's hand closed around the doll with surprising strength. He waved it and crowed happily.

Though Eve had meant her words to be too soft for anyone but the baby to hear, Reno did. His eyes narrowed as he searched Eve's face for any sign that she was trying to get his sympathy. He saw only the gentleness that came over her expression whenever Ethan looked at her and cooed his delight.

Frowning, Reno looked away and reminded himself that all women—even conniving saloon girls—had softness in their hearts when it came to babies.

Willow came out of the kitchen, took Ethan, and headed for the bedroom. Immediately the coos became unhappy cries.

"I don't mind walking him around the room for a while," Reno offered.

"If he's still crying in a few minutes," Willow said firmly.

"How about if I sing him to sleep?"

Willow laughed and gave in. "It's a good thing you're going gold hunting. You spoil your nephew shamelessly."

Smiling, Reno followed his sister into the bedroom. A few moments later, the gentle strains of a hymn floated out into the room, sung by Reno's fine baritone. Willow's clear soprano joined in a few moments later in flawless harmony.

Eve's breath came in with surprise and pleasure.

"Had the same effect on me the first time I heard them," Caleb said. "Their brother Rafe sings like a fallen angel, too. I've never met the other three brothers, but I imagine they're the same."

"Think of sitting next to them in church. . . ."

Caleb laughed. "Something tells me the Moran boys ran more to fighting than to sitting in church."

Absently Eve smiled, but it was the voices that claimed her attention. Music had been one of the few pleasures in the orphanage, and had been practiced under the demanding yet patient choirmaster from the nearby church.

Eyes closed, Eve began humming to herself. She didn't know the particular verse they were singing, but the tune was familiar. Automatically she took the counterpoint, letting her smoky alto voice weave through the simple harmony created by brother and sister.

After a few minutes, the music claimed Eve, making her forget where she was. Her voice soared, skimming between the light of Willow's soprano and the deep shadow of Reno's baritone, enriching both like a rainbow stretched between sunlight and storm, radiant with all the hopes of man.

Eve didn't realize what she had done until the harmony stopped abruptly, leaving her voice alone. Her eyes snapped open.

She found herself being stared at by Caleb, Reno, and Willow. Color rose in Eve's cheeks.

"Forgive me. I didn't mean to—"

"Don't be a goose," Willow interrupted quickly. "Where on earth did you learn that gorgeous harmony?"

"The church choirmaster."

"Could you teach Caleb to play that on the harmonica?"

"No time," Reno cut in. "We've got journals to work on tonight, and we're leaving at first light tomorrow."

Willow blinked at the roughness in her brother's voice. It hadn't escaped her that Reno was reluctant to involve Eve in his family. Willow couldn't imagine why.

The look in Reno's eyes told her not to ask.

"I found where the journals cross," Caleb said into the uncomfortable silence.

"Good," Reno said.

"I doubt it," Caleb said dryly.

"Why?"

"It leaves you with half the West to explore for gold."

Reno took the chair on the other side of Eve and sat down.

Bracketed by the two men, Eve felt frankly petite. As she was every bit of five feet, three and one-half inches tall, the feeling was unusual; most of the men she met were barely a hand taller than she was.

Trying not to touch either of the pair of wide shoulders she was wedged between, Eve reached for the old Spanish journal.

So did Reno. Their hands collided. Both jerked back with a muttered word—an apology in Eve's case and a curse in Reno's.

Caleb looked away so that neither of his companions would see the broad smile on his face. He had a good idea what was making Reno so touchy. Wanting a particular woman very badly and not having her had been known to shorten the tempers of men much more easygoing than Reno Moran.

And Reno looked like a man who was wanting a particular woman. Badly.

"Now," Caleb said, clearing his throat, "you say the Cristóbal expedition came up from Santa Fe to Taos. . . ."

"Yes," Eve said quickly.

She reached for the journal once more, hoping that the slight tremor in her fingers didn't show.

Her skin burned where Reno had touched it.

"Some of the early expeditions went past the Sangre de Cristos and into the San Juans before turning west," Eve said in a carefully controlled voice.

As she spoke, she turned pages, tracing routes on maps that had been drawn by men long dead.

"They crossed through the mountains about . . ."

She turned to Caleb's journal.

". . . here. They must have passed very close to this ranch."

"Wouldn't surprise me," Caleb said. "We're on the flats, and only a fool climbs mountains."

"Or a man looking for gold," Reno said.

"Same thing," Caleb retorted.

Reno laughed. He and Caleb had never seen eye to eye on the subject of hunting gold.

"But here the trail gets hard to follow," Eve continued.

Beneath her slim finger a page in the Spanish journal showed the major route unraveling into a network of trails.

"That symbol means year-round water," Eve said, pointing to one.

Caleb picked up his father's journal and began thumbing through it rapidly. Year-round water was rare in the stone canyons. Any source his father had discovered would have been carefully mapped and marked.

"What does that symbol mean?" Reno asked.

"A dead end."

"What does the sign in front of it mean?" Reno asked.

"I don't know."

Reno gave Eve a sideways glance that was just short of an accusation.

"Tell me more about the other symbols," Caleb said, glancing between the two journals. "That one, for instance."

"That means an Indian village, but the sign just to the right of it means no food," Eve explained.

"Maybe the Indians were unfriendly," Caleb said.

"There was a different symbol for that."

"Then it's probably some of the stone ruins," Reno said.

"What?" asked Eve.

"Towns built of stone a long, long time ago."

"Who built them?"

"Nobody knows," Reno said.

"When were they abandoned?" Eve persisted.

"Nobody knows that, either."

"Will we see any of the ruins? And why don't the Indians live there today?"

Reno shrugged. "Maybe they don't like scrambling up and down a cliff to get water, or to hunt, or to grow food."

"What?" Eve asked, startled.

"Most of the ruins are smack in the middle of cliffs that are hundreds of feet high."

Eve blinked. "Why on earth would anyone build a town in a place that hard to get to?"

"Same reason our ancestors built castles on stone promontories," Caleb said without looking up from his father's journal. "Self-defense."

Before Eve could say anything, Caleb laid his father's journal down next to the other one and pointed at a page in each.

"This is where the journals go separate ways," Caleb said.

Reno looked quickly between the two hand-drawn maps.

"You sure?" he asked.

"If Eve is right about that sign meaning a dead end, and that one meaning an abandoned village . . ."

"What about white cap rock?" Reno said, pointing to Caleb's journal. "Does your father mention it?"

"Only well north of the Chama. Red sandstone is what he saw most of."

"Cliffs or arch-forming?" Reno asked.

"Both."

"How thick? And what about mudstone?"

"Lots of it," Caleb said. He pointed to the Spanish journal. "Here and about here."

"Were the layers thin or thick, slanted or level?" Reno asked quickly. "How about slate? Granite? Chert?"

Caleb bent to his father's journal once more. Reno did too, talking phrases that were more like code to Eve. With every minute, it became more obvious to her that Reno hadn't spent all his time in gunfights and looking for gold. He was a man of rather formidable geological learning.

After a few minutes Reno made a sound of satisfaction and tapped a page of the Spanish journal with the clean, short nail of his index finger.

"That's what I thought," Reno said. "Your father and the Spaniards were on opposite sides of this big neck sticking out into the canyon country from the main body of the plateau. The Spaniards thought it was a separate plateau, but your daddy knew better."

Caleb studied the two journals, then nodded slowly.

"Which means," Reno continued, "that if there's a way to cross over the neck about here, we don't have to go all the way to the Colorado River to pick up the Cristóbal trail."

"Where do you want to cross?" Caleb asked.

"Right here."

Eve leaned forward. The hasty knot she had made at the nape of her neck after giving Ethan her scarf came loose. A long lock of her hair escaped and spilled across Reno's hand. The individual strands gleamed in the lantern light like the very gold he had spent his life seeking.

And like gold, Eve's hair was cool and silky against his skin.

"Sorry," she mumbled, hastily redoing the knot.

Reno said nothing at all. He didn't trust himself to. He knew his voice would reveal the sudden, hard running of his blood.

"Maybe you're right," Caleb said.

He looked intently between the two journals.

"But if you're wrong," he added after a minute, "you better pray there's more water than either journal shows."

"That's why I'm hoping Wolfe won't mind if I run off with a couple of his mustangs for pack-horses."

"Take the two Shaggies," Caleb said. "And get Eve a desert mount, too. Her old pony wouldn't make it."

"I was thinking of the lineback dun," Reno said. "She didn't foal this year."

Caleb nodded, then said bluntly, "Horses are the least of your problems."

"Water," Reno answered.

"That's one, but not the worst."

Eve made a questioning sound.

"The worst problem," Caleb said, "is finding the mine—if the damned thing exists. Or were you expecting to find a sign saying, 'Dig here'?"

"Hell no. I was expecting a carnival barker and dancing elephants to point the way," Reno drawled. "Now, don't you go telling me there won't be any. It will plumb break my poor little heart."

Caleb laughed and shook his head.

"All fooling aside," he said a moment later, "how do you expect to find the mine?"

"Mining leaves marks on the land."

"Don't count on it. It's been two hundred years. Long enough for trees to grow right over any signs of mining."

"I'm not a bad geologist," Reno said. "I know what kind of rock to look for."

Caleb looked at Eve. "What about you? Think you can come close enough with that journal to find a mine?"

"If not, there's always the Spanish needles," she said.

"What?"

Eve reached into the front pocket of her faded dress. A moment later she brought out a small, leather-wrapped bundle. When she unrolled the leather, two slim metal rods fell into her palm with a musical sound.

"These," she said.

"Spanish dip needles," Reno explained to Caleb. "They're supposed to find buried treasure, not metal ore or water." Reno looked at Eve. "Where are the other two?"

She blinked, then understood. "Don said his ancestors had figured out that two worked as well as four, and were easier to use."

"Hell's fire," Caleb said in disgust. "You'd be lucky to find the floor with those."

"What do you mean?" Eve asked.

"They're damned hard to use," said Reno. "I've never tried it with two, though. God knows it can't be worse than four." He looked at Eve. "Have you ever used them?"

"No."

Reno held out his hand. She dropped the small rods on his palm without touching his skin with her fingers.

"Look close," Reno said to Eve. "The idea is to keep the needles touching on the forked end."

"At the tips?" Eve asked.

"No. At the base. Interlocked but moving easily, able to respond to the least change."

Eve watched, frowning. The notch of each Y was so shallow that it offered no real aid in keeping the rods together.

Delicately Reno brought the narrow metal sticks together until they barely met at the base of the wide Y. Breathing very lightly so as not to break the contact, he held them out for Eve to see.

"Kind of like this," Reno said. "Just kissing, mind you. No real pressure."

"Doesn't look all that hard," Caleb said.

"Not when one person is holding both rods. But they don't work that way. Takes two people, one rod each."

"No fooling?" asked Caleb. "Give me one of those."

Eve watched while Reno handed over one slim metal stick and kept the other. They indeed looked like needles when held in the men's large hands.

Large, but not clumsy. Reno and Caleb had unusually fine coordination. Eve had seen both men use their fingers with the delicate precision of a butterfly landing on a flower.

Indeed, very quickly Caleb had matched the flattened notch on his needle with the one on Reno's. Keeping them barely touching was more difficult. Even so, it was only a moment before Caleb mastered it.

"See. Nothing to it," Caleb said.

"Uh-huh," drawled Reno. "Now let's take a walk around the table."

Caleb gave him a startled look. "With the needles touching?"

"Every step of the way," Reno said. "Just kissing, mind you. No shoving."

A grunt was Caleb's only answer. The two men stood, matched needles, and looked at each other.

"On three," Caleb said. "One . . . two . . . three."

They took a step.

Instantly the small rods separated.

The second time, Caleb tried applying more pressure when he took a step.

The rods crossed like swords.

The third time the men tried, the rods clashed, slipped, and drew apart.

"Damn," Caleb said.

He flipped the dowsing rod end over end on his palm several times, then shot it toward Reno without warning.

Reno's free hand flashed out and snagged the flying needle. With no break in the motion, he flipped a rod in each hand like a circus juggler.

Whatever the problem in using the rods, lack of dexterity on the part of the men wasn't it.

"Good thing you've read enough geology books to stock a university," Caleb said. "Those needles are as useless as teats on a boar hog."

Eve's hand shot out, catching one of the dowsing rods as it somersaulted obediently above Reno's palm.

"May I?" she asked calmly.

The question was unnecessary. She had already leveled the forked end of the rod in Reno's direction. The metal stick was balanced between her palm and her thumb, so lightly held that a breath could sway the metal.

Reno hesitated, shrugged, and carelessly pointed the forked end of his rod toward her. He held the rod as she did, balancing it between his palm and his thumb.

Eve moved her hand slightly. The notches met, brushed, and came back together like lodestone and iron.

As they caught and held each other, a ghostly current rippled through the rods to the flesh holding them, startling both people.

With a gasp, Eve let go of her needle. So did Reno.

Caleb caught both pieces of metal before they hit the floor. Giving Eve and Reno an odd look, Caleb returned the rods to them.

"Something wrong?" he asked.

"I was clumsy," Eve said quickly. "I knocked the rods together."

"Didn't look clumsy to me," Caleb said.

Reno said nothing. He simply watched Eve through narrowed green eyes.

"Let me try it this time," Reno said.

Eve positioned her needle and held still. "Ready."

Reno brought his rod close, then closer, then closer still, brushing the prongs and then the cup of the Y on the end of Eve's Y.

Ghostly currents rippled.

This time Reno and Eve managed to hold on to the rods, but their breath came in hard and fast. Even that small a motion should have jerked the needles apart.

It didn't.

"On three," Reno said.

His voice was unusually deep, a sound like black velvet. The tone was a caress as intangible and undeniable as the subtle currents flowing through the Spanish needles, stitching together two halves of an enigmatic whole.

"Yes," Eve whispered.

Reno counted. As one, they took a step forward.

The prongs interlocked yet moved readily, as though faintly magnetized.

Deliberately Reno jerked his hand. Instantly the needles came apart.

"Again," he said.

The needles came to each other as though alive, eager, hungry for the fragile currents that would both join and define them.

"I will be damned," Reno whispered.

He looked up from the oddly shimmering

needles to the woman whose eyes were the color of purest gold.

And he wondered what it would be like to be buried within Eve, feeling her shiver as delicately and as completely as the two rods touching, two halves interlocked, moving freely, joined by currents of fire.

8

Long before first light, Eve was awake, dressed, and sneaking quietly out of the house. Carrying her saddlebags and bedroll, she headed for the barn. She expected to find Reno already there, getting the horses ready, for she had heard Caleb get up earlier and leave the silent house. A few minutes later she had caught the faint rumble of men's voices coming from the barn.

Despite the fact that Eve had slept little the night before, she had been too restless to stay in the Blacks' guest room a moment longer. She had told herself she was simply excited at starting the hunt for gold that had both possessed and eluded generation after generation of the Leon family.

Yet it wasn't gold that had haunted Eve's waking dreams. It was the memory of two dowsing rods touching and ghostly currents flowing.

The barn door was open. Just outside, two tall men were working over four horses. A lantern suspended on a nearby corral pole glowed pale gold against the fading darkness of night.

As Eve quietly approached, she could hear Caleb talking.

". . . coming down out of the high country. Most of them are too busy moving to winter camp to be a problem, but keep a sharp eye out. The warriors are raising hell with the army, and the shamans are all off looking for a powerful new vision."

Reno grunted.

"And then there's the rest of it," Caleb continued.

"The rest of what?"

"Oh, I just feel that as your friend—and brother-in-law—I should warn you what can happen when a man takes a pretty girl into wild country," Caleb drawled.

"Save your breath," Reno said. Then, dryly, "Not you, Darlin'. If you hold your breath, you're going to find my knee in your belly right quick."

Eve smiled. She had learned on the trail that Reno's mustang had a sly way of sucking in a lot of air before the cinch was tightened, then letting it out afterward. If Reno hadn't been aware of the mare's little trick, he would have found himself riding upside down half the time.

Leather slid over leather with a rushing sound as Reno drew his mare's cinch strap up tight. She snorted and stamped her foot in displeasure.

In the stillness of predawn, each sound was unnaturally clear.

"All the same," Caleb said, "I took a job guiding a pretty girl into the San Juans to find her brother, and I ended up married."

Leather snapped against leather as Reno tied off the mare's cinch with smooth, strong motions.

"Willow was one thing," Reno said finally. "Eve is a horse of an entirely different color."

"Not that different. Sure, her hair is darker than Willow's, and her eyes are gold rather than hazel, but—"

"That's not what I'm talking about," Reno interrupted curtly.

"You remind me of a mustang stud feeling a rope for the first time in his wild life," Caleb said.

Amusement rippled plainly in his voice.

Reno grunted.

Laughing aloud, Caleb settled a pack saddle onto a wiry little bay. The bay's thick mane fell to its shoulders, and the tail was so long it left marks on the dusty ground.

Another bay mustang stood patiently beside the first. The two animals were twins. Because it was hard to tell them apart, they were simply called Shaggy One and Shaggy Two, depending on which horse was closer to the speaker at the time. The geldings were inseparable. Where one went, the other followed.

The second Shaggy was already fully loaded. In addition to the usual trail gear, there were large, empty canteens and two small barrels of black powder tied on either side of the pack saddle.

"Surly as a fresh-caught stud," Caleb continued cheerfully. "Wolfe was the same way at first. He came around, though. Smart men know when they've got something good."

Reno acted as though he hadn't heard.

"Take my word for it," Caleb said, "whatever you think you have now isn't a candle against the sun to what a good woman will give you."

Reno smacked his mustang on her warm haunch.

"Stand on your own feet, Darlin'," he muttered.

"Mine have their work cut out as it is."

"She can cook, too," Caleb pointed out. "That apple pie was like eating a slice of summer."

"No," Reno said curtly.

"Bull. If you didn't like it, why did you have thirds?"

"Damn it, that's not what I meant, and you know it."

"Then what did you mean?" Caleb asked wryly.

Reno swore beneath his breath. He ducked under Darlin's neck and went to the last horse in line, a dun-colored mare with black socks, black mane and tail, and a black line down her spine.

Now the two men were working so closely they were all but stepping on each other, which made it harder for Reno to pretend that he wasn't hearing Caleb's low, casual voice. Working quickly, as though anxious to be on the trail, Reno curried the lineback dun with muscular sweeps of his arm.

Just as Eve thought it would be safe to walk into the lantern's ring of light, Caleb started speaking again.

"Willow likes Eve. Ethan took to her right away, and he's cool with strangers."

Reno froze with the brush just above the dun's barrel. The mare snorted and nudged him, wanting more of the currying.

"She's bright and she's spirited," Caleb said. He laughed softly. "She'll be a real handful, and that's a fact."

"The dun? Maybe I better use her as a packhorse and give one of the Shaggies to Eve to ride."

Caleb's grin flashed. "She'd run rings around most men, but she's a good match for you."

"I like Darlin' better."

Caleb chuckled. "I thought my two horses were

my best friends. Then Willow taught me that—"

"Eve isn't like Willow," Reno interrupted, his voice cold.

"That's it, boy. You just keep on fighting that silk rope."

Reno said something brutal under his breath.

"Fighting won't do you any good," Caleb said, "but no man worth his salt ever gives up without a fight."

With a hissed curse, Reno turned and faced Caleb.

"I should be whipped for bringing Eve into my sister's house," Reno said flatly.

A chill settled over Eve. She knew what Reno would be saying next. She didn't want to hear it.

But even more, she didn't want to be caught eavesdropping, no matter how innocently. She began retreating one slow step at a time, praying that she would make no sound to give her away.

"You asked me how I met Eve, and I ducked the question," Reno said. "Well, I'm through ducking."

"Glad to hear it."

"I met her in a Canyon City saloon."

Caleb's smile vanished. "What?"

"You heard me. She was dealing cards at the Gold Dust. Slater and a gunnie called Raleigh King were at the table."

Reno stopped talking, walked around the lineback dun, and began brushing away dust.

"And?" Caleb prodded.

"I took cards."

The only sound in the next minute was that made by the brush moving over sleek hide. Then came the muted bawling of cattle as dawn slowly began stealing stars from the sky.

"Keep talking," Caleb said finally.

"She was cold-decking and bottom-dealing."

Again Caleb waited.

Reno was silent.

"Christ, it's like pulling teeth," Caleb muttered. "Spit it all out."

"You've got the meat of it."

"Like blazing hell I do. I know you, Reno. You wouldn't bring a whore into your sister's house."

"I said Eve was peeling cards, not men."

There was a taut silence followed by the snap of a saddle blanket as Reno shook it out.

"Talk," Caleb said bluntly.

"When it came time for Eve to deal, she gave me a pat hand."

Caleb whistled through his teeth.

"When Raleigh went for his gun, I dumped the table in his lap. Eve grabbed the pot and ran out the back, leaving me in a shoot-out with Raleigh and Slater."

"Crooked Bear's whore said nothing about Slater being dead. Just Raleigh King and Steamer."

"Slater didn't draw on me. They did."

Shaking his head, Caleb said, "Be damned. Eve doesn't look like a saloon girl."

"She's a card cheat and a thief, and she set me up to die."

"If any man but you said that, I'd call him a liar."

Without warning Reno turned and looked into the darkness beyond the lamplight.

"Tell him, saloon girl."

Eve froze in the act of taking a step backward. After a sharp struggle with herself, she controlled the impulse to turn and flee, but there was nothing she could do to put color in a face gone as pale as salt. Head high, she walked into the circle of lantern light.

"I'm not what you think I am," she said.

Reno grabbed the saddlebags Eve was holding, opened one of them, and yanked out the dress she had worn in Canyon City. It hung from his fist in scarlet condemnation.

"Not as heart-tugging as a dress made of flour sacks, but a damn sight more truthful," Reno said to Caleb.

Color returned to Eve's cheeks in a crimson tide.

"I was a bond servant," she said in a thin voice. "I wore what I was given."

"So you say, *gata*. So you say. You were wearing this in a saloon when I met you, and your bond masters were dead."

Reno jammed the dress back into the saddlebag, flipped the joined bags over the corral rail, and went back to saddling the lineback dun.

"Have you eaten?" Caleb asked Eve.

She shook her head, not trusting her voice. Nor could she look Caleb in the eye. He had taken her into his house, and what he must think of her now that he knew the truth made her wish to be somewhere else. Anywhere else.

"Is Willow up yet?" Caleb asked.

Eve shook her head again.

"Not surprising," Caleb said easily. "Ethan was cranky all last night."

"Teething."

The word was barely a whisper, but Caleb understood.

Reno swore under his breath. That, too, carried in the stillness of dawn.

"Cloves," Eve whispered a moment later.

"Beg pardon?" Caleb said.

Eve cleared her throat painfully. "Oil of cloves. On his gums. It will sweeten his temper."

"I'd a hell of a lot rather kick his butt around the barn," Caleb said, "and I don't mean Ethan."

Reno's head came up. He gave Caleb a hard look. Caleb gave it right back.

"Yuma man," Reno said coldly. "I'd think you'd be the last one to be taken in by a pretty face."

Reno reached under the dun's belly, shot the long leather strap through the cinch ring, and began tightening the cinch with hard, quick motions of his hands. His words were the same—hard and quick.

"You went into the wilderness with Willy, an innocent girl who wanted love."

Leather hissed over leather.

"I'm going into the wilderness with an experienced little cheat who wants half of a gold mine."

Reno snapped the stirrup into place. The creak of leather was like a cry in the silence.

"If we find the mine, I'll have to look sharp or she'll steal me blind and shoot me in the back, or leave me to be shot up by the likes of Jericho Slater," Reno concluded harshly. "She's done it before."

From the house came the sound of an iron triangle being struck with a metal wand as Willow called the men in for breakfast.

Reno yanked Eve's saddlebags off the corral fence, took the bedroll from her hands, and secured both behind her saddle. When he finished, he spun around, picked Eve up, and dumped her in the saddle.

Only then did he turn to Caleb.

"Tell Willy good-bye for us."

Reno sprang into the blue roan's saddle like a big cat. A swift motion of his hand jerked Shaggy One's lead rope free of the corral rail. He wheeled Darlin' around and touched her with his spurs.

The mustang headed out of the yard at a brisk

canter. The two Shaggies and the lineback dun followed.

So did Caleb's voice.

"Run while you can, you hardheaded son of a bitch. There's nothing stronger than a silk rope. Or softer!"

RENO knew they were being followed. He pushed the horses hard from dawn until dusk, covering twice as much ground as a normal traveler would, hoping to wear down Jericho Slater's horses.

Right now Slater had the advantage, for his long-legged Tennessee horses were faster than the mustangs. In the desert, the advantage would quickly switch. The mustangs could go faster and longer on less food and water than any horse Slater had.

Not once through the long hours of riding did Eve complain about the pace. In fact, she said nothing at all except in response to a direct question, and Reno had very few of those.

Gradually Eve's anger gave way to curiosity about the land. The high, open country was slowly filling her with both peace and a heady sense of being on the edge of a vast, undiscovered land.

To her left a high, ragged mesa rose, covered with piñon and juniper. To her right were the rolling slopes of low, pine-covered ridges. Behind her was a beautiful valley bounded by granite peaks, rugged ridges, and the immense, shaggy mesa with its cliffs of pale stone.

Even without the journal to guide her, she knew they were slowly descending from the green and granite heights of the Rockies. The land itself was changing beneath the agile feet of the mustangs.

Foothills melted into plateau tops separated by steep, stream-cut ravines. Rocky stream banks had been replaced by dirt banks deeply cut and sandy tongues in river bends. Sandstone and shale had replaced granite and slate.

Graceful aspens and dense stands of fir and spruce had given way to cottonwoods and pines, piñon and juniper. Scattered, big sagebrush appeared in place of scrub oak. Clouds gathered and thunder rolled down from the peaks, but no rain fell at the lower elevations.

And over all loomed the dark mesa. Eve could not take her eyes from the ragged thrust of land, for she had seen nothing like it before. Plants grew on the mesa's steep sides, but not enough to conceal the starkly different layers of stone beneath. No rivers or creeks drained its ragged length. No water winked from its ravines. No tall trees grew on its crest.

The map in the Spanish journal hinted that the mesa was only the beginning of the changes. It was the lip of an enormous, high plateau that was as big as many European nations. Ahead, beyond the setting sun, the plateau's highlands fell away in immense stone steps that ultimately unraveled into countless stone canyons.

Eve couldn't see the stone maze, but she sensed it just over the horizon, an end to the mountainous terrain that had begun in Canyon City and had continued for hundreds of miles.

The stone maze was a land of awesome dryness where no rivers flowed except after storms, and then only briefly. Yet at the bottom of the deepest canyon was a river so mighty that it was like death itself; none who crossed its boundaries returned to speak of what lay on the other side.

Eve wanted to ask Reno how such a thing could

be, but did not. She would ask for nothing from him that wasn't part of the devil's bargain they had struck.

And the thought of having to keep that bargain—of giving herself to a man who thought her a liar and a cheat—was like ice congealing in her soul.

Surely Reno can't keep on believing that. The more we're together, the more he must see that I'm not what he thinks I am.

As Reno had all through the day, he turned and checked the back trail. At first Eve had thought it was concern that she would cut and run that kept Reno so alert. Gradually she had realized it was something else entirely.

They were being followed. Eve sensed that at the same instinctive level as she sensed the woman-hunger in Reno whenever he looked at her.

She wondered if Reno was like her, remembering the two rods touching, clinging, joined by secret currents, shimmering with unknown possibilities. She had never felt anything like it in her life.

Throughout the long hours on the trail, the memory haunted Eve. Each time it returned, it sent frissons of wonder and excitement through her, undermining her anger at Reno.

How could she be angry at a man whose very flesh and soul matched hers?

He felt it as clearly as I did.

He can't believe I'm no better than my cheap red dress.

Surely he understands. He just too mule-stubborn to admit he was wrong about me.

The thought was as alluring to Eve as the possibility of Spanish gold somewhere ahead in the wilderness, hidden from all other people, waiting to be discovered by whoever was brave or foolish enough to risk the dangerous stone maze.

"WAIT here."

Reno said no more. Nor did he need to.

Eve reined in her tired mount, took the lead rope of Shaggy One, and watched Reno leave without asking where he was going or why. She simply sat on her horse and waited for his return with a patience that came from exhaustion. Around her, the last colors of the day drained from the sky, leaving twilight behind.

It was full dark when Reno reappeared as silently as a wraith. The Shaggies and the dun were too busy cropping the scant grass to bother calling a greeting to their trail mate. The blue roan felt the same way about wasting energy on ceremony; as soon as Reno allowed, she fell to grazing with the hunger of a mustang that had grown up rustling its own feed.

Reno waited for Eve to ask where he had been and why. When she didn't, his mouth tightened with irritation.

"Are you going to sulk all night, too?" he asked.

"Why do you care what a liar, a cheat, and a saloon girl does?" Eve asked wearily.

She pretended not to hear the word Reno hissed beneath his breath as he dismounted. He began unsaddling Darlin' with quick, angry motions. After he upended the saddle on the ground to let the fleece dry, he turned to face Eve with his fists on his lean hips.

"Beats me why women get upset when a man calls them what they are," he said bluntly.

Eve was too tired to be polite, much less cautious.

"I can understand how a rude, blind, stubborn, cold-blooded lecher like you might feel that way," she said.

There was a taut, electric silence while she dismounted.

And then Reno laughed.

"Sheathe your claws, *gata*. You're safe from me tonight."

Eve gave him a wary, sideways look.

"I may be lecherous," he said dryly, "but I'm not a fool. As long as Slater is on my trail, I'm not going to get caught with my pants undone."

Eve told herself she wasn't disappointed that she would get none of Reno's disturbing, compelling touch that night—or any night soon. It was better that way.

Only one thing a man wants from a woman, make no mistake about it. Once you give him that, you better be married, or he'll go off down the trail and find another foolish girl to spread her legs in the name of love.

Yet even the echoes of Donna Lyon's bitter advice couldn't keep Eve from seeing Reno with his nephew, smiling and gentle, and with his sister. The love in him had been strong enough to touch.

Eve wanted to touch it. She wanted to make with Reno the home she had always dreamed of, the safe haven from a world that didn't care whether she lived or died, and the babies no one could take from her arms and send away.

The realization of how deeply and in how many ways she yearned for Reno frightened Eve. Unlike the Spanish needles, she wasn't made of iron. They weren't hurt by the eerie currents that joined them. She doubted that she would be so lucky if she gave in to her complex, unexpected hunger for Reno.

Eve dismounted in a rush. As she stood and flipped the stirrup up over the saddle horn, Reno's arm went around her waist, pulling her close. Suddenly she felt the muscular length of his body molded against her from shoulder blades to thighs. A hard ridge of flesh pressed against her hips.

"Cold-blooded is the last thing I am," Reno said. "Especially with you around to keep me hot."

First his mustache teased her sensitive ear, then the tip of his tongue, then the edges of his teeth. The restraint of the caresses was at odds with his heavy arousal.

The combination of intense masculine hunger and equally intense self-control was both disarming and compelling to Eve. She had never known a strong man who had exercised any restraint when it came to taking what he wanted.

Except Reno.

Maybe the longer he's with me, the more he sees I'm not a saloon girl to be bought and sold on a man's whim.

The idea was profoundly alluring. Eve wanted Reno to look at her and see a woman he could trust and respect, a woman he could build a home with, have children with, share a life with.

A woman he could love.

Maybe when he sees that I keep my word, too, he'll look at me with more than desire. Eve thought yearningly. *Maybe and maybe and maybe . . .*

If I don't try, I'll never know.

Table stakes. Five-card draw. A royal heart flush or a bushed heart flush.

Ante up or get out of the game.

As Reno felt the subtle softening of Eve's body, both hunger and relief swept through him. He hadn't meant for her to overhear his conversation with Caleb. Nor had he meant to hurt her by rubbing Caleb's nose in the fact that Eve wasn't the sweet country innocent she appeared to be. But Caleb hadn't left Reno any other choice.

"Does this mean Slater is far enough back that you're not worried about being, er, distracted?" Eve asked.

"No," Reno admitted reluctantly, releasing her. "I'm afraid we'll have to have a cold camp tonight, in more ways than one."

"Is Slater that close?" she asked.

"Yes."

"Lord, how could he be? After a day on the trail like we had, even our shadows were complaining about following us."

Reno's smile gleamed in the moonlight.

"How did he know where to find us after he lost my trail out of Canyon City?" she asked.

"There aren't that many ways over the Great Divide."

Eve sighed. "I guess the country isn't as empty of people as it looks."

"Oh, it's empty, all right. I've gone months at a time in the high country without seeing a soul. Just the crossroads and passes get kind of crowded."

"Not to mention human nature," Eve said, stretching.

"What?"

"Even if we took a hard way over the Great Divide, if Crooked Bear has a woman who's also keeping company with one of Caleb's riders, Slater would find out real quick where I'd been."

"That's the way I figured it," Reno said. "We've got an edge, though."

"What?"

"The mustangs. Most of Slater's boys are riding Tennessee horses."

"Those horses beat everything on four legs in Canyon City," Eve pointed out.

Reno's grin was as hard as his voice.

"We're not in Canyon City anymore. Our mustangs are going to walk Slater's Tennessee horses right into the ground."

9

By day Reno rode with the rifle across his saddle. By night he and Eve slept with the mustangs picketed around their remote, hidden campsites. As a further precaution, he scattered dried branches along the obvious approaches to the campsites.

Several times a day Reno would send Eve and the packhorses on ahead while he backtracked along the trail to a high point. There he would dismount, pull out his spyglass, and study the land they had ridden over.

Only twice did he catch sight of Slater. The first time he had six men with him. The second time he had fifteen.

Reno collapsed the spyglass, mounted, and cantered quickly to catch up with Eve and the packhorses. At the sound of hoofbeats, she turned. He saw the golden flash of her eyes beneath her hat brim and the intense honey color of her hair beneath the hot August sun. He also saw the subtle lines that fatigue and worry had drawn around her curving lips.

When Reno reined in beside Eve, the temptation to lean over and taste once more her subtle blend of salt and sweet and heat almost overwhelmed his control. He scowled savagely at his own growing, unruly hunger for the girl from the Gold Dust saloon.

"Are they closer?" Eve asked anxiously, looking at Reno's grim face.

"No."

She licked her dry lips.

Eyes like green crystal followed the tip of her tongue.

"Are they falling back?" she asked hopefully.

"No."

Her mouth curved down. "I guess those Tennessee horses are tougher than you thought."

"We're not in the desert yet."

Eve made a startled sound and looked at the surrounding land. They were riding down a long, troughlike valley that was bracketed for its entire length by two flat-topped ridges. So little vegetation grew on the ridges that their layered stone bodies showed clearly through the scattered brush and piñon. As a result, the ridges took on a dappled sandy color that owed more to stone than to plants.

"Are you sure we aren't in the desert?" Eve asked. "It's so dry."

Reno looked at her in disbelief.

"Dry? What do you think that is?" he demanded, pointing.

She looked beyond his hand. Winding down the center of the valley was a ribbon of water that was more brown than blue, and so narrow a horse would have to work to get all four feet wet at the same time when crossing it.

"That," Eve said, "is a poor excuse for a creek. More sand than water."

With a wry grin, Reno took off his hat, wiped his forehead on his sleeve, and resettled his hat.

"By the time you see that much water again, you'll think it's God's own river," he promised.

Dubiously Eve looked at the thin, dirty ribbon of water coiling through the dry valley.

"Really?" she asked.

"If we find the shortcut, yes. Otherwise, we'll see a river that owes more to hell than to God."

"Rio Colorado?"

Reno nodded. "I've known a lot of men who like wild country, but I've never known a man to cross the Colorado where it runs through the bottom of the stone maze, and come back to tell the tale."

A sideways glance at Reno convinced Eve that he wasn't teasing her. But then, it was too hot and dusty for anyone to have any energy left for teasing.

Even Reno was feeling the heat. The sleeves of his faded blue chambray shirt were rolled up, and the collar was open for several buttons. Sweat glittered like tiny diamonds in the thicket of black hair revealed by the half-undone shirt. Three days on the trail had left a thick, black stubble of beard that made his smile savage rather than reassuring.

No one looking at Reno now would have been misled into thinking him anything but what he was—a hard man with a reputation for coming out on the winning end of gunfights.

Yet despite Reno's threatening appearance and the currents of sensual tension that coiled invisibly between herself and him, Eve had never slept more securely than she had in the past few days.

For the first time since she could remember, she was not the one who had to sleep lightly, listening for every noise, ready to grab whatever weapon was at hand and defend those who were weaker than she was from whatever predator was prowling the night beyond the campfire or cheap hotel room.

Being able to depend on someone else was such a simple thing, yet the realization that she could depend on Reno kept rippling through Eve like currents through a river, changing old certainties.

Reno saw Eve take in a breath and let it out, then do it again as though breathing deeply were a luxury.

"Looks like the thought of going dry doesn't bother you," he said.

"What? Oh." She smiled slightly. "It's not that. I was just thinking how nice it is to sleep through the night without worrying."

"About what?"

"About a bully or a lecher trapping one of the younger kids in bed at the orphanage, or about outlaws stumbling over the Lyons' campsite." Eve shrugged. "That sort of thing."

Reno frowned. "Did much of that happen?"

"Bullies and lechers?"

He nodded curtly.

"They learned to leave me alone after a while. But the younger kids . . ." Eve's voice faded. "I did what I could. It was never enough."

"Was old man Lyon a lecher?"

"Not at all. He was kind and gentle, but . . ."

"Not much good in a fight," Reno said, finishing Eve's sentence.

"I didn't expect him to be."

Reno's eyes narrowed in surprise. "Why? Was he a coward?"

It was Eve's turn to be surprised.

"No. He was simply kind. He wasn't as quick

or hard or strong or mean as most men are. He
was too . . . civilized."

"He should have lived back East," Reno muttered.

"He did. But when his hands started slowing
down, and Donna was too old to distract men with
her looks, they had to come to the West. People
out here were more easily entertained."

"Especially once they bought you off the orphan
train and taught you to 'distract' the men and deal
the cards," Reno said roughly.

Eve's mouth thinned, but there was no point in
denying it.

"Yes," she said. "They lived much better after
they had me."

Reno's expression told Eve that he had little sympathy to spare for the Lyons' difficulty in making
a living.

She hesitated, then spoke again, trying to make
him understand that the Lyons hadn't been vicious
or cruel to her.

"I didn't like what they made me do," Eve said
slowly, "but it was better than the orphanage. The
Lyons were kind."

"There's a word for men like Don Lyon, and it
sure as hell isn't *kind*."

Reno lifted the reins and cantered on ahead before Eve could answer. He didn't trust himself to
listen to her defending her whoremaster.

He was kind and gentle.

Yet no matter how quickly Reno rode, he
couldn't leave behind the sound of Eve's voice, for
it echoed within the angry silence of his mind.

They lived much better after they had me.

I didn't like what they made me do.

He was kind.

The thought of Eve being so lonely that she welcomed the smallest crumbs of human decency and called it kindness disturbed Reno in ways that he couldn't name. He could only accept them as he accepted other things he didn't understand, such as his desire to protect a saloon girl who had been carefully taught to lie, cheat, and "distract" men.

A girl who trusted him so much that she had slept better in the past few days than she had in years.

I was just thinking how nice it is to sleep through the night without worrying.

Reno knew the thought of giving the girl from the Gold Dust saloon that kind of peace shouldn't touch him.

But it did.

THE mountains receded behind Reno and Eve like a cool blue tide, leaving nothing but the memory of heights where water danced in crystal beauty and trees crowded so closely together that a horse couldn't walk between. There was plenty of room for horses in the dry washes and on the spare plateau tops where the two of them rode now. There was nothing but room for miles and miles.

"Look!" Eve said.

As she spoke, she reached across the small space between her horse and Reno's, grabbed his right arm, and pointed.

"There."

Reno stared beyond Eve's fingertip and saw only tawny, curving outcrops of sandstone, like the bones of the land itself pushing up through the thin skin of earth.

"What?" he asked.

"Over there," Eve insisted. "Can't you see it?

Those stone buildings. Is that one of the ruins you talked about?"

After a moment, Reno understood.

"Those aren't ruins," he said. "They're just layers of sandstone shaped by wind and storms."

Eve started to argue, then thought better of it. When Reno had first told her that they would be riding through whole valleys where no creek drained the highlands and no water collected in the lowlands, she had thought that he was teasing her.

He hadn't been. There were such valleys. She had seen them, ridden through them, tasted their sun-struck dust on her tongue. She was riding in one of them now.

For Eve, the transformed land was a constant source of wonder. In all the years she had read the journal of Cristóbal Leon, she had never truly understood what it must have been like for the Spanish explorers to ride out into the unknown desert, following rivers that grew smaller and smaller until they disappeared entirely, leaving only thirst behind.

Nor had she imagined what it would be like to look a hundred miles in all directions at once, and see not one creek, not one pond, not one lush promise of shade and water to ease a thirst as big as the dry land itself.

Yet even more than the lack of water, Eve was astonished by the naked, multicolored, fantastically shaped rocks that rose out of the land. Taller than any building she had ever seen, drawn in shades of rust and cream and gold, the massive, seamless stone formations fascinated her.

Sometimes they resembled sleeping beasts. Sometimes they resembled mushrooms. And sometimes, like now, they resembled the picture she had once seen of a Gothic cathedral with flying buttresses of solid stone.

Reno stood in the stirrups and looked over his shoulder. The mountains were no more than a dark blue blot against the horizon. He could have covered them with his hand. The long, dry valleys he had led the way through offered few chances of concealment, whether for him or for the men who pursued him.

Yet since dawn Reno had seen nothing move over the face of the land but cloud shadows, and very few of those.

"Looks like Slater's horses finally gave up," Eve said, staring out over their back trail.

Reno made a sound that could have meant anything.

"Does that mean we can camp early?" Eve asked hopefully.

He looked at her and smiled.

"Depends," he said.

"On what?"

"On whether that spring Cal's daddy marked is still flowing. If it is, we'll fill up the canteens and make camp a few miles away."

"Miles?" Eve said, hoping she had heard wrong.

"Miles. In dry land, only a fool or an army camps next to water."

She thought about it and sighed.

"I see," Eve said unhappily. "Camping by water would be like camping in the center of a crossroads."

Reno nodded.

"How far is the spring?" she asked.

"A few hours."

When Eve was silent, Reno glanced aside at her. Despite the hard miles on the trail, she looked good to him. The shine of her hair was undiminished, her color was high, and the quickness of her mind hadn't changed.

Even more pleasing to Reno, Eve shared his fascination with the austere land. Her questions showed it, as did her long silences while she studied the layers of stone he pointed out, trying to imagine the forces that had built them.

"How big is the spring?" she asked.

"What did you have in mind?"

"A bath."

The thought of getting Eve naked in a pool of water had a rapid, pronounced effect on Reno's body. With a silent curse he forced his thoughts away from the memory of her nipples drawn taut and shiny from the searching caresses of his mouth.

Reno tried very hard not to think about Eve in that way at all. It was too damned distracting. He was a man of unusual self-control, yet he had very nearly reached for her at dawn that morning, and to hell with worrying about the outlaws on their trail.

"You might get a basin bath out of the spring," he said evenly.

The purring sound of pleasure Eve made did nothing to decrease Reno's sensual awareness of her.

"Is it at the end of this valley?" Eve asked.

"This isn't a valley. It's the top of a mesa."

She looked at Reno, then at their back trail.

"Looks like a valley to me," she said.

"Only if you come at it from this direction," he said. "You come at it from the desert, you have no doubt. It's like climbing up onto a big, broad step, then another and then another until you come to foothills and then real mountains."

Eve closed her eyes, recalling the maps from the journals, thinking of how different the land had looked to her than it had to the Spanish, who often were approaching from a different direction than she and Reno took.

"That's why they called it Mesa Verde," she said suddenly.

"What?"

"The Spanish. They first saw the mesa when they were in the desert. And compared to the desert, the mesa was as green as grass."

Reno took off his hat, resettled it, and looked over at Eve with a smile.

"That's been bothering you for days, hasn't it?" he asked.

"Not anymore," she said with satisfaction.

"The Spanish might have been fools for gold, but they weren't crazy. What something looks like depends on how you come at it, that's all."

"Even red dresses?" Eve asked.

The instant the words left her mouth, Eve regretted them.

"You just never give up, do you?" Reno asked coolly. "Well, I've got bad news for you. Neither do I."

For a long time after that, nothing broke the silence but the sound of hooves striking the ground in a rhythm so familiar, it was like a heartbeat, unnoticed unless it changed suddenly.

The valley that wasn't really a valley began to descend with increasing steepness. As it slanted down to the stone maze, the land changed, rising slowly on either side of the dry wash Reno had chosen to follow.

The wash was lined with stunted cottonwoods whose leaves were a dusty green that gave shade but little coolness. Plants that required surface water to survive had long since flowered, gone to seed, and died back to brittle stalks that rustled with every breeze, waiting for the seasonal rains to come.

The farther the wash went to the west and north, the higher the walls on either side became, and the more narrow the passage between. After a time, Reno slipped the thong that held his six-gun in the holster and pulled his repeating rifle from its saddle scabbard. He levered a round into the firing chamber and rode with the rifle across his lap.

Reno's actions told Eve that there was no other way to go but the one ahead. And that one led farther and deeper into what was rapidly becoming little more than a crack in the dry body of the land. She pulled the old double-barreled shotgun from its worn scabbard and checked the load.

The dry, metallic sound the shotgun made as Eve broke it open to put a shell in each firing chamber turned Reno's head. She closed the gun and rode as he did, with a gun across the saddle, its muzzle pointed in the opposite direction of Reno's rifle. The look on her face was intent and wary, but not frightened.

At that moment Reno was reminded of Willow, who once had stood with her back to him and a shotgun in her hands, waiting to see if the next person coming out of the forest would be Caleb or a member of Jed Slater's savage gang.

It had been Caleb who came out of the forest, but Reno had no doubt that Willow would have shot anyone else.

He didn't doubt Eve's courage, either. Not in that way. She had spent too many years defending herself to flinch from what must be done.

They learned to leave me alone.

Reno's eyes moved ceaselessly, probing shadows and the random turnings of the stream bed. The blue roan mustang he rode liked the narrowing wash no better than he did. Her ears swiveled and pricked at the least sound. Despite the long trail behind, she carried herself lightly, muscles coiled, ready to leap in any direction at the first appearance of danger.

The lineback dun was equally edgy. Eve could feel the mare's wariness in her quick movements and nervously lashing tail. Even the two Shaggies were skittish. They crowded up on the dun's heels as though taking no chance on being left behind.

Dry watercourses came in from the right and the left, yet still the main channel narrowed, eating deeper and deeper into the land. The bluffs on either side became cliffs that rose high enough to cut off the sun.

Abruptly Reno reined the mare into one of the side channels. The other horses followed. When Eve would have spoken, he gestured curtly for silence.

Long minutes later, a small band of wild horses trotted past the mouth of the narrow side canyon. The sound of their passage was all but smothered by the sandy ground. The horses were heading back the way Eve and Reno had come.

Eve felt the dun's barrel swell as the horse drew breath to whinny. Immediately she leaned forward in the saddle and clamped her fingers around the mustang's nostrils.

The motion caught Reno's eye. He saw what Eve had done, nodded approvingly, and went back to watching. Long after the last wild mustang had gone by, he waited.

Nothing else moved.

Reno considered the tiredness of the horses, the

time of the day, and the map in his mind.

It didn't take long to decide.

"We'll camp here."

THE spring was marked only by the shocking green of growing things. Where water overflowed, there was a narrow ribbon of fern and moss that gave way almost immediately to plants better suited for surviving the relentless sun. Yet even those plants didn't last long, for the air drank water more quickly than any growing thing. Fifty feet from the spring, the trickle of water vanished into sand and pebbles.

Reno sat on his heels, studying the tracks leading to and from the water hole. Deer had been to drink. So had coyotes, rabbits, ravens, and horses. None of the horses showed clear signs of being shod, but something about the tracks disturbed Reno just the same.

He had used various herds of wild horses to hide the tracks left by his own horses. There was no reason to think that Slater was any less clever at disguising his own tracks. But Reno couldn't prove that it had happened here.

Reluctantly he stood, mounted Darlin', and rode back up the wash to the place where Eve and the packhorses waited. After a hundred feet he turned to look at his own back trail. Darlin's shod hooves left clear marks in the damp, churned earth at the fringes of the spring.

"Has Slater been here?" Eve asked with outward calm as Reno rode up.

He had been expecting the question. The hours and days on the trail had taught him that Eve was accustomed to using her eyes and her brain. Even though there was no trail marked in the journals that Slater could have taken to get in front of them, that possibility still remained.

The Spanish hadn't found all the ways through the wild land. Nor had the U. S. Army. The Indians had; some of the men who rode with Slater might easily know things that no white men did.

"Couldn't prove it by the tracks," Reno said.

She let out a silent breath of relief.

"Couldn't disprove it, either," he continued. "Not all of Slater's men are riding shod horses."

"They were in Canyon City." Then, before Reno could say it, she added dryly, "But we're not in Canyon City anymore."

The corner of his mustache lifted in a smile.

"Comancheros aren't welcome in Canyon City," Reno pointed out.

"Couldn't the tracks you saw have been made by mustangs?"

"Some of them were. And some of them were cut deep into the ground."

"Like a horse carrying a man?" Eve asked.

"Or a horse digging in to shy away from an irritable neighbor. A lot of nipping and squealing goes on at a water hole this small."

Eve made a sound of exasperation and licked her dry lips.

"Don't worry, *gata*," Reno said. "I'm not planning on making you go without your bath."

She smiled with delight. As she did, she realized that somewhere along the hot, hard trail to Spanish gold, she had lost her displeasure over Reno's nickname for her.

Or maybe it was simply that his voice had lost its cutting edge when he called her *gata*. Now his tone was darkly caressing, as though she were indeed a wary cat being coaxed closer and closer to his hand for a thorough petting.

The thought brought a flush to Eve's cheeks that

had nothing to do with the heat radiating from the canyon's stone walls.

"Cover me from here while I fill the canteens," Reno said. "When I'm finished, I'll water the horses one by one."

By the time the canteens, the humans, and the horses had drunk their fill and returned to the small side canyon, the sun no longer touched even the highest edges of the rock walls. The air was hushed, for no breeze disturbed the hidden canyon. Shadows flowed out from every crevice, pooled, and rose in a soundless tide. Overhead the sky flushed darkly with the passionate hues of sunset.

While Reno took care of the horses, Eve built a small fire against a boulder. By the time the smoke rose to the boulder's top, nothing remained to give away the camp's presence but a faint fragrance of piñon fire and coffee. With the meager light of the flames to aid her, Eve ate quickly and gathered up what she would need for a "bath."

Silently Reno watched Eve walk out into the darkness with a canteen, a small metal pan, a soft rag, and a piece of soap. The faded dress made of old flour sacks was draped over her shoulder. He couldn't decide if she was going to wear it back to camp or use it as a towel.

"Don't go far," Reno said.

Though he had spoken quite softly, Eve froze.

"And take the shotgun with you."

Reno followed the small sounds Eve made as she picked up her shotgun and walked once more into the darkness. She didn't go far. Just enough to be well beyond the reach of light from the fire.

Reno heard the muted splash of water and told himself he could not possibly hear the subtle whisper of cloth against skin as Eve undressed. Nor could he hear her sigh of pleasure as the cool water caressed her. He most certainly couldn't hear her breath shiver when her nipples peaked in response to the wet cloth. But he could imagine it.

And he did.

10

THE air felt sleek and cool on Eve's damp skin as she finished her bath. She shivered, but not from chill. Like the half-wild, wary mustangs, Eve sensed she was no longer alone. She shook out her flour-sack dress and hurriedly pulled it on over her head.

"Finished?"

Reno's voice came from only a few feet away.

Eve spun toward him, her eyes wide. He was standing within reach. Clean clothes were bunched in one hand.

"Yes," she whispered. "I'm finished."

"Then you won't mind if I use the basin."

"Oh . . ."

Eve took a shaky breath and told herself she wasn't disappointed that Reno had followed her merely because he, too, wished to refresh himself after the long ride. Quickly she held out the basin.

"Here," she said.

"May I use your cloth, too?"

The husky darkness of Reno's voice heightened Eve's awareness of him until it was almost painful. Her skin tingled as though it had been stroked.

"Yes, of course," she said.

"And your soap?"

She nodded.

The motion of her head set her carelessly bound hair free of its loose knot. Moonlight tangled in the tawny locks that fell below her waist.

"And your hands, *gata*. May I use them, too?"

Reno heard the break in Eve's breathing and wished that he could see her eyes. He wanted to know whether curiosity or dread, sensuality or fear, had caused that soft, tearing intake of breath.

"I know that wasn't part of our bargain," he said, "but I would appreciate a shave. Heat makes beard stubble itch like the very devil."

"Oh. Yes, of course," she said hurriedly.

"Have you shaved a man before?"

Moonlight gleamed and ran like liquid silver through Eve's hair as she nodded.

"And cut hair," she said. "And gave manicures."

"Another way you earned your keep, is that it?"

The edge in Reno's voice made Eve flinch.

"Yes," she said.

Then, knowing what he was thinking, she added, "And none of them touched me."

"Why? Did it cost extra?"

"No. I had a razor at their throat," Eve said succinctly.

Reno remembered how he had seen her a few minutes ago, naked in the moonlight, all glistening silver and black velvet, with curves that made a man ache. He wanted to believe that she was as pure as she looked.

But he couldn't.

Even night and shadow didn't conceal Reno's skepticism. Eve saw it clearly. Her expression changed, becoming as cool and remote as the moon.

"I never sold myself, gunfighter."

Reno smiled rather grimly. He wanted to believe Eve the way he wanted to take his next breath. He would have given up heaven and taken on hell if it would have made Eve half as innocent as she had seemed as she stood naked, shimmering with moonlight and water.

The depth of his desire to believe that Eve had never been bought and sold shocked Reno. Yet he could no more deny his futile wish than he could control his primal response to something as simple as watching her move around the campfire.

Nor could Reno understand his reaction to Eve. He had never fancied saloon girls. Nor had he ever used them. He had preferred to go without rather than to slake his thirst at a tainted water hole. Yet he wanted Eve like hell burning, no matter how many other men she might have had in her young life.

That was why he had taken cards in the Gold Dust Saloon. A single look at Eve's steady eyes and trembling mouth had drawn him straight across the room. He hadn't cared if the two outlaws at the table with her objected to having a stranger join them for a few rounds of draw poker. He would have fought just to sit near her. He would have killed.

And he had.

Abruptly Reno turned and went to the smooth, blunt shelf of sandstone that Eve had used as a table for her basin of water. He sat on the rock ledge, put the clean clothes aside, and started undoing his shirt with quick, angry motions of his hands.

"Do you have a razor with you?" Eve asked.

Reno reached back to his hip pocket and took out a folding straight-edge razor. Without a word he handed it to Eve, for he didn't trust his voice not to reveal how much he disliked the idea of her hands moving over other men's faces, their hair, their hands; and all the while the men would be looking at her lips and her breasts, breathing in the scent of lilacs from her skin, undressing her in their minds, opening her thighs. . . .

Warily Eve came closer to the dangerous man who watched her with eyes made colorless by moonlight. Years of living in the Lyons' Gypsy wagon had taught her how to wash herself and others with a minimum of fuss and water. She wet Reno's hair and heavy beard stubble and began to work soap into both.

Normally she stood behind a man to do this, but Reno was sitting on a smooth stone outcropping rather than a chair. She had no choice except to stand in front of him.

And, Eve admitted silently to herself, no real desire to stand elsewhere. She liked watching Reno's closed eyes and knowing that her touch was pleasing him.

Slowly, subtly, Reno shifted his position as Eve worked. Before she quite understood how it had happened, she found herself standing between his legs. She made a startled sound.

As though she had stumbled, Reno's hands came up to steady her.

"Perdition," she whispered.

His eyes opened. "I beg your pardon?"

"The manicure. I forgot your hands."

Reno raised a single black eyebrow and flexed

his hands, sinking his fingers into the lush flare of
Eve's hips. He felt the heat of her body clearly, for
there was only one layer of cloth between his skin
and hers. She was quite naked under the flour-
sack dress.

Eve's breath rushed in and stayed until she felt
dizzy. She had never imagined that there would
be pleasure in a man's hands on her hips.

"Your hands," she said.

Reno smiled and flexed his fingers again.

"My hands," he agreed. Then he bent forward
and whispered against Eve's breasts, "Where else
would you like them?"

"That wasn't what I meant."

She turned away quickly, stepping beyond
Reno's reach. Using the canteen he had brought,
she poured just enough water in the basin to cover
his hands.

"Here," Eve said, putting the basin in Reno's
lap. "Soak your hands."

Wryly Reno moved his knees together to make
a platform for the basin. As he did, he wondered
if Eve really thought putting his hands in a basin
would keep them off her warm curves.

The feel of Eve's fingers rubbing his scalp made
gooseflesh ripple over Reno's body. In the silence
of his mind he cursed his unruly response to this
one woman, but he said nothing aloud. If Eve
chose to ignore his arousal, he wasn't going to call
attention to it.

He wanted to give her no more hold over him
than he already had. The feel of her fingers buried
in his hair and rubbing his scalp was arousing him
to the point of pain.

"Are you cold?" Eve asked when she sensed a
faint tremor in Reno.

"No."

Reno's voice was too husky, but he couldn't change that any more than he could help watching the play of moonlight and shadow over Eve's face as she bent and turned, working over him with hands that were surprisingly strong.

Belatedly Reno remembered the ragged sores he had seen on Eve's hands from burying the Lyons in a trailside grave. He grabbed one of her hands and turned it over, holding it in the moonlight. Though nearly healed, the skin still showed the cruel marks of the shovel. So did her other palm.

"Does it hurt?" Reno asked.

"Not anymore."

He released Eve's hands without a word.

She gave him a wary look before she turned to the razor. The small sound the folding blade made as she opened it seemed almost loud in the hushed night. She tested the razor's edge delicately. Despite her care, the razor sliced a shallow line in her skin.

"Perdition," she muttered. "Don't make any sudden movements. The razor is very sharp."

Reno's smile was like a thin slice of moonlight.

"Cal honed it for me," Reno said. "That man could put an edge on a brick."

Though nothing showed on Eve's face, Reno sensed the inner tightening of her body.

"Now what's wrong?" he asked.

She looked at him warily, wondering when he had learned to read her so well.

"Don't do anything to, er, startle me," Eve said finally.

"Such as?"

"Touch me."

"I thought you'd never ask," Reno drawled, lifting his hands from the water.

"That's not what I meant," Eve said hastily, stepping back out of his reach. "Well, it is, but not that way."

"Make up your mind."

"I meant that you shouldn't touch me."

Reno's whole body became still.

"We have a bargain, *gata*. Remember?"

Eve closed her eyes.

"Yes," she said. "I remember. I think of little else."

Table stakes. Five-card draw. A royal heart flush or a busted heart flush.

Ante up or get out of the game.

"I'm not trying to go back on our bargain," she continued, "but if you start touching me, I'll get nervous, and this blade is hellishly sharp."

Cautiously Eve watched the man who was sitting so still, watching her with a hunger that even darkness couldn't disguise.

"I'll sit very still," Reno said in a deep voice.

"All right."

She drew a deep, steadying breath and let it out.

Reno barely hid the shiver of response that went through him at the warm rush of her breath over his bare chest.

"Ready?" she asked.

He laughed. "You have no idea just how ready I am."

Eve bent and began shaving Reno with deft, neat motions, wiping the blade on the washcloth every few strokes. As she worked, she tried to tell herself that this was just like a thousand other times when she had shaved Don Lyon. Don had sworn that her hands were his secret luck. They made him look sharp and prosperous before he talked his way into a card game with little more than his aristocratic good looks and a handful of silver coins that wouldn't bear close examination.

"Be very still now," Eve cautioned in a low voice.

"Like a rock," Reno promised.

She pushed his chin up and ran the razor over his throat with light, even strokes. When she finished, she heard the long breath he let out. Gingerly he touched his neck.

"I didn't cut you," Eve said quickly.

"Just checking. That blade's so damned sharp, I wouldn't know I'd been killed until I saw the blood running down to my belt buckle."

"If you're that worried about my skill," she said tartly, "why did you want me to shave you in the first place?"

"I've been asking myself the same question."

Eve hid her smile as she rinsed the rag in cool water. She was still smiling when she turned back to him with the wet rag between her hands. His breathing hesitated, then resumed more deeply as she rinsed his face once, then again for good measure.

While Eve worked, small drops of water dripped onto Reno's shoulders and tangled in the dark thicket on this chest. When he breathed, the drops trembled and gleamed like translucent pearls. The temptation to touch a drop was so great that it startled her.

"Something wrong?" Reno asked huskily.

Eve shook her head too hard. Her hair spilled over her shoulders and across Reno's chest. His breath hissed in as though he had been burned.

"Sorry," she said.

"I'm not."

She gave him a startled look, then gathered up her hair and twisted it into another knot at the nape of her neck.

"I like it better when it's free," Reno said.

"It's in the way."

"Not for me, *gata*."

"Lift your hands," was all Eve said.

Reno moved his hands and waited while Eve poured more water into the basin and rinsed him thoroughly from crown to collarbones.

"Not a single cut," she said with satisfaction. "While you finish your bath, I'll get some witch hazel."

Before Reno could object, Eve was hurrying back to camp.

The thought of stripping, bathing, and waiting naked for her to return tempted him. The thought of the deeply cut hoof marks by the water hole told him how foolish he was being even to consider it.

He could divide his attention long enough to taste Eve's cool skin and hear her breath break with desire; but if he had his pants off when she came back, the next thing he would be wearing would be soft, sultry woman.

Cursing silently, Reno stripped, washed himself, pulled on the clean underwear he had brought with him, and yanked his pants back on. Only then did he begin on his chest. He was just reaching for his clean shirt when Eve's voice came from the darkness.

"Reno?"

"Come ahead. I'm decent."

She walked close enough to see the faint shine of his damp, naked shoulders and the dark silhouette of his jeans.

"Thank you," she said.

"What for?"

"Not shaming me."

"An odd choice of words for a . . ."

Reno found he couldn't finish the sentence. He

didn't like thinking of Eve as a saloon girl. With an irritated sound he turned his attention back to straightening out his shirt so he could put it on. Then he had a better idea.

"Fix this, would you?" Reno asked, holding out his shirt.

When Eve hesitated, he said sarcastically, "Never mind. It wasn't part of our *bargain*, was it?"

She took the shirt and shook it vigorously. He watched with eyes moonlight had transformed to the color of hammered silver. It was obvious that men's clothing was almost as familiar to her as her own.

"You're real good at that," Reno said.

"Toward the end, Don couldn't get into his clothes, much less fasten them," Eve said.

"Then you wouldn't mind helping me out?"

Surprised, she said, "Of course not. Hold out your arms."

He did, and she slipped the shirt on.

"Fasten it for me?" he asked blandly.

Eve gave him a wary look.

"You don't have to," he said. "It's not part of—"

"Our bargain," she muttered, reaching for the first button. "Perdition. I suppose you'll want me to undress you, next."

"Hell of an idea. Are you volunteering?"

"No," she said instantly. "It's not part of—"

"Our bargain."

She looked up sharply. He smiled.

Eve concentrated on the buttons. As she worked, she tried not to notice how different his powerful body was from Don Lyon's frail, age-twisted form.

It was impossible. Health and strength radiated from Reno's big body.

"Why didn't his wife take care of Lyon?" Reno asked.

"Donna did what she could, but a lot of the time her hands were worse than his."

The smell of lilacs rose from Eve's hair, infusing Reno with her fragrance more deeply than even the scented soap had.

The matter-of-fact skill with which Eve worked told Reno she had spent a lot of time caring intimately for a man who couldn't—or wouldn't—care for himself.

It's just as well that cheating whoremaster is dead, Reno thought grimly. *The temptation to kill him might have put my good sense in the shade.*

"There. All finished," Eve said.

"Not quite. It's not tucked in."

"You'll manage."

"What's wrong? It's not like I'm asking you to undress me."

When she gave him a skeptical look, Reno smiled.

"Guess you'd rather I went back to touching you, huh?" he asked.

"Perdition."

Before Eve could think better of it, she reached for Reno's waist. As his belt was already undone, it was only an instant's work to open the metal buttons. Moving quickly, she began tucking in his shirt as she had Don Lyon's, starting at the back and working forward.

Moments later, Reno's breath hissed in as he felt the pressure of Eve's fingers slide across his aroused flesh. She made a startled sound and tried to jerk her hands out of his jeans.

Reno was faster. He caught Eve's wrists and held

her fingers where they were, where he had wanted them to be for so long he almost lost control at her mere touch.

"Let me go!"

"Easy, *gata*. There's nothing down there that's going to bite; and you've unfastened enough pants to know it as well as I do."

The shocked look Eve gave Reno made him want to laugh, but the ache of his hunger was too fierce.

"I'm tempted to have you pet me a little, but it would be too damned distracting. I'll settle for a kiss or two. . . ." Reno said.

Eve struggled against his grip. It only served to rub her fingers over his aroused flesh.

Reno couldn't stifle a groan of pleasure and need. He looked hungrily at the soft lips that were only a few inches from his mouth.

"Be still—" he began roughly.

"Let go of—"

"—or else I'll pull off my pants," Reno continued in a hard voice, "and make you finish what you started, and to hell with anyone who might be following us."

"What *I* started? You were the one who—"

"Be still!"

Eve froze.

Reno let out a strained breath. He started to ease her hands from his pants, then stopped, for her balled fists made it difficult.

"Open your hands," he said.

"But you said not to mo—"

"Do it," he interrupted. "Slowly, *gata*. Very slowly."

Eve uncurled her hands. As she did, she found herself measuring Reno inch by hard inch.

A thread of sound came from Reno, as though

he were being drawn on a rack. He eased her hands from his pants, but instead of releasing her wrists, he pulled them up and over his shoulders.

"Stop fighting me," he said. "It's time to show me how well you can keep your word."

Fear and the memory of the pleasure she had found in his kisses fought for control of her body.

Maybe when he sees that I keep my word, he'll look at me with more than desire. Maybe . . .

"You'll keep your word, too?" she asked.

"I won't take you unless you want it," he said impatiently. "Is that what you mean?"

"Yes, I—"

Reno's mouth closed over Eve's. His tongue slid between her lips, cutting off the possibility of talking.

Other than a startled sound, she made no protest. Despite his obvious strength and hunger, he wasn't being hard on her. Quite the opposite. Once he understood that she wasn't going to struggle against him, he held her rather gently.

The sensitive edges of Eve's lips were caressed by the silky thickness of Reno's mustache. The tantalizing currents of awareness that had shimmered into life the instant she had first seen him became stronger as the kiss inevitably deepened. Warmth flared in the pit of her stomach, making her shiver with a delicious awareness. She had wanted this without knowing it.

But she knew it now.

Eve's eyes opened, wide and curious, wondering if Reno was feeling the same unexpected warmth. All she could see of Reno was the dense black eyelashes any woman would have envied. Their softness reassured Eve.

Tentatively she touched Reno's tongue with her own, rediscovering the textures of his mouth, the velvet and the silk and the heat. For a moment she forgot all about fear and bargains and her hopes for the future. She simply savored the kiss in a hushed, trembling silence that was like nothing she had ever known.

Unexpected heat splintered through Eve, a single current of sensation that went from her breasts to her knees. She liked the taste and feel of his intimate kiss. It sent currents of pleasure to hidden parts of her body, teaching her things about herself that she had never suspected.

The slow, repeated rasp of Reno's tongue over hers was dizzying, making it hard for Eve to breathe. Instinctively her grip on him tightened even as she pulled back.

Reno made a thick sound of protest.

"I can't breathe," Eve explained.

It was the huskiness of her voice that told Reno more than her words. He caught her lower lip between his teeth and bit with great care, drinking her startled gasp.

"Give it back to me, *gata*."

"What?"

"I like it hot and deep."

Reno's arms tightened, arching Eve closer to his hungry mouth.

"Remember?" he asked.

Before she could answer, he caught her lips under his own. His head moved abruptly, opening Eve's mouth.

The sensual rubbing of Reno's tongue over hers drew a small sound from the back of her throat. Her body tightened, but not in protest of the increasing force of the embrace. This time she liked being held hard against Reno's muscular body. More than that, she needed it in a way she didn't even question.

The tentative touches of her tongue against his changed as she became accustomed to the sensual fencing. She probed more deeply into his mouth, tasted him more fully, stroked his tongue completely with her own. The sensation of his tongue tangling rhythmically with hers made her head spin. Her breath wedged in her throat until she could barely breathe.

Reno made a thick sound and pulled Eve closer, taking and giving a kiss that made him realize he had never really kissed a woman before—not like this, two hungry flames burning, twisting, straining toward each other across the barriers of flesh and clothing.

When Eve finally tore her mouth from Reno's, her breathing was ragged and her mouth felt empty without him. She looked at him with dazed eyes. His smile was dark, hot, and as male as the power in his body. His fingers sank into the resilient flesh of Eve's hips as he dragged her against himself, letting her feel the fire she had started.

Then Reno was kissing Eve again, sending the night spinning darkly around her. She was aware only of his strength, of his heat, of his tongue's rhythmic stroking over hers. Holding him as tightly as she could, she let his heat sink into her.

"*Gata*. You're burning me alive."

"No. It's you. Burning me."

Reno lifted Eve, holding her suspended in his arms, while his mouth made hot entreaties to hers. He wanted to take her down to the ground and bury himself in her warm and willing body, but knew it would be foolish.

Even worse, it could be fatal.

Damn Slater, Reno raged silently. *I should have killed him in Canyon City. Then I wouldn't have to spend every minute looking over my shoulder.*

Reno's arms tightened and he took Eve's mouth as he wanted to take the rest of her sultry body. Without breaking the kiss, he carried her the two short steps to the weathered sandstone ledge and sat down.

Eve made a surprised sound when the world shifted and she found herself sitting across Reno's legs. Quickly he pulled his six-gun and set the weapon within reach on the ledge. With a stone wall at his back and a lap full of warm woman, he was as safe as he was going to be.

Not very damned safe, Reno thought sardonically.

But when Reno lowered his mouth to Eve's once more, Jericho Slater seemed very far away. Her kiss was as wild as his, making and meeting sensual demands.

Neither skilled nor coy, Eve's kiss told Reno that she wanted him enough to forget for the moment all the cold tricks women played on hungry men, tantalizing them until they would agree to anything to get at the hot lure that was burning just beyond their reach.

Reno had never had a woman want him so much that she forgot the coy game of tease and retreat and ended up burning in her own fire. Knowing that Eve wanted him that much made Reno shake with a hunger greater than he had ever known.

"Sweet God," Reno said heavily. "It's a good thing that dress doesn't have any buttons."

"W-why?"

"I'd have it down around your waist before you could blink. And that would be a mistake."

Before Eve could say anything, Reno's mouth fastened almost savagely on hers. The cloth of the dress she wore was frail with long use, and so thinned by age that it was little barrier to his caresses. She wore nothing underneath but the heat that radiated up to him, stripping away his restraint.

The feel of Reno's fingers shaping and stroking her breasts made Eve tremble. Heat bloomed within the darkness of her body. The pleasure his kiss gave her was heightened by the sensual, shifting pressure of his hands caressing her.

Then Reno's mouth replaced his hands, testing and tugging at Eve's sensitive flesh through the cloth. Her nipples hardened in a rush of sensation that dragged a low cry from her. Surprise and currents of pleasure arced through her body, making her feel as though she had been struck by tender lightning.

The husky sounds Eve made sent Reno very close to the breaking edge of his restraint. His hands tightened reflexively as he fought to control the unexpected fury of his need. As his fingers clenched, the worn-out cloth of her dress gave way at the shoulder seams. A flap of material fell forward, revealing one perfect breast.

Reno groaned. He hadn't meant to tempt himself like this. But having done it, he couldn't resist.

He lowered his head and took the hard peak deep into his mouth. She tasted of hot summer nights, of lilacs and hidden springs and secret pleasures. The husky sound he drew from her throat was a siren song urging him to forget whatever danger might wait in the surrounding darkness.

The rest of the dress gave way with a soft sound that was lost in the rippling cries Eve made while Reno's mouth and hands drew her breasts into a sensitivity that was almost painful. She knew she should protest the intimacy, yet the pleasure he gave her was so great she couldn't make herself draw back.

Eve didn't realize that Reno had eased his hand between her legs until only the fragile barrier of old cloth separated his fingers from her hidden softness. All she knew was that she had never felt the way she did now, a fire spiraling and burning, reaching toward something unknown, something both fierce and beautiful, something she must have or die from its loss.

Passion burst though Eve, drenching her in liquid heat, yet there was no relief from the urgency driving her. She twisted like a flame on Reno's lap, seeking a release from the searing need she had never before felt.

"You're killing me," Eve whispered raggedly.

Reno laughed almost painfully. "No. You're killing me. Do it again, sweet *gata*."

"What?"

His hand moved once more, tightening around the soft flesh that wept passionately at his lightest caress.

Eve gasped and felt liquid fire spread from her body to Reno's hand.

Abruptly Reno lifted and turned Eve until she sat astride his thighs. When he pushed up her skirt, she saw that his pants were undone. The blunt evidence of his arousal gleamed in the moonlight between her thighs.

Too late Eve understood what the fire had been reaching for, and who would ultimately burn with regrets.

Only one thing a man wants from a woman, make no mistake about it.

"No," Eve said. "Reno, no!"

"You want it as bad as I do. You're shaking with it."

"No!" Eve said frantically. "You promised you wouldn't take me if I didn't want it. I don't want it!"

Reno hissed words that made Eve turn pale. Without warning he shoved her off his lap so fast she barely caught her balance against the stone ledge. She yanked her dress up and faced him with an anger that was as great as her passion had been.

"You have no right to call me names!" she said in a shaking voice.

"The hell I don't! You teased me and—"

"Teased you!" she interrupted wildly. "I wasn't the one taking off your clothes and putting my hand between your legs and—"

"—you were all over me like spilled honey," Reno snarled, talking over her.

"I didn't—didn't mean to," Eve stammered. "I don't know what—what happened."

"I do," Reno said savagely. "A cheating little tease found herself dangling at the end of her own damned rope."

"I'm not what you think!"

"You keep saying that, *gata*. Then you keep proving yourself a liar. You wanted me."

"You don't understand."

"The hell I don't."

Eve closed her eyes and clutched the worn, ragged cloth against her body with fingers so tightly clenched they hurt. All of her ached and trembled, and she wanted to scream.

"Why do men want only one thing from a woman?" she asked angrily.

"Honesty?" Reno retorted. "Damned if I know. I don't think it's in a woman to be honest."

"And I don't think it's in a man not to take what he wants and then walk away without a thought to what he's done!"

"What did you have in mind—marriage?"

Reno's sardonic question was like a whip.

Eve opened her mouth, but no words came out. Pain rippled through her as she realized Reno was right. She wanted a man to love her enough to build a life with her. But she was too smart to speak about love with the gunfighter whose nakedly aroused body gleamed in the moonlight.

"I want a man to care for me," Eve said finally.

"That's what I thought," Reno said. "Your comfort and to hell with his."

"That's not what I meant!"

"Horseshit."

"I was talking about being loved," she said passionately, "not about being kept like a princess on a satin cushion!"

Hastily Eve backed up as Reno stood and began fastening his pants with angry, abrupt motions. He cursed steadily, disgusted with himself and with the saloon girl who could make him ache like no other woman ever had.

"No matter how hard you get me," Reno said in a savage voice, "you won't make me beg for the cold chains of marriage."

Reno reached down, swept up his six-gun, and spun its cylinder to check the load. His words were like the gun itself, cold, hard, unrelenting.

"Women sell themselves into marriage the same way whores sell their bodies for an hour at a time," Reno said. "Women never just give themselves out of love to a man who has promised them nothing in return but his own love."

"Is that how it was with Willow and Caleb?" Eve challenged.

Reno's mouth shifted into a cold smile. "They're the exception that proves Reno's Golden Rule."

He holstered the gun with a single smooth motion and looked at her. The bleak expression on his face made her shiver.

"What rule?" Eve asked, knowing as she spoke that she wouldn't like the answer.

She was right.

"You can't count on women," Reno said, "but you can count on gold."

BEFORE dawn was more than a vague promise along the eastern horizon, Reno and Eve were on the trail. All morning he divided his attention between the landscape and the journals. He hadn't spoken two words to Eve since he had told her about his own version of the Golden Rule.

By noon, Eve was becoming tired of her one-sided conversations with the lineback dun. The two Shaggies weren't any better. In fact, they were worse. They wouldn't so much as flick an ear in her direction when she spoke to them.

"Part mule, just like he is," Eve said clearly.

If Reno heard—and she was sure he had—he didn't even bother to look in her direction. He just kept opening first one journal, then the other, bracing the books on his thigh while he tried to find something.

"Can I help?" Eve asked finally.

Reno shook his head without looking up.

Another mile went by with no change except that

171

Reno stopped long enough to get out his spyglass and take a good look at the land ahead and behind. Then he collapsed the glass and urged Darlin' forward.

In the days past, the silence of the trail hadn't bothered Eve at all. In fact, she had found it peaceful. It gave her as much time as she wanted to look at the colorful, ever-changing rock formations and imagine how they had come to be as they were.

This morning was different. Reno's silence goaded Eve in a way she didn't understand.

"Are we lost?" Eve asked finally.

Reno didn't answer.

"Now who's sulking?" she muttered.

"Dry up, saloon girl. I'm just looking for a way around that."

Eve looked beyond Reno's finger and saw nothing but another dry watercourse winding down to another notch in the land, one more step in what she privately called God's Staircase down to the bottom of the stone maze of canyons.

"We've gone through worse," she said.

"The back of my neck itches."

"Maybe I didn't get off all the soap."

Reno turned and looked at her with glittering green eyes. "Are you offering to try again?"

"Your throat in one hand and a razor in the other?" Eve asked sweetly. "Don't tempt me, gunfighter."

Reno looked at the girl who last night had been a summer storm, wild and sultry. Just the memory of it made his blood run savagely, swelling and hardening him in a torrid rush. But in the end she had refused him the very thing she had held out as a lure.

At least he had the bitter satisfaction of knowing that he wasn't the only one who had slept restlessly last night, raked by claws of unfulfilled desire.

"Wait here," he said. "I'm going to see if there are any tracks heading into the notch. If anything happens to me, turn and run for Cal's ranch."

It wasn't the first time Reno had left Eve in order to reconnoiter, but it was the first time he had so flatly warned of danger. She watched anxiously while he quartered back and forth on either side of the most obvious routes into the notch.

Finally Reno signaled Eve forward. While she brought the packhorses up, he drew his six-gun, spun the cylinder once to check the load, and holstered the gun again. Then he reached back and pulled another six-gun and two spare cylinders from a saddlebag. With them came an odd harness, rather like a Mexican bandolier rigged to hold more than just ammunition.

The second pistol was already fully loaded. So were the two extra cylinders. The spare gun went into a holster on the bandolier. The extra, loaded cylinders went into special loops.

Eve watched the preparations with unhappy eyes as he checked the ammunition loops one by one.

"Is there something you aren't telling me?" she asked.

Reno's mouth turned up at one corner. "Hardly. I've always told you exactly what was on my mind."

"You didn't use a second pistol before," Eve said.

"Cal's journal mentions a passage up ahead so narrow you can't swing a cat."

"Can a horse get through?"

"Yes, but my repeating rifle is no good in a box like that," Reno said calmly.

"I see."

Nervously Eve took off her hat, tucked up wisps of hair, and looked everywhere but at Reno's ice green eyes. She didn't want him to know how fearful she felt.

And how alone.

"What about my shotgun?" she asked after a moment.

"Use it, but make damn sure you hit what you aim at. A ricochet cuts you up worse than a regular bullet."

Eve nodded.

"Are your reins still tied together?" Reno asked.

She nodded again.

"Take Shaggy One off the lead and put the packhorses between us," he said.

Eve's head turned swiftly toward him. "Why?"

Reno saw the shadows in her golden eyes and felt like pulling her into his arms to reassure her.

But reassurance would be a lie. The way ahead was dangerous, and Reno's instincts were riding him like iron spurs. Reassuring Eve wouldn't be a kindness. She would need all her wariness. So would he.

"There are a lot of tracks," Reno said. "The ground is too sandy to be sure if it's mustangs or shod horses. If Slater's up ahead, he'll be shooting at me. If you're too close, you could catch a bullet. So put the packhorses between us."

"I'll take my chances on a bullet."

Reno's left eyebrow rose in a black arc. "Suit yourself. Either way, take off the lead rope."

"If I were going to suit myself," Eve said distinctly as she began working over the lead rope, "I'd stay away from the notch."

"It's the only route to the Spanish mine marked in your journal, unless you want to go all the way back through the Rockies and take the route up from Santa Fe."

"Perdition," Eve muttered. "It would be spring before we got back here."

"This route also leads to the only sure water."

Eve sighed. She had never realized how much water it took to keep horses going, and how precious water could be.

"Maybe Slater gave up," she said.

She leaned over in the saddle and tied the lead rope around Shaggy One's neck.

"He might have given up on punishing a cheating saloon girl, but I don't think he'll give up on gold. Or," Reno added sarcastically, "on the man who helped to shoot his twin brother's gang to pieces."

"You?"

Reno nodded. "Me, Cal, and Wolfe."

"Caleb Black? My God—what if Slater goes after Caleb instead of us?"

"Old Jericho is smarter than that. Cal has some hard men riding for him, especially those three freed slaves. Two of them were Buffalo Soldiers. The third one is called Pig Iron. He's half Seminole and pure poison mean."

Eve frowned.

"Except with Willow," Reno added, seeing the uneasy expression on Eve's face. "She tended them after they ate bad meat. They think the sun rises and sets in her. So do their women—including the Comanchero squaw who can't make up her mind between Crooked Bear and Pig Iron."

"Are they armed?"

"Hell, yes. What use is an unarmed man?"

"All the same," Eve said, "Slater has a lot of men."

"That's not the same as having *good* men. Don't you worry about Cal. He's a one-man army all by himself. Wish to God I had him at my back right now."

With that, Reno reined the blue roan toward the notch. The lineback dun followed immediately. The two Shaggies fell into place despite the absence of lead ropes.

Reno didn't have to tell Eve to be silent. She rode the way he rode, alert to every shadow, wary of every bend in the river bottom that could conceal riders waiting in ambush. The shotgun across her lap gleamed in the rare patches of sunlight.

The heat of day slowly gave way to a hushed kind of twilight as rock walls rose on either side of the track. Layers of stone piled one upon another until the sky retreated to scarcely more than a wide, cloud-ridden banner high overhead. There was no sound but that of creaking leather, the dry swish of a horse's tail, and hoofbeats softened by sand.

Small finger canyons joined the larger one from time to time. All of them were dry.

Finally the strip of cloudy sky overhead began to widen, telling Eve they were almost out of the dry riverbed that separated the towering walls of stone. Just ahead, the wash bent to the right around one more nose of rock. Behind her and to the left, another side canyon opened.

Suddenly the blue roan tried to leap out of her tracks. Reno yelled at Eve to take cover.

Then men were shouting and shots were hammering as lead whined and screamed between stone walls. Some of the shots were Reno's. In a wild drumroll of sound, he fired at the men who had leaped from hiding behind the wall of stone that lay just ahead of his horse.

Reno's speed in drawing and shooting both guns

took the ambushers by surprise. His deadly accuracy shocked the men who survived the brutal thunder of the first twelve shots. The outlaws who were still able to move dove for cover in a tangle of flailing limbs and vicious curses.

With movements so fast they blurred, Reno swapped empty cylinders for loaded ones and began shooting again before the men could recover.

"Behind us!" Eve screamed.

The last part of her cry was lost in the deafening thunder of the shotgun as she triggered both barrels. The two outlaws who had been concealed in the underbrush of the side canyon shouted in pain as buckshot whipped and whined around them.

Reno spun the blue roan and fired so quickly the sound of his bullets was buried beneath the shotgun's noise. The men dropped where they were and didn't move again.

"Eve! Are you hurt?"

"No. Are—"

The rest of Eve's question was cut off by the ragged thunder of horses' hooves echoing down between stone walls. The sound came from behind and from ahead, rising like a tide.

"We're trapped!" Eve shouted.

"Go left!"

As Reno spoke, he spurred the blue roan toward the narrow side canyon, sweeping Eve and the packhorses before him. They hurtled the bodies of the two outlaws and raced into the small opening. Within twenty feet, the tributary canyon took a steep bend around a fin of red rock.

Eve clung to the lineback dun with knees and heels, trying to reload the shotgun while the mustang took the obstacle course of the dry stream bed at a dead run. She managed to get one shell into the shotgun.

She was trying for a second shell when it spurted from her fingers as the dun skidded on a patch of bedrock rising up through the thin layer of sand. The mustang went down to her knees, then righted herself with a force that sent sparks flying as steel shoes clashed against rock that was harder than sandstone.

After that, Eve forgot about loading the shotgun and concentrated on keeping herself and her mustang right side up.

A mile later the stream bed began to rise more steeply beneath the horses' pounding hooves. No more cottonwoods whipped by at the edge of Eve's vision. There were few bushes to hurtle or avoid, and even those were stunted.

The layered rock walls pinched inward. Sand thinned into patches and pools with stretches of water-polished rock in between. The trail became dangerously slick and uneven. Even the tough, agile mustangs nearly came to grief more than once.

"Pull up!" Reno called finally.

Gratefully Eve reined in the hard-running mare. She turned to ask a question, but all she saw was Reno spurring the blue roan back the way they had come.

The two Shaggies crowded around Eve's mustang as though needing reassurance. She fumbled a second shell into the shotgun before she bent over in the saddle to check the rigging on the packhorses. Nothing had shifted. Nothing had come undone. Even the awkward little barrels on the outside of the tarpaulins were still in place. So were the picks and shovels. Reno was as thorough in caring for the animals as he was in caring for his weapons.

Gunfire echoed up the canyon in a staccato cataract that seemed to go on forever. The Shaggies snorted and crowded closer, but showed no inclination to bolt. Eve's heart was hammering so hard she was afraid it would burst from her chest.

More gunshots echoed. The silence that followed the echoes was worse than any thunder.

After Eve counted to ten, she could bear no more. She kicked the dun hard and went racing back to see what had happened to Reno. The mustang laid back her ears, flattened out, and began to gallop despite the uncertain footing. Head low and tail high, the dun tore over the dangerous ground.

The sound of hoofbeats alerted Reno. He reined his horse around just in time to see Eve flying toward him on the back of a hard-running mustang. The dun leaped a spur of rock, sprayed sand through a soft spot, and nearly went down on a stretch of slickrock.

Reno thought that would slow Eve, but as soon as the dun had all four hooves under her again, Eve set the mustang at a dead run once more.

"Eve!"

She didn't hear him.

Reno spurred his roan out into the open. Eve's horse reared as she was hauled back on her hocks in a skidding, sliding stop.

"Of all the damn fool—" yelled Reno.

"Are you all right?" Eve said urgently.

"—things to do. Of course I'm—"

"I heard gunfire and then silence, and I called your name and you didn't answer."

Anxious golden eyes searched Reno for injury.

"I'm fine," he said in a clipped voice. "Except that you damn near gave me heart failure running your horse over that ground."

"I thought you were hurt."

"What were you going to do—trample Slater's

bunch right into the sand?"

"I—"

Reno kept on talking. "If you ever pull a damn fool stunt like that again, I'll turn you over my knee."

"But—"

"But nothing," he interrupted savagely. "You could have galloped right into a cross fire and been cut to ribbons."

"I thought that was what had happened to you."

Reno let out a breath and damped down the temper that threatened to flash out of control. He had been in a lot of tight places and been shot more than once, but he had never been as plain scared as when he had seen Eve run her mustang flat out over the sand and slickrock.

"It was my ambush this time," Reno said finally. "Not theirs."

A ragged sigh was Eve's only answer.

"It will be a while before they come asking for more," he continued. "We better hope it isn't too long, though."

"Why?"

"Water," he said succinctly. "This canyon is stone dry."

EVE looked up anxiously as Reno rode back in from his short exploration of the tributary canyon. The grim line of his mouth told her that he hadn't discovered anything useful.

"Dry," he said.

She waited.

"And blind," he added.

"What?"

"It's a dead end."

"How far ahead?"

"Maybe two miles," Reno said.

Eve looked down the narrow wash where Slater's men waited for their quarry.

"They need water, too," she pointed out.

"One man can lead a lot of horses to water. The rest will stay put, waiting for us to get thirsty enough to do something stupid."

"Then we'll just have to get past them."

Reno's smile wasn't comforting.

"All in all," he said, "I'd rather take my chances on climbing the head wall of the canyon than get caught in that kind of a cross fire."

Eve looked beyond Reno to the stone wall that piled layer on layer to the sky.

"What about the horses?" she asked.

"We'll have to turn them loose."

What Reno didn't say was that a man on foot in a dry land didn't have much chance of surviving. But as small as that chance was, it was better than the odds of successfully running a gauntlet of Slater's guns through the narrow canyon.

"Let's go," Reno said. "We only get thirstier from now on."

Eve didn't argue. Already her mouth was dry. She could imagine the thirst of the mustangs, who had run an obstacle course through the hot canyon.

"You first," Reno said. "Then the packhorses."

The dry stream bed narrowed until it was little more than a sculpted, water-smoothed opening snaking through solid stone. Overhead, the clouds flowed together and thickened into a turbulent lid over the dry land. Thunder rolled distantly, following invisible lightning.

Reno saw Eve glance longingly at the clouds.

"You better pray it doesn't rain," he said.

"Why?"

He gestured to the canyon wall that was only inches beyond his outstretched hand.

"See that line?" he asked.

"Yes. I've been wondering what it was."

"High-water mark."

Eve's eyes widened. She looked at the line that ran the length of the canyon well above their heads. Then she looked back at Reno.

"Where does it all come from?" she asked.

"Up on the plateau. During big storms, rain comes down faster than it can sink in. And in some places, it can't sink in at all. So it just runs off all at once. In these slot canyons, it gets real deep real fast."

"What a country," Eve said. "Eat sand or drown."

The corner of Reno's mouth lifted slightly. "I've come close to both, one time or another."

Yet he had never had his tail in quite as tight a crack as he did right now—a dead end ahead, outlaws behind, and thirst in between.

Silently Reno examined the walls of the side canyon where he and Eve were trapped. Something about the rock layers nagged at his mind.

"Pull up," he said to Eve.

She reined in and looked over her shoulder. Reno was sitting with both hands on the saddle horn, studying the narrow little canyon as though he had never seen anything quite so interesting in his life.

After a minute Reno urged the blue roan forward, squeezed past the two Shaggies and Eve's dun to the tiny slot canyon he had discovered on his first reconnoiter up the canyon. He had dismissed the slot as a runoff channel. But now he thought he might have been too hasty.

"Is your shotgun loaded?" Reno asked.

"Yes."

"Ever used a six-gun?" he asked.

"Sometimes. I can't hit the side of the barn with one at much over thirty feet."

Reno turned and looked at Eve. The smile he gave her made her realize all over again what a good-looking man he was.

"Don't worry, *gata*. No barns will be sneaking up on us."

Eve laughed.

Reno pulled out his second six-gun and removed one bullet from the revolving cylinder before he put the weapon back in the bandolier.

"Here," he said, handing the bandolier to Eve. "The firing pin is on an empty chamber, so you'll have to pull the trigger twice to fire."

The bandolier fit Eve the way a greatcoat fits a child. When Reno reached forward to adjust the buckle, the back of his fingers accidentally brushed over one of her breasts. Her breath came in hard and fast. The sudden motion had the effect of brushing her breast against his hand once more. The twin touches hardened her nipple in a rush.

Reno looked up from her breast to the vivid golden eyes of the saloon girl who haunted even his dreams.

"You're so damned alive," Reno said almost roughly. "And you came so damned close to dying. . . ."

He adjusted the bandolier as much as possible on her. Telling himself he wouldn't, reaching for her even as he told himself not to, Reno slid his hand around the nape of Eve's neck. He pulled her toward him as he leaned down.

"I'm going to check out that slot canyon," he said against her lips. "Keep an eye on the back trail while I'm gone."

"Be careful."

"Don't worry. I plan to live long enough to enjoy

every last bit of what I won in the Gold Dust Saloon—and that includes you."

The kiss Reno gave Eve was like lightning, hot and untamed, striking to her core, lasting only an instant.

Then Reno was gone, leaving her with his taste on her lips, his hunger racing in her blood, and his words shivering through her, warning and promise in one.

I plan to live long enough to enjoy every last bit of what I won in the Gold Dust Saloon—and that includes you.

12

A FEW hours later, Eve, Reno, and the horses were still scrambling up layer after layer of stone, following a precarious way out of the blind canyon. Many times the passage threatened to vanish against one cliff or another, stranding them, but it never did.

Not quite.

"Don't look down."

Reno's order was unnecessary. Eve wouldn't have looked down if someone had held a gun at her head. In fact, she might have considered being shot a blessing, if it meant that she would never again have to lead a mustang along an eyebrow trail high above the canyon floor.

"Are you sure you're all right?" Reno asked.

Eve didn't answer. She didn't have any energy to spare for words. She was too busy staring at her feet, willing herself not to stumble.

The coarse grain of the sandstone was engraved on Eve's mind. She was certain the texture of it

185

would inhabit her nightmares for years to come. Pebbles the size and shape of marbles were scattered all over the surface of the ledge, ready to send a careless foot sliding and skidding.

The mustangs had little difficulty with the trail. They had four feet. If one slipped, there were three to take its place. Eve had nothing but her hands, which were already sore from catching herself the last time she had tripped.

"See the white rock ahead?" Reno asked encouragingly. "That means we're getting closer to the lip of the plateau."

"Hallelujah," Eve whispered.

The lineback dun snorted and jerked her head down to rub off a pesky fly.

Eve barely stifled a scream as the reins yanked at her hand, threatening her precarious balance.

"It's all right," Reno said in a low, calm voice.

The hell it is.

But Eve didn't have the breath to waste on contradicting Reno aloud.

"That was just a fly bothering your horse," he said. "Put the reins over her neck. She'll follow you without being led."

A jerky nod was the only answer Reno got.

When Eve lifted the tied reins over the mustang's neck, her arms were trembling so much that she nearly dropped the reins.

Reno's hands balled into fists. Ruthlessly he forced himself to relax one finger at a time. If he could have walked the trail for Eve, he would have. But he could not.

Bleakly Reno resumed the climb. Eons of rain and wind had rounded the rock and worn nearly perpendicular channels through it. The higher he climbed, the deeper and steeper became the many channels cutting across the pale, smooth surface of the stone. Sometimes he had to double-back and find a way around a particularly wide channel.

Reno scrambled up and onto another slickrock terrace. The blue roan was hard on his heels, as surefooted as a cat. The other mustangs were equally agile. He walked forward quickly, anxious to meet and overcome the next obstacle.

He didn't notice that Eve had sent her mustang on ahead at the first wide spot in the trail. He was intent on the next scramble and then the next. Until he climbed the last pale slickrock terrace and saw a mesa top opening before him, he wouldn't know whether they had struggled upward all this way only to reach a dead end at the foot of a cliff. He was impatient to find out, for he didn't want to retrace his steps in failing light.

Eve kept her eyes on the small marks the horses' hooves had left on the stone. Each time she came to one of the hundreds of runoff channels that criss-crossed the massive layer of white rock, she took her courage in both hands and stepped across, ignoring the black abyss beneath her feet.

She no longer looked to the right or to the left or even straight ahead. She definitely didn't look behind. Each time she looked over the back trail, her skin tightened at the sight of layer after layer of rock dropping steeply into a blue haze. She couldn't believe she had climbed that far. She couldn't believe she had to keep on climbing.

Breathing hard, Eve stopped to rest, hoping some strength would flow back into her weary legs. She would have given a great deal for a drink of water, but she had left the heavy, awkward canteen tied to the dun's saddle.

Sighing, she rubbed her hands over her aching thighs and scrambled up onto the next terrace to see what awaited her. Just a few feet away, the rock sloped to another runoff channel. This one was shaped rather like a funnel with the far side cut away. There was a steep descent to a small ledge. From there the channel sliced endlessly down through the white rock, dividing it into separate masses.

Reno and the horses were on the other side.

"It's no more than a yard wide," Eve told herself through stiff lips. "I can step across it."

It's more than a yard. I'll have to jump.

"I jumped farther than that across the creek just for fun."

It didn't matter if I fell in the creek. If I fall now . . .

The weakness in Eve's knees frightened her. She was thirsty, exhausted, and nervous from spending hours expecting to slip and fall with every step. And now this black canyon to cross.

She couldn't do it. She simply could not.

Stop it, Eve told herself harshly. *I've done harder things the last few hours. The crack is only a few feet wide. All I have to do is give a little jump and I'll be on the other side.*

Repeating it made her feel better, especially as her eyes were closed. It would have helped if she could have seen Reno or the horses on the other side, but she couldn't. From where she was, she could see nothing but the steep slope at her back and the chasm ahead.

Eve ran her dry tongue over her equally dry lips. She was tempted to walk back a hundred yards and drink out of one of the many, odd hollows in the solid stone where water lingered from a recent rain. The hollows held anywhere from a cup to several gallons of water.

In the end, Eve decided not to go back, because she didn't want to walk one more yard than was absolutely necessary. Besides, the hollows were alive with tiny swimming creatures.

Eve took a deep breath and approached the black opening that lay between her and the horses. From the marks she could see on the rock, the mustangs had sat on their hocks, skidded down to the ledge, and then stepped or jumped to the other side of the channel. There was no slope to scramble up on the far side. She could fall flat when she landed and it wouldn't matter.

Easy as jumping down a stair. Nothing to it.

Taking another breath, Eve walked forward.

A pebble turned under the ball of her foot, throwing her off balance. She turned as she fell, her arms wide, her fingers reaching for anything that would stop her fall. There was nothing to grab but air.

The force of the fall knocked the breath out of Eve and sent her rolling rapidly toward the black gap. There was no bottom, no top, nothing to cling to. She was flailing down a slide made of stone, hurtling toward an endless night.

"Reno!" Eve screamed.

First her feet, then her knees, bumped over the ledge, then her thighs. Somehow her hands found enough purchase on the rock to halt her tumbling. She lay with her cheek against the rock, her arms shaking, and her legs dangling over eternity. When she tried to pull herself up out of the abyss, she nearly lost what grip she had upon the stone.

An instant later Eve felt herself being torn free of the rock. She fought wildly before she realized that it was Reno lifting and turning her, pulling her back from the abyss. He braced his feet apart and held her against his body.

"Easy, *gata*. I've got you."

Trembling in every limb, Eve sagged against Reno.

"Are you hurt?" he asked urgently.

Eve shook her head.

He looked at the pallor of her face, the trembling of her lips, and the shiny trails tears had left on her skin.

"Can you stand?" he asked.

She took a shuddering breath and put more of her weight on her own feet. He released her just enough to find out if she could stand. She could, but she was shaking.

"We can't go back," Reno said. "We have to go on."

Though he tried to speak in gentle tones, the race of adrenaline in his system made his voice harsh.

Nodding to show she understood, Eve tried to take a step. Immediately she was betrayed by the shaking of her legs.

Reno caught her and brushed his mouth lightly over hers. The kiss was unlike any he had given her, for it asked nothing of her in return. He eased her down onto the stone and sat beside her, cradling her while she shook with a mixture of fatigue and exhaustion, fear and relief.

Reno took off the canteen he wore slung down his back. The rasp of a canteen stopper was followed by the silvery music of water trickling out as he dampened his bandanna. When the cool cloth touched Eve's face, she flinched.

"Easy, little one," Reno murmured. "It's just water, like your tears."

"I'm n-not crying. I'm . . . resting."

He poured a bit more water on his dark bandanna and wiped Eve's pale, tear-stained face. She let out a ragged breath and sat quietly while he removed the evidence of her tears.

"Drink," he said.

Eve felt the metal rim of the canteen nudge her lips. She sipped lightly, then with more interest as the water slid over the parched tissues of her mouth.

A low sound of pleasure came from her as she swallowed. She hadn't known anything could taste so clean, so perfect. Holding the canteen with both hands, she drank greedily, ignoring the tiny trickle that escaped at one corner of her mouth.

Reno blotted the extra water with his bandanna at first, then with his tongue. The warm caress so startled Eve that she dropped the canteen. He laughed and caught the canteen, stoppered it, and slung it across his back once more.

"Ready to go?" he asked softly.

"Do I have any choice?"

"Yes. You can take that gap with your eyes open and me right beside you, or you can take it unconscious over my shoulder."

Eve's eyes widened.

"I wouldn't hurt you," he added.

Gently his hands circled her throat. His thumbs found the points where blood flowed into her brain.

"A bit of pressure and you'll faint," Reno said calmly. "You'll wake up within seconds, but you'll be on the other side by then."

"You can't carry me over that," she protested.

"You're like a cat. Sleek and lithe. But for all their speed and grace, cats don't weigh much."

Reno stood, pulling Eve to her feet and then off them in a smooth, easy motion. He shifted his grip, holding her balanced against his hip with one arm. It all happened so quickly, she didn't have time to draw a breath.

Eve's eyes widened in shock as she realized how much of Reno's strength he had kept in check when he touched her. She had always known he was stronger than she was. She just hadn't known how much stronger. An odd, strangled sound escaped her lips.

Reno frowned.

"I didn't mean to frighten you," he said.

"It's not that," she said faintly.

He waited, watching her.

"It's just..." Eve made a sound that was half laugh, half sob. "I'm used to being the strong one."

There was a long silence while Reno held Eve and thought about what she had said. Slowly he nodded. It explained a lot, including why she hadn't told him how close to the end of her rope she was. It simply hadn't occurred to her. She was used to being with people who had less strength and stamina than she did, not more.

"And I'm used to traveling alone," Reno said. "I've pushed you too hard. I'm sorry."

Carefully he set Eve on her feet again.

"Can you walk?" he asked.

Eve sighed and nodded.

One of Reno's arms slid around her waist.

"Tired little *gata*. Put you arm around me and lean. It's not far."

"I can—"

Abruptly Reno's hand came down over Eve's mouth, shutting off her words.

"Quiet," he whispered against her ear. "Someone is coming."

Eve froze and strained to hear beyond the wild beating of her heart.

Reno was right. The lazy breeze was carrying the sound of someone cursing savagely.

"Damnation," hissed Reno. "Get down!"

Eve had no choice about it. He had her pressed

on her stomach against the rock before she could blink.

"Keep your head down," he said in a very soft voice. "They won't be able to see you until they're at the top of the slope above us."

Reno took off his hat, handed Eve the canteen, and drew his gun. She watched as he began crawling on his stomach up the ten-foot slickrock incline.

On the other side were three Comancheros leading wiry mustangs. They were headed straight for Reno. Crooked Bear was in the lead. He spotted Reno immediately. When the Comanchero shouted, bullets started whining and ricocheting off the pale stone, sending sharp chips of rock flying.

Instantly Reno returned the fire, picking targets with care, for the range was better suited to a rifle than to a six-gun. There wasn't much cover, but the Comancheros made good use of every irregularity. They flattened themselves in the shallow basins, dove behind hardy piñon, or threw their bodies into one of the many cracks on the seamed surface of the slickrock.

Unfortunately, all except Crooked Bear were beyond the range of Reno's six-gun. The Comanchero took a bullet in his arm, but the wound wasn't bad. The most it would do was slow the big Indian down a bit.

Reno slithered back down the slope to Eve and pulled her to her feet.

"They'll stay put, but not for long," he said. "Get ready to run."

Eve wanted to object that she couldn't run, but a look at Reno's jade green eyes made her change her mind. His fingers wrapped around her right arm just below the shoulder.

"Three steps, then jump," he said.

There was no time for Eve to waver or worry. Reno was thrusting her forward. She took three running steps and jumped like a doe. He was right beside her, flying over the black channel, landing, holding her upright when her foot slipped. Seconds later they were running flat out over the slickrock.

Eve had never moved so fast before in her life. Reno's powerful hand was clamped around her arm, lifting her, hurtling her forward, then lifting her again the instant her feet touched the ground.

They were almost to the horses when rifle bullets began crashing and whining around them, screaming off the slickrock. Reno made no attempt to take cover. He simply tightened his grip on Eve and ran faster toward the ravine ahead. He knew their best chance of survival lay in reaching the ravine where the horses were hidden before Slater's Comancheros reloaded their single-shot rifles.

Breath tore in and out of Eve's lungs as she sprinted beside Reno, captive to the iron grip on her arm. Just when she thought she could run no farther, a bullet ricocheted nearby. She ran faster than before, trusting Reno to catch her if she stumbled.

Suddenly the rock sloped away beneath their feet. Together Eve and Reno skidded down the steep incline. The mustangs snorted and shied with alarm as he threw her into her saddle, vaulted onto his own horse, and headed up the ravine at a gallop.

All too soon the way began to narrow and climb steeply toward yet another slickrock terrace. Reno kept the horses pointed uphill, not stopping even when the way became so narrow that stirrups scraped against stone. Scrambling and clawing like cats, the agile mustangs climbed through stony debris.

Abruptly they were in the clear. A wide mesa opened up before them. Reno didn't stop to congratulate himself on their good luck at not finding themselves smack up against a slickrock cliff. He spun the blue roan around and raced back to the Shaggy that carried the small barrels. He jerked one barrel free, grabbed a leather sack from the pack saddle, and turned to Eve.

"I'm going to try to close the trail," he said curtly. "Take the horses about a hundred yards up the draw and hobble them."

She grabbed Darlin's reins, kicked the dun, and took off up the shallow, grassy ravine that drained the plateau. The two Shaggies followed. A scant one hundred yards later, Eve threw herself off the dun, hobbled her, and ran back to Darlin'. The mustang snorted in alarm but was too tired to bite when strange hands slapped hobbles around her forelegs. The two Shaggies were already cropping grass eagerly. They were hobbled before they knew what had happened.

Eve yanked the repeating rifle out of Reno's saddle scabbard, grabbed her own shotgun, and ran back to where Reno worked at the lip of the plateau.

"Can you see them yet?" she asked breathlessly.

He spun toward her in surprise. "What are you doing here? I told you to—"

"They're hobbled," Eve interrupted.

"They better be, or we'll be afoot."

Reno bent over the ground once more. Working quickly, he poured black powder into a second tin can.

"What are you doing?" she asked.

"Getting set to bring a chunk of slickrock down

around those boys' ears."

The sound of voices came up the ravine.

"Hell's fire, but they're fast," muttered Reno. "Can you shoot a rifle?"

"Better than a six-gun."

"Good. Keep those Comancheros pinned down while I finish. Leave the shotgun with me."

As Eve started for the lip of the mesa with Reno's rifle, he grabbed her.

"Keep down," Reno ordered in a low, hard voice. "Go on your stomach for the last few yards. There are three of them, and they don't have a repeating rifle, but it takes only one bullet to put you six feet under."

Eve crawled to the lip of the mesa and stared down the narrow ravine. No men were in sight yet, but their voices carried clearly, as did the sound of hooves on stone.

"The next time goddamn Jericho wants me to go chasing goddamn Reno Moran, I'm gonna make goddamn damn sure I—*goddamn!*"

The sound of Eve's shot echoed and reechoed through the narrow ravine. She levered in another shot and fired again. The bullet whined and caromed from stone to stone. She fired one more shot for good measure.

No one fired in return. They were all too busy diving for cover.

Eve looked over her shoulder. Reno was hammering the edges of the second can shut with the butt of his six-gun. A two-foot fuse dangled from each can.

"Keep them pinned down," he said.

With a silent prayer, Eve sent bullets flying down the ravine while Reno crawled over to a ledge of smooth rock that jutted out to one side of the ravine. Carefully he shoved both cans into a deep crack.

"Keep firing," Reno said.

While rifle shots echoed, he struck a match and lit both fuses.

Eve kept firing until she was snatched to her feet and set to running flat out away from the ravine. Scant seconds later, a sound like double thunder came from behind them. Reno took Eve down to the ground and covered her with his body while rock exploded and fell in a hard, sharp-edged rain.

Behind them a piece of the plateau sheared away. Skidding, bouncing, grinding, groaning, the stone avalanche went down the narrow ravine until it hit a barrier and piled up in a boiling cloud of dust and grit.

"You all right?" Reno asked.

"Yes."

Reno rolled aside and came to his feet in an easy motion, bringing Eve with him. He approached the edge of the plateau cautiously and looked over.

The ravine was choked with stones of all sizes.

"Be damned," he said. "That crack must have gone farther down than I thought."

Numbly Eve stared, astonished at the change two cans of black powder had made.

Above the sound of random debris settling along the slope came the rhythmic beat of hooves. The sounds retreated farther and farther down the ravine as the mustangs fled the unexpected thunder.

"Even if those boys survived, they've got a long walk ahead of them," Reno said with distinct satisfaction.

"Then we're—safe?"

Reno gave Eve a rather dark smile.

"For a time, yes," he said. "But if there's another

way onto this plateau, Slater's Comancheros will know about it."

"Maybe there isn't," Eve said quickly.

"You better hope there is."

"Why?"

"Because their way up is our way *down*," Reno said succinctly.

Eve rubbed her dusty forehead against her equally dusty sleeve and tried not to show her dismay at the thought of being trapped on top of the plateau.

Reno saw anyway. He squeezed her arm reassuringly just before he turned away.

"Come on," he said. "Let's go see how well you hobbled the horses."

13

EVE watched the blue roan scramble back up the head of the steep ravine. It was the fifth chute down the plateau Reno had tried in the past two hours. So far, each ravine had ended in a cliff that horses couldn't descend.

This time, however, Reno had been gone at least half an hour. Though Eve didn't say anything, she couldn't keep a look of hope from her face. Without realizing it, she ran her tongue over her lips. No shine of moisture followed.

"Take a drink," Reno said as he rode up. "You're as dry as stone."

"I can't drink when my horse is so thirsty, she tries to crawl in my pocket each time I pick up the canteen."

"Don't let the sweet-faced fraud fool you. She sucked one of those little *tinajas* dry while you were a quarter mile back, trying to fall into that big slot."

"*Tinajas*?" Eve frowned, then remembered what the Spanish word meant. "Oh. Those holes in the

199

rock where rainwater collected. Is the water good?"

"The mustangs liked it."

"You didn't drink any?"

"The horses needed it more than I did. Besides," Reno admitted with a slight grin, "I wasn't thirsty enough to strain all those little critters between my teeth."

Eve's laughter surprised Reno. She was dusty, worn-out, scuffed from crawling over rock . . . and he had never seen a woman who appealed to him more. He tucked a tawny lock behind her ear, ran his fingertip over the line of her jaw, and touched her lips with the ball of his thumb.

"Mount up," he said softly. "There's something I want to show you."

Curious, Eve stepped into the stirrup and rode alongside Reno as far as the trail allowed. To her surprise, the shallow ravine didn't get deeper right away as the others had. Instead, it got wider and wider, descending gently through piñons and cedar.

Gradually the slickrock became buried under dirt. More and more small gullies joined the ravine, widening it, until they were riding through a valley that was nearly surrounded by steep walls of stone.

Eve turned and looked at Reno with hope on her face and a question in her eyes.

"I don't know," Reno said quietly. "But it looks good. I rode another mile and nothing changed."

Eve closed her eyes and let out a breath she hadn't even known she was holding.

"No water, though," Reno added reluctantly.

For several miles there were no sounds but that of an eagle keening on the wind, the creak of leather as the horses walked, and the muffled beat of hooves on the dry earth. Though it was late in the afternoon, the sunlight still held an amazing amount of heat.

Clouds gathered into groups high overhead. Their color ranged from white to a blue-black that promised rain. But not on the plateau. It wasn't high enough to trap these clouds. Only the mountains were. Nowhere had Eve seen running water on the plateau.

"Reno?"

He made a rumbling sound that said he had heard.

"Does it rain here?"

He nodded.

"Where does it all go?" she asked.

"Downhill."

"Yes, but where is it? We're downhill from something, and there's no water."

"The streams only run after a rain," he said.

"What about the mountain streams?" she persisted. "It rains there all the time, and snow melts. Where does the water go?"

"Into the air and into the ground."

"Not down to the sea?"

"From here to the Sierra Nevadas of California, I know of only one river that gets all the way to the sea before it dries up—Rio Colorado."

Eve rode silently for a few minutes, trying to understand how there could be land and no water.

"How far is it to California?" she asked.

"Maybe six hundred miles as the crow flies. Hell of a lot farther the way we do it."

"And only one river?"

Reno nodded.

Eve rode in silence for a long time, trying to comprehend a land so dry, you could ride for weeks and find only one river. No streams, no creeks, no brooks, no lakes, no ponds, nothing but red rock, creamy stone, and shades of rust where any vegetation stood out like a green flag on the dry land.

The thought was both frightening an oddly exhilarating, like waking into a landscape seen before only in dreams.

As the valley slowly dropped down to an unknown end, the buff-colored cliffs that rose on either side became more and more of a barrier. From time to time Eve turned and looked over her shoulder. If she hadn't known that a way onto the plateau existed behind them, she wouldn't have guessed it from the view. The rock wall looked seamless.

Gradually the valley changed, becoming more narrow as the stone ramparts closed in once more. Twice they had to dismount and lead the mustangs over a particularly difficult patch of land, squeezing between massive boulders and sliding down gullies floored with water-polished stone.

The sun descended as they did, but with more ease. Long shafts of light gilded the stones and painted dense velvet shadows behind the least irregularity of the land.

"Look," Eve said suddenly, her voice low. "What's that?"

"Where?" Reno asked.

"At the base of the cliff, just to the left of the notch."

Silence, then Reno whistled softly and said, "Ruins."

Air rushed out of Eve's lungs. "Can we get over there?"

"We're sure going to try. Where there are ruins, there's usually water somewhere nearby."

He glanced sideways at her and added, "But don't count on it. Some of the Indians depended on cisterns that have long since cracked and let out all the water."

Despite Reno's warning, it was hard for Eve not to show her disappointment when they finally worked their way through the piñon and juniper to the rubble-strewn base of the cliff and found no sign of permanent water.

As the sun descended beyond the rim of the canyon, she sat on her tired mustang and looked at the broken walls, oddly shaped windows, and walled-up rooms of the ruins. The silence in the canyon was complete, as though even the animals avoided the broken reminders of people who had come and gone like rain over the face of the land.

"Maybe that's what happened to them," Eve said. "No water."

"Maybe," Reno said. "And maybe they lost too many battles to hold on to what they had."

Half an hour after the sun slid behind stone ramparts, the sky overhead was still bright with afternoon light. Gradually the breeze shifted, coming from a different quarter. One after another, the mustangs threw up their heads, pricked their ears, and sniffed the wind.

Reno's six-gun appeared in his hand with startling speed, but he didn't fire.

Gooseflesh prickled over Eve as she saw an Indian walking toward them from the direction of the ruins.

"I thought Indians avoided places like this," she said softly.

"They do. But sometimes a very brave shaman will go to the old places on a medicine quest. From the looks of his silver hair, I'd guess he's come to ask his last questions of his gods."

Reno's six-gun went back into its holster as soon as the Indian was close enough for Reno to see that he was painted for making medicine rather than war. The once colorful paint was cracked and dusty, as though the shaman had been a long, long time in his quest. Reno reached back into a saddlebag for the small sack of trade goods he always kept, pulled out a pouch of tobacco, and dismounted.

"Stay put," he said. "Don't speak to him unless he speaks to you first."

Eve watched curiously as Reno and the shaman silently exchanged greetings. The sign language they used was oddly graceful, as fluid as water. After a time, the pouch of tobacco was offered and accepted. Privately Eve thought that food would have been a better gift; the shaman looked drawn and worn, as lean as a mustang that had never known the touch of a man.

And like a mustang, the shaman was alert, aloof, fierce in his freedom. When he turned and looked directly at Eve, she felt the force of his presence as clearly as she had felt Reno's when they held the Spanish needles.

It seemed like a long time before the shaman looked away, freeing her from his clear, uncanny eyes.

When the old man faced Reno once more, the Indian's arms and hands described graceful arcs, quick lines, flashing motions that Eve could barely follow. Reno watched intently. His very stillness told Eve that something unexpected was happening.

Without warning the Indian turned and walked away. He didn't look back.

Reno turned and looked at Eve strangely.

"Is something wrong?" she asked.

He shook his head slowly. "No."

"What did he say?"

"Near as I can tell, he came here to see the past and instead saw the future. Us. He didn't like it, but the gods had answered his quest, and that was that."

Eve frowned. "How odd."

"Shamans usually are," Reno said dryly. "The really curious thing was his medicine paint. I've never seen an Indian use the old signs from the rock walls."

Reno looked over his shoulder. The shaman was gone. Frowning, he looked back to Eve.

"He told me there was water ahead."

"Good."

"Then he told me the gold I was seeking was already in my hand," Reno continued.

"What?"

"Then he told me I couldn't see the gold, so he would tell me how to get to the Spanish mine."

"He knew?" she asked.

"Seemed to. The landmarks match."

"And he just told you?"

Reno nodded.

"Why?" Eve asked.

"I asked the same thing. He said it was his revenge for seeing a future he didn't want to see. Then he walked off."

Reno reclaimed the blue roan's reins and mounted in a muscular surge.

"Revenge. Dear God."

"Let's see if he was right about the water," Reno said. "Otherwise we may not live to worry about the revenge."

He turned Darlin' toward the long shadows flowing out from the base of the cliffs.

"Deer sign," Reno said after ten minutes.

Eve looked, but could make out nothing in the dusk.

"No sign of wild horses," he continued. "Strange. Damn few water holes that a mustang can't find."

As the sky and clouds overhead became touched with scarlet sunset, a narrow side canyon opened in the stone cliffs. Reno turned the blue roan in to it. Within minutes the side canyon narrowed so much that they had to go in single file. After a few yards of sand, the floor of the channel became smooth, water-polished stone. A shallow pool shimmered in the failing light.

Darlin' tugged at the bit eagerly.

"Slow down, knothead," Reno muttered. "Let me check it out first."

While Eve held the horses, Reno read the sign left in the very fine silt that bordered the shrinking pool. He came back to the horses, stripped off canteens, and began filling them. When he was finished, he stepped back.

"Let them in one at a time," Reno said.

While Darlin' drank, he watched the level of the pool intently.

"All right, girl. That's enough. Let the dun have a turn."

Under Reno's quick eyes, the four horses were allowed to drink their fill. When they were finished, little remained but a churned, silty puddle barely a quarter the size that the shallow pool had been before the horses arrived.

"Will it fill again?" Eve asked.

Reno shook his head. "Not until the next rain."

"When will that be?"

"Could be tomorrow. Could be next month."

He looked beyond the puddle to the place where the stone walls pinched in.

"Look!" Eve said.

Reno turned to her. Silently she pointed to the

wall behind him. There, on the rusty face of the rock, someone had chipped out a symbol. It was the same as one of the symbols in the Spanish journal.

"Permanent water," Eve translated.

Reno looked at the puddle and then at the dry, unpromising slot that was so narrow he would have to enter it sideways.

"Take the horses back to grass and hobble them," Reno said. "Sleep if you can."

"Where are you going?"

"To look for water."

THE following day Reno slept until a rising tide of sunlight crested the high canyon walls and flowed through the hidden valley. He awoke as he always did, all at once, with no fuzzy twilight between sleep and full alertness. He rolled on his side and looked across the ashes of the small campfire at the girl who slept on her side with her hair a tawny glory spilling across the blankets.

Desire tightened Reno's body in a rush as silent and deep as the sunlight filling the valley. With a whispered curse, he rolled out of bed.

The crackle of the campfire startled Eve. She awoke in a rush, sitting up so suddenly that blankets scattered.

"Easy, *gata*. It's just me."

Blinking, Eve looked around. "I fell asleep."

"That you did. About fourteen hours ago." Reno looked up from the fire. "You woke up when I came in."

"I don't remember."

Reno did. When he had covered her, she sleepily kissed his hand and then snuggled deeper into the blankets, for the nights were always crisp.

The trust implicit in Eve's caress had burned

through Reno like lightning through night. He had almost slid in bed beside her. The amount of self-control it had taken not to peel off the blankets and run his hands all over her had shocked Reno.

It told him how much he wanted a girl who didn't want him. Not really. Not enough to give herself to him out of sheer passion.

"Did you find water?" she asked.

"That's why we're not on the trail right now. The horses need rest."

So did Eve, but Reno knew she would insist they get on the trail if she thought he was stopping only for her. The exhaustion implicit in her deep sleep last night had told Reno how close Eve was to the end of her strength.

They ate breakfast in a lazy kind of silence that was more companionable than any conversation could have been. When they were finished, he smiled at her as she hid a yawn.

"Feel up to a little walk?" he asked.

"How little?"

"Less than a quarter of a mile."

Eve smiled and got to her feet.

She followed Reno into the narrow slot at the head of the feeder canyon. Her shoulders fit without walking sideways, which gave her an easier time of it for the first few yards. Then she, too, had to wriggle and twist to make any progress. Gradually the stone passage widened until two people could walk abreast. The rock walls became cool and damp. Puddles gleamed on the solid rock floor of the canyon.

Twisting, turning, the slot canyon widened as it snaked through layers of rock. Small pools appeared. Some were only inches deep. Some were a foot or more. The water was cool and clean, for it was held in basins of solid stone.

The sound of falling water came from somewhere ahead. Eve froze, listening with her breath held. She had never heard anything so beautiful as the musical rush of water in a dry land.

Moments later Reno led Eve into a bell-shaped opening in the slot canyon. A stream of water no wider than Reno's hand leaped from a shelf ten feet high and fell into a plunge pool carved from solid stone. The sound the water made was cool, exquisite, a murmur of prayer and laughter combined. From every crevice, ferns trailed, their fronds a green so pure it burned like emerald flame against the stone. Rays from the overhead sun touched the mist-bathed opening, making it blaze with a million tiny rainbows.

Eve stood for a long time, lost in the beauty of the secret pool.

"Watch your step," Reno said in a hushed voice as he finally started forward.

Moss softened the stone floor, making the footing tricky. The small marks left by Reno's passage on the previous day were the only sign that anything living had visited the pool for a long, long time.

But men had come there before. Indians and Spaniards had picked out messages and names in the surface of the sheer sandstone walls.

"Fifteen-eighty," Reno read aloud.

Next to the date, a man had written his name in an arcane, formal script: Captain Cristóbal Leon.

"My God," Eve breathed.

She traced the date with fingers that trembled, thinking of the man who had left his mark centuries before. She wondered if he had been as thirsty as they were when they found the first pool, and if he had been struck by the uncanny beauty of the final pool veiled in thousands of shimmering rainbows.

There were other marks on the rock wall, figures that owed nothing to European traditions of art or history. Some of the drawings were easy enough to puzzle out—stick deer with spreading antlers, arrowheads, a ripple that probably meant water or river. Other figures were more enigmatic. Faces that were not human, figures that wore ghostly robes, eyes that had been open for thousands of years.

The shaman had worn such drawings. Perhaps other men had once. But now no men built stone cities and came to drink from the pool. No women came to dip gourds and water jars in the cool silence of the canyon. No children wet small fingers and made fleeting drawings on the rock walls.

Yet there was an odd peace within the crystal laughter of the pool. Orphaned or not, saloon girl or saint, friend or friendless, Eve knew she was part of the vast rainbow of life that stretched from the unknowable past to the unforeseen future. Hands like hers had created enigmas on rock walls countless centuries ago. Minds like hers would try to solve the riddles countless years ahead.

Reno bent down, found a cobble the size of his palm, and began hammering carefully on the rock wall. With each strike of stone against stone, the thin black veneer that time and water had left upon the stone chipped away, revealing the lighter stone beneath.

Within a surprisingly short time, he had picked out the date and the name Matthew Moran.

"Is your name really Evening Star?" Reno asked without turning around.

"My name is Evelyn," she said in a husky voice. "Evelyn Starr Johnson."

Then she blinked back tears, for she was no longer the only one alive who knew her real name.

EVE floated on her back, watching the sapphire sky overhead and the inky shadows that shifted slowly against sheer rock walls. The ripples made by falling water rocked her gently. From time to time she steadied herself with a hand on the smooth stone or on the cool bottom of the pool a few feet beneath her body.

Suspended in time as well as water, turning as slowly as the day, Eve knew she should go back to camp, but she wasn't ready to leave the pool's peace just yet. She wasn't ready to face the smoldering green of Reno's eyes as he watched her with a hunger that was almost tangible.

Eve wondered what Reno saw in her own eyes when he turned suddenly and found her watching him. She was afraid he saw a reflection of her own hunger for him. She wanted to know again the surprising, sweet fire that came when he held her close.

Yet she wanted more than Reno's passion. She wanted his laughter and his dreams, his silences and his hopes. She wanted his trust and his respect and his children. She wanted everything with him that a man and a woman could share: joy and sorrow, hope and heartache, passion and peace, all of life ahead of them like an undiscovered country.

And most of all, Eve wanted Reno's love.

He wanted her body. And nothing more.

I'll keep the ring and the pearls until I find a woman who loves me more than she loves her own comfort.

And while I'm at it, I'll find a ship made of stone, a dry rain, and a light that casts no shadows.

Eve closed her eyes on a wave of unhappiness. Yet no matter how tightly she shut her eyes against the truth, it was there behind her eyelids, haunting her.

There was one way to convince Reno that he was wrong about her. One way to convince him that she wasn't a cheater and conniver, a strumpet in a red dress. One way.

Give herself to him, paying off a bet that never should have been made and betting her future once more at the same time.

Then he'll see that I didn't lie about my innocence, that I keep my word, that I am worthy of his trust. Then he'll look at me with more than lust. He'll want more from me than the use of my body until we find the mine.

Won't he?

There was no answer to that question except to bet herself once more. A chill coursed through Eve at the immensity of the risk she would be taking.

What if he takes everything I have to give and gives nothing in return but his own body?

That was the danger, the risk, and the probable outcome. Part of Eve knew it with the cool logic of an orphan who had learned to survive whatever life threw her way.

And part of Eve had always believed there was more to life than simple survival. Part of her believed in miracles such as laughter in the face of pain, the joy of a baby discovering raindrops, and a love great enough to overcome distrust.

She's a card cheat and a thief, and she set me up to die.

Unhappily Eve finished her bath, dried herself, put on the shirt Reno had lent her, and walked back to camp.

Reno's eyes burned with hunger when he looked at her.

"I left the soap there for you," Eve said. "And the towel."

He nodded and walked past her. She watched until he disappeared into the slot before she went to the clothesline that had been rigged between two piñons.

Eve turned Don Lyon's black twill pants over on the clothesline. The white ruffled shirt wasn't quite dry. She shook it out and draped it over the rope again. She turned Reno's dark pants over as well, envying him the luxury of a change of clothing. Since her flour-sack dress had fallen apart, she had nothing but Don Lyon's second-best gambling clothes to wear, for she had buried him in his best.

There's always the red dress.

A grimace went over Eve's face at the thought. She would never again wear that dress in front of Reno. She would rather go naked.

Then she wondered if Reno was naked now, bathing as she had bathed in the rainbow pool. The thought was unsettling.

Eve's restless glance fell on the journals lying side by side on Reno's bedroll. Eve grabbed them and sat cross-legged, tucking the long shirttails between her knees. Beyond the narrow slot that held the pool, the sun was still a hot, slanting presence across the late afternoon sky. The clear, pouring light made the journals easy to read.

The spare prose of Caleb's father said much about the centuries the Indians had spent under Spanish rule . . .

> *Bones poking up through the desert pavement. Femur and part of a pelvis. Looks to be a child. Female. Scraps of leather nearby.*
>
> *Bent Finger says the bones belong to an Indian slave. Only the children could fit into the dog holes the Spaniards called mines.*
>
> *Spanish sign on the rock. Crosses and initials.*

Bent Finger says the scattered stones were once a vista, a kind of small mission. Tiny copper bell found with the child's bones. It was cast, not hammered.

Spanish didn't call them slaves. Slavery was immoral. So they called it the Encomienda. The savages owed the Spanish for Christian teaching. Pay off in coin or pay off in labor.

War was immoral, too. So the King had a Requerimiento, a requirement that had to be read before fighting commenced. It told the savages that anyone who fought God's soldiers placed himself beyond the pale.

Upshot of the Requerimiento was any Indian who fought the Spanish was declared a slave and sent to the mines. Since Spanish was gibberish to the Indians, they didn't understand the warning.

Not that it mattered. Indians would have fought anyway.

Spanish priests ran the mines. Slave labor. Men lasted about two years. Women and children a lot less.

Hell on Earth in the name of God.

Coolness condensed along Eve's spine as she thought of the ruins she had seen back up the valley. The descendants of the people who had built those many-storied dwellings weren't dumb animals to be enslaved by other men.

But they had been enslaved, and no war had been waged for the sake of their freedom. They had lived, endured brutal labor, died young, and been buried like rubbish in unmarked graves.

Eve felt a kinship with the forgotten dead. More than once in the past few days, she and Reno had come close to dying alone and unnoticed, their graves no more than whatever piece of earth they fell upon when they drew their last breath. The lesson of mortality was as old as man's expulsion from Eden. Life was brief. Death was eternal.

Eve wanted more from life than she had known so far. She wanted something she couldn't name.

Yet even without a name, Eve knew that it awaited her within Reno's arms.

14

WHEN Reno came back to camp, Eve was dressed in camisole, pantalets, and one of his dark shirts. She was also curled up on his bedroll, asleep. Slowly he took the journal from her relaxed fingers and set it aside. She stirred sleepily and looked up at him with eyes that reflected sunlight and darkness.

"Move over, *gata*. I'd like a nap, too."

When Reno stretched out beside Eve, she smiled.

"You smell like lilacs," she murmured. "I like it."

"You should. It's your soap."

"You shaved," she said, touching a place on Reno's neck where he had nicked himself. "I wouldn't have cut you. Why didn't you ask me?"

"I get tired of demanding things from you," he said simply.

Eve's eyes opened and she looked at Reno, hearing all that he wasn't saying.

"I like shaving you," she whispered.

216

"What about kissing me? Do you like that, too?"

The green of Reno's eyes was hot enough to burn, yet he made no move toward Eve.

"Yes," she whispered. "I like that, too."

Slowly Reno bent and put his mouth over Eve's. She made a soft sound of revelation and remembrance in one. The warm, hungry questing of his tongue made her shiver with pleasure. For long, sweet seconds she relearned the velvet rhythms of penetration and retreat, knew once more the textures of his deep kiss, felt again the heat of him spreading through her in wave after wave of pleasure.

Reno cupped Eve's face in his hands, letting the warmth of her skin radiate through him in a shimmering rush that was hotter and sweeter each time he felt it. Her warmth, her taste, her soft mouth opening beneath his, set fire to him.

"*Gata*," he whispered. "You burn me."

Her only answer was a broken cry and a shiver of pleasure as his teeth scored lightly over her neck.

The passionate cry was a razor fraying the cords of Reno's restraint. He wanted to strip Eve's few clothes away and bury himself in the sultry softness he knew waited for him within her body.

But even more than that, he needed to bring her to the point where she wanted him at least as much as he wanted her. He needed her crying and clawing and demanding that he take her. He needed her to forget all her cold feminine calculations and come to him without restraint, a golden fire burning him to the marrow of his bones.

Then he would burn her in return, leaving a mark on her that she would never forget. No matter how many men she had known before, she would never take another without remembering what it had been to be Reno's lover.

He didn't ask himself why it should matter that Eve never forget him. He simply accepted it as he had the uncanny currents of the Spanish needles, a mystery that didn't have to be understood to be used.

Slowly Reno lowered his mouth over Eve's once more, letting the rising currents of passion swirl back and forth between them, joining them in a quest that ultimately could have only one end.

Eve's fingers slid deeply into Reno's thick, cool hair, seeking the elemental warmth beneath. Her nails drew lightly over his scalp. The low sound he made was both reward and goad. She flexed her fingers again, and again felt the response that rippled through his muscular body.

"Such sweet little claws," Reno said.

He bit Eve's lower lip with careful restraint. She made a sound of surprise and pleasure. Smiling, he released her lip so slowly she could feel the tiny serrations of his teeth caressing the smooth, sensitive skin.

She leaned closer as he withdrew, for she wanted more of the gentle torment. He laughed softly and turned aside, denying her his mouth. When she tried to follow him, he held her face still between his hands. Her lips were parted, glistening with sunlight and desire, trembling lightly.

"Reno?"

He made a questioning sound that was rather like a purr of satisfaction.

"Don't you want to kiss me?" Eve whispered.

"Do you want to kiss me?" Reno countered.

She nodded her head.

Golden strands slid forward over his hands, caressing him with a cool fire. His suddenly indrawn breath filled his throat.

"Then do it, *gata*. Do it now."

Eve saw the banked fire in Reno's eyes, heard it in his low voice, felt it in the tension of his arms. Knowing how much he wanted her kiss made a strange heat coil deeply within her.

"Do you want to taste me?" she whispered. "Is that how you want it?"

But Reno couldn't answer, for Eve had matched her mouth to his. The delicate explorations of her tongue made him groan.

She lifted her head.

"More," he said huskily.

Eve gave Reno what he asked for, because it was what she wanted, too. The taste of him was familiar, her own mouth and his combined. His textures lured her, making her feel both dizzy and strangely powerful. She strained against him, needing an even deeper tasting of him. She wanted to hold him so tightly that she became a part of him, never to be wholly separate again.

With an urgency Eve didn't understand, her hands stroked from Reno's head to his shoulders as she leaned closer and closer to him. He neither advanced nor retreated, letting her come to him. Restlessly her arms tightened around his neck.

An exquisite sensation shot through Eve as her breasts met the muscular warmth of Reno's chest. She hadn't known how she ached for that contact until she felt it. Instinctively she began to twist slowly against him, dragging the hardening peaks of her breasts over the tense muscles of his chest.

The sound Reno made was both encouragement and sensual demand. She sank her nails into the tightly corded muscles of his back, wanting to feel his powerful arms around her, wanting to be held against him more tightly than her arms alone could manage.

When he didn't respond as she wished, she made a frustrated noise.

"What?" Reno asked in a low voice.

Eve tried to draw his mouth down to hers once more, but he was far stronger than she was. He held his lips just above hers, teasing her with the kiss he withheld just as he was withholding his strength from her passionate demands.

"What do you want?" he whispered.

"To kiss you."

He brushed her mouth with his lips.

"Like that?" he asked.

"No. Yes."

"No and yes?"

The tip of Reno's tongue teased Eve's lips while she struggled to be closer.

"Yes," she said, shivering at the touch of his tongue.

And then he withdrew.

"No," she said quickly.

"Yes and no. Make up your mind, sweet *gata*."

"Reno," Eve said urgently. "I want . . . more."

His breath came in as though she had flicked him with a whip.

"Open your mouth," Reno said in a deep voice. "Kiss me that way. Let me see that you want it as much as I do."

Sunlight glistened on Eve's lips and on the tip of her tongue. Reno made a low sound and tightened his arms, lifting her face up to his.

"More," he said, brushing his parted lips over hers.

Eve trembled and did as he asked.

Reno's mouth closed over hers, and his tongue slid into the warmth that had opened for him. He took her mouth as he meant to take her body, completely, a seamless melding of flesh and honeyed heat.

The feathering touch of air across Eve's skin when Reno unlaced her camisole was like the edge of his teeth, an exciting contrast to the satin heat of desire.

Eve didn't know how much her breasts ached to be stroked until Reno's hands cupped and his thumbs prodded nipples into proud peaks. She didn't know he was lying half over her until his fingers plucked the taut nipples and streamer after streamer of fire shot through her, making her arch into unexpected contact with his body.

She would have cried out at the sensual pleasure of her body against his, but the only cries the deep mating of mouths allowed were small noises from the back of her throat. He drank the passionate whimpers and silently demanded more, teasing and kneading her sensitive breasts. Long fingers stroked and shaped and tugged until she twisted almost wildly beneath him.

Only then did Reno shift again, flowing completely over Eve, giving her what she had needed without knowing it. His hips pressed against hers, sinking into her until she moved her legs apart in an instinctive effort to match the aching softness between her thighs with the rigid proof of Reno's hunger.

Eve didn't know who made the hoarse sound of discovery when Reno fitted himself against her. She knew only that fire spiraled wildly, burning her. Her nails dug heedlessly into the flexed muscles of his back as she gasped, in the grip of a pleasure that burned.

Reno didn't object to her nails. He simply groaned his response and dragged his hips over her in passionate reflex. The liquid fire of her response spread between their straining bodies.

Surprise froze Eve until Reno's hips moved
again, sending wildfire racing through her body in
a burst of heat she could neither deny nor conceal.
When he repeated the movement, his tongue shot
into her mouth in a possession that was total yet
so tantalizing in its lack of completion that Eve
wept.

One of Reno's hands moved between their bodies. The sound of his pants coming undone was
lost in the passionate protests that came from Eve
when he lifted his weight from her hips.

"It's all right, *gata*," Reno said thickly as he eased
himself from the confinement of cloth. "I'm not
going anywhere."

Eve barely heard the words. She knew only that
Reno's weight was settling back on her, but just
missing the part of her that ached for the pressure
of his body. She twisted against him, wanting more
than he was giving her. No matter how she moved,
he managed to evade her.

"Reno," she said raggedly.

"What?" he asked when she said no more.

As he spoke, he raked his teeth lightly over her
neck.

Eve had no words to answer him, for she had
never felt as she did now, wild for something she
couldn't name.

Reno smiled darkly, for he knew just what she
was missing.

"What is it?" he asked again.

Then he listened to the splintering of Eve's voice
as his teeth closed with more force on her smooth
skin.

"I can't . . . I don't . . ." she gasped.

He caught her nipples in his fingers once more
and tugged. Her breath came out in a hoarse sound

as she arched like a bow. The motion made him settle more deeply onto her legs, yet still not where she wanted him. Her hands clenched in unbearable frustration. She twisted up against him in unknowing demand.

"Open your legs," he whispered.

As Reno spoke, he moved his hips just enough to brush against Eve's fire. The caress drew a ragged cry and a rush of heat from her. She shifted, wanting more of the sweet violence he had teased from her.

"More," he said thickly. "Let me see that you want me."

Eve shifted again.

"More, *gata*. You know you'll like it. Draw your knees up on either side of me."

She did as Reno asked, opening her legs until he lay easily between her thighs. Slowly he began teasing her nipples, watching her as he plucked the sensitive, rosy peaks.

"Yes," Reno said when Eve lifted her hips blindly toward him. "Like that. Tell me you want me."

The sensual torment of his hands on her breasts was no longer enough. Eve's head moved as restlessly as her hips, seeking release from the vise of need that was closing around her.

"Reno, I . . ." Eve bit her lip and shivered.

"I know. I can see it."

The pantalets had no center seam, allowing Reno's fingertips to flick over her unprotected secrets, touching all but one.

"And I can feel it," he said in a low voice.

Eve gasped in a combination of fear and passion as she realized that she lay undefended before Reno.

Deliberately he plucked the tender bud that had

swelled with desire. The rush of pleasure Eve felt was so intense she cried out sharply and melted over him.

"Again," Reno said, rubbing his thumb all around her, teasing her with what he was once again withholding.

She made a broken sound.

"Let me feel your pleasure," he whispered. "Now."

Then he touched her and she gave him what he had demanded. The hoarse sound of his satisfaction was another light caress, another delicate flick of passion's whip across her intensely sensitive flesh.

"You're like a spring welling up at my touch," Reno said in a low voice.

His fingertip caressed again, drawing forth another rush of pleasure.

"I like that, *gata*. I like it the way I like to breathe."

His fingers moved, barely brushing her slick, hot flesh.

Eve wept and writhed with the honeyed teasing that sent savage streamers of fire through her. She didn't know when Reno's fingertips were replaced by blunt, satin flesh. She knew only that he wasn't touching her the one place she must be touched. Her nails raked down his back in a demand she couldn't help making.

Reno regretted that his shirt kept him from feeling the sharp edges of his cat's passionate claws. He smiled and teased Eve some more, circling the tender nub without quite touching it. Her hands raked again, and he laughed deep in his throat despite his own unanswered need.

The twisting motion of Eve's hips beneath Reno made a fine sweat break all over his body. He had never had a woman want him so completely, her whole body crying her need. The slightest brush of his fingers sent her response spilling over again. He enjoyed it with savage intensity, bathing himself in her passionate heat, wanting to take her so much that his body shook with his need.

Yet no matter how hard she twisted and fought to make him touch the hungry bud he had drawn from her softness, he eluded her.

"Why?" Eve asked finally.

"I want to hear you ask for more."

She made a frustrated sound and twisted again, and again Reno left her barely touched, wholly aching.

"More," Eve said, trembling.

Reno brushed against her swollen, sultry flesh.

"Harder," she said raggedly.

Her fist struck his shoulder as she strained toward the unattainable fire that withdrew just as she reached for it.

"That's not enough," she said urgently.

"What if I say that's all there is?"

"No! There has to be more!"

Reno touched her again, drawing his nails with exquisite care over the swollen bud. She gasped and liquid fire overflowed.

Teeth clenched against the need shaking him, Reno took a deep breath, seeking the self-control that was sliding away. The primal scent of Eve's passion swept through him. It was like breathing fire.

"Reno," she whispered. "I—"

Her voice broke as she twisted.

"This?" he asked.

Flesh that was both smooth and hard pressed sensually against her, parting her even as she melted over him.

"Yes," she said brokenly. *"Yes."*

With a smooth, powerful motion, Reno drove into Eve, expecting a sleek, seamless ease to the coupling, for there was no doubt of her arousal.

What he found was a barrier that was breached almost the instant it was discovered. Almost, but not quite. The difference was a tearing of flesh and a moisture that owed nothing to passion.

Eve's eyes flew open as pain rather than pleasure stabbed through her whole body.

"You're hurting me!" she said hoarsely.

The motions of Eve's body as she tried to dislodge Reno stripped away his control. He tried to hold her still, but it was too late, he was far too aroused to deny himself the tight satin paradise he had entered. Release swept through him, burning him with pulses of pure fire.

The wild shuddering of Reno's body moved him within Eve, but there was no pain for her this time. Instead, tongues of fire licked up from the place where their bodies were joined.

The sharp ripples of passion surprised Eve, as did Reno's hoarse groans and the rhythmic pulses of his flesh deep within her. She closed her eyes, let out a broken breath, and waited for him to release her.

Yet Reno made no move to do so, even when his breathing slowed. The rise and fall of his chest was enough to move him within Eve. Each small motion sent more currents of unwelcome fire through her body. She no longer enjoyed the sensation, for she knew now where it led—to a feeling of pain and edgy despair.

She had been one of those foolish women Donna talked about, the kind who spread their legs in the name of love. But Reno didn't want a saloon girl's love. He wanted only her body.

And he had taken it.

"Get off me," Eve said finally.

The flatness of her voice angered Reno. She had been so hot, so willing, and now she couldn't wait to be rid of him. She couldn't have told him more clearly how little she had enjoyed coupling with him.

Yet he had enjoyed it so much he had lost control too quickly. That had never happened to him before. The knowledge that he had wanted her much more than she wanted him made him furious.

Then Reno remembered the fragile barrier, the tearing an instant before he could take Eve completely. He remembered, but he could not believe it. He could not believe a saloon girl was a virgin.

It must have been a long time since her last man.

That would explain the sleek constriction of her body, a sensual pressure that still caressed him every time either one of them breathed.

Reno realized anew how slender Eve was, how delicately made. He wasn't either slender or small. He was an unusually large, potent man. He hadn't meant to hurt her, but he must have. The knowledge simultaneously shamed and angered him, for it underlined the difference in their level of mutual desire.

"Don't tell me you didn't want it," Reno said harshly. "Hell, you asked for it as plain as day."

Color stained Eve's cheeks as she remembered her own wanton behavior. He was quite right. She had asked for it.

"I'm not asking for it now," Eve said tightly.

With a hissed word, Reno shifted to roll aside. Eve's breath wedged and a shudder went through her body as he caressed her violently sensitive flesh in the act of leaving her.

Blood glistened in the sun, scarlet testimony to a truth Reno could barely believe. She had felt like wild, sun-warmed honey. He had been so eager for her that he hadn't even undressed her or himself. He had taken her wearing his boots and pants as though she were no more than a whore bought for a few minutes of ease.

And she had let him. She had begged him.

Reno looked at Eve as though he had never seen her before. And he hadn't. Not the way he was seeing her now. He hadn't allowed himself to look past the scarlet dress to the innocent girl beneath; because he had wanted that girl too much to turn aside, no matter what the truth of her innocence was.

"*Virgin.*"

"That's right, gunfighter," Eve shot back. "I'm a virgin."

Suddenly her mouth drew down in an unhappy curve.

"Well, I *was* a virgin," she said. "Now I'm just one more ruined girl who should have known better."

The word rang in Reno's mind. Ruined.

Like Savannah Marie had been ruined. Like Willow had been ruined.

A decent man marries an innocent girl if he ruins her.

Suddenly Reno felt cornered. Like any cornered animal, he fought to be free. His fingers wrapped around Eve's shoulders.

"If you think you just traded your maidenhead for a husband," he said, "you're dead wrong. I won you in a card game. I took what was mine. That's all the payment that's required."

"Thank God," Eve said between her teeth.

For the second time, Eve had shocked Reno. He had expected an argument, a torrent of words telling him how it was his duty as a decent man to marry the girl his lust had ruined. It was an old trick, the oldest and most potent in the arsenal of the war waged between marriage-minded girls and freedom-minded men.

Yet Eve wasn't using it.

"Thank God?" Reno repeated numbly.

"Damn straight," Eve shot back. "Thank God I've paid off the bet fully and you won't want to do that again, because—"

"What the hell are you talking about?" he interrupted.

"—now I know why women get paid for it!"

Eve's furious words hung in the air for a long, taut moment before Reno trusted himself to answer.

"You liked it and you know it," Reno said in a low, lethal voice. "I didn't rape you."

"You didn't rape me. And I didn't like it!"

"Then why did you beg for me?" he retorted.

Humiliation and anger burned on Eve's cheeks. Her lips trembled, but her voice was as steady as her eyes.

"I'll bet if you asked a baby bird how it liked flying, it would sing happily all the way down to the ground that breaks its stupid neck!"

For an instant Reno was silent. Then he laughed despite his anger at taking a saloon girl and discovering he had made a passionate virgin bleed.

"Flying, huh?" he asked deeply.

Eve gave Reno a wary look, not trusting the sudden, velvety darkness of his voice one bit. With small, subtle motions, she tried to ease away from his grip. His long fingers tightened just enough to let her know that she was well and truly held.

"Not flying," she said in a clipped voice. "Falling. There's a big difference, gunfighter."

"Only in the landing. Next time you'll land on your feet like the sleek little cat you are."

"There won't be a next time."

"Are you going back on your word?" Reno challenged smoothly.

Eve's smile was like a piece of winter.

"I don't have to," she said. "You can handle me until fire freezes solid. I won't ask again to be hurt until I bleed."

"It's only like that the first time. And if I had known you were a virgin, I—"

"I told you I'd never let a man under my skirts," she interrupted. "But you didn't believe me. You thought I was a slut. Now you know I'm not."

Then realization came to Eve. Her mouth turned down in a bitter curve.

"I wasn't a slut," she corrected. "But I am now."

Anger coiled in Reno.

"I did not make you a slut," he said, biting off each word.

"Really? How does it happen, then? One time is a mistake and two times makes a slut? Or is it three? Maybe four?"

"*Damnation.*"

"Precisely," she hissed. "How many times does it take before a girl magically becomes a slut? Do tell me, gunfighter. I'd hate to use up more than my God-given share of *fun*."

"What am I supposed to do?" he asked furiously. "Marry you? Would that make it right again?"

"No!"

"What?" Reno asked, wondering if he had heard correctly.

"Nothing would make what we did right but love," Eve said bitterly, "and getting love from a man like you is about as likely as finding 'a ship made of stone, a dry rain, and a light that casts no shadow.' "

Hearing his own words come so harshly from Eve's tongue told Reno that he had hurt her in more than the breaching of her maidenhead.

"You thought you were in love with me," Reno said, shocked.

Eve went pale. "Does it matter?"

"Hell, yes, it matters! You responded to me because you're very much a woman, not because of any girlish crap about love."

With a twisting movement, Eve pulled free of Reno's grasp. She drew his shirt closer around her body and watched him with feral yellow eyes.

It occurred to Reno that he could have been more tactful on the subject of love. A lot more tactful.

She had been innocent, and innocence believed in love.

"Eve . . ."

"Fasten your pants, gunfighter. I'm tired of seeing my blood on you and knowing how foolish I was."

15

E VE knew without turning around that Reno had followed her to the pool where water danced and whispered. She had sensed him behind her every step of the way from camp.

Her hands hesitated as she began to peel off the shirt. Beneath it she wore only underclothes whose sheer cotton provided scant protection from Reno's eyes.

It's a little late for maidenly modesty, Eve told herself mockingly. *Very much like locking the barn door after the horse is long gone.*

With quick, edgy motions, Eve stripped off the big shirt and threw it aside.

Reno's breath came in with a sharp sound as he saw the bright scarlet stain on Eve's pantalets that had been hidden by the long tails of her borrowed shirt.

"Eve," he said in a raw voice. "I didn't mean to hurt you."

She said nothing. Nor did she look over her shoulder at Reno.

Soundlessly he came up behind Eve and put his hands on her shoulders.

"Do you think me such an animal that I get my pleasure hurting women?" he asked harshly.

Eve wanted to lie, but saw nothing except more hurt in it for her. Reno was relentless when it came to the subject of truth and saloon girls.

"No," she said flatly.

The rush of his expelled breath stirred the hair at the nape of Eve's neck. Gooseflesh rippled down her arms.

The treacherous response of her own body infuriated her.

"Thank God for that much," Reno muttered.

"God had little to do with it, gunfighter. More like the devil."

"You begged for me."

"How kind of you to remind me," Eve said. "It won't happen again."

Her whole body was rigid beneath Reno's hands. He cursed his quick tongue and the savage anger that came when Eve reminded him of how little she had enjoyed being his lover.

Yet for him, it had been a pleasure both sweet and violently intense, right up to the instant when he realized he had taken a virgin. Then there had been a fury as deep as his passion.

"It *will* happen again," he said, "but it won't be a mistake. You'll like it this time. I'll be certain of it."

"A no-account gunfighter once told me I'd like it so much, I'd scream with pleasure." Eve's shrug was a parody of her usual grace. "He was half-right. I screamed."

Reno said something brutal under his breath before he managed to rein in his anger. Keeping his temper had never been so difficult. Eve had a way of getting underneath his control that would have frightened him if she had been coldly manipulative. But she wasn't. She was the most passionate woman he had ever had the joy of touching.

Unfortunately, at the moment, she fairly radiated outrage and . . . frustration.

Reno took in a long breath and let it out in a soundless sigh as understanding came to him. He hadn't meant to tease her and leave her raw and knotted with hunger, yet he had done just that. He could hardly blame her if she wanted a few strips of his hide to nail to the nearest tree.

Calmly Reno turned Eve around so that she faced him. He slid his hands beneath the camisole, preparing to lift it over her head.

"What do you think you're doing?" she demanded.

"Undressing you."

Eve said something that normally would never have crossed her mind, much less her lips.

Reno barely hid his smile beneath his mustache. His hands paused underneath the camisole on either side of her breasts. He could see the change in her nipples as they tightened in passionate reflex to his presence.

"We've both agreed that you're the kind of girl who keeps her word," he said. "And we've both agreed that you gave me your word I could touch you."

Barely veiled mutiny glittered in Eve's eyes. Never had she looked more like a cat than she did now, watching him without blinking, her lips thinned as though ready to draw back in a spitting snarl.

"You're going to keep your word, aren't you?" Reno asked.

Eve didn't answer.

"I thought so," he said.

Slowly he slid his hands from beneath the partially laced camisole.

"But the undressing can wait," he continued. "Hand over the soap and washrag."

She had forgotten the piece of lilac-scented soap and cloth she had brought to the pool. With difficulty, she forced herself to unclench her hands.

Reno took the ragged square of flour sack and the pale lump of soap from her.

The deep marks left by Eve's nails on the soap and on her other palm gave silent proof of the effort she had made not to lose what little control she had over herself.

The evidence of her own uncertain temper appalled Eve. She had never thought of herself as a particularly passionate or violent person. The orphanage had taught her never to lose control of herself, for if she did, she would be at the mercy of others.

Just as she had been at Reno's mercy, reaching for love and getting nothing in return but pain.

Pity I had to learn the lesson all over again.

Reno looked at the crescents Eve's nails had cut in the soap and in her own skin. Then he looked at her eyes. There was nothing of laughter or passion or curiosity in them now. Her eyes were as bleak as a winter sunset.

"Eve," he whispered.

She simply watched him out of yellow cat's eyes.

"I'm sorry I hurt you," he said. "But I'm not sorry about having you. You were silk and fire. . . ."

Reno's voice died. Eve's innocent passion had

been a revelation that his mind still had trouble accepting.

His body had no such problem. Though he had just had her, he wanted her again. She wanted him, too. He was certain of it. Her body was crying out its hunger and frustration.

But Eve was too innocent to understand the source of her anger. Reno knew better than to try to convince her with words. She was in no mood to listen to him on any subject, least of all the subject of her own needs as a woman.

Besides, there were better ways than words to teach an innocent like Eve, more pleasurable ways. For both of them. All he had to do was convince her to trust him with her passion again.

A difficult task, but not an impossible one. Her body was already on his side.

"Since you're feeling shy, I won't undress you," he said calmly.

Surprise widened Eve's eyes. She hadn't expected Reno to allow her any slack at all.

His smile told her that he knew very well the source of her surprise. He tucked the washrag into the waist of his pants and shoved the soap into a pocket.

"Into the pool," Reno said.

"What?"

"Come on. You'll feel better after a bath."

Eve said nothing. She just waded until the waterfall's cool silver braids twisted down less than a foot away from her. Water lapped to midthigh and swirled around her legs in patterns of rainbow bubbles.

To Eve's surprise, Reno walked into the pool right behind her. He didn't undress, as she had feared he would. He looked just as he had when he had rolled off her—half-buttoned shirt, bare feet, and dark pants.

At least his pants were fastened now.

Heat climbed Eve's cheeks as she remembered how Reno had looked before, his pants undone, the evidence of her virginal stupidity gleaming scarlet in the daylight for everyone to see.

"Your hair is as clean as sunshine," Reno said, "but I'll wash it if you like."

Eve shook her head tightly.

"Then I'll tuck it up out of the way."

"No," she said instantly, not wanting to be touched. "I'll do it."

Hurriedly Eve caught up her long hair and twisted it into a knot on top of her head. A few tendrils slithered back down. She ignored them. The look on Reno's face as she lifted her arms and dealt with her hair told her that he liked watching her breasts shift and sway with each movement of her body.

And if the look on his face weren't enough, there was the frank bulge in his pants to give away his thoughts. Hastily she glanced away.

"Ready?" Reno asked.

"For what?"

He bent and scooped up water in his cupped hands.

"To get wet," he said simply. "You can hardly take a bath when you're dry, can you?"

Reno's reasonable tone of voice was at odds with the smoldering sensuality of his eyes.

"I don't need any help getting wet," Eve muttered.

He laughed softly and let water from his hands trickle down the front of her camisole.

"Some things are better when they're shared," Reno said in a husky voice.

"Baths?" she asked sarcastically.

"I don't know. I've never shared one."

Eve looked surprised.

"It's true," he said.

"I believe you."

"Do you?"

"Yes."

She shivered as water that was neither warm nor cold trickled down between her breasts.

"Why?" he asked, curious.

"You wouldn't bother to lie to a slut."

Reno closed his eyes and grappled with the rage that stabbed him like black lightning, threatening to rip away his control.

"I suggest," he said distinctly, "that you never use that word again in my hearing."

"Why not? You're so damned fond of the truth."

He opened his eyes. "Baiting me won't make you feel better. I can guarantee it."

Eve made an involuntary sound and looked away. The grim shadows and raw fury she saw in his glance reminded her too much of her own seething turmoil. In any case, Reno was right. Baiting him hadn't made Eve feel better. It had made her feel worse, on the breaking edge of her own control. She felt like biting and clawing and screaming. The depth of her own wildness was frightening.

"And that's all you're doing," Reno added. "Baiting me. We both know you're not a slut."

Eve said nothing.

The temptation to push Eve until she agreed with him nearly overwhelmed Reno, but he managed to keep his silence. Barely. He scooped up more water, letting it fall in sparkling liquid necklaces over Eve until her camisole and pantalets were drenched.

Eve closed her eyes and pretended that she was washing herself beneath one of the barrel showers Don Lyon had rigged before his hands became too crippled for such things.

The cool glide of the water down her body made her shiver, but not with cold. The day was too hot for that, and the sun's heat was both absorbed and reflected by the high rock walls.

Eve flinched at the first touch of Reno's hands on her shoulders. He whispered her name unhappily. Through a screen of thick bronze eyelashes, she saw the painful line of Reno's mouth.

"I won't hurt you," he said with aching control. "I would never have hurt you the first time, if I had known. . . ."

Eve's breath came out in a long, ragged sigh. She nodded, believing him, for it was the simple truth. She had sensed that about Reno the instant he sat down at her table in Canyon City; despite his size, despite his strength, despite his lethal speed, he wasn't the kind of man who enjoyed cruelty.

"I know," she said in a low voice. "It's why I dealt cards to you. You weren't what Slater and Raleigh King were."

Reno let out breath that he wasn't aware of having held. He brushed his lips over Eve's forehead in a soft caress that ended before she could be sure she had felt it at all.

"Let me bathe you," he said.

She hesitated, then reached up to remove her camisole. Hands sleek with lather closed over her wrists, holding her gently.

"Let me," Reno said.

She hesitated again.

"I won't take you," he said. "Not unless you ask me to. I just want to make you . . . hurt less."

Unable to bear the intensity of Reno's eyes, Eve

closed her own and nodded. For several moments she waited in an agony of suspense, but when Reno touched her, it was only to wash her face as gently as he had his nephew's.

Yet Eve didn't feel like a baby. Reno's touch made an almost painful pleasure course through her. She hadn't known how sensitive her face was. The ritual of soaping and washing and rinsing made frissons of pleasure ripple over her.

"Was that so bad?" Reno asked.

Eve shook her head. A long tendril of hair floated free. Reno tucked it behind one ear.

"How about this?" he asked.

He bent and began tracing every clean curve of Eve's ear with his tongue and then his teeth, biting with exquisite care, enjoying the ragged intake and breaking of her breath. When the tip of his tongue probed and tested, spiraling down, retreating, returning, caressing, she made an odd sound in her throat and clung to his arms for balance.

Reno lifted his head and looked down into Eve's wide, surprised eyes.

"Is something wrong?" he whispered.

"I..." She swallowed. "I never know what to expect from you."

"Your boyfriends must have been, er, unimaginative."

"I never had one, imaginative or otherwise."

"No boyfriend?" Reno asked. "Not even for a few stolen kisses out by the barn?"

Eve shook her head. "I never wanted a male near me. Until you."

"My God."

The realization of just how innocent Eve had been went through Reno in a shock wave of pleasure and surprise. So innocent, yet she had been a passionate spring welling up at his touch, his word, his lightest caress.

So innocent . . . so passionate. The possibilities for mutual pleasure were enough to make him light-headed. He hardly knew where to begin.

Reno's glittering green glance swept over Eve. Her underwear was nearly transparent, clinging to every curve and valley of her body. The taut crowns of her breasts stood out clearly, as did the luxuriant triangle of bronze hair that both shielded and outlined her essential femininity.

"My God," he said again, reverently. "No man has ever touched you at all, has he?"

"Not quite," she whispered.

"Who?" he demanded.

"You've touched me," she said simply. "Only you."

In a hush that seethed with the small songs of water, Reno washed Eve to the waist. He tried not to linger over her breasts, but it was impossible. The velvet hardness of her nipples lured him irresistibly. He returned to them again and again, until they stood out urgently against the camisole, drawn taut by more than the cool water.

Saying nothing, Reno pulled Eve under the gentle waterfall, rinsing her. When he was finished, he slowly pulled off her camisole and tucked it into the waistband of his pants. Then he bent and tasted the freshness of her skin until she made small noises and clung to him.

"I shouldn't let you do this," Eve said huskily.

"Am I hurting you?"

"No. Not . . . yet."

"Not ever," Reno said, nuzzling her breast. "Not ever again."

Eve couldn't answer. The sight of Reno's mouth so close to the rosy peak of her breast took away the ability to speak. The tip of his tongue circled her, stabbing softly. He sheathed his teeth with his lips and bit down.

The ragged sound Eve made owed nothing to pain and everything to a sudden, bright pleasure. Before she could become used to it, the caress changed. Heat surged through her, making it hard to hang on to her anger, for her body sensed a different outlet for the emotions churning beneath her control.

Eve didn't know whether to be relieved or unhappy when Reno finally, slowly, lifted his head and resumed washing her.

"I should have taken the time to tell you how beautiful you are," Reno said. "You have the kind of skin poets write sonnets to. But I'm not a poet. I never wanted to be, until now."

Reno bent and brushed his lips over first one breast, then the other. "I don't know the words to describe you."

Long fingers smoothed soap over Eve's pantalets, waist and hips and thighs. When his palm rubbed against the lush delta, she made a frightened sound.

"Easy," he murmured. "That doesn't hurt you, does it?"

Her lips were trembling. She shook her head.

"Move your legs a bit," Reno said, pressing gently. "Let me wash all of you, especially there, where I hurt you."

He waited, watching her face, wanting her to give so that he wouldn't have to take.

Slowly Eve shifted position, giving Reno the freedom that he wanted. In a silence seething with memory and possibility, he bathed away every last trace of the virgin she had been and would never be again.

"If I could take back the hurt, I would," he whispered. "But I wouldn't take back the rest of it. I've dreamed all my life of finding a passion like yours."

Eve shivered and bit back a throaty sound as Reno's fingers unfastened her pantalets and eased them down her legs until he was kneeling in the pool at her feet.

"Brace yourself against my shoulders," he said huskily.

He felt the trembling of her hands as they settled on his naked shoulders, and wondered if passion or fear moved her.

"Lift your right foot," Reno said.

The pressure of her hands on his shoulders increased. He slipped one leg of the pantalets free.

"Now the other."

She moved, only to stop, frozen by the touch of his fingertips. When he traced the delicate skin, sweet lightning rippled through her. She closed her eyes and held on to his shoulders so hard that her fingers pressed deeply into muscle.

"Does that hurt?" Reno asked, looking up.

"No," she whispered through trembling lips.

"Does it please you?"

"It s-shouldn't."

"But it does?"

"Yes," she whispered on a rush of air. "Dear God, yes."

Reno leaned his forehead against Eve and let out a long breath of relief. Only then did he admit how afraid he had been that he had irrevocably driven her away. That was why he had followed her to the pool. Fear, not passion.

"Such tight petals," Reno whispered, touching Eve delicately, "yet so full. Like a bud in spring. And I was expecting a flower full-blown by a hundred suns."

Eve didn't answer. She couldn't. Heat was sweeping through her body, making her forget everything but the rushing instant and the man who caressed her so tenderly.

Turning his head from side to side, Reno stroked her belly and thighs with his cheeks and the thick silk of his mustache.

"So smooth," he whispered. "So warm. Open for me, sweet Eve. Let me show you what it should have been for you. No hurt, no bleeding, just the kind of pleasure you'll die remembering."

Eyes closed, Eve responded to the gentle pressure between her legs, allowing Reno greater freedom. A warm, lightly probing caress was her reward. Its silky heat astonished her, loosening her knees. She made a ragged sound of pleasure and tried to catch her balance.

"That's it," Reno said, smiling, urging her legs farther apart as he bent to her. "Hold on to me."

Only when Eve felt the heat of Reno's breath did she understand why the caress had been so sleek and hot.

"Reno."

His answer was a tender movement of his tongue that dragged another husky cry from her.

"Don't fight me," Reno breathed. "You gave me what you had given no other man. Let me give you what I've given no other woman."

"My God," Eve whispered as his caresses turned her very bones to honey.

Reno made a husky sound of discovery and pleasure in one as he found the satin knot rising from her softness.

"The bud swells," he whispered. "This time you will flower, too."

Eve couldn't answer. She had no voice, no thoughts, nothing but the sensual lightning licking up through her body, taking it from her control, giving it to the man who both cherished and consumed her in fiery silence.

Reno sensed the storm that was claiming Eve, convulsing her secretly. The scent of her was an elemental perfume singing to him of dark fires and wild release, luring him unbearably.

When the sensual storm broke, her taste was that of a desert rain, sultry and mysterious, bringing life to everything it touched. And after the storm passed, she was the earth itself, flushed with the miracle of rain, all contrasts heightened, radiant in completion.

Reluctantly Reno released the sweet, captive flesh and stood up, holding Eve, for she was barely able to stand. He tucked her head against his chest and rocked her slowly while she came back to herself.

After a long time Eve gave a shivering sigh and looked up at Reno with dazed golden eyes.

"That's what it's all about between men and women," Reno said, kissing Eve gently. "The kind of pleasure you would kill or die for. Not a childish notion of love."

A painful shudder went through Eve.

"You're saying I'd feel that with any man?" she asked, her voice strained.

The violent denial that leaped to Reno's lips made him uneasy. He had never been a possessive kind of man, yet even the thought of Eve allowing another man the freedom of her silky body enraged Reno.

"Reno?" Eve asked, her lips trembling and her eyes steady.

"Some people are better together than others," he said finally. "You make me hotter than any woman ever has. I make you hotter than any man ever has."

Reno looked down into Eve's clear golden eyes. "That's why you gave yourself to me. Not the poker bet. Not love. Just passion, pure and simple and hot as hell."

"That's why men and women marry?" Eve persisted. "Passion, pure and simple?"

Again, Reno hesitated.

"It's why men marry," he said after a moment. "Damn few women have enough passion in them to burn."

"But—"

"Otherwise they wouldn't be able to hold out long enough to get a man to the preacher," Reno continued, ignoring Eve's interruption. "But the little dears do somehow manage, don't they?"

Reno saw the pain in Eve's expression, and winced. He hadn't meant to hurt her with his blunt declarations about the nature of men and women and the illusion called love. But he had hurt her.

Again.

"Sugar child," he said, kissing her temple softly. "Would you feel better if I told you sweet lies about love?"

"Yes."

Then Eve laughed sadly and shook her head.

"No," she amended. "Because I'd want to believe you so much, I'd do it, and then I'd wake up one day and find you saddled up and ready to leave, and I'd know the words for the lies they were."

"I'm not saddling any horses."

"We haven't found the mine yet, have we?"

Gently Eve pushed away and looked up at Reno with steady eyes and a smile that threatened to turn upside down. She stood on tiptoe to brush her lips over his.

"Thanks for the teaching, sugar man. Now maybe we better get to work finding that mine. I've had about all the learning I can bear in one day."

16

THE next day Reno and Eve followed the shaman's directions, heading for an old, nearly forgotten way down the plateau. Late in the afternoon, Reno turned to Eve, breaking the companionable silence that had grown between them as they rode through the wild land.

"The shaman said I had to be sure to take you to a special place up ahead," Reno said.

"Where?" Eve asked, surprised.

"About a mile from here. You stay put while I check it out. I don't want you getting caught in some old shaman's revenge."

It didn't take Reno long to reconnoiter. No more than ten minutes went by before he was back. He reined in next to Eve, saw the unasked questions in her eyes, and reached for her. He leaned over and wrapped his hand around her nape, pulling her to meet the quick, fierce claiming of his mouth. When he released her, she gave him a look that was both startled and . . . hungry.

He smiled. "Did you think that, once satisfied, it would go away?"

Bright color rose in Eve's cheeks.

"I don't think thinking had much to do with it," she said, remembering her headlong abandon yesterday, when Reno had bathed her in the hidden pool.

Reno laughed and nibbled lightly at her mouth.

"You're so sweet to tease," he said. "It's a burning wonder I didn't wake you up this morning the way I wanted to."

"How was that?"

"From the inside out."

The color deepened in Eve's cheeks, but she couldn't help laughing.

Reno had been so different with her today, almost as though he were courting her. Then Eve remembered what he once had said about courting, and her laughter faded.

Courting is for a woman you want to make your wife. That was a little rolling around before breakfast with a saloon girl.

"But I decided it was too soon," Reno continued. "You're such a tender little bud. I don't want to bruise you."

Though Reno's words were teasing, his eyes weren't. Eve knew that he still blamed himself for hurting her the one time he had taken her.

"I'm fine," she said.

And it was true. She had awakened this morning determined to enjoy what she had rather than crying after what she didn't have. Life had taught her that tomorrow would come soon enough, and with it all the regrets for yesterdays that were forever beyond her reach—her dead mother, her gentle and helpless father, the offhanded cruelty of life to the very children who were least able to defend themselves.

Whatever comes with Reno, I won't regret it. Whether he believes it or not, love exists. I know. I feel it.

For him.

And maybe, just maybe, he can feel it for me. He loved once, foolishly. He can love again, wisely. He can love me.

Maybe . . .

"You certain?" Reno asked.

Eve looked startled, then realized he hadn't somehow guessed her thoughts. He was simply pursuing the subject of how she felt today.

"Yes," she said. "I'm fine."

"Even after all these hours in the saddle?" he pressed.

She looked away from the crystal clarity of Reno's eyes, trying to conceal the depth of her feelings at his concern. He didn't love her, but he did care if he hurt her. That was something.

It was the world. No one who was stronger than Eve was had ever cared about her like that.

After a moment Eve touched Reno's cheek with her fingertips and tried to reassure him that he hadn't hurt her yesterday, when he had torn the veil of her innocence and replaced it with a sensual knowledge that permeated her blood like champagne.

"The only thing wrong with me," she said, "is that I get all shivery and have trouble breathing when I think about what we . . . about what you . . . about what I . . ."

Eve made an exasperated sound and wished her hat were big enough to cover her flaming face. It didn't help that she sensed Reno's silent amusement as clearly as if he had thrown back his head and laughed to the clouds.

"You're laughing at me," she muttered.

The back of Reno's fingers smoothed down Eve's cheek in a gentle caress.

"No, sugar girl. I'm laughing because you go to my head like straight whiskey," he said. "I like knowing you're as aware of me as I am of you. It makes me want to pull you off your horse and take you right here, right now, sitting up and watching you."

"Sitting up on a horse?" Eve asked, too startled to be embarrassed. "Is it possible?"

"Damned if I know. I'm real tempted to find out, though. I've been aching for you since about ten minutes after I first had you."

Reno pulled lightly on the reins. Darlin' backed up quickly, removing her rider from temptation.

"Come on," he said to Eve. "The shaman and I have a surprise for you."

"What?"

"If I told you, it wouldn't be a surprise, would it?"

Smiling, Eve reined the dun around to follow Reno. His new ease with her made her happy. He hadn't been so quick to smile since his sister's ranch, where he had been able to let down his guard among friends and family.

That was how he was treating Eve now. As though he trusted her. The heady combination of teasing and frank sensuality kept her senses fully alert, her body quickened in anticipation of the next caress, the next instant of laughter. She couldn't remember ever having smiled so much in her life.

Eve was still smiling when her horse came alongside Reno's. He smiled in return, wondering at the resilience of the girl who was fresh and eager to venture into new country after having barely escaped with her life from the twin hazards of outlaws and a forced exploration of uncharted land.

Not to mention the hazards of innocence and a gunfighter who had wanted her for so long he was having a hell of a time keeping his hands off her now.

"Close your eyes," Reno said huskily.

Eve gave him a sideways look.

"Uh-oh. The dark velvet voice again," she teased. "Is this where you snatch me from the saddle and attempt dubious things while riding a bad-tempered mustang?"

Reno threw back his head and laughed with delight.

"Sugar girl, you do tempt a man. But you're right about Darlin's disposition. She'd unload both of us into the nearest pile of rocks. So close your eyes and don't open them until I tell you. You're safe . . . for now."

Laughing quietly, Eve closed her eyes, knowing that her horse would follow Darlin' without guidance.

For a few minutes, all Eve was aware of was the subtle creak of leather, the lazy rhythms of the lineback dun, the warmth of the sun, and the unique smell of sage and evergreen permeating the dry air.

"Can I peek yet?"

"Uh-uh."

"Sure?" she teased.

"I sure am."

Eve heard the smile in Reno's voice and wanted to laugh out loud with her own soaring pleasure. She loved the lazy teasing that had grown between them since yesterday. She loved being able to turn around and find Reno watching her with warmth in his eyes instead of anger or raw desire. She loved hearing pleasure in his voice and knowing that he was enjoying just being with her. She loved . . .

Reno.

"No peeking," he warned.

Reno tugged Eve's hat brim down over her eyes and ran the back of his fingers along her jawline.

"I wasn't going to cheat," she said quietly. "No matter what you think, I'm not a cheater by nature."

Reno felt her hurt as though it were his own. Leaning over, he lifted Eve from her horse and settled her sideways across his lap, holding her like a child.

"Hush. I wasn't thinking about anything when I pulled on your hat but an excuse to touch you."

Eve turned her face in to Reno's chest, knocking her hat aside. It dangled from its chin strings until he pushed it over her shoulder and stroked her hair.

"I didn't mean to hurt you," he said after a time.

Eyes still closed, she nodded.

"Eve?"

"I'm sorry," she whispered. "I know I shouldn't be so touchy. But . . . I am."

He tipped up her face and gave her the lightest of kisses. Then his arms tightened around her, holding her close when Darlin' shied at the shadow of a soaring hawk.

"Take it easy, knothead," Reno said.

"Watch who you're calling names," she muttered.

There was an instant of surprised silence, then Reno laughed and gave Eve a hard kiss before he urged Darlin' forward.

A few minutes later, Reno reined in and kissed Eve's eyelids gently.

"Open your eyes."

When the warm sensation of his lips vanished,

Eve opened her eyes and looked at Reno. With a gentle smile, he gestured to the view. She turned her head.

A low sound of wonder and disbelief escaped her. A few feet in front of the horses, the land dropped abruptly away. In the distance, rank after rank of smaller plateaus and mesas rose in a series of irregular steps. Those in turn unraveled into an immense stone maze painted in shades of red and gold, pink and mauve.

In place of the dance of streams and rivers, there were columns of stone, cliffs of stone, tables of stone, castles of stone, cathedrals and arches of stone, vast walls and layer cakes of stone, ridges and valleys and hills and flats of stone, a rainbow labyrinth of stone piled upon stone until land and sky merged into a purple sameness so far away that the curve of the earth could be sensed like the distant coming of night.

Clumps of clouds ranged in color from blindingly pure white to dense indigo. Solitary storms stalked the land on stilts of lightning, dragging ragged veils of rain behind, yet the wind brought no smell of rain. The maze was so vast that storms came in across it like squall lines across an unimaginable sea.

"Is that where we're going?" Eve whispered.

Reno looked at the landscape where the bones of the earth itself pressed up through the thin skin of life. There were no living flashes of water, no wide green valleys calling to a weary traveler, no trails or wagon tracks, no hearth fires sending messages of settlements ahead.

The land was untamed. It was wildfire wrought in stone, frozen flames reaching forever to the sky while a dry wind blew, bringing clouds whose rain never reached the ground, leaving the fire to rage unquenched, motionless, eternal.

"I won't go there if I can help it," Reno said finally. "I'll leave that kind of foolishness to my brother Rafe."

Eve nodded her understanding even as she said, "It's beautiful in a wild kind of way."

"So is the sun, but you'll go blind looking at it."

Reno kissed the nape of Eve's neck. His heartbeat speeded at the shiver of response that coursed through her in the wake of the light caress.

"I'm surprised you think it's pretty," Reno said against her skin. "You didn't like the view from the slickrock one bit."

"Not at first. But toward the end, it wasn't as scary. Especially after Slater's men started shooting," Eve added dryly. "Something about those bullets flying around took my mind right off the view."

Reno laughed aloud, hugged Eve hard and quick, and reminded himself of all the reasons he shouldn't move his hands just a few inches and feel the warm weight of her breasts filling them.

"We saved at least fifty miles, maybe more, by crossing that neck of slickrock," Reno said. "Even so, we've got the devil's own trail ahead of us."

"Is there water?" she asked.

"Seeps, springs, potholes, and seasonal creeks." He shrugged. "It should be enough if we're careful."

"And if you don't mind your horse drinking out of your hat?" Eve suggested.

She smiled as she spoke, remembering how they had emptied canteen after canteen into their hats because the way to the hidden pool was too narrow for a horse to take.

Reno kissed the corner of Eve's smile and said, "Be glad we're riding mustangs. They drink less than anything except a coyote."

Eve watched him with sensual memories in her eyes and a hungry fullness to her mouth. Not trusting himself to accept the unknowing invitation of her parted lips, Reno turned Eve until she was facing forward with her back to him.

The confinement of the saddle made her hips press intimately against the inside of his thighs. He hardened in a rush that made him ache. Long fingers wrapped around her thighs, savoring the resilience of her flesh. He pulled her close against him and then released her with a whispered word he hoped she didn't hear.

Reno slid off Darlin' in a rush. He stood close enough to Eve that she felt the heat of his chest against her leg as clearly as she had felt the heat of his thighs against her own. She had felt something else as well, but doubted her own senses. Surely a man couldn't become aroused so quickly.

A glance told Eve she had indeed been correct. Once, Reno's bold arousal would have embarrassed or unnerved her. Now it simply made heat splinter delicately through her. She remembered what it had felt like to give herself to Reno's heat and strength and heady sensuality.

"Sugar girl, you do tempt a man," he said in a deep voice.

"I do?"

"You sure do."

"I'm just sitting here," she pointed out.

"And looking at me like you're wondering how I'd taste with butter and maple syrup," Reno drawled.

Eve flushed, but couldn't help laughing. She was still laughing when Reno pulled her out of the saddle and gave her a kiss that made her dizzy.

"I like having you look at me that way," Reno

said against her mouth. "I like it too damn much."

He carried Eve the few steps to her horse.

"Mount up, *gata*. I'm going to have hell riding as it is."

As Reno spoke, he lifted Eve into the saddle. Then he let go of her and turned away quickly, heading for his own horse once more.

"I didn't mean to tease," she said.

A curt nod as Reno mounted was his only answer.

"Couldn't we..." Eve's voice faded, then strengthened along with the color in her cheeks. "You're hurting and I'm all right and there's no reason we can't... is there?"

Reno reined Darlin' over to Eve and looked at her for the space of several heartbeats.

"There's a reason we can't," he said.

The calm of Reno's voice was belied by his smoldering green glance.

"Slater?" guessed Eve unhappily.

Reno shook his head. "I figure it will be at least two days before Crooked Bear cuts our sign again. The shaman figured it about the same, and he knows the land better than the Spaniards and Cal's daddy combined."

"Then why can't we...?"

Despite the hunger knotting his guts, Reno smiled at the bright red on Eve's cheeks.

"Because, sugar girl, the next time I get my hands on you, I'm not going to let go until neither one of us has enough strength left to lick our lips."

EVE sat with her chin on her knees and her arms around her legs. A few feet beyond her boots, the land sheered away.

At the moment, Reno was exploring the head of the ravine that the shaman had told them would take them across a fringe of the stone canyon and then join with one of the old Spanish trails. If the trail was clear enough, they would ride by the ghostly light of the moon. If not, they would make a dry camp here, at the edge of the plateau.

Off to the west, the sun hovered a few degrees above the horizon. Below and in the distance, long, dense shadows flowed out from countless stone formations. Like the sun, the shadows moved, changing everything they touched, making and re-making the landscape in a slow-motion kaleido-scope of shifting colors and breathtaking vistas.

When footsteps approached, Eve didn't have to turn around to know that it was Reno rather than some stranger walking up behind her. The unique rhythms of Reno's steps had become a part of her, as had the sweet memories of a hidden pool and water braiding down cliffs of solid stone.

"Penny for your thoughts," he said.

Smiling, Eve looked back out over the slow trans-formations of stone and shadow and sunset.

"I keep wondering," she said, "how the maze got here and why it's so different from everything I've ever seen."

"I felt the same way the first time I saw it. I came across a government paleontologist about eight years ago, and he—"

"What's that?" Eve interrupted.

"A paleontologist?"

She nodded.

"It's a four-dollar word for a man who hunts bones so old, they've turned to stone."

Eve made a sound of disbelief. "A stone bone?"

"It's called a fossil."

"Where do the bones come from?"

"Animals that lived a long, long, long time ago."

A vague memory came to Eve, left over from a

time when she had attended the orphanage school.

"Like the 'terrible lizards'?" she asked.

Reno looked surprised. "Yes."

Eve put her chin back on her knees.

"I thought the older kids were teasing me, but one of them showed me a photograph in a book," she said dreamily. "It was a skeleton of a lizard standing on its hind legs. It was taller than a church steeple. I wanted to read the book, but somebody stole it before I could."

"I've got the same book back at Willy and Cal's ranch," Reno said, "along with about fifty others."

"Do any of them tell you how that happened?" Eve asked, gesturing toward the stone maze far below.

"Ever see a river undercut its bank until the bank topples, making a new shape to the river?"

"Sure. Floods do it even faster."

"Think how it would look if the river cut through stone rather than dirt, and every tributary creek and stream cut through stone, and stone banks slowly were worn away, widening all the ravines more and more. . . ."

"Is that what happened here?"

Reno nodded.

"It must have taken a long time," Eve said.

"Longer than anyone but God can imagine," he said simply.

Into the silence came the slow exhalation of a wind that had touched nothing but time, distance, and stone.

"Somewhere out there lie the bones of animals so strange, they can scarcely be believed," Reno said. "Out there are sand dunes turned to rock, and with them the tracks of animals that died a thousand thousand years before anything like man ever lived."

"Eden," Eve whispered. "Or Hades."

"What?"

"I can't decide if this is a demanding kind of paradise or a seductive kind of hell," she said.

Reno smiled strangely. "Let me know when you decide. I've often wrestled with that question myself."

In silence they watched patterns of light and darkness shift and re-form until the distant mesas looked like stone ships anchored in a shadow sea.

"It's so unbelievable...." Eve's voice faded into silence.

"It's no stranger than men building a boat that carries four people and goes *under* water."

Eve gave Reno a startled look, but before she could say anything, he was talking again.

"It's no stranger than the New Madrid earthquake that changed the course of the Mississippi," he said. "It's no stranger than Mount Tambora blowing its top and bringing the Year Without a Summer to Britain."

"What?" she asked.

"It's true. Byron even wrote a poem about it," Reno said.

"Good Lord. If one little volcano was worth a poem, what would he have written about this?" she demanded, gesturing to the view in front of her.

Reno smiled wryly. "I don't know, but I would have enjoyed reading it."

The smile faded from Reno's face as he said, "The world is all of a piece, all connected. It's big, but it's still only one place. Someday Rafe will figure it out and stop roaming."

"And until then?"

"Rafe will be like the wind, alive only when he's moving."

"What about you?" Eve asked softly.

"I'll be what I've always been, a man who puts his faith in the only thing that's as valuable as it is incorruptible . . . tears of the sun god, the transcendent brought down to earth, the one thing that a man can count on in life. Gold."

There was a long silence while Eve looked out on the land with eyes that would rather have cried. She should have expected Reno to say nothing else, but the depth of her pain told her that she had.

She had been seduced by passion and love. The passion had been returned to her redoubled.

The love had not.

Becoming Reno's woman had changed the world for Eve. But not for him. He still had only one Golden Rule:

You can't count on women, but you can count on gold.

Reno stood and held out his hand to Eve. He pulled her to her feet with an ease that made her wonder if he ever grew tired, ever felt he couldn't take one more step, ever knew hunger or cold or sleeplessness.

"Time to go, sugar girl."

"We're not camping here?"

"No. The shaman was right about the trail. It's so easy, we can do it by moonlight."

As Reno walked back to the horses, Eve looked out over the beautiful, enigmatic maze once more.

"Ships of stone," she whispered. "Why can't Reno see you?"

17

EVEN after the moon set, the
stars burned in such radiant profusion that ghostly
shadows formed. Though as sheer as a veil, the
shadows were nonetheless real.

Unhappily Eve concluded that, no matter how
vague, starlight wasn't exempt from Reno's list of
impossible demands.

*A stone ship, a dry rain, and a light that casts no
shadow.*

She might have found an armada of stone ships,
but the dry rain was as unattainable as ever. The
shadowless light was also beyond her reach.

One of the hobbled horses snorted, disturbing
Eve's gloomy thoughts. She turned in her bedroll,
blaming her sleeplessness on the hard ground
rather than on her depressing reflections.

But the ground wasn't any harder than it had
ever been. Turning over didn't make her more
comfortable. It simply gave her a better view over
the ashes of the campfire.

Reno's powerful, broad-shouldered silhouette was looming unmistakably against the stars. His bare chest and feet were a lighter shade of darkness. Obviously he was ready for bed but not ready for sleep.

Reno was standing quietly, watching Eve rather than the slow wheeling of the stars overhead. She wondered where he had been, and why he had told her to go to sleep when he walked out of camp alone, and if he knew she was awake now.

Then he spoke to her, answering one question; he knew she was awake.

"Can't sleep?" Reno asked in a low voice.

"No," Eve admitted.

He walked over and sat on his heels next to her bedroll.

"Know why?" he asked.

She shook her head and asked, "Can't you sleep?"

"No."

"Know why?" she asked, echoing him.

Reno's smile flashed faintly in the starlight.

"Yes," he said.

"Are you worried about Slater?"

"I ought to be."

"But you aren't?" Eve persisted.

"Not enough to keep me awake."

"Then why aren't you sleeping?"

"You."

Eve propped herself up on her elbow and stared at the darkness and thin starlight that hid as much as they revealed of Reno's expression.

"Am I that noisy when I roll over?" she asked wryly.

He laughed. "No. You're as graceful and quiet as a cat."

Eve waited, watching him with eyes that

gleamed in the dim light.

"But every time you move," Reno continued, "I get to thinking how warm you are under the blankets, and how much I'd like to be lying beside you, touching all that sweet warmth."

"I thought you didn't want..." Eve's voice faded.

"You?" Reno asked.

"Yes," she whispered. "You hardly even looked at me while we made camp."

"I didn't dare. I wanted you too much."

"Why does that make you angry? Do you think I'll refuse you?"

Reno let out his breath in a stifled curse.

"I haven't been like this since I was a boy," he said roughly. "I don't like it one damn bit."

"I'm not teasing you. I lov—" Eve corrected herself instantly, "I *want* you too much to be a good tease."

She held the blankets aside in silent invitation.

"You're tired, and so am I," Reno said in a curt voice. "Tomorrow is going to be another long day. I should have enough self-control not to bother you."

"I want you," she repeated.

"Eve," Reno whispered, trying and failing to control the wild rush of heat that had taken him at her words.

With an almost soundless groan of hunger and need, he knelt and then stretched out next to Eve beneath the blankets. She felt the fine trembling of his hands on her face and was amazed that she could affect his strength so much.

"I don't want to hurt you," he said hoarsely. "I want you so damn much, and you were so tight. . . ."

"It's all right."

Eve moved her head, kissing both of Reno's hands in turn while he breathed her name into the fragrant warmth of her hair.

"It's all right," she repeated with each brush of her lips over his skin. "I want to be a part of you again."

"Sugar girl," he whispered. "Sweet and hot."

He discovered within the yielding luxury of her mouth a feminine hunger and demand that raced through his blood and brain like straight whiskey. The kiss began gently but quickly changed, becoming a hungry, searching prelude to the deeper joining that would soon come.

Reno tried to rein in the wild need that had been eating at him since he had first tasted Eve in the liquid embrace of the pool, but control kept sliding away from him. He took the velvet heat of her mouth with deep, repeated movements of his tongue, probing and stroking, wanting her with a violence that was like nothing he had ever known before.

When Reno finally forced himself to end the kiss, he was wholly, painfully aroused. He braced himself on his elbow and closed his eyes, fighting for control.

It was impossible. Every breath he took was infused with the delicious scent of lilac and a woman's secret warmth.

"Reno?"

The huskiness in Eve's voice was another caress, making him want to groan. He touched her cheek with fingers that weren't entirely steady.

"I hope you want me half as much as that kiss suggested," he said in a low voice.

Eve took his hand and slowly moved it down to her breasts. Reno's breath broke when he felt the nipple changing at his touch, becoming a tight velvet peak in a single rushing instant.

"I wish it were full sunlight," he said.

"Why?"

Instead of answering, Reno bent and caught the tip of Eve's breast between his lips, then took her deep into his mouth, pulling on her with hot, shifting pressures.

She made a throaty sound as her back arched in passionate reflex. His hands slid beneath her, holding her while he fed on the sweet flesh she had offered him. Her breasts were seduced and shaped by his mouth until they were full, flushed, and crowned by nipples that stood up hungrily against the sheer camisole.

Reno raised his head and looked at the proof of Eve's desire. The sight did nothing to cool the savage hunger of his body.

"That's why I wish it were sunlight," he said huskily. "I want to see the pink buds swelling on top of your breasts."

He laughed softly when he felt the wave of heat climb tangibly up Eve's body at his words.

"And the sweet blush that comes when I talk about what I'm doing to you," Reno said. "I'd like to see that, too."

Eve made a sound that was half laughter, half embarrassment. Smiling, he bent down and took between his teeth one of the laces that tied her camisole. With small motions of his head, he tugged until the bow came undone.

"Take off your clothes, sugar girl."

Reno felt the tremor that went through Eve as clearly as she did.

"I could do it," he coaxed softly, "but then I'd have to let go of you. I don't want to do that. You feel too damn good right where you are."

He flexed his hands and tightened his arms,

deepening the arch of Eve's back until her nipples just brushed against his mustache. His smile was a lighter shade of night as he watched her shiver and twist restlessly, seeking a deeper caress.

"*Gata*," Reno said thickly. "All supple and graceful. Undress for me. Want me as much as I want you."

Eve's fingers were clumsy as she undid the camisole. But even when wholly unfastened, the cloth didn't slide free of her body. Damp from his mouth, the cotton clung to the hard nipples Reno had drawn from her breasts.

Hesitantly Eve peeled the thin fabric from her body. While she did, Reno kissed her breasts, her throat, her lips, taking tiny bites of her in between each nuzzling caress. He shifted just enough to allow her to get free of the camisole, but he never released her completely.

Soon the camisole lay beside the bedroll like a pale reflection of starlight.

"Keep going," Reno whispered. "This time I want you to be completely naked."

With shaking fingers, Eve undid her pantalets and pushed them slowly down her legs until she was as Reno wanted her, completely naked. Her skin glowed like the creamy petals of a night-blooming flower.

"Yes," Reno whispered. "Like that. You're beautiful. You should always be as God made you."

He drew his mustache across Eve's breasts as he lowered her back to the warm blankets. She shivered and bit back a cry of pleasure as heat shimmered through her in the wake of his caress. When the tip of his tongue fenced with her taut nipples, she twisted again, harder, wanting more than his teasing.

Reno gave Eve what she asked for, his mouth

both caressing and demanding, his hand sliding down her body, seeking the sultry, delicate flesh that lay concealed between her legs. When he found her and touched her once, very lightly, she cried out.

Instantly Reno withdrew, for the memory of making Eve bleed haunted him. He clenched his teeth against the pain of wanting her and not having her.

"I'm sorry," Reno said, sitting up. "I never meant to hurt you."

"You didn't."

"You cried out."

Eve touched his chest with fingers that trembled.

"Did I?" she asked huskily.

"Yes. Did I hurt you?"

"Hurt?" She shivered. "No."

The masculine textures of muscle and hair lured Eve. She stroked Reno, liking the feel of him beneath her palm.

"Lie next to me again," she whispered. "You make me too dizzy to sit up. Especially when you touch me like you just did. If I cried out, it was because your touch took the world away."

Reno's eyes narrowed against the sudden clenching of desire deep in his loins, a knife turning, bringing pain.

"You aren't tender?" Reno asked.

As he spoke, he touched the thicket of hair that shielded Eve's hidden warmth. Her breath came in brokenly, soft echo of the tongues of fire licking up at his touch.

"Sugar girl? Talk to me. Are you sore?"

"No. I ache, but it's not..." Eve's voice faded. "That is, it isn't..."

"Isn't what?"

"I..." She took a ragged breath. "I can't...I

don't know how . . . to say it."

"Embarrassed?" Reno asked gently.

She nodded.

"Try to tell me," he coaxed. "I want to know if I do anything that hurts you."

"How could you?" she muttered. "You're not doing anything at all."

Reno's soft laughter was a rush of warmth across Eve's breasts as he bent down to her. When he kissed the hardened tips, they tightened even more.

Sensual lightning went from Eve's nipples to the pit of her stomach and beyond. In the wake of lightning came a twisting need that was close to pain.

"I ache, but not from what you've done," Eve said, biting back a moan. "I ache from what you *haven't* done."

"Are you sure?"

"Yes!"

Still Reno hesitated, remembering the bright blood and the terrible realization that he had taken a virgin too hard, too fast, tearing the very flesh that gave him such pleasure.

With great care he stroked Eve, smoothing over the tawny cloud that looked dark in the starlight. He heard the hesitation in her breath, the break, the ragged sigh as his fingertips sought and found the soft, warm petals.

"Do you like that?" Reno whispered.

A small, throaty cry was her answer.

He brushed his fingertips over her thighs, pressing lightly. Her legs shifted until they no longer protected her from a more intimate caress. When he traced the shadowed crease between her legs, he felt her pleasure as a hot kiss over his fingertips. The heady fragrance of her response sank into him like sweet talons, raking him into an arousal that was pain and pleasure savagely combined.

Before Reno realized what he was doing, he had unfastened his pants. When he realized how close he was to taking Eve, he rolled away and surged to his feet in a single movement.

Fists clenched at his side, he breathed hard and fast, as though he had run for miles to get where he was. He looked down at the girl lying at his feet, watching him with night-darkened eyes. The quick rise and fall of her breasts with each breath she took made him want to tear off his few clothes and bury himself in her.

The violence of Reno's need was greater now than it had been when he first took Eve. The knowledge shocked him. He shouldn't want her that much. He had sworn never to want a woman that much again.

"Reno?" Eve whispered.

"I'm afraid of hurting you," he said roughly. "I want you too damn much."

She held out her arms.

"Eve . . . damn it . . . you don't know what you're doing!"

Yet Reno's hands stripped away his clothes even as his mind told him to leave Eve alone until he was less aroused, more certain of his own control.

Through half-lowered eyelids, Eve watched Reno undress. His body gleamed with heat. Power rippled darkly beneath his skin each time he moved. When he peeled away the last of his clothing, the evidence of his arousal stood out boldly.

"Finally afraid?" Reno asked, his voice rough.

She shook her head.

"You should be," he said flatly. "I've never wanted a woman like this."

Eve's only answer was a sinuous movement of

her body. Her hips lifted in silent plea.

Slowly Reno knelt between her legs.

"You don't know..." he said, but he couldn't finish.

"Then teach me," she whispered.

With a word that was both profane and reverent, Reno reached for Eve. He forced himself to move slowly despite the hammering of his own blood. The back of his hands caressed her from ankle to inner thigh, sensitizing her skin and parting her legs even more. He tried to resist the scented temptation that opened to him, but he could not prevent himself from stroking her just once.

Eve was softer than silk, hotter, and she trembled at his touch. Reno eased his fingertip between the sleek petals. A fragrant, searing rain licked over him as he slid into her.

Slowly Reno withdrew, knowing that he was shaking and knowing there wasn't a damn thing he could do about it. He hadn't expected her to be so ready to take him, so hungry for the coupling that had hurt her before.

"I'll try to be gentle," Reno said through clenched teeth.

"I know," Eve whispered. "But don't try too hard. Cats have more than one life."

He smiled despite the sweat sliding down his spine from the fierce tension of his body.

"You'll be the death of me, *gata*." Then, his voice harsh, he added, "Help me."

"How?"

"Bring your knees up."

Long legs shifted.

"Higher. Yes, like that. God," Reno said heavily, "I wish I could see you."

Eve made a stifled sound as she felt his fingertips trace every part of the night-blooming flower that was fully revealed to him. It was as though he wanted to memorize with touch what he couldn't clearly see.

Delicately Reno tested the satin nub he had found hidden within her petals.

Eve's breath came in with a husky sound that could have been pleasure or pain.

"Talk to me," Reno said. "Tell me if I hurt you."

He circled the sensitive knot with his fingertips before he caught it and plucked gently.

Eve stiffened as though he had taken a whip to her.

"Eve?"

She couldn't answer. Pleasure raced through her body from Reno's touch, making it impossible to think or speak. A broken breath, a stifled moan, and a scented rain were the only answer she could give him.

It was enough. It told Reno that Eve wanted him as profoundly as he wanted her.

He pressed lightly into her again for the sheer pleasure of feeling how much she hungered for what he could give her. The hot rush of her response clung to him, shimmering in the vague light, making him dizzy with the answering surge of his own blood. He shifted, bringing his aroused flesh very close to her, pushing lightly, testing her ability to take him.

The testing was also a caress. Eve made a sound of wonder as pleasure rippled through her. Sensual heat licked over Reno's violently aroused flesh, dragging a ragged groan from him. His hips moved reflexively, pushing between hot petals, seeking an even deeper joining.

Eve's eyes opened as the pressure between her legs intensified, Reno's body slowly stretching her with a gentle, measured movement that was at odds with the harsh lines of his face.

"Tell me," he said hoarsely.

Reno wanted to say more, but he couldn't. He was feeling Eve too intensely, sleek heat and sultry rain and a loving glide of flesh over flesh. She was feeling him in the same way, her eyes heavy-lidded, watching him as he took her and gave himself to her in the same deliberate movement.

Never had Reno known such a sensual merging of body with body, heat with heat, breath with breath. There was no barrier, no cry of pain, no sudden attempt by Eve's body to reject him.

She gave way before him like a summer storm, luring and surrounding him as he pressed into her hot center. No matter how deeply he probed, there was only liquid heat and a satin constriction caressing him in secret, teaching him what it meant to be fully, passionately joined with a woman.

The hot perfection of sheathing himself so slowly within her nearly undid him. Blood hammered through his veins, filling him until thought he must burst or die.

"Eve..."

Reno's voice was ragged, all but throttled by the wild race of his blood.

Eve heard him and knew that he was trying to ask if he was hurting her. She would have answered, but the slow, heavy penetration was transforming her.

Rings of fire pulsed up from the point where her body joined his. The tiny, secret convulsions brought a pleasure so great she could only give herself to it and to the man who was so deeply a part of her that he felt each silky pulse distinctly. And with each pulse came a sensual rain that eased his way even more, luring and welcoming and caressing him profoundly.

Reno felt his control being stripped away by the sweet rhythms of Eve's pleasure. He measured himself once within her, then twice, before the firestorm within him burst. He arched into her welcoming heat and gave himself to her in a shuddering rush that left him spent.

The weight of Reno's body against Eve's sent another wave of passion through her. She made a sound deep in her throat and twisted against him as her body was impaled by a shaft of ecstasy.

The sinuous, gliding pressure of Eve over his buried flesh sent tongues of fire licking sharply through Reno. He moved slowly within her and savored her shimmering response.

Watching her, he moved again, enjoying her throaty cries and the melting of her body around him. He had never known a woman to enjoy so clearly his presence within her. He had never guessed how much satisfaction there could be in watching his smallest motion transformed into sensual feminine pulses and a silent, sinuous pleading for more of him.

Nor had he known what his own body was capable of, the rushing transformation repeated, sweet needles of fire pricking delicately, deeply, until he was consumed by a need that was all the sweeter for having been ignited while he was fully sheathed within her.

"I hope you're right about having lots of lives, *gata.*"

Eve's lashes lifted, showing eyes that were still glazed with pleasure.

"What?" she asked huskily.

Her voice broke before the question was finished, for Reno was moving slowly within her, filling her.

"Do you like this?" he asked, withdrawing and returning once more.

"Dear Lord, yes."

"It doesn't hurt?"

Soft laughter was Eve's answer. Her hands caressed the length of Reno's spine. She paused to comb through the scattering of silky hair in the small of his back before she went on to his buttocks. The taut muscles intrigued her, as did the swift, ripping breath he took when her hand strayed between his thighs. She repeated the caress, drawing another shudder from him.

"No more of that," Reno said, dragging Eve's hand back to his flank.

"Don't you like it?"

"Too damn much," he admitted. "Save it for next time."

"Next time?"

"Yes, *gata*. Next time. I may need it then. I sure don't need it now."

"I don't understand."

Reno moved again within Eve, caressing and stretching her in the same motion.

"If I get any harder," he said, "it will be over too soon. I want this one to last a long, long time."

"Oh."

He bent down and put his cheek next to hers. The heat of her skin amazed him.

"Are you blushing?" he asked.

Eve buried her face in his neck and hit his shoulder lightly with her fist.

"How anyone can be so abandoned and yet so shy..." Reno's voice faded into a soft laugh. "Never mind. You'll get over it."

A muffled comment told him that she doubted it.

"Look at me, sugar girl."

When she shook her head, he gently pried her face from his neck.

"Shy little night-blooming flower," Reno said, dropping tiny kisses over Eve's hot face. "If you knew how rare you were, you wouldn't blush."

He saw the narrow gleam of Eve's eyes as she peeked through her lashes at him.

"And you are rare," he breathed against her lips.

"I'm just a . . ."

Whatever Eve was going to say was lost in the slow penetration of his tongue until he filled her mouth just as he filled her body. The tiny, throaty cry she gave affected him the way a burning match affects dry straw. He retreated and returned with exquisite control from her body, measuring both of them simultaneously, intimately. Then he withdrew again.

With a ragged sound that was Reno's name, Eve moved her hips, trying to reclaim him.

"You make me feel like the man who first discovered fire," Reno said in a low voice, watching her.

He rocked slowly against her, leaving none of her untouched, moving with the deliberate rhythms of a storm that has eternity to gather and break.

"Hurt?" he asked softly.

Her answer was a rippling sigh of pleasure.

"Tell me if I hurt you," Reno said.

Smoothly he shifted, sliding his arms beneath her knees, bending and lifting her legs, pressing them gently back against her body, moving in slow motion, joining them more deeply than she would have believed possible.

"Eve?" he whispered.

"Dear God," she said, shivering with pleasure.

As Reno moved, a hot, gentle vise closed around

Eve, a burning so soft she knew it only in after-thought. A long, sweet shimmering began to steal through her, making her want to laugh and cry at the same time.

Reno withdrew, taking the sensual pressure with him.

"No," Eve said.

"I thought I was hurting you."

"Only when you left."

She made a low, ragged sound as Reno slowly returned, rocked against her, then retreated as deliberately as he had taken her. The ghostly shimmering returned, delicate currents of fire claiming her softly.

"I think . . ." Eve whispered.

He moved again, and flames licked gently, stealing her voice.

"What do you think?" he asked.

"I think . . . a woman . . . discovered fire," Eve said. "With you . . ."

Tender fire leaped, consuming her.

Reno heard the echoes of ecstasy in Eve's voice, felt it in the rhythmic shivering of her body, and wanted to shout his triumph at the stars.

But he had no breath to shout, for the flames that he had nurtured in her were spreading outward, licking over him in the silken rhythms of her release. He held himself utterly still, fighting against the need to join her. He didn't want that yet, not before he had plumbed the depths of her ability to respond to him.

The lure of Eve's body was too great to withstand. When she twisted slowly, repeatedly, against him, Reno felt the world unravel in a series of soft explosions. With her name breaking on his lips, he came undone a single heartbeat at a time, giving himself to her in a long, rippling current of fire.

Eve's breath caught and sighed out in wonder as she held Reno, savoring the gentle shuddering of his body. For long, sweet minutes, her slender fingers caressed his back and shoulders. The breadth and power of him were obvious even now, when he lay with his head between her breasts, breathing slowly, utterly relaxed.

Smiling, Eve stroked Reno's back with slow sweeps of her hands, savoring the strength of him and the knowledge that she had never been so close to anyone.

It was more than the fact of their interlocked bodies. She loved Reno as she had never loved anyone in her life.

Eve didn't know she had spoken her thoughts aloud until Reno lifted his head and turned it from side to side, stroking her breasts with his cheek as he spoke.

"Love is an illusion, sugar girl," he said. "But passion isn't."

She felt the slow drawing of Reno's tongue over her nipples. With each delicious movement, his body stirred within her, redoubling the effect of his caresses. An answering heat splintered through her, making her breath break audibly.

Reno heard Eve's response and felt it in the swift rise of her breasts. His laughter was velvety, dark, exultant.

"Passion is very real," he said, biting delicately at Eve's taut nipples. "We're good together, you and I. Hell, we're better than good. There's no word for what we have when we're like this."

"What do you mean?" she whispered.

"Little innocent," Reno murmured, drinking the tender shivering of her flesh as his teeth raked lightly. "You don't even know, do you?"

"What?"

"This."

His hips moved and he drove into her as though he would fuse their bodies into a single seamless whole. A throttled cry and an urgent twisting of her hips answered him. Laughing with sheer pleasure, he twisted against her in turn and listened to his name come from her lips in a rush.

"Yes," Reno said. "It's me. Again. But don't blame me, *gata*. I've never been like this before in my life."

Another twist, another cry, another sultry wave melting through Eve to lick over Reno, fueling his passionate fire, driving him higher, urging him to drive her higher as well.

Reno moved heavily, sparing Eve nothing of his power. Nor did she ask for less. She moved in urgent counterpoint, meeting strength with fluid grace, hunger with desire, fire with searing fire.

When sweat misted her skin, he bent his head and licked salty drops, bit flesh that strained to become part of him. He seduced her breasts with his teeth and tongue, demanding and receiving a hard bud from each while his hips moved relentlessly, demanding a different kind of flowering.

His hand slid down between their slick, hot bodies until he found the satin bud. He circled, pressed, raked with shattering delicacy.

"What are you . . ." Eve said brokenly. "Dear God . . . *Reno*."

Pleasure burst in her with the force of a blow, arching her body as fierce currents swept through her, driving her even higher.

Reno held Eve wild and shivering while he moved over and within her relentlessly, riding the fierce passion he had called from her. He punctuated each heavy thrust with a savagely restrained caress that demanded everything of her, plucking at the delicate bud until it began to flower one dark petal at a time.

Eve cried out as her body experienced an ecstasy that had no beginning and no end, shattering her, transforming her. If there had been room in her for fear, she would have been terrified; but there was room only for Reno's driving body and the dark words of desire and demand he poured over her.

She cried out in abandon, sinking her nails heedlessly into his back as she arched like a drawn bow, succumbing to the sweet violence he had called from her.

Reno's smile was as untamed as Eve's cries. He held himself utterly motionless, absorbing her violent trembling into his strength. When she was still once more, he bent his head, drew his teeth over her shoulder in a fierce caress, and began moving inside her again.

Eve gasped as passion ravished her body once more.

"Reno."

"I warned you," he said in a low voice. "Until we can't even lick our lips."

Reno moved powerfully, pulling the night down around them like a cloak of black fire.

And like fire, they burned.

18

THE jumbled waste of rock, sand, and tough shrubs looked like it went on forever in all directions, but Reno knew it didn't. It was simply another wide step down in the long descent from the Rockies to the place more than a hundred miles to the west, where the mysterious, powerful Rio Colorado coiled invisibly between stone banks.

If it weren't for Slater hovering on the horizon like a vulture, I'd be happy to camp by fresh water and not move for a few weeks.

Or months.

Reno smiled wryly at his own thoughts. For the first time in his life, he was in no real hurry to find Spanish treasure. He was having too much pleasure in other explorations, charting the undiscovered territory of a dual sensuality that was both savage and sublime, violent and tender, demanding and renewing. He didn't want it to end until both of them had drunk the dark wine to the last heady drop.

Until we find the mine, you'll be my woman whenever I want you, however I want you.

Eve had kept her end of the bargain with a generosity that was as unexpected and consuming as the sweet violence of their joined bodies. The thought of never again reaching for her in the darkness was unsettling to Reno. Whenever the thought came, he pushed it away.

Sufficient unto each day the troubles thereof.

The old advice echoed in the silence of Reno's mind. He had no argument with it. He had enough troubles for this or any other day.

By now, word of the presence of a man and a woman riding along the edges of the stone maze would have gone out along the mysterious, efficient grapevine that existed throughout the West wherever strangers met at a water hole or crossroads, or shared a cup of coffee over a tiny campfire.

Hope Rafe hasn't forgotten all the old signs we used to leave each other when we hunted as boys.

And I hope Wolfe hears I'm out here with a woman looking for gold. He knows the country. He'll know I need a good man at my back if I find the mine.

Damn Slater and his hawk-eyed half-breed tracker. Anybody else would have given up a week ago.

By the end of the following day, Reno and Eve were camped at the base of a red sandstone formation that rose against the sky like a sail hewn from a single piece of stone. High up on the side of the cliff, rock had weathered away more quickly than in other parts of the formation. The result was a window set like a gem in the solid rock wall. A shaft of light from the setting sun speared through the opening, gilding everything it touched with deepest gold.

Yet even more astonishing than a window in stone was the muted murmur of fresh water nearby. They had climbed out of the stone maze and were riding once more through a landscape where mountains were close enough to make out individual peaks. The camp they made was between a series of sunny river bends.

Reno had been right about Eve's reaction to water after having ridden through a rock desert. The first time she saw a trickle of water twisting through the center of an arid valley, she talked excitedly about riding next to a "river" again. Reno had teased her about it, but he hadn't objected when she asked to camp at the point where the small stream spread out into a series of sun-warmed pools bordered by whispering cottonwood trees.

At sunset and dawn, the land looked like an illustration for a mythic tale from a book men had forgotten how to read. It made Eve wonder if she had stumbled into an enchanted land where time stood still.

"It looks like it's been here forever," Eve said.

Reno followed her glance to the golden window time had carved from stone.

"Nothing lasts forever," he said. "Not even rock."

Eve looked at Reno, then back to the sail of stone rising improbably against the endless sky.

"It looks like it does," she said softly.

"Looks don't count for much. That window gets a bit bigger each day as grain after grain of the sandstone is chiseled out by the wind," Reno said.

Eve listened, and sensed what lay beneath the

words, change coming whether it was wanted or not.

"Someday that little window could be a full-blown arch," Reno said. "Then the arch will get worn thin over time until it collapses, leaving a notch behind in the rock wall. Then the notch will be cut deeper and wider by wind and rain, until finally nothing is left but red rubble and blue sky."

Eve shivered again. "I can't imagine this land worn down like that."

"That's where the sandstone came from in the first place," Reno said, looking at the soaring red wall. "Mountains that were worn down a grain at a time and piled by the wind into ancient dunes or washed down to seas so old even God has forgotten them."

The quality of Reno's voice drew Eve's eyes from the fantastic rock formations. Motionless, she watched him as he watched the land and spoke calmly of unimaginable eons passing into eternity.

"Then the sand became stone again," he said, "and the earth shifted and new mountains were lifted to the sky to be worn down by new winds, new storms, new rivers running down to new seas."

"'Ashes to ashes, dust to dust...'" Eve whispered.

"It's the way of the world, sugar girl. Beginnings and endings all tangled together, like the pictographs on a canyon wall, Indian and Spanish and us, different symbols, different people, different times."

Slowly Eve looked back to the red stone that seemed so massive and enduring. Then she faced the man who refused to acknowledge that anything endured, even stone.

Or love.

As Reno and Eve followed the old Spanish trail, each valley or basin they rode through had more water and less rock than the previous one. The climb was so gradual that it was understood only at rare vistas where men could look back down toward the stone maze.

Slowly sagebrush gave way to piñon forests, and piñon gave way to pine. Red cliffs sank back down below the surface of the earth as sandstone gave way to different layers of rock that had come from deep beneath the surface of the earth, where heat transformed sandstone into quartzite, and limestone into marble.

Only one thing didn't change. Each time Reno looked out over the back trail, there was a thin veil of dust miles and miles behind them.

"Somebody is still dogging us," Reno said, putting away the spyglass.

"Slater?" Eve asked unhappily.

"They're raising a lot of dust, so it's either Slater's men or an Indian raiding party."

"Some choice," Eve muttered.

Reno shrugged. "On the whole, I'm thinking it's Slater. We don't have anything Indians want enough to spend two days following us to get."

"Are we going to try to lose him?"

"No time," Reno said bluntly. "See those yellow patches high on the mountainsides?"

Eve nodded.

"Aspens are turning," he said. "I'll bet those clouds we're looking at will leave a dusting of snow in the high country tonight."

"How long do we have before everything gets snowed in?"

"Only God knows. Some years the high country closes the first week in September."

A startled sound escaped Eve. "But it's that late now!"

"And other years it can be open clear up to Thanksgiving, or even later," Reno added.

Eve made a relieved sound. "Then we're all right."

"Don't count on it. A storm can blow up and drop snow chest-high to a Montana horse in one night."

Silently Eve remembered the warnings in the journal about the short summers and long, brutal winters in the country around the mine. Don Lyon had speculated that if the Indians hadn't killed his ancestors, the mountains had.

"Those mountains won't give up their gold easily," Reno continued, as though following Eve's thoughts.

"If mining gold were easy, someone else would have cleaned out the Lyons' mine long ago," she pointed out.

Reno stood in the stirrups, looking out across their back trail again.

"Why is Slater hanging back?" Eve asked.

"I suspect old Jericho's greed finally got the better of his lust for vengeance," Reno said dryly.

"What do you mean?"

"He didn't think much of the notion that the journal led to a real gold mine."

"Raleigh King did."

"Raleigh King was a braggart, a bully, and a fool. Whatever he believed wouldn't mean spit to Jericho. But about the time we cut Spanish sign along the trail, Jericho must have begun thinking."

"About gold," Eve said glumly.

Reno nodded. "But he can't read the signs. We can. He can't find the mine. We can."

She looked unhappily over their back trail.

"And even if his Comancheros can read the sign," Reno continued, "I'll bet Jericho got to thinking about how much plain hard work gold mining is."

"It didn't make him give up."

"No. He's just going to wait for us to find the mine and get a bunch of gold together," Reno said. "Then he's going to come down on us like a blue norther'."

Silence followed Reno's calm words.

Finally Eve asked faintly, "What are we going to do?"

"Find the mine and the gold and hope to God above that Cal or Wolfe or Rafe gets wind of Slater before he gets impatient and kills us, and to hell with the gold."

"What good would Caleb or one of the others be? It would still be three of us against however many Slater has."

"He's got at least two men scouting us, and the rest are raising enough dust for an even dozen. And the longer he's on the trail, the more the word goes out. But he's replaced the men he lost in that ambush three times over."

"Do you think there's much chance of Caleb following us?"

"More chance than there is of us finding Spanish gold," Reno said succinctly.

"How will he know where we are?" Eve asked.

"News travels fast in a wild land, and Cal is a listening kind of man."

"Then Slater could know about other people following us, too."

"He could," Reno agreed.

"You don't sound worried."

"Cal isn't hunting me with death on his mind," Reno said. "Slater knows Cal as the Man from

Yuma. He'll be real unhappy about having Cal on his trail. Cal, Wolfe, and I caught Jericho's twin brother in a cross fire. What happened to Jed would have been a lesson to a man smarter or less mean than Jericho Slater.''

Two days later, Eve was still watching the back trail as often as the way ahead. Hand shading her eyes beneath her hat brim, she stood in the stirrups and she looked out over the way she and Reno had come.

She thought she saw a thickening in the air way back where the Abajos began rising from the last broad step up from the stone maze, but it was hard to be certain. In the dry air, it was possible to see eighty or a hundred miles. At that distance, things smaller than mountains and mesas tended to flow together in a muted rainbow blur.

The slight haze she thought she saw could have been caused by a group of wild horses that had been startled by something and had galloped off, leaving a cloud of dust to rise behind.

The vague darkening in the air could also have been caused by wind blowing up dust, but it was beneath one of the blue-black clumps of cloud that were marching over the land. Dust and rain didn't seem a likely combination.

It could have been simply a trick played on her by eyes tired from straining forever into the distance, seeking something that might or might not be there.

Or it could be Slater and his gang, dogging Reno and Eve's trail with unnerving patience.

Eve turned away from her scrutiny of the back trail.

She felt a distinct thrill of pleasure as she watched Reno ride closer. He called her *gata*, but

he was the one who moved with feline quickness
and grace in everything he did.

Even before Reno spoke, Eve sensed his buried
excitement in the way he held himself. It was a
difference few people would have noticed, but she
had come to know him very well during the long
days and passionate nights on the trail.

"What did you find?" Eve asked before Reno
could speak.

"What makes you think I found anything?" he
asked, reining in alongside her.

"Don't tease," she said eagerly. "What is it?"

Smiling, Reno reached back into a saddlebag.
When his hand emerged again, he was holding a
piece of curved wood wrapped in rawhide that was
cracked with age and dryness, and bleached nearly
white by the sun.

Eve looked at the junk lying on Reno's palm.
Then she looked at him, perplexed by his excitement.

Smiling, he hooked his arm around her neck,
pulling her close for a brief, hard kiss before he
released her once more and explained.

"It's a piece of stirrup," Reno said. "The Spanish
didn't always use iron stirrups. This one was
carved from a hardwood tree that grew half a world
away from here."

Hesitantly Eve touched the fragment of stirrup.
When her fingertips brushed the smooth, weath-
ered wood, she felt a spectral chill down her spine.
Awe and curiosity rippled through her.

"I wonder if the man who used this was a priest
or a soldier," Eve said. "Was his name Sosa or
Leon? Did he write in the journal, or did he watch
while another man wrote? Did he have a wife and
children in Spain or Mexico, or did he give himself
only to God?"

"I was thinking the same things," Reno admitted. "Makes you wonder if someone two hundred years from now will find that broken cinch ring we left next to the campfire ashes yesterday, and if they'll wonder about who rode there and when and why, and if we'll somehow know someone is thinking about us hundreds of years after we died."

Eve shivered again and withdrew her hand.

"Maybe Slater will find the cinch ring and use it for target practice," she said.

Reno's head came up sharply. "Did you see sign of him and his gang?"

"I couldn't be sure," Eve said, pointing. "It's so far back."

Standing in the stirrups, Reno stared along the back trail. After a long minute, he sat once more and looked at Eve.

"All I see in that direction are some storm clouds trying to rain," he said.

"I thought it might be the wind kicking up dust," she said, "but the clouds were right over that spot, and it looked dark almost all the way to the ground. Rain and dust don't mix."

"They do here. In the summer it's so hot and thirsty that rain from a small storm like that never reaches the ground. The drops just dry up in midair and vanish."

Eve looked back at the clouds. They were the color of slate on the bottom and cream on the top. A ragged, slanting veil of lighter gray came from the base of the little storm.

The longer she stared, the more Eve was certain that Reno was right. The veil became thinner and thinner as it approached the ground. By the time the surface of the earth was reached, there was no moisture left.

"A dry rain," Eve said wonderingly.

Reno shot her a sideways look.

When Eve realized he was staring at her, she gave him an odd, bittersweet smile.

"Don't worry, sugar man. You're safe. I've seen ships made of stone and a dry rain, but even the smallest light casts a shadow."

Before Reno could think of an answer, Eve urged her horse forward, heading deeper into the mountains, searching for the only thing the man she loved would count on.

Gold.

For two more days they followed a trail that was so old it appeared only to the half-focused eye or very late in the day, when sunlight slanted steeply and was the color of Spanish treasure. The valleys they rode through became smaller and steeper the higher they rode in the mountains. Every afternoon thunder rumbled through the mountains while first one peak and then another played host to the elemental dance of lightning. Rain came down cold and hard, running off the trees in veils of silver lace.

Between storms, aspens on the highest slopes lifted their golden torches to the indigo sky. Deer and elk were everywhere, fleet brown ghosts that withdrew before the horses. Creeks of startling purity abounded, filling shadowed ravines with the sound of running water. Only game trails were visible. There were no tracks of wild horses or man, for there was nothing on the steep slopes or in the rugged mountain canyons that couldn't be found more easily at lower elevations.

When Reno and Eve came to the last, high valley

described by both the shaman and the Spanish journal, they rode its length silently, looking all around.

There was no sign of Cristóbal Leon's lost mine.

19

"**I**T's hard to believe we aren't the first people to see this land," Eve said as they came back to the mouth of the small valley.

"Feels that way," Reno agreed, "but there's plenty of signs that men have been through here."

He reined in, hooked his right leg around the saddle horn, and lifted the spyglass again, but not to look at the meadow. Slowly he surveyed the green patchwork of forest and meadow falling away to the dry lands below, seeking any sign of the men he was certain were following them. The brass casing of the spyglass glowed in the muted light with every shift in direction.

"What signs?" Eve asked after a minute.

"See that stump at the edge of the meadow, right in front of that big spruce?"

Eve looked. "Yes."

"You get close enough and you'll see ax marks."

"Indians?" she asked.

"Spaniards."

"How can you be sure?"

"Steel ax marks, not stone."

"Indians have steel axes," Eve said.

"Not when that tree was chopped down."

"How can you tell?"

Reno lowered the spyglass and gave his attention to Eve. He had come to enjoy her curiosity and quick mind as much as he did her feline grace.

"That big spruce has roots that were shaped around the fallen log that came off that stump," Reno said. "Since the spruce has been there a long time, the log must have been there, too."

"Why would someone go to all the trouble of chopping down a tree and not take it?"

"Probably they were forced to leave by weather or Indians or news that the Spanish king had double-crossed the Jesuits and they could look forward to going home in chains." He shrugged. "Or maybe they only wanted the top of the tree to use as thatching or to make a chicken ladder for the mine."

Eve frowned. "What's a chicken ladder?"

"If I could find the damned mine, I'd probably be able to show you one," muttered Reno, putting the spyglass to work again.

"If you stopped looking over our back trail, maybe you'd find the mine," she said dryly.

With an impatient movement, Reno collapsed the spyglass and straightened in the saddle.

"There's nobody there," he said.

"I think you'd be happy about that."

"I'd be a lot happier if I knew where they were."

"At least they can't be preparing an ambush up ahead," Eve pointed out. "There's only one way into this valley."

"Which means there's only one way out."

Distant thunder rumbled from a peak that was

buried in a mound of clouds. Wind twisted through the forest like an invisible river, stirring everything within reach of its transparent currents. The air smelled of evergreens and an autumn chill sliding down from the heights, riding the crest of a golden wave of aspens.

Reno looked around with narrowed green eyes, bothered by something about the high valley that he couldn't quite define.

Yawning, Eve closed her eyes, then half opened them, enjoying the rich color of the late afternoon light and the knowledge that they would be making camp soon. Lazily she looked around, trying to guess if Reno would choose this place to camp or press on beyond the head of the valley to see if there was a way through the massed peaks.

An odd pattern of meadow growth caught Eve's attention, plants arrayed in a nearly perfect circle. She knew that natural outlines were rarely geometrical. Man, not nature, had invented formal gardens with precise curves, right angles, and hedges pruned into unlikely shapes.

The circular patch of plants lay near one of several small springs that formed the headwaters of a branch of the creek that drained the valley. Eve reined the lineback dun closer to the plants. Dismounting, she went to check the circle on foot. At its edges the ground was bedrock covered by a thin skin of soil. Yet in the circle itself, there was a profusion of plants that usually preferred richer ground.

When Reno turned to say something to Eve, he saw that she was on her hands and knees at the edge of the meadow. In the next instant he realized what had seemed wrong to him about the landscape.

Beneath the growth of grass and trees, there

were angles and arcs that suggested man had once cut, cleared, and built in the meadow.

Reno dismounted in a rush, grabbed a shovel from the outside of one of the pack saddles, and headed for Eve. She looked up as she heard him approach.

"There's something odd about this," she began.

"There sure is."

He positioned the shovel, rammed it home with his boot, and struck stone six inches down. He went to another part of the circle and then another. Each time it was the same—six inches of plants and soil, and then solid stone.

Reno walked slowly toward the center of the circle, testing the depth of the soil every few inches. When he got to the center, the shovel bit deeply but didn't find stone.

"Reno?"

He turned to Eve with a slashing grin and pure excitement dancing in his green eyes.

"You found yourself an *arrastra*, sugar girl," he said.

"Is that good?"

Reno's laughter was as bright and golden as the sunlight.

"It sure is," he said. "Next best thing to finding the mine itself."

"Really?"

He made a purring, rumbling sound of satisfaction.

"This is the center hole," Reno said, gesturing with the shovel for emphasis. "It supported the mill that dragged the stone over the ore, crushing it as fine as sand."

Before Eve could ask a question, Reno bent and began digging once more, working methodically until he had bared a section of rock.

"They worked this crusher long and hard," he said. "The millstone wore the bedrock down so much that it left a circular trough for plants to grow in once the mine was abandoned."

"What turned the millstone?" she asked. "Even with a dam, there isn't enough water in the little springs to do the job."

"No sign of a dam anywhere nearby," Reno said.

The shovel scraped against bedrock, gouging away dirt, leaving bare stone behind. Cracks and seams in the surface were marked by soil that was darker than the stone.

"They could have used horses to turn the mill," Reno continued. "But likely it was slaves. They had more of them than they had horses."

Eve rubbed her hands over her arms. Though she wore one of Reno's dark shirts over Don Lyon's old gambling shirt, she felt chilled. It was as though the very ground were infused with the cruelty of the Spaniards and the misery of the slaves.

Reno went down on one knee, used the shovel blade to ream out a crack, and made a triumphant sound.

"Quicksilver in the cracks," he said succinctly. "No doubt of it. This *arrastra* was used on metal ore."

"What?"

"The Spaniards used quicksilver on the crushed ore. The mercury stuck to the gold but not the ore itself. Then they heated the amalgam, vaporizing the quicksilver and melting the gold. Then they poured the gold into molds."

Brushing off his hands, Reno stood and stared around intently.

"What are you looking for?" Eve asked after a time.

"The mine. The Spaniards weren't stupid. They

didn't move the ore one more foot than they had to before they refined it.''

"There's supposed to be a trio of big fir trees just to the left of the mine opening when you're standing with the sun at your back at three o'clock on the third Saturday in August," Eve said eagerly.

He grunted and kept looking.

"Reno?"

"There are a lot of big fir trees growing three to a bunch no matter what time of the day or month it is," he said after a few moments.

Frowning in concentration, Eve tried to remember the other clues from the journal. She and Don had once taken turns reciting them to each other while Donna sat nearby, smiling and shaking her head at the dream of wealth that wouldn't die.

"There's a turtle carved on a gray rock fifteen paces to the right of the mine," Eve offered.

"A pace can be anywhere from two feet to three, depending on the height of the man doing the pacing. But if you want to look at every boulder for a turtle, I won't get in your way."

Eve grimaced. The little valley was carpeted with boulders of all sizes and shapes.

"A burn scar on the north side of—" she began.

"Burn scars heal," Reno interrupted. "Little trees grow into big ones. Big ones die and get blown down. Lightning starts new fires. Downed trees rot or are overgrown with brush. Landslides change the shape of the mountain."

"But—"

"Look up there," Reno said, pointing.

Eve looked and saw a pale scar on the mountain where rock and thin soil had sheered away, scouring down a ravine and finally filling it, burying whatever might have been a landmark before.

"That could have happened twenty years ago or

two hundred and twenty years ago," Reno said.
"Without evergreens or aspen growing in the scar,
it's hard to tell. Fireweed and willow or alder can
grow in a few seasons and regrow each season
forever. Landmarks that rely on plants are damn
near useless."

"Then how are we going to find the mine?" Eve
asked in dismay.

"The same way you found the *arrastra*. Look for
something out of place, and keep on looking for it
until it jumps up and slaps you in the face."

For the rest of that day and all of the next, Reno
and Eve quartered the valley like patient hounds,
crossing and recrossing the area around the overgrown *arrastra*. They found a rectangle whose out-
line had once been logs and now was little more
than a mulch in which various plants flourished.
They found bits of leather nearly petrified by long
exposure to the dry, cold mountain air.

They found no sign of the mine itself.

Eve scrambled up a rubble slope and found a
shallow alcove tucked beneath a wall of rock, protected from all but the most violent storms. With
an eye sharpened by hours of searching, she noted
that the lines of rotting wood that came out from
the alcove were too orderly to be accidental. Once
there had been a lean-to or shed extending outward.

In the farthest recess of the alcove Eve found a
pile of rubble and a crushed sack made of woven
leather strips. Nearby were the charcoal remains
of an ancient fire. Quickly she went to the ledge
and called across the meadow.

"Reno! I've found signs of men up here!"

A few minutes later Reno came up the slope like
a cat, fast and surefooted. He took in the alcove
with a swift glance that missed nothing.

Bands of different rocks made faint patterns on the walls and ceiling and floor. He ran his fingertips over the surface of the ceiling, feeling the marks men had left when they used picks and hammer stones to widen and deepen the natural alcove.

The shelter could have been a mine head, a living space, or a storage area. Near the remains of the ancient fire were pieces of crude pottery and a rotted wooden shape that might have been a spoon. That suggested a cooking fire, which suggested that men had lived in the alcove rather than mined it.

Turning to the leather sack, Reno sat on his heels and poked at the stiff leather weave. Bits of white stone were caught between pieces of leather. Frowning, he looked again at the rock that made up the alcove's walls and ceilings. No streaks of white caught his eye.

"Is it the mine head?" Eve asked when she could no longer stand the suspense.

"Could be, but it looks more like slave quarters."

"Oh."

"See this long strap attached to the *tenate?*"

"*Tenate?* What's that?"

"A sack or basket for carrying ore. See this thick strap? The padded part rested on the slave's forehead. The rest of the strap went back over his shoulders and attached to the sack."

Eve frowned. "That's an odd way to carry anything."

"It works better than you'd think," Reno said. "You lean forward and take the weight of the *tenate* on your forehead and back. That leaves your hands free for mining or climbing or balancing on the chicken ladders. You can carry a hundred pounds like that all day long."

She looked dubious.

"In fact," Reno continued, "I've carried more than that, back when I was young and foolish enough to try mining rich man's gold with a poor man's tools."

"Maybe you could carry a hundred pounds all day," Eve said wryly. "I'd be lucky to lug half that for a few hours."

Reno's mustache shifted over a quick smile, but he said no more. Instead, he sat on his heels again and began digging at the remains of the woven leather.

"What are you after?" she asked.

"Pieces of ore are still caught in the weave."

Eagerly Eve bent forward. "Really? Let me see!"

He pried out a piece of the pale, opaque quartz. Whistling softly between his teeth, he turned the fragment of ore over and over on his palm. The jagged bit of quartz was no bigger than the ball of his thumb.

"Pretty, isn't it?" Reno murmured.

"It is?" Eve asked, unimpressed.

Smiling, Reno turned and held his palm closer to Eve's eyes.

"See the bright specks mixed in with the white?" he asked.

She nodded.

"That's gold," he said.

"Oh." Eve frowned. "Goodness, it couldn't have been a very rich mine."

The disappointment in her voice made Reno laugh out loud. He tugged lightly on a stray lock of her hair.

"Sugar girl, it's a good thing you dealt a gold prospector that pat hand back in Canyon City. You could have walked right over the strike of a lifetime and not known it."

"You mean this is worth mining?" Eve asked,

flicking her fingernail against the quartz.

"It's one of the richest pieces of ore I've ever seen," Reno said simply.

Eve gave him a startled look.

"If the vein was more than a few inches thick," he said, "the Spanish priests had themselves one hell of a gold mine somewhere around here."

"Somewhere. But where?"

Thoughtfully Reno tucked the ore into his pocket, went to his saddlebags, and pulled out an odd hammer. Shaped like a small pick at one end and a squared-off hammer on the other, the tool was handy for knocking off chunks of rock to see what lay beneath the weathered surface.

Steel rang against stone as Reno raked and gouged at various points along the alcove's ceiling and walls, testing the different layers of stone. The unweathered fragments that came away were lighter in color than the surface rock, but none was as light as the fragment of ore.

Eve peered at one of the gouges Reno had abandoned.

"Look!" she said suddenly. "Gold!"

Reno didn't even pause in his hammering. He had already seen and dismissed the flecks of shiny stuff that were exciting Eve.

"Pyrite," he said. "Fool's gold."

Steel rang fiercely against stone.

"Not real gold?" she asked.

"Not real gold," he answered. "Wrong color."

"You're sure."

"It's the first thing a prospector learns."

Rock showered down like a sharp rain. Reno looked at the fresh gouges.

"Slate, through and through," he muttered.

"Is that good?"

"Only if you're building a house. Some people

fancy a roof or a floor of slate.''

"Do you?" she asked, curious.

He shook his head. "More trouble than it's worth, far as I'm concerned. Wood is easier, prettier, and smells better."

Reno went to the back of the alcove where the ceiling sloped sharply down to the rubble pile. He kicked at some of the smaller stones. They were a mixture of the same rock layers that made up the alcove itself.

Putting his fists on his hips, Reno looked at the unpromising stone layers and the equally unpromising meadow beyond the alcove. He and Eve had found all the proof anyone would need that Don Lyon's Spanish mine existed—except the mine itself. That had eluded them. Nor had Reno been able to find any promising outcroppings of rock.

And during the night, the aspens just above the head of the valley had turned gold. If he was going to find the mine this season, he would have to be quick about it.

"Now what?" Eve asked.

"Now we go over the perimeter of the meadow again. Only, this time, we'll use the Spanish needles."

CLOUDS billowed upward in seething mounds turned gold by the afternoon sun. Lightning licked delicately over the face of a distant peak while rain fell in a shining veil. Over everything, even the storm, arched a cobalt blue sky. In the sunlight the temperature was hot enough to raise a sweat. In the shade it was as cool as quicksilver rain.

Reno and Eve appreciated the shade. They had already made one circuit of the valley, to no avail. Walking and keeping the rods in contact had

proven to be exacting work. It was also oddly exhilarating, even though nothing had been found.
The intangible, eerie currents kept Eve and Reno
alert and aware of both each other and the sensuous riches of the high mountain day.

"Once more," Eve said.

Reno looked at her, sighed, and agreed.

"Once more, sugar girl. Then I'm going to try
my hand at catching trout for dinner. That way the
whole damn day won't have been wasted."

Hobbled horses grazed at the mouth of the
meadow, standing sentry even as they ate. When
Reno and Eve stepped from the lacy shadows cast
by a small stand of aspen, the lineback dun threw
up her head to test the air. She quickly recognized
their familiar scents and went back to cropping
grass.

"Ready?" Eve asked.

Reno nodded.

They moved their hands slightly. Metal notches
met. Ghostly currents flowed.

No matter how many times it happened, the tin-
gling, shimmering sensation made Eve's breath
catch. It was the same for Reno, a hesitation in
breathing as the world shifted with immense sub-
tlety, making room for the impossible merging of
self with other.

"On three," Reno said in a low voice. "One . . .
two . . . three."

Slowly, with carefully matched steps, Reno and
Eve worked their way down the margin of the small
valley. Hours ago they had started working with
the needles here, then had gone on to other parts
of the valley.

Only in retrospect had this section of the valley's
perimeter seemed different. Here the needles had

been fairly humming. Here they had kicked and shivered and jostled.

Reno and Eve had assumed it was their own lack of skill rather than anything else that had made the needles so twitchy. Now they wondered if it might have been the presence of hidden treasure that had animated the slender dowsing rods.

To Eve's right a small ravine opened, choked with brush and rubble from an old rockslide. To Reno's left lay the valley itself. Ahead of them and around a rocky nose was the alcove where an Indian slave had laid down his *tenate* for the last time.

Silently, intently, Reno and Eve worked their way along the edge of the valley. Rarely did the needles come apart, despite the rocky, uneven terrain and the detours around trees or fallen logs. With each step, the metal sticks shivered almost visibly.

"Stop pulling to the right," Reno said.

"Stop pushing," she retorted.

"I'm not."

"Neither am I."

As one, Reno and Eve halted and looked at the needles. Hers was pointing almost straight ahead instead of lying along her hand. His was at a right angle, as though pushing—or being pulled.

Slowly Eve turned to her right. Reno followed, matching his movements to hers as though he had spent his life sharing her breath, her blood, her very heartbeat.

When the needles were straight once more, the debris of the old landslide confronted Reno and Eve. Step by careful step, they walked along the landslide's raggedly curving edge. The needles pivoted slowly, as though pinned to a point uphill and beneath the pile of rubble.

"Up," Reno said tersely.

Together they scrambled up the slide, moving in unison despite the uneven terrain, like two cats chasing the same mouse with sinuous, nearly matched strides. Despite that, it should have been impossible to keep the needles in touch.

It proved to be impossible to keep them apart.

Suddenly the needles dipped, jerked, and pointed down, vibrating so fiercely, it was all Eve could do to hang on to hers.

"Reno!"

"I feel it. My God, I feel it!"

He slipped the hammer from a loop on his belt and jammed the handle into the rubble where the needles pointed, marking the spot.

"Keep going up," Reno said.

They clambered up the last ten feet of the landslide. The needles grew calmer the higher up the slope they were carried.

"Back down to the hammer," he said.

When they were back at the hammer, Reno looked around, orienting himself.

"Left," he said, pointing with his free hand. "Toward the alcove, but stay as much on a line with this part of the slide as you can. Ready?"

"Yes."

As they stepped forward, Eve's tawny eyebrows came together in a frown of concentration that made Reno want to pull her close and kiss away the small lines. But he knew better than to reach for her while they were holding the Spanish dowsing rods. The one time he had put his hand on her when the rods were touching, desire had flooded through him so hotly it had almost brought him to his knees.

Although Reno didn't understand the energy that coursed so fiercely through the slender metal sticks, he no longer doubted it. Sunlight wasn't tangible either, but when focused through a magnifying glass, it could set fire to wood. In some uncanny way, the Spanish needles focused the intangible currents flowing between himself and Eve.

As Reno and Eve moved away from the rockslide, the pull on the needles diminished, but not as quickly as it had in the uphill direction. When they retraced their steps and walked in the opposite direction, the pull fell off quickly, leaving the metals sticks feeling almost lifeless in their hands.

In silence they walked out into the meadow and looked back at the rockslide.

"It felt strongest to me about two-thirds of the way up the rockslide," Eve said finally.

"Same for me."

Reno checked a compass reading.

"Going toward the nose is the next best pull," she added.

He nodded and took another compass reading.

"What does it mean?"

He put away the compass and looked at Eve. Beneath the shadow of her hat brim, her eyes glowed as golden as a harvest moon. The curve of her lower lip reminded him of how sweet it was to run the tip of his tongue over the soft flesh and feel the shiver of her response.

"Well, sugar girl, I'll tell you," Reno said in a deep voice. "I'm damn glad it was Jesuit priests who used these needles before us. Otherwise I'd worry about pacts with the devil and my immortal soul."

Reno smiled wryly after he spoke, but Eve knew he was quite serious.

"Me too," she said simply.

He took off his hat, raked his fingers through his hair, and put his hat back on.

"If we can believe the needles," he said, "there's

a concentration of pure gold somewhere under that rockslide."

Eve glanced at the rubble. "Does it look like ore to you?"

"It looks like what was above the mine head before the king of Spain double-crossed the Jesuits and they blew the mine's entrance to hell."

20

For the third time that day, the sound of man-made thunder reverberated through the valley, battering the two people who were crouched behind a tree, their hands over their ears. Pulverized stone boiled up into the air and then fell in a jagged, dusty rain over a quarter of the small meadow.

When the last echo had faded and no more rocky debris pelted down, Eve cautiously lowered her hands. Despite the fact that she had covered her ears, they still rang from the force of the blast.

Reno straightened and looked out at the ravine that had been choked by rocky debris. As he watched, a ragged black hole in the mountainside emerged from behind veils of dust. Elation speared through him. He took off his hat and threw it into the air with a whoop of triumph.

"We did it, sugar girl!"

He pulled Eve to her feet and into his arms as he spun around and around until she was dizzy with laughter. He kissed her hard and fast, then set her on her feet and held her until she found her balance once more.

"Come on, let's see what we have," he said.

Grinning widely, Reno grabbed Eve's hand and headed for the mine, moving with a long-legged stride that had her half running to keep up.

As he had hoped, the blast had removed most of the debris from the mouth of the mine tunnel. A tongue of jagged rubble stuck out from the opening. Grit and dust still hung in the air inside. Reno dropped Eve's hand and pulled his dark bandanna over his nose.

"Wait here," he said.

"But—"

"No," Reno said, cutting off whatever Eve was going to say. "It's too dangerous. There's no way of telling what shape the mine was in before the blast, much less after it."

"You're going in," she pointed out.

"That's right, sugar girl. I'm going in. Alone."

Reno lit the lantern, ducked low, and stepped into the opening. Almost immediately he stopped, raised the lantern, and began examining the walls of the mine.

They were solid rock. Though seamed by natural cracks in the rock beds, the tunnel seemed strong enough. When he used his hammer on the surface, very little stone came free.

Cautiously, bent nearly double, Reno went farther into the mine. Very quickly the walls of the shaft changed. A vein of pale quartz no wider than his finger appeared. Tiny flashes of gold embedded in matrix answered every shift of the lantern.

Had the quartz been a creek, the gold within would have been panned as dust. But stone wasn't water. Getting the tiny specks of gold free of their quartz prison would take black powder, hard labor, and a man who was willing to risk his life in dark, rock-bound passages beneath the earth.

"Reno?" Eve called anxiously.

"It looks good so far," he answered. "Stone walls and a small vein of gold ore."

"Rich man's gold?"

"Yes. And not a whole lot of it."

"Oh."

"Don't get disappointed yet. I'm only fifteen feet into the mine."

Eve heard the amusement in Reno's voice and smiled despite her anxiety.

"Besides," he said, "didn't the Spanish journal talk about rough ingots of gold that had been cast but not carried off to New Spain yet?"

"Yes. There were sixty-two of them."

A whistle floated back out of the mine.

"You never told me that before," he said.

"I started to last night, but you distracted me."

Laughter echoed in the tunnel as Reno remembered just how he had distracted Eve.

She had been bending over the campfire, tending a venison stew and talking about a badly spotted page in the journal she had just puzzled out. He hadn't been listening closely, for the lush curve of her hips had claimed his full attention. They had barely managed to get all their clothes off before he pressed into her with the fire crackling on one side, the cool night air on the other, and in the center a smooth, liquid heat that fit him more perfectly than any glove.

"No, you were the one who distracted me," Reno said.

Laughter was Eve's only answer.

The floor of the mine shaft began to slant steeply beneath Reno's feet. The vein of gold ore also dipped sharply, telling him that the tunnel was the result of following a bigger vein of ore rather than of any particular planning on the part of the Spaniards.

Reno moved quickly but carefully into the tunnel, shining the lantern all around as he went. The mine was sound except for the places where it cut through softer rock that hadn't been cooked deep with the fires of the earth. Where the walls were in soft or heavily fractured rock, the Spaniards had put in beams to brace the tunnel.

There were many branching, seemingly random side tunnels that were too narrow for anyone but a child to get through. Those openings hadn't been braced. Reno looked into each small hole, but didn't find one that tempted him to explore it.

"Reno! Where are you?"

The sound of Eve's voice thinned and echoed as it sank down through the mine.

"Coming," he said.

Reno scrambled back up the steep incline and down the tunnel to the mine's mouth. Eve was waiting just outside, a lantern in her hand.

"I told you to stay out," Reno said curtly.

"I did. Then your light disappeared and didn't come back. When I called out, no one answered. I didn't know if you were all right."

Reno looked at Eve's level gold eyes and knew he wasn't going to succeed in keeping her out of the mine unless he roped and hog-tied her like a calf for branding.

"Stay behind me," he said grudgingly. "Don't light your lantern, but keep some matches handy in case something goes wrong with the one I'm carrying. I have candles, but only for an emergency."

Eve nodded and let out a hidden breath, glad

that she wasn't going to have to fight Reno over entering the mine. But fight him she would; she simply couldn't bear to wait on the outside not knowing if something had gone wrong deep in the mine.

"This early part is safe enough," Reno said.

Lantern light dipped and quivered and flowed as though alive when he gestured to the rock walls, ceiling, and floor.

"I thought all mines had some kind of wooden supports," Eve said, eyeing the bare stone distrustfully.

"Not in solid rock. You don't need it, unless the ore body is huge. Then you just leave some of the ore in place to act as pillars."

A flash of white caught Eve's eye.

"What's that on the right?" she asked.

"A small vein."

"Gold?"

Reno made a rumbling sound of agreement. "Just like the chunk I took out of that *tenate*."

"How did the Spanish know the gold was here if they couldn't see it from the outside of the mountain? Did they use the needles?"

"Maybe. And maybe the vein showed on the surface somewhere else."

Reno pointed to the wall. "This is the end of a shaft rather than the beginning. The nature of the rock changes about ten feet this side of the opening. The way the vein is dipping, it might come out close to that alcove you found."

For a few steps there was only the sound of boots scuffing over the uneven floor of the tunnel.

"Watch it," Reno cautioned. "It goes down steeply for about twenty feet."

Eve looked. The nature of the walls seemed unchanged.

"Why did they suddenly take a notion to dig deeper?" she asked.

"Oldest mining technique in the world," he said. "Find a vein, follow its drift, and leave tunnels wherever you take out ore or look for new veins."

Wherever a tunnel branched off, there was an arrow pointing away from it. Each time Reno took a tunnel, he marked the shaft of the arrow so that he wouldn't explore the same opening twice.

Some of the tunnels were numbered. Most weren't. The result was a three-dimensional maze bored through rock that was hard as steel in some places, and nearly as soft as fruitcake in others.

"Why do all the arrowheads point away from the tunnel mouths?" Eve asked.

"In a mine, everything points to the way out. That way if you get lost, you don't wander deeper and deeper."

Just before the steep descent, there was a place where supporting beams had been brought in. The timber was roughly hewn. Some pieces still had fragments of bark clinging. Others were simply small logs that had been cut and dragged underground.

Small side tunnels branched out in all directions and levels. Two of them had caved in. Rubble in the bottom of the others warned of unstable ceilings or walls.

"What are those little holes I keep seeing?" Eve asked. "Most of them don't seem to go anywhere but a dead end."

"They're called coyote holes. They were dug to find the drift of the vein. Once the miners struck the vein again, or found a better one, they abandoned the side tunnels and concentrated on widening the one that led to ore."

"Such narrow tunnels. I'd barely fit in one. The

Indians must have been even smaller than Don Lyon."

"Only the children were. They're the ones who dug the coyote holes."

"Dear God," Eve said.

"More like the devil's work, despite the presence of Jesuit priests. Watch your head."

She ducked and continued walking bent partway over. Reno had to bend much more deeply to avoid the ceiling.

"The boys would dig the holes, load *tenates*, and carry ore up to the surface," Reno said. "This must have been a wide vein, because they didn't dig an inch more than they had to."

Reno paused, examined the face of the tunnel carefully, and went on, crouching to avoid the ceiling.

"When the ore was brought to the surface," he continued, "girls and smaller boys would hammer on it with rocks until everything was in pieces about as big as the ball of your thumb. Then it would go into the *arrastra*, to be ground into dust by the adult slaves."

Black, ragged holes radiated out again from floor, walls, and ceiling.

"Lost the drift again here," Reno muttered.

"What happened?"

"The vein took a turn or was pinched off or was displaced by a fault line."

"I always imagined veins as being straight."

"That's every miner's dream," Reno agreed, "but damn few are straight. Most gold deposits are shaped like a maple tree or like lightning. Branches every which way in all directions for no reason a man can see."

The lantern swung as Reno bent over one of the yawning mouths set into the floor of the tunnel.

Light washed into one of the coyote holes that was at waist level off to the right. The hole had been clogged with debris that had since dribbled out into the main tunnel.

"What's that?" Eve asked.

"Where?"

"Hold the lamp a little higher, where the side of the coyote hole collapsed. Yes. Right there."

Eve peered into the crumbling side tunnel. When she realized what she was looking at, she swallowed convulsively and backed up so quickly she bumped into Reno.

"Eve?"

"Bones," she said.

Reno stepped around her and held the lantern up to the coyote hole. Something gleamed palely inside. It took a moment for him to realize that he was looking at fragments of a leather sandal wrapped around a foot bone that could have been no more than six inches long. The dry, cold air of the mine had preserved the bones very well.

"Is it one of Don Lyon's ancestors?" Eve asked quietly.

"Too small."

"A child," she whispered.

"Yes. A child. He was digging and the wall gave way."

"They didn't even bother to give him a decent burial."

"It's less dangerous to fill in the front of a bad tunnel than it is to dig out a dead body," Reno said. "Besides, slaves were treated worse than horses, and even a Spaniard didn't bury his horse when it died."

The lantern swung away, returning the coyote hole to the darkness of the grave it was.

Eve closed her eyes, then opened them quickly.

The darkness was unnerving, now that she knew it was inhabited by bones.

"You asked what a chicken ladder was," Reno said a few moments later. "Take a look."

A long log poked up from one of the holes. Notches had been cut into the sides of the log to serve as footholds. The shaft wasn't straight up and down, but the slant was so steep that passage wouldn't have been possible without the log.

"Some of them are made with branches poking out instead of notches cut in," Reno said. "Either way, they work."

The wood felt rough and cool beneath Eve's hand, except where the notches were. So many feet had passed over the notches that they were smoothed to a satin finish.

"Hold the lantern," he said.

Eve took the light, then watched with her breath held while Reno tested the chicken ladder. Soon she could see only his broad shoulders and hat.

"Solid," Reno said, looking up into the golden light. "Unless water is around, wood lasts a long time at this altitude."

The primitive ladder led to another level of the old mine where more coyote holes branched off in all directions. Many of them were too small for Reno's shoulders to fit in the opening. A few were so narrow that Eve barely could find room to shove the lantern ahead of her.

"Anything?" Reno asked.

He hadn't wanted Eve to go poking into every coyote hole, but the logic of it was inescapable. She could go farther, and do it faster, than he could.

"It keeps going," she said, wriggling out breathlessly. "But once you're past the bend, another tunnel comes in. It's twice the size of this one."

She stood and brushed herself off. "There's

something funny about that big tunnel, though. The arrows point the other way. At least, they used to. Someone scratched out the head of the old arrows and put a new head on the tail."

Reno frowned, pulled out his compass, and checked.

"Which way does the coyote hole turn?" he asked.

Eve pointed. "The other tunnel comes in from that direction, too."

Reno turned to orient himself with the hidden tunnel and its twice-drawn arrows.

"Same angle, or does that change, too?" he asked.

"It goes up about like this," Eve said, holding her hand at a slant.

"Are you bothered by those tight tunnels?"

She shook her head.

"You sure?" Reno pressed.

"Very. I'll take tunnels over ledges perched like God's eyebrow over a thousand-foot drop," Eve said wryly.

Reno's smile flashed in the lantern light. "I'm just the opposite. I'd rather be on God's eyebrow than down in coyote holes any day of the week."

She laughed. "Want me to see where that double-headed tunnel leads?"

He hesitated, then reluctantly agreed. "But only if the walls are rock. I don't want you crawling through any of the crumbling stuff we've seen. Understand?"

Eve understood perfectly. While the coyote holes didn't bother her the way heights did, she had no desire to end as the slave child had, buried alive.

"Go on, then," he said reluctantly.

Before she turned to leave, Reno pulled her close and kissed her hard.

"Be careful, sugar girl," he said in a rough voice. "I don't like this one damn bit."

Reno liked it even less as the sounds of Eve's passage through stone faded into silence and the minutes crawled by as though nailed to the stone floor. The third time he dug out his watch, stared at it, and discovered that less than thirty seconds had passed, he swore and began counting slowly.

Finally he heard the sound of Eve half crawling, half scrambling through the coyote hole. As soon as her head and shoulders appeared, he pulled her out and gave her a hug that all but squeezed the breath from her.

"That's the last time you go into a coyote hole alone," Reno said flatly. "I aged ten years waiting for you."

"It was worth it, sugar man," Eve said breathlessly, laughing, kissing him. "I found it! I found the gold!"

        Two gold ingots gleamed in the firelight, gold as pure and uncorrupted now as the moment when slaves had first poured the molten metal into molds to cool. Reno looked from the ingots to the girl whose eyes were the exact shade of the Spanish treasure she had found hidden in darkness.

Eve looked back at Reno, smiled, and then laughed softly.

"I can't believe there are sixteen more just like that one," she said. "You should have let me go back and get them. I could have had them all out in the time it took you to widen the coyote hole that connects the two big tunnels."

"The gold has waited this long. It will wait until tomorrow."

"With both of us working, it shouldn't—"

"No," Reno said flatly, cutting across her words. "You're not going into that coyote hole again. The part where it cuts the second tunnel is too damned dangerous."

"But I'm smal—"

"The reason they closed out that second big tunnel," Reno said over her, "is that the middle section isn't stable. It collapsed more than once. Each time they cut a coyote hole around the cave-in and kept digging until they mined out the good ore, and things kept on caving in. Finally they came at the ore from the other side, where we started."

"Do you really think that second big tunnel goes all the way to the alcove?"

He shrugged. "The rock layers looked the same."

"Dear Lord." Eve shivered. "That mountain must be honeycombed with holes."

"Are you cold?" Reno asked, noting the shiver that had passed over Eve.

"No," she whispered. "I was just wondering how many slaves died for those eighteen ingots of gold."

"Not to mention the other forty-four ingots that are hidden somewhere down there," he said.

Another shiver passed over Eve. She knew that Reno was going to search for the missing ingots. The thought of him hunting through the mountain's lethal coyote holes for gold that might or might not be there made her wish they had never found the mine.

"I didn't see any other coiled-snake symbols chiseled in the wall," Eve said. "Maybe the Jesuits took most of the gold with them. Maybe it would be a waste of time to search."

"Maybe they didn't have time to spend chiseling snakes into rock walls to mark where treasure was buried," he said dryly. "Maybe they just piled the ingots in a coyote hole and got the hell out of there before the king's soldiers came and dragged them back to Spain in chains."

Reno finished the last of his coffee and began scattering the embers of the small fire. Soon there was no illumination but that of the moon.

"It's worth staying until the weather changes to look for forty-four gold ingots, isn't it?" Reno asked.

The dark velvet of his voice acted on Eve like a caress. Suddenly she knew he wasn't asking about staying for the gold; he was asking if she would stay here with him awhile longer.

Until we find the mine, you'll be my woman.

And the mine had been found.

"With or without gold, I'd stay," Eve said softly.

Reno held out his hand. When she took it, he kissed her palm, and led her to the place where he had cut evergreen boughs to make a bed. It was several hundred feet away, for any intruders would expect to find them by the campfire.

The tarpaulin rustled as Reno and Eve sank down on the bedroll together.

"I'll never forget the smell of lilacs," he whispered against her neck. "Or the taste of you."

Before Eve could answer, Reno took her mouth in a long, deep kiss. By the time it ended, both of them were breathing quickly and flushed with heat. Long fingers moved over Eve's shirt, baring her to the waist. The camisole gleamed like silver in the moonlight. Slowly he bent and brushed his lips over the rapid pulse in Eve's neck.

"The first time I saw you in your camisole," Reno said, "I wanted to take it off and bury my face in your breasts."

Smiling, Eve unlaced the camisole and shrugged it aside.

"Lilacs and rosebuds," he whispered. "God, but you're sweet."

"It's my soap."

Reno smiled slowly. "No, sugar girl. It's your breasts."

Reno kissed first one tip, then the other. The silky caresses of mustache and tongue drew Eve into velvet peaks. She made a murmurous sound of pleasure that became a gasp when he began taking tiny, gentle, repeated bites of her.

"I could eat every bit of you," he said. "Head to heels and back again. Would you like that, *gata*?"

"Do I get to nibble on you, too?"

For an instant Reno went still. Then a sensual shudder went through his whole body.

"You don't have to," he said. "I've never asked that of a woman."

"I want to," Eve whispered. "I want to know you every way a woman can know a man."

Between kisses and gliding caresses, they undressed each other until nothing lay between them but moonlight and the crisp air of mountain night. Reno pulled a blanket over them as he wrapped Eve in a long, naked hug.

"I wanted to do this, too, that first time I saw you," he said. "I wanted to feel your body all bare against mine."

Eve tried to speak, but the shiver of pleasure that went through her as the heat of Reno's skin pressed against her whole body took her voice, making words impossible.

Her silent response was enough. A low, ragged sound came from Reno's chest as he felt Eve's delicate trembling.

"Each time it's better," he whispered. "Only you

affect me like this. I don't understand it, but I don't care anymore. I need you tonight, Eve. More each time. Only you."

"Yes, I can feel it. More each time . . ."

Reno barely heard. The feel of Eve's fingers wrapped around his aroused flesh was like having golden flames licking all over him. The pleasure was so intense his whole body tightened.

Then Eve pushed the blanket aside, slid slowly down his body, and taught him what it was like to be loved by fire.

Her name came in fragments from his lips as she tasted him with all the curiosity and delicacy of a cat. The satin roughness of her tongue licked and teased each difference in masculine texture from rigid base to blunt satin tip.

When Eve circled him with her mouth, Reno tried to speak, but couldn't. She had taken the breath from him and left seething, searing currents in its place. Sweat broke out all over his body as he fought to control the firestorm coiling in his loins. Fists clenched, he made a raw sound of passion and restraint.

"Reno?" Eve asked in a low voice. "Did I hurt you?"

His laugh was as broken as his breathing.

"No, sugar girl. You're killing me, but you're not hurting me one bit."

Her sigh washed over his moist, sensitive skin, sending a visible pulse of pleasure through him.

"Did it feel good?" she asked.

"There's only one thing that ever felt better."

"What?"

"When I sheathe myself in your sweet . . ."

The rest of Reno's words were lost in the groan that was dragged from his lips as Eve caught him up in the loving firestorm once more. He took as much as he could, and then more, because it was a wild, sweet ecstasy he didn't want to end.

Suddenly he could bear no more.

"Eve, I . . ."

Reno shuddered, ravished by fire.

She whispered against him, telling him how much she liked his taste.

Another satin pulse escaped his control before he dragged her up his body until she straddled his hips, his waist, his chest.

"Higher," Reno said huskily. "Higher. Make it easy for me. That's it. Right there . . . so sweet . . . Stay there, sugar girl."

The sleek questing of his tongue licked over Eve like sensual lightning. She made a husky sound that ended in a moan as a long finger tested her and found her sultry readiness.

Knowing that Eve had truly enjoyed the intimate caresses she had given him made Reno laugh with sheer pleasure. He redoubled his presence within her body, hearing her response in her broken breathing, feeling it in the slick heat of her body.

"You liked tasting me," Reno said, nuzzling against Eve's hot, soft skin.

"Yes, I . . ."

Her words became a broken sound as his teeth closed delicately over her most sensitive flesh. She barely succeeded in controlling the liquid heat bursting through her.

"Don't fight it," Reno said huskily. "Let it come."

"But . . ."

Teeth raked with exquisite care, and tongue caressed.

"Share with me, sugar girl."

Ecstasy stole softly through Eve's body, claiming it. Reno felt it, tasted it, and laughed against her, caressing her again and again, savoring the silken rain of her response. When she could bear no more, he lifted her and turned over, stretching her out beneath him. She clung to him until the wild shivering subsided.

When Eve opened her eyes, Reno was propped up on his elbow, fully aroused, watching her. The two slender dowsing rods were in his hand. He bent, kissed her gently, and waited, a question in his eyes. Without hesitation, she reached for one of the rods.

It was warm from his body heat.

Slowly Reno settled between Eve's legs even as she drew them up around him, yielding her warmth to him. He paused just before he fitted himself to her.

"Are you sure?" he whispered. "It could make me . . . wild."

Eve smiled and shifted her hips, taking Reno even as he took her. The rod tips met, meshed, shimmered . . . and blossomed in a soundless explosion of fire. The world receded as they joined more deeply than they ever had before, knowing no difference between their bodies. They kissed each other and were kissed at the same time, caressed and were caressed, until rapture both delicate and elemental coursed through their interlocked bodies, fusing them into a single flesh, a single being, a single life.

As one they learned that ecstasy was like fire itself, changeless and yet never the same, burning everything but itself, a mysterious Phoenix reborn in its own flames, soaring upward to fly and die and be born yet again.

21

THE horses had been restless when Reno and Eve emerged from the mine the previous day, and were restless much of the night. Shortly after dawn, Reno and Eve were awakened by the sound of three rapidly fired shots from a six-gun.

Without a word, both of them got up and dressed quickly. Instead of wearing boots, Reno pulled on knee-high moccasins of the kind favored by Apaches, some Comancheros, and Caleb Black, who was the quietest man on the stalk that Reno had ever seen.

Wish I were that good, Reno thought grimly. *I'd send him out to find out what's riling the horses while I did what I'm good at—shooting and mining, not sneaking around like a shadow.*

Reno shoved the spyglass in his belt, strapped on his six-gun and bandolier, and picked up his repeating rifle.

"Stay with the horses," Reno said.

"But—"

"Promise me," he interrupted urgently. "I don't want to shoot you by mistake."

"What if I hear more gunfire?"

"When I come back to camp, I'll come in from the opposite direction. Shoot anything that comes in from the front of the valley."

Eve closed her eyes, then opened them and looked at Reno as though she were afraid it was the last time.

"How long will you be gone?" she asked.

"I'll be back before dark."

Reno turned away, then turned back and gave Eve a kiss that was both tender and fierce.

"Don't follow me. Be here when I get back, sugar girl."

Eve's arms tightened painfully around Reno before she let go and stepped back.

"I'll be here."

Without another word, Reno turned and began walking toward the mouth of the valley. He moved quickly over the meadow, keeping to the cover provided by the forest. The horses threw up their heads when they spotted him, then returned to their restless grazing when they recognized his scent.

Quickly Reno came to the place where the valley narrowed and the stream became a white cascade shooting between pincers of black rock. A game trail wound along one side of the cascade. Above the trail was a stand of squat, wind-blown spruce. Below it, at the end of the cascade, was a tiny, marshy meadow, another cascade, and then another, much larger valley with a rock-ribbed lake at one end.

Reno eased among the spruce trees and waited, motionless, until the birds and small animals returned to their normal patterns of movement. A fitful wind blew up the mountainside. The smell of smoke rode the wind.

So did the sound of men's voices.

Reno settled more deeply into cover and waited. A short time later, two men appeared along the middle cascade. Their horses were gaunt, stringy, and tough as a boot. The riders were the same. They watched the ground and the surrounding countryside by turns. Each man wore a six-gun and had a rifle in a saddle scabbard.

One of the men was familiar to Reno. The last time he had seen Short Dog, it had been over the barrel of a six-gun at Jed Slater's camp high in the San Juans, where Willow had been held prisoner. Short Dog had lifted his rifle, Reno had shot first, and Short Dog had fallen. But when the time came to bury bodies, Short Dog hadn't been among them.

The other man was known to Reno only by reputation. Bandanna Mike was a stage robber and small-time gunnie who thought he was God's personal gift to womanhood. His trademark was a black and red silk bandanna that was big enough to use as a picnic cloth. At the moment, the bandanna was lying at ease around his dirty neck.

Conversation came with the wind, phrases and bits that Reno had to piece together.

"Nobody been here...days," Bandanna Mike said. "Why in hell..."

"Eat beans up here, eat beans down..." Short Dog said. "Same beans."

There was silence punctuated by the occasional sound of a pebble rolling as the horses scrambled up a rocky piece of trail just below the spruces.

Reno was afraid the Comancheros' horses would scent him if they kept climbing until Reno was upwind of them, but the men dismounted at the far end of the grove, perhaps thirty feet away. Unless the wind shifted, the horses wouldn't catch Reno's scent.

"No point to settin' up here on a rock when we could be layin' back there in grass," Bandanna Mike grumbled. "They cain't git out without walkin' plumb through our camp, and even a skunk-drunk mestizo couldn't miss 'em then."

"Talk Slater," Short Dog said.

"Might as well shoot myself and git it over with as talk to him," grumbled Bandanna Mike.

"Shoot and Slater come hell-running you bet," Short Dog said. "End same Walleye Jack."

"Jericho had no call to shoot old Walleye. He was just funnin' with that snake."

"All same, Walleye Jack dead meat you bet. Snake same."

"Jericho is a mean 'un," Bandanna Mike agreed.

It was quiet for a few minutes. Then came the sound of a cork being pulled from a bottle. The satisfied gasping and coughing sounds that followed told Reno that it wasn't water or coffee being passed around.

"What do you think happened to Crooked Bear?" Bandanna Mike asked.

Short Dog belched. "Dead or gone see squaw. Same thing."

"Damn, but the thought of gold gets a feller to itchin'," Bandanna Mike said after a moment. "Think they got it yet?"

"No leave yet. No gold yet," Short Dog said succinctly.

For a time there was only silence and the sound of the restless wind. A horse snorted and stamped its foot.

Reno waited, motionless.

"You think that there Reno feller is as good with a six-gun as they say?"

"Goddamn straight fast hell-shooter you bet," Short Dog said emphatically.

Silently Reno wished that he had shot just a bit straighter when he had had Short Dog in his sights. It would have meant one less Comanchero to deal with now.

On the other hand, there was never any lack of lazy, greedy, or cruel men to fatten the ranks of gangs led by men like Jericho Slater.

"What about thet gal? Did you see her? Is she a pretty 'un?"

"Squaw all same. Hell bad you bet."

Bandanna Mike laughed. "Hell bad is goin' without. Hope I'm one of the first. Ain't no fun if'n there ain't no vinegar left in a gal."

There was another silence, another round of coughing and gasping as the men took a pull on the bottle, and then more silence.

"Acey-deucey?" Bandanna Mike asked.

Short Dog grunted.

The sound of cards being shuffled carried in the stillness.

Reno waited with the patience of a man whose life depended on it—and while he waited, he wished again that he had Caleb's ability to move over terrain without making a sound. He would have given a great deal to slide up and cut Bandanna Mike's dirty throat.

For an hour Reno listened to the two outlaws argue over cards. Then he withdrew slowly, using the fitful wind to cover any sounds he might make.

When Reno got back to camp, he circled around and came in from the back. Eve was waiting with the shotgun leveled and both barrels loaded. As soon as she saw him, she set down the gun and ran to him. He wrapped her up in his arms and held on hard. When he finally released her, she watched him with eyes that read him too well.

"Slater," Eve said.

It wasn't a question.

"Slater," Reno confirmed. "He's got two men guarding that little marshy meadow just below this one. The rest of his men are camped in the big meadow further down."

"What are we going to do?"

"Hunt for gold, sugar girl."

"And then?"

Reno smiled coldly. "Then I'm going to teach those boys about black powder."

And pray very hard that Cal, Wolfe, or Rafe is on the way.

EVE waited at the point where the coyote hole came into the main tunnel. Reno's work yesterday had widened the hole enough that he could squeeze through. It wasn't comfortable, but it got the job done; it took him to the place where sixteen ingots had been buried centuries before.

The sound of Reno crawling closer reassured Eve, but she still wanted to hear his voice. She flattened out on the floor of the tunnel and called out.

"Reno? Is everything all right? I thought I heard something fall."

His answer came quickly, distorted by the curves of the wormhole he was crawling through.

"Just me pushing junk out of the way," he said.

It was half the truth, but it was the only half Reno planned to tell Eve. The middle of the old tunnel was unstable as hell. Widening the coyote hole had triggered two small slides. Loose rock was still raining down. A real slide could come at any moment. The longer he spent in either tunnel or coyote hole, the greater the danger was.

But Reno knew if he told Eve, she would insist on helping him get the gold out. He didn't want her anywhere near the crumbling tunnels.

In fact, he hadn't wanted her anywhere near any part of the mine this time, but she had gone mule-stubborn on him. In the end he had agreed that she could come into the mine, but only as far as the solid rock of the main tunnel went. After that, she was to stay put.

"Stand back," Reno said. Then he added wryly, knowing that standing wasn't possible, "Crawl out of the way, *gata*. I'm coming through."

Eve pushed away from the opening that still looked too small to admit Reno's broad shoulders. As she watched, two gold ingots appeared. They gleamed in the lantern light as though freshly poured.

With a muscular twist of his body, Reno emerged from the small opening. His face was streaked with sweat and grit. So were his clothes. His weapons were clean, however. He had stacked them to one side of the coyote hole before he crawled in.

Reno picked up a heavy ingot in each hand and placed them with the others he had retrieved.

"Sixteen down and two to go," Reno said, stretching.

"Let me get th—"

"No."

Reno heard the flat rejection in his voice and prayed Eve didn't hear the fear for her safety that lay just beneath it. He forced himself to smile as he tilted her face up for a quick, hard kiss.

"I'll be back before you know it, with a gold bar in each hand."

Eve wanted to argue even though she knew it would be futile. Instead, she made herself smile as she brushed her fingertips over his lips.

"Hurry back, sugar man," she whispered.

After Reno disappeared back into the coyote hole, Eve crouched by the black opening and prayed.

She was still praying when she heard a rumbling, grinding sound. A burst of air gusted out from the mouth of the coyote hole, bringing with it a cloud of grit and the sound of rock rushing down.

The coyote hole had collapsed.

"Reno!" Eve yelled. *"Reno!"*

Nothing came back to her but the gnashing sounds of rocks as they found a new place to lie.

When Eve looked into the coyote hole, there was no gleam of light from Reno's lantern. Frantically she grabbed her own lantern and crawled into the narrow tunnel, pushing the light in front of her. There was so much dust hanging in the air that the light looked as though it had been wrapped in gauze.

Within seconds Eve was coughing and choking from the swirling dust. She yanked her bandanna up and wriggled forward as fast as she could, ignoring the rocks that scraped and bruised her body.

With every breath Eve took, she called Reno's name. No answer came but the raw echoes of her own screams.

The lantern hit something and refused to budge. Crying, calling for Reno, Eve battered blindly at the unexpected obstacle. Finally she realized what was wrong. Where the coyote hole should have emerged into the older, wider tunnel, the ceiling had given way. Now there was nothing but a wall of debris.

Eve clawed at the loose rubble, pushing it away down both sides of her body. For every handful she removed, two more took its place.

"Reno."

There was no sound in the tunnel but that of her own broken sobs.

It was the same an hour later, when Eve finally realized that she didn't have the strength to dig through the cave-in alone.

DIRTY, disheveled, wild-eyed, Eve crept past the point where Reno had said Slater's guards were posted. Though twice she sent pebbles rolling, no man called out or came after her. She hardly noticed her good luck. She was intent on what had to be done, bribing Jericho Slater with a combination of gold ingots and lead bullets.

They want the gold, they can have it. But first they have to dig Reno free.

And I'll be standing over them with a loaded shotgun every inch of the way.

A small corner of Eve's mind knew that her plan was so foolish as to be suicidal. The rest of her mind just flat didn't care. She wasn't strong enough to dig Reno out of the mountain. Slater's gang was.

So she would go to Slater, and let the devil take the hindmost.

Eve went through the marshy area like a gritty wraith. Her once white shirt was the gray-black color of the rocks. So were her pants. So was everything else but the guns she carried. She had wiped them down with a care Reno had taught her. The weapons were clean, fully loaded, and ready to fire.

The second cascade was bordered by forest and brush. Silence was impossible, but that didn't matter; the water was making enough noise to drown out a mustang stampede. Automatically Eve shifted the shotgun and bandolier so they wouldn't catch on the shrubs and trees that reached out to snag her.

Just before the cascade spread out across the boulder-strewn mouth of the larger valley, the water took one final leap over a slate ledge. Eve wriggled out on the rock to get a look at the camp. She had already decided that Jericho Slater was the first prisoner she should take. It was just a matter of finding out where he was.

A quick look over the ledge told Eve she was lucky not to be a prisoner herself. Slater's gang was camped about a hundred feet from the waterfall, back in a thick grove of evergreens. Horses were picketed around the meadow. A quick count gave her a total of twenty.

Despair curled blackly in Eve's bones. Ten men, she might have managed to watch. Even twelve.

But twenty?

There's no help for it. Grab Slater, cut a deal, and get on with it. No matter how bad it looks for me, what Reno's facing is worse, trapped in there without light or food or water.

And he never liked the tunnels. He feels the same way about them that I do about those eyebrow trails over slickrock.

I've got to get to him soon. I can't leave him there alone.

Eve refused to think about the possibility that Reno was already dead under tons of rubble, buried as the slave child had been buried, one more sacrifice to the golden tears of the sun god. Eve was certain she would know if he were dead. She would feel it just as surely as she felt her own life now.

Wiping her eyes against her sleeve, she looked again at the camp. A swirl of pale gray caught her attention. Jericho Slater still wore the wrist-length cape of the Confederate army. The white planter's hat was also familiar; he hadn't removed it even when he sat at her table to play cards.

I wonder how Slater feels about tunnels. Hope he hates them. Because until Reno is free, Slater is going to be spending a lot of time in the dark.

Smiling grimly, Eve eased back off the slate overlook and into the cover of the trees.

As soon as the green boughs folded around her, a man's hand shot out and clamped over her mouth. Simultaneously a powerful arm clamped around her waist, pinning her arms to her body. Though she was holding a shotgun, she had no chance to use it.

An instant later Eve was lifted off her feet, helpless but for her wildly kicking feet.

"Slow down, wildcat," a deep voice said quietly in Eve's ear. "It's Caleb Black."

Eve went still, then looked over her shoulder.

Caleb's whiskey-colored eyes looked back at her. The warmth she remembered in his eyes was lacking. He looked just like what Reno had once called him, a dark angel of vengeance.

Eve nodded to show that she understood she was safe. Slowly Caleb set her down. When she was standing on her own feet, he jerked his thumb, silently telling Eve to get deeper into cover.

As soon as she did, another man stepped forward. His hair was the same black as Caleb's, but the resemblance ended there. Caleb's hair had a slight curl. Wolfe Lonetree's was straight as a ruler. His eyes were an indigo so dark as to be nearly black. His face showed the high cheekbones of his Cheyenne mother and the sharply defined mouth of his Scots father. Though not as big as Caleb or Reno, Wolfe moved with a physical confidence that was more impressive than size alone would have been.

Caleb's hands moved in sign talk that was as graceful as it was precise. Wolfe nodded and moved past Eve, touching his dark hat in silent greeting as he did. The hand he lifted to his hat was holding two boxes of shells. His other hand was wrapped around two repeating rifles.

Eve stared for an instant, then eased farther back into the trees, pulled by Caleb's hand on her arm. As soon as it was safe to speak, she did.

"There was a cave-in. Reno's trapped. There are two guards at the next cascade."

Caleb's eyes narrowed. "Is he alive?"

She nodded, unable to say anything for the fear drawing her throat tight.

"Is he hurt?" Caleb asked.

"I don't know. I couldn't get to him."

"What did he say?"

"Nothing. He couldn't hear me."

Caleb didn't ask how Eve knew Reno was alive. He had seen both the wildness and the soul-deep determination in her eyes.

"I took care of the guards," Caleb said. "Go back to the marshy area and wait. We'll be along shortly."

"But Reno—"

"Go. We can't do a damn thing for Reno as long as Jericho Slater is settin' up to shoot us in the back."

Caleb turned away, then stopped and looked over his shoulder at Eve.

"Rafe Moran is somewhere around here. So if you see a man as big as Reno coming at you, blond hair, easy-moving, with a bullwhip in one hand

and a six-gun in the other, don't shoot him."

Numbly Eve nodded.

"There's a pint-sized redhead called Jessi Lonetree about a mile back down the trail," Caleb continued. "She's supposed to stay put, but she might take a notion to come looking for her man after the shooting stops."

"Jessi? Then that was Wolfe?"

Caleb grinned. "Sure was. Now, go on up to the marsh and wait for us. With Wolfe and a repeating rifle up on that rock preaching to them about the wages of sin, Slater's boys will soon see the error of their ways. There will be a regular stampede of converts heading down the mountain."

"I can help."

"You sure can," Caleb agreed. "You can get your rump up to the marsh and stay safe. If anything happens to you, no one would know where to look for Reno."

"Then I'll go back to the mine. He might be calling for me."

"Don't go inside that mine until I'm there," Caleb said flatly.

Eve opened her mouth to argue.

"I mean it, Eve. I'll tie you like a chicken for the spit if I have to."

"But—"

"Get it through your head," Caleb said roughly, overriding her attempts to speak. "Without you, we don't have a chance in hell of helping Reno."

Slowly Eve nodded and turned away, not even noticing the tears that were once again making silver trails through the dirt on her cheeks.

She was halfway up the cascade when Wolfe Lonetree opened up with his rifle. Shot after shot screamed through the high mountain air, echoing back from stone peaks. From below, other rifles returned fire in a crescendo of noise.

By the time Eve reached the marsh, the rifle shots were coming less frequently. As she climbed the second cascade, a six-gun opened up in measured intervals. Silence returned to the mountain before she reached the tiny valley that held the mine.

Caleb had been right. Slater's gang hadn't liked facing Wolfe Lonetree's lethal skill with a rifle.

22

"**Y**OU'RE not making sense," Eve said flatly.

Hands on her hips, she faced the three hard-looking men and the slender red-headed woman who had gathered in front of the mine.

"You're the one who isn't making sense," Caleb said. "First you were going to take on Slater's bunch with a shotgun, and now you're talking about going down alone into that hellhole and—"

"I went after Slater because I didn't care if I killed some of his gang digging out Reno," Eve interrupted. "You have a wife and child waiting for you."

She turned to Wolfe. "And you have a wife right here who needs you. I'm the only one who knows how to get to Reno, and I don't have a soul who looks to me for anything at all. Besides, there's only room for one to dig at a time. When I can't dig anymore, you can draw straws."

As Eve spun around to go inside, a bullwhip

snaked out and curled tightly around her knees, holding her in place without hurting her in the least.

"Wait up, miss. I'm going with you."

Eve spun and confronted the big, blond man who smiled and spoke and moved so much like Reno, she could hardly bear to look at him. The color of the eyes was different, gray rather than green, but their catlike tilt and clarity were so similar, it was like a knife in her heart.

And like Reno, Rafe's eyes could be as cold as winter ice when he was determined to get something.

"Don't waste my time arguing," Rafe said bluntly. "Either I go with you or I go alone. I'm no stranger to mines and Reno's trail signs. I'll find him."

Eve didn't doubt it.

"All right," she said in an aching voice. "I'd be obliged. I'm not nearly as strong in the shoulders as you are."

Rafe flicked his wrist. The long bullwhip fell away from Eve. Ignoring Wolfe's and Caleb's objections, she grabbed a lantern and went into the mine's entrance. Rafe dropped the whip and followed, pausing only long enough to grab a shovel and a lantern.

Caleb and Wolfe were right behind them, sharing a third lantern between them. Jessi stayed just inside the mouth of the mine with a shotgun, standing guard on the off chance that one of Slater's Comancheros had run the wrong way when the bullets started flying.

Eve heard the sounds of more than one person following her, looked over her shoulder, and felt warmed. Though there truly wasn't room for more than one man at a time to dig, it made her feel better just knowing that so many hands would be available to help.

Rafe ducked lower and lower as the ragged ceiling of the mine came down. At every branching of the tunnel, he noted the signs Reno had left.

Eve went through the big, rockbound tunnel with a speed that set the lantern to swinging. Rafe followed her like a large, muscular shadow. Caleb and Wolfe kept back a bit, marking the branching tunnels in their own way.

A dust as fine as talcum powder still hung in the air back where the collapsed coyote hole cut away from the main tunnel. Rafe took in the place with a single glance. When he saw the pile of gold bars, his eyes widened. He looked swiftly at Eve. She paid no more attention to the gold than she would have to a similar pile of river rocks.

"This goes back about ten feet before it's blocked," Eve said, pointing to the coyote hole. "I shouted and shouted, but he didn't answer."

Rafe's mouth thinned, but all he said was, "Let me try it. My voice carries a lot farther than yours."

Eve nodded tightly and watched as Rafe knelt and set aside the lantern. The coyote hole looked about as inviting as a grave. He glanced down at the shovel. In that narrow opening, he would be lucky to have enough room to use it as a bludgeon.

"Surprised Reno went in here," Rafe muttered. "He never cared much for dark, tight places."

"Maybe he never had Spanish gold waiting on the other side," she said tersely.

"There's more?" Rafe asked as he crawled over the stacked ingots and into the dark, tight hole.

"Two ingots that we know of. Supposed to be a lot more buried somewhere down here. For all of me, they can stay buried."

The only sound that came from Rafe was a low

curse as he forced himself over the ingots and into the narrow coyote hole.

Eve sank to her knees and leaned against the cold wall of the tunnel. Distantly she realized that she was trembling. When Caleb touched her shoulder, she started wildly.

Rafe's deep voice boomed through the coyote hole as he called for Reno. Silence followed. Rafe called again. More silence followed. It was no different the third and fourth time Rafe yelled his brother's name.

"Cal, Wolfe, cart that gold up to Jessi," Rafe said after a minute. "It's just in the way down here."

The sound of a steel shovel blade ramming into rocky rubble came back through the tunnel as Rafe began to dig.

"You'll need someone to haul rubble out of your way," Caleb said.

"It will have to be Eve. Two men just flat won't fit in here."

Wolfe bent, shone the lantern into the coyote hole, and began swearing in a combination of Cheyenne and British English.

"He's right, Cal. The bloody thing fits Rafe like a stone skin."

Caleb bent, looked, and began picking up the heavy gold ingots, swearing fit to raise blisters on the rock about the connection between fools, gold, and the kind of hell you didn't have to die to discover.

The rhythm of the shoveling never varied as Rafe dug through loosely piled stones and crumbling rock, pushing the debris to either side of his body and praying that the rest of the coyote hole would hold.

While Rafe bored through the darkness like a grim, living drill, Caleb and Wolfe came and went until a stack of big ingots grew at the mouth of the mine. Eve barely noticed the absence of the bars except that it made her job easier as she crawled into the hole and dragged debris out, giving Rafe a bit more room to work.

"Send Eve when you need someone to spell you," Wolfe said as he picked up the last ingot.

Rafe grunted an answer and kept digging.

In time, the first spectral flickers of lantern light gleamed through the rubble piled in front of Rafe.

"I see light!" Rafe called back.

"Is Reno there?" Eve called.

"Can't tell. The ceiling keeps—"

Rafe's words were cut off by a shower of stones. He cursed in the kind of searing invective learned in the toughest ports on earth. And as he cursed, he dug, knowing with every stroke of his shovel that he could be digging his own grave.

No matter how hard Rafe dug, he could not keep a hole open that was big enough to crawl through. The grim set of his mouth when he wriggled back out into the tunnel where Eve waited told her more than she wanted to know.

"The more I dig, the farther away I get," Rafe said bluntly, wiping sweat from his eyes. "I got the biggest rocks out of the way, but the small stuff keeps coming down. It's like digging through a riverbed. I can barely open up enough space for a cat, much less for a man my size."

"Any sign of Reno?"

Rafe looked at Eve's shadowed golden eyes and pinched face. He stroked her tangled hair with surprising gentleness.

"I got the shovel through to air twice," Rafe said. "More stuff came down each time. I shouted through the opening, but . . ."

He looked away, unable to confront the anguished hope in Eve's eyes.

She didn't ask for any more information. If Reno had called out in return, Rafe would have heard.

"Well, we're better off than we were," Rafe said. "At least we know there's new air going in through the hole, and enough space on the other side to echo when I shout, and there was enough air all along to keep Reno's lantern burning."

Eve nodded, but her attention was on the coyote hole.

"If he wasn't killed outright," Rafe continued, "he's probably knocked out or in another part of the mine, looking for a way out."

"Shall I get Caleb or Wolfe?"

"No," Rafe said curtly. "You were dead right. That hole is no place for a family man."

"Rest for a few minutes," Eve said in a shaking voice. "There's water in the canteen. It's yesterday's, but I don't suppose you'll mind."

Rafe's teeth were a white flash against his grit-and sweat-streaked face.

"I sure won't," he agreed.

He set aside the shovel and went to the canteen, which Eve had put back up the tunnel, out of the way.

As soon as Rafe picked up the canteen, Eve grabbed the shovel and scrambled into the coyote hole. By the time he turned around and realized what she had done, she was beyond his reach.

"Come back here!" Rafe yelled. "It's too dangerous. That ceiling is set to come down at the first excuse!"

Eve's only answer was, "I can get through any hole a cat can. Ask Reno. He calls me *gata*."

Rafe slammed his open hand against the rock wall and swore viciously.

But despite his anger, he didn't crawl into the

coyote hole and drag Eve back. If she could get through the opening, she was Reno's best chance of survival.

And if Reno was dead, Eve could find out that, too, before Caleb or Wolfe got killed trying to dig out a man who was no longer alive.

Eve crawled and clawed her way through the rubble, lured by the haze of lantern light ahead. The last foot was the hardest, for the cave-in all but filled the opening. There was just enough space for her to put one arm and her head through. Using her feet to push, she drove herself through the hole.

Abruptly the ceiling gave way.

For an instant Eve felt a crushing weight. Then a tongue of rubble shot forward, taking her with it. She sprawled across the uneven floor of the tunnel and fought for breath.

The first thing Eve saw was Reno's lantern. The second was Reno's head and shoulders sticking out of a pile of rubble left by the series of cave-ins. The third thing she saw was that Rafe had accidentally done what the Spanish had done many times by design; he had dug a new coyote hole connecting to the big tunnel.

Eve didn't know she was crying Reno's name until the broken echoes came back at her. Coughing dryly, she pulled her bandanna into place and crawled toward Reno through the swirls of dust stirred by the new cave-in.

"Eve!" Rafe yelled. "Are you all right?"

"I found Reno!"

"Is he alive?"

Eve reached out to Reno, but her hand was shaking so badly, she couldn't tell if there was a pulse in his neck. Then she saw blood welling slowly from a cut on his forehead.

Distantly Eve became aware of Rafe shouting her name.

"He's alive!" she yelled back.

"Praise God. Watch out. I'm coming through."

Moments later another shower of rubble spurted from the unstable wall where coyote holes riddled the old tunnel. Stones as big as Eve's fist hammered down. One of them struck the lantern, knocking it over and extinguishing it. Another struck Reno, who groaned softly. The remainder of the rocks added another layer to the mound covering him.

"Stop!" Eve yelled. "Rafe, stop! Every time you move, Reno gets buried deeper!"

"All right. I'm stopping. What happened to the light?"

"A stone knocked it over and spilled the fuel."

Rafe swore.

Eve groped in darkness through her pockets. Finally she found the stub of candle that Reno had insisted she carry in case something happened to her lantern.

Suddenly light from Rafe's lantern poured through the small opening that was all that remained of the coyote hole.

"Can you see now?" he asked.

"Yes. Wait."

A match sizzled. Soon a candle flame burned cleanly against the enveloping darkness. Eve crawled deeper into the old tunnel and wedged the base of the candle into a crevice.

"I've got light now," she said.

"How bad is Reno hurt?"

"I don't know. He's facedown, buried from his heels to his ribs. He's got a cut on his forehead."

Rocks fell and rolled as the mine adjusted to its new shape.

"Can you get him out of reach of another cave-in?" Rafe asked urgently.

Eve put her hands beneath Reno's arms and pulled. He groaned again. She closed her eyes and pulled harder.

The rocks covering Reno barely stirred.

"I've got to get the rubble off him first," Eve said.

"Be quick about it. That opening is damned unstable."

She worked frantically, pushing rocks until Reno was free to his hips.

"Eve?" Rafe called.

"I've got all but his legs uncovered."

"Want me to try to come through and help?"

Even as Rafe spoke, more rocks came raining down on Reno.

"Stop digging!" Eve said frantically.

"I didn't move!"

Rocks bounced and groaned and rattled.

"Get up the tunnel as far back from the coyote hole as you can," Rafe ordered.

"But Reno—"

Another wave of rubble lapped out from the unstable wall as a low, grinding sound vibrated through the mine.

"You can't help him now!" Rafe yelled savagely. "Save yourself!"

As though in a dream, Eve saw the wall shiver and shift minutely as it began to unravel.

Adrenaline poured through her in a wild cataract. She didn't stop to think or worry or wonder. She just hooked her hands under Reno's arms and pulled with every bit of strength and determination she had, dragging him in a single lunge away from the rubble and the unstable wall.

Rocks ground and gnashed and poured out in a wave of debris that lapped at Reno's boots. Desperately Eve kept backing up, dragging him with her until she stumbled and fell. She struggled to her feet and kept pulling, but her frenzied burst of strength was spent, leaving her unable to budge him. Still she kept tugging and tugging, crying and calling brokenly to Reno.

"It's all right, Eve. You can let go. You pulled him far enough."

For a wild second she thought Reno was talking to her. Then she realized that it was Rafe kneeling next to her.

"How . . . ?" Eve's question ended in a cough.

"When the wall went, it opened up a whole new passage. I don't know how long it will last, though. Can you walk?"

Shakily Eve got to her feet.

"Take the lantern," Rafe said. "We'll be right on your heels."

He bent, levered his brother into place across his broad shoulders, and followed Eve. Soon they met Caleb and Wolfe, who had heard the rumble in the gut of the mine and had come running.

Fresh air and the jostling that came on the way through the mine revived Reno. He regained consciousness in a haze of pain and dizziness just as he was carried out of the mine. Sunlight was a hammer blow in his eyes. Groaning, he closed his eyes and wondered why the world was bumping so badly.

"Lie still," said Rafe's voice. "You've been hurt."

Other voices came to Reno, men's voices, Caleb and Wolfe talking as they carried him into the shelter of the camp.

Nowhere did Reno hear Eve's voice, her touch, her scent. When he opened his eyes, sunlight blinded him.

"Eve?" he asked hoarsely.

"Other than being crazy enough to try to cut a deal with Slater, she's fine," Caleb said dryly. "Let's set him down over here. Feet first, Wolfe."

Reno heard nothing but the words about Eve. They echoed in his mind like the waves of concussion, pounding home the old truth about men and women and betrayal.

Tried to cut a deal with Slater. Cut a deal with Slater. Cut a deal . . .

The words echoed terribly in Reno's mind, bringing a pain in their wake that was like nothing he had ever known. When he had felt the tunnel collapsing around him, his last thought was that at least Eve would be safe.

Her first thought had been to take the gold and cut a deal with Jericho Slater, leaving Reno to die in the mine.

"Should have learned . . . Savannah Marie," he said bitterly.

"What?" Caleb asked.

"Did that cheating saloon girl . . . leave any gold?"

Before Caleb could answer, Reno passed out again.

Eve wished she could have done the same. She stumbled as though the ground had been taken away from beneath her feet.

Rafe caught her before she fell.

"Easy there," he said kindly. "You're at the end of your rope."

She simply shook her head and said nothing.

"Who's this Savannah Marie?" Caleb asked Rafe.

"A girl back home who used to drive boys crazy with her teasing. For a while there, Reno was young enough to think he loved her," Rafe said as he set Eve back on her feet. "Who is the cheating saloon girl?"

"I am," Eve said tonelessly.

Abruptly Caleb realized that his words about Eve cutting a deal with Slater had been misunderstood by Reno.

"Reno's out of his head," Caleb said roughly. "When he wakes up, I'll set him straight."

"It doesn't matter," Eve said, turning away.

"Eve," Caleb said. "Wait."

She shook her head and kept walking.

Everything that mattered had already been said. Reno might have enjoyed her company, might have been gentle with her, might have shared the most intense kind of passion with her; but he didn't love her.

He never would. Love required trust, and Reno would never forget that Eve had been a card cheat and a saloon girl.

I understand that women have to make up in cunning what they lack in strength. Understanding isn't the same as liking.

You can't count on women, but you can count on gold.

Sugar child, would you feel better if I told you sweet lies about love?

While the others hovered around Reno, Eve went into a grove of trees and washed the grit of the mine from every bit of her, and while she did, she wished she could wash away the past at the same time.

But she couldn't. She could only leave the past behind her, like the dirty water she was pouring from the basin onto the stony ground.

With a calm that came from a loss so deep it numbed her ability to feel pain, Eve pulled on her only remaining clothing—the red dress with jet buttons and a bullet hole in the hidden pocket where she carried her derringer.

Mechanically she went about her preparations. The most difficult part was figuring out how to carry the gold. Finally she brought her mount over to the mouth of the mine, tied on her empty saddlebags, and loaded them. Reno's saddlebags, she tied around the saddle horn. Then she loaded them, too. Gold bars clanked and shifted within the heavy leather pouches.

Only Caleb noticed Eve's transformation from grubby miner to tawny-haired saloon girl. He watched with brooding amber eyes that shifted between the half-conscious Reno and Eve's quick, efficient preparations.

Abruptly Caleb stood up and went over to her. "You're getting ready to pull out," he said.

She nodded.

"Where are you going?" he asked.

She shrugged. "Canyon City, I guess. It's the nearest saloon."

"You'll need someone to ride shotgun. I'll be ready in a few minutes."

"I'll pay you."

"Like flaming hell you will. I was planning to get back to Willow as soon as I could anyway. Pig Iron is a fine guard, but he's a mite short on social graces."

Caleb stalked off, whistling shrilly. A black gelding stopped grazing in the meadow and trotted over to him. He saddled and bridled the horse with swift motions before he came back to camp to pick up his saddlebags. Their unexpected weight nearly yanked him off balance.

He spun toward Eve just as she mounted the lineback dun in a flurry of scarlet silk and rode across the meadow toward the people gathered around Reno.

Rafe and Wolfe looked up at her, saw the dress

and the tightly drawn beauty of the girl with shining hair and golden eyes, and were too shocked to speak.

Jessi saw, too. Her eyes widened, but she said only, "Reno is much better. Steady pulse, good deep breaths. He'll be coming around soon. I don't think he's badly injured at all. He's strong as an ox."

Eve's smile was the saddest Jessi had ever seen.

"Yes," Eve said softly. "He's very strong."

Caleb rode up, reined in beside Eve, and waited, saying nothing.

Jessi came to her feet and stood next to the girl who looked as though she had been pushed beyond her last reserves. Jessi knew what it was like to be pushed that hard by life.

"Caleb told me," Jessi said in a low voice. "Reno didn't know what he was saying. When he wakes up, he'll call himself ten thousand kinds of fool."

The compassion in Jessi's blue eyes made Eve want to laugh and cry at the same time.

"You're very kind," Eve said huskily. "And very wrong. Reno knew exactly what he was saying. He's said it often enough before."

Jessi bit her lip and shook her head unhappily.

Eve continued speaking in an unnaturally calm voice.

"My half of the gold came to eight bars. I left two for you and Wolfe and two for Rafe. Caleb already has his."

Wolfe and Rafe started to speak at the same time.

Eve ignored them. With breathtaking speed, she bent over and yanked Caleb's belt knife from its sheath. The lethally sharp blade flashed, slicing through the tie that held Reno's saddlebags to the saddle horn. They landed with a weighty thump a few feet from Reno's legs.

"That gold belongs to Reno," Eve said. "He can count on it."

The lineback dun spun on its hocks and leaped forward as once again Eve left Reno behind in a drumroll of hoofbeats and a wild swirl of scarlet skirts.

23

Reno sat quietly in the shade of a fir tree, watching the meadow through narrowed eyes. For the first time in five days he wasn't dizzy in the least. The ringing in his ears was gone, as was the nausea that had plagued him. Though his mouth was drawn in a flat line of pain, his headache had subsided until it was little more than a nuisance.

It wasn't the headache that was hurting Reno. It was thinking about a girl who had loved her own comfort more than she had cared whether he lived or died.

Reno hadn't seen Eve since he came out of the mine. When he had asked where Caleb was, Rafe told him that Caleb had taken Eve back to Canyon City. Reno hadn't mentioned her name again. Neither had anyone else.

The sound of Wolfe laughing came back through the clean air, followed by the silvery music of Jessi's laughter as her husband lifted her off the ground and spun her around and around. Finally he sank down with Jessi and disappeared in the meadow's long, lush grass.

A bitterness that Reno refused to acknowledge as grief twisted through him, memories like razors slicing him, making him bleed in secret.

Once he had chased Eve through this meadow, caught her, and pulled her laughing down into the grass. Once, but no longer. Now even the memory of their shared passion was a pain he couldn't face, so he shoved it down in his mind, condemning it to darkness.

Yet the pain remained, reflected in the new brackets on either side of his mouth.

Tried to cut a deal with Slater. Cut a deal with Slater. Cut a deal . . .

Slowly Reno became aware of his brother standing nearby, watching him with shrewd gray eyes, holding a pair of saddlebags over his arms.

"Sure is a wonder to hear Wolfe laughing," Rafe said. "Makes a man feel good just watching them together."

Reno grunted.

Rafe's smile was a warning any man other than Reno would have heeded. Rafe had been waiting impatiently until concussion and physical pain no longer hazed his brother's eyes. Rafe wanted to be certain that Reno would hear and understand each word with great clarity.

The waiting was finally over.

"How's your head this morning?" Rafe asked blandly.

Reno shrugged.

"Glad you're feeling better, baby brother," Rafe said. "We were all real worried about you."

The look Reno gave his older brother didn't invite conversation. Rafe ignored it and kept talking.

"Yessir," he drawled, "the story went through the countryside like wildfire. A gunfighter called Reno, a Spanish treasure map, and the girl from the Gold Dust Saloon."

Reno's eyelids flinched at the mention of Eve, but he made no other response.

If Rafe hadn't been looking closely for a reaction, he would have missed it. But he missed nothing. His smile widened without becoming a bit warmer.

"I was in the Spanish Bottoms when I heard you were trapped in a blind canyon and were going to be cut to bloody rags by Slater and a passel of Comancheros," Rafe said.

"They tried."

"By the time I got there, nothing was left but coyote bait."

Reno's smile was a cold match for his brother's. "It was a near thing."

"That's what Caleb said. He came up on me when I was reading sign after the fight, trying to figure out which way to go. That man's like a ghost. Near scared me out of my boots."

More laughter floated up from the meadow, a man and woman's voices joined in celebration of the sheer joy of being alive.

Reno looked away from the sunlight and grass, trying to forget the time when he had laughed and breathed in the heady fragrance of lilacs from Eve's hair, her skin, her breasts.

"Seems word had gotten to Cal through that Comanchero squaw one of his men keeps," Rafe continued. "I'll tell you, brother, that was one hair-raising trail you found out of the blind canyon."

"It was better than what Slater had waiting for me."

"Well, Cal and I decided on the sensible route.

We took after Slater. He left a lot wider trail than you did."

"I didn't expect friends to be following me," Reno said dryly.

"You left signs for me."

"Just covering my bets."

"Bets, huh?" Rafe said sardonically. "Appears you've turned into quite a gambler since Canyon City. Must have been Eve's bad influence."

Reno's mouth thinned even more beneath the black stubble that covered his cheeks.

Rafe pretended not to notice his brother's grim reaction each time Eve was mentioned.

"We hooked up with Wolfe and Jessi on the far side of that mesa you blazed a trail over," Rafe continued. "One of Wolfe's Indian friends had told him you were in too much trouble to shoot your way out of alone, so Wolfe and Jessi came on the run."

Reno barely heard. He was too busy trying to shut out the sound of laughter coming from the meadow where Wolfe and Jessi enjoyed the sunlight and the day and each other.

The rippling music of feminine laughter haunted Reno, reminding him of everything he wanted to forget.

". . . Caleb came on Slater's guards just after they were changed," Rafe said. "No sooner had he taken care of them than he heard someone go by. Turned out it was Eve, on her way to spy on Slater's camp."

Abruptly Reno started to get up.

Rafe uncoiled. A single swift motion of his foot brought his brother down. The blow was as unexpected as it was precise.

Reno looked at his brother in shock.

"Settle down, baby brother," Rafe said flatly.

"You're not going anywhere until I've had my say. You want to fight about it, you go right ahead. I'll beat you, and you know it."

"You and those damned Chinese wrestling tricks," Reno said angrily.

"I'll teach you every one of them when you're well. But right now you're going to listen to me."

Reno looked into the icy gray eyes that were so like his own. Though none of the coiled readiness left Reno's body, he nodded curtly.

Rafe backed away with a lazy motion and sat on his heels with the saddlebags beside him. The appearance of being relaxed didn't fool Reno. If he showed any sign of getting up again, he would be brought down just as swiftly as he had been the first time.

"Cal snagged Eve before Slater saw her," Rafe said. "Seems she had some damn fool notion about taking Slater at gunpoint and offering him gold if his men dug you out."

"Is that was she told Cal?"

Rafe nodded.

"And he believed it?" Reno asked sarcastically.

Rafe nodded again.

A mockery of a smile curved Reno's mouth.

"Marriage has softened Cal's brain," Reno said in a flat voice. "That little saloon girl was going to trade for *her* life, not mine."

"The less you say, the fewer words you'll have to eat," Rafe retorted. "But don't let that stop you from running off at the mouth. When you get tired of eating your words, I'm looking forward to feeding them to you one by one."

Green eyes narrowed into glittering slits, but Reno said no more. He was in no shape at the moment to take on his brother, no matter how badly he wanted to. Both of them knew it.

"After we took care of Slater's gang, we went to the mine," Rafe said. "Eve stood there covered with dirt from head to heels, cut and scraped and bleeding from trying to dig you out. She refused to let Wolfe or Caleb go into the mine. Said it was too dangerous."

Tension began to steal through Reno's body once more as he listened.

"She said she wouldn't have minded killing Comancheros to dig you out," Rafe drawled coolly, "but she wouldn't risk family men. Said she was going to do it herself, because she had no family waiting for her."

"You didn't let her go back in the mine, did you?" Reno asked in a harsh voice.

"She was the only one who knew where you were," Rafe said flatly. "She led me to the cave-in, and I dug like hell burning, not knowing if you were alive or dead, and that goddamned ceiling kept coming down on me like a hard rain."

Reno gripped his brother's arm. "Christ! You should have gotten out. The rock in that coyote hole was as rotten as fruitcake!"

"Would you have gotten out if I were stuck down in some godforsaken hole?" retorted Rafe.

Reno shook his head. "Not a chance."

Rafe's expression softened for a moment. Of all his brothers, he had been closest to Reno.

"I finally opened up a hole a cat would have had trouble getting through," Rafe said. "I saw light, but you didn't answer my yells. Every time I tried to make the hole bigger, the ceiling came down."

"Then how did you get to me?"

"I didn't. Eve did."

"What?"

"Somehow she shoved herself through that little hole. She started uncovering you, and then the whole damn shooting match started groaning and grinding. I yelled at her to leave you and save herself."

Reno's hand clenched on his brother's arm hard enough to leave bruises.

"But she didn't," Rafe continued harshly. "Somehow she managed to drag you out of the rubble before the wall caved in. When I got to her, she was still pulling on you, crying your name, trying to save your life and to hell with her own."

Reno opened his mouth, but no words came through the constriction in his throat.

"You may have found that girl in a saloon," Rafe continued in a savage voice, "but she's worth more than any gold you ever dug out of the ground."

Eyes closed, Reno fought for control.

"She hung around long enough to hear you run off at the mouth about cheating saloon girls," Rafe said. "Then she washed up, put on a fancy red dress, and took that lineback dun out of here like its heels were on fire."

Reno put his head in his hands. He had thought he could hurt no more than the moment when he had learned of Eve's betrayal.

He had been wrong.

But Rafe was still talking, and Reno was still learning how much he could hurt.

"She left you a message," Rafe said.

With a deceptively easy motion, Rafe upended the saddlebags he had brought with him. Gold bars tumbled out and clashed to the ground.

"Here's your gold, brother. *You can count on it.*"

The agonized expression on Reno's face made Rafe regret his harshness. He reached toward his brother, but Reno was already on his feet, walking away from the gleaming gold bars.

"Where are you going?" Rafe asked.

Reno didn't answer.

"What about the gold?" Rafe called.

"To hell with it," Reno said savagely. "There's more where it came from."

But there was only one woman who had ever loved him more than she loved her own comfort, and he had lost her.

"PLEASE stay in the big house tonight," Willow said. "That little cabin is so drafty."

"Thank you, but no," Eve said. "I've put you to enough trouble. I'll be on my way in the morning."

"You've been no trouble at all," countered Willow quickly. "I enjoy having another woman around."

Eve turned to Caleb. "I wish you would let me pay you for—"

"Evelyn Starr Johnson," Caleb interrupted, "if you weren't already hurting so much, I'd turn you over my knee for bringing that up again."

A wan smile flickered over Eve's face. She stood on tiptoe and brushed a kiss over his cheek.

"You're a kind man, Caleb Black," she whispered.

"That will come as news to a lot of folks," he said dryly. "Since you're so all-fired set on leaving, we'll go at first light. Otherwise you'll go off alone, and this is no country for a woman alone."

"Thank you."

"You're welcome," Caleb said. "But when Reno gets all shooting mad about having to ride to Canyon City after you, be sure to tell him it wasn't my idea."

"Reno wouldn't ride across a pasture for me, much less across the Great Divide."

Eve turned and walked quickly toward the cabin

where Caleb and Willow had lived while they built the big house.

Unhappily, Willow watched Eve until she went into the cabin and shut the door behind her.

"Why won't she stay in the house with us?" Willow asked.

"I suspect it's the same reason she won't stay, period. She knows how Reno feels about having a saloon girl mixing with his sister."

"Eve may have worked in a saloon, but she isn't a saloon girl!" Willow said in exasperation. "Good God. How can he be so blind?"

"Same way I was with you for a time. Same way Wolfe was with Jessi."

"Just because you're men?" Willow suggested tartly.

Caleb laughed. His arm snaked out, drawing her close.

"All the same, I could shake Reno by his ears," she muttered as she put her arms around Caleb's lean waist.

"Don't worry, honey. I left that job for Rafe. He was looking forward to it so much I almost feel sorry for Reno."

Before Willow could speak, Caleb kissed her. It was a long time before he lifted his head.

"Is Ethan asleep?" Caleb asked.

"Yes," she whispered.

"You interested in learning more about the fine art of catching trout with your bare hands?"

"Who gets to be the trout this time?" Willow asked with a hidden smile.

Caleb laughed softly. "We'll take turns."

EVE sat at the only table in the one-room cabin, watching moonlight and lantern light send conflicting shadows across the table's wooden surface. As she watched, she mechanically shuffled a deck of cards. Each time she shuffled, several cards escaped and slithered across the table.

Frowning absently, Eve flexed her fingers. They were much better than they had been when she arrived at Caleb's ranch a few days ago. Even so, they were still clumsy, stiff from the terrifying time she had spent in the mine, digging frantically through rubble for something far more valuable than gold.

Did that cheating saloon girl leave any gold?

Slowly Eve's hands became fists. Just as slowly they uncurled. She put her palms down on the table and pressed so that the trembling that came when she remembered Reno's words wouldn't show.

After several moments Eve took a deep breath and gathered up the cards. She squared them off carefully and began shuffling again. When cards slipped free, she ignored them. After several shuffles she flexed her hands, rounded up all the cards, and shuffled some more.

Eve knew she should be sleeping, for the ride to Canyon City would be long and tiring. Yet sleep eluded her. Whenever her eyes closed, she would hear rocks grinding and breaking over Reno in a long, brutal wave.

From the direction of the barn came the low rumble of male voices. Eve cocked her head, looked at the angle of the moon, and decided that Pig Iron was making his nightly rounds a bit early.

She flexed her fingers absently, picked up the cards that had escaped, and stared at them. The more she worked her hands, the more supple they became, but she had nothing like her normal dexterity.

A cool breeze came from the front of the cabin

just as Eve was trying very hard to shuffle cards without losing one of them. Startled, she looked up.

Reno was standing in the open door, looking at Eve as he had in the Gold Dust Saloon, taking in the red dress, the steady golden eyes, and the mouth that trembled.

Drawn from the long trip, his face still cut and bruised, he was even more handsome than she had remembered; and his eyes were a hungry green fire.

When Reno walked toward Eve, cards shivered and overflowed from her hands in an untidy burst. Blindly she began gathering them up once more, but her hands were shaking too much. She balled them into fists and hid them in her lap.

Reno pulled out the other chair at the table and sat down. With a sweep of his arm, he cleared the table. Cards fluttered like autumn leaves to the floor. He unbuttoned his jacket and pulled a fresh pack of cards from his shirt pocket.

"Five-card draw," he said huskily, "two-card limit, table stakes, five-dollar ante, my deal."

The words were familiar to Eve. They were the exact words she had spoken to Reno a lifetime ago, when he had pulled out a chair, sat between two outlaws, and taken cards at her table in the Gold Dust Saloon.

Eve tried to push back from the table, but could not. Her arms refused to respond. She looked at the patterns of shadows rather than at Reno. She couldn't bear looking at him and knowing what he saw when he looked at her.

Saloon girl. Card cheat. Something bought off a train.

"I don't have any money on the table," Eve said. Her voice was thin, flat, a stranger's.

"Neither do I," Reno said. "Guess we'll have to

bet ourselves to stay in the game."

Eve watched in disbelief as Reno dealt cards. When five cards lay before her, she reached for them automatically. Just as automatically she threw away the card that didn't fit with the rest. One more card appeared in front of her. She picked it up and looked.

The queen of hearts looked back at her.

For a heartbeat Eve couldn't believe what she was seeing. Slowly all the cards slid from her fingers one by one.

Reno reached out and turned over the cards that had fallen facedown in front of Eve. Within moments a ten, jack, queen, king, and ace of hearts gleamed in the lantern light.

"Beats anything I have, now or ever," Reno said, throwing in his hand without looking at it. "I'm yours, sugar girl, for as long as you want me, any way you want me."

He reached into his shirt pocket and brought out the emerald ring.

"But I'd rather be your husband than your fancy man," Reno said in a low voice.

He held the ring out to Eve on his palm, silently asking that she take it. Tears gathered in Eve's eyes. She put her hands in her lap to reduce the temptation to take the ring and the man.

"Why?" she whispered painfully. "You d-don't trust me."

"I didn't trust myself," Reno said tightly. "I'd been such a fool over Savannah Marie that I vowed never to give a woman that kind of hold over me again. Then I saw you."

"I'm a card cheat and a saloon girl."

Reno gestured to the pat hand he had dealt to Eve.

"I'm a card cheat and a gunfighter," he said.

"Sounds like a good match to me."

When Eve's hands remained in her lap and she said nothing, Reno closed his eyes on a wave of pain. Slowly he got up and sat on his heels beside her, putting one hand over her cold fingers.

She looked at the table rather than meet his eyes.

"Can't you even look at me?" Reno whispered. "Did I kill every bit of what you felt for me?"

Eve took a deep, shaking breath. "I showed you stone ships and a dry rain . . . but I'll never find a light that casts no shadow. Some things are just impossible."

Reno stood with the stiff motions of an old man. Once his hand moved as though to touch Eve's hair, but he didn't. Instead, he reached toward the heart flush he had dealt her.

As the gold ring dropped soundlessly onto the cards, lantern light revealed the fine trembling of his fingers. Reno looked at his hand as though he had never seen it before. Then he looked at the girl whose loss would haunt him for the rest of his life.

"You should have left me in the mine," he whispered.

Eve tried to speak, but tears closed her throat.

He turned away swiftly, heading toward the door, unable to bear anymore.

"No!" Eve cried.

Suddenly she was on her feet, running to him.

Reno caught Eve up in his arms and buried his face against her neck, holding her as though he expected her to be torn from him. When she felt the scalding caress of his tears against her skin, her breath stopped, then came out in a ragged sound that was his name.

"Don't leave," Eve said in a shaking voice. "Stay with me. I know you don't believe in love, but I love you. I love you!"

Reno's arms tightened even more. When he could speak, he lifted his head and searched Eve's eyes.

"You showed me ships made of stone and a dry rain," Reno whispered, kissing her gently, taking her tears, "and then you showed me the light that casts no shadow."

Eve trembled and then went very still, looking at him with a silent question in her eyes.

"Love is the light that casts no shadow," Reno said simply. "I love you, Eve."

🐾 Epilogue

BEFORE the last aspens were transformed into topaz sentinels burning against the autumn sky, Reno and Eve were wed. When they stood before their friends and vowed to share their lives with each other, Eve was wearing Reno's gift to her: a gleaming rope of pearls, an ancient Spanish ring of emerald and pure gold, and a radiance that made Reno's throat ache until he could barely speak.

They stayed with Caleb and Willow through the cold brilliance of winter, laughing and working together while they shared Ethan and sang Christmas carols in a harmony that tempted angels into envy.

When spring came, Reno and Eve rode west for a day, to the place where a shaggy green mesa and snowy mountains stood guard over a long, rich valley. On the banks of a rushing river, the two of them built a home that was shelter against winter, haven against summer heat, and scented with the lilac bushes that were Reno's gift to Eve on the birth of their first child.

The children of Reno and Eve knew what it was to walk free upon a wild land. They felt the untamed sun of the stone maze and stared in wonder at signs hammered into rock by a culture and a people long dead. Two of the children became ranchers. Another learned to hunt mustangs with Wolfe Lonetree. A fourth lived among the Utes, writing down their language and legends before they, too, passed from the land.

A fifth stood with an ancient journal in one hand, a broken cinch ring in the other, and all around him the elegant, enigmatic stone ruins left by a civilization so old that no one remembered its true name. His sister stood beside him, her eyes filled with wonder. In her hands was a sketchpad filled with the mythic landscapes of the stone maze whose deepest mysteries only God knew.

In time, each in his own way, the children of Eve and Reno Moran took the measure of dreams made and dreams lost, pain endured and pleasure remembered. But above all, each child discovered the truth of stone ships and dry rain, and the name of transcendent light that casts no shadow.

And the name was love.

THE MOST SENSUOUS VOICE IN ROMANTIC FICTION
BRENDA JOYCE

"Brenda Joyce has a distinctive style
that captures and doesn't let go."
Johanna Lindsey

THE GAME	77573-5/$5.99 US/$6.99 Can
AFTER INNOCENCE	77572-7/$5.99 US/$6.99 Can
PROMISE OF THE ROSE	77140-3/$4.99 US/$5.99 Can
SECRETS	77139-X/$5.99 US/$7.99 Can
SCANDALOUS LOVE	76536-5/$5.99 US/$7.99 Can
THE FIRES OF PARADISE	76535-7/$5.99 US/$7.99 Can
FIRESTORM	75577-7/$5.99 US/$7.99 Can
VIOLET FIRE	75578-5/$4.99 US/$5.99 Can
INNOCENT FIRE	75561-0/$4.99 US/$5.99 Can
BEYOND SCANDAL	78146-8/$5.99 US/$7.99 Can

Coming Soon
CAPTIVE
78148-4/$6.50 US/$8.50 Can